# SNOW FALLS OVER
# STARRY COVE

# SNOW FALLS OVER STARRY COVE

Nancy Barone

*An Aria Book*

First published in the UK in 2022 by Head of Zeus Ltd,
part of Bloomsbury Publishing Plc

9 7 5 3 1 2 4 6 8

A catalogue record for this book is available from the
British Library.

ISBN (E): 9781803284378
ISBN (PB): 9781803284385

Cover design: Nina Elstad

Typeset by Siliconchips Services Ltd UK

Printed and bound in Great Britain by
CPI Group (UK) Ltd, Croydon CR0 4YY

Head of Zeus Ltd
First Floor East
5–8 Hardwick Street
London EC1R 4RG

WWW.HEADOFZEUS.COM

To you, my dear Readers, who have made
all this possible.

# Prologue

*Twenty years ago*

'Jago Moon!' the old man called across the glistening cove, his voice echoing over the deserted waves. 'You get back here with my granddaughter right now!'

Huddled behind a rock at the far end of the inlet, young Jago and Miranda tried to stifle their giggles.

'No more games! Jago!' Nano tried again. 'You know you're the only person I trust her with!'

At that, Jago peeked round the corner to see Nano scratching his head, face crumpled against the Cornish morning sun, and his heart lurched with guilt. Nano had always been kind to him. He'd been the father he'd never had.

'My word, if you've taken her out on my barge again, I'll personally kick you all the way down the coast!'

'Enough, Miranda,' Jago said, his heart softening as he moved to spring up. 'He's getting really worried now...'

'It's *fine*!' Miranda hissed, grabbing him by the wrist. 'We're just having a bit of fun.'

Biting his lip, Jago looked over at his old friend, who

was now negotiating the boulders blocking his path. 'I don't want to upset him, with his heart troubles and all. Let's go.'

'Not yet,' Miranda commanded. 'Kiss me again first...'

Jago glanced down at the love of his young life and felt his heart melt instantly. There was nothing he could refuse her.

Shaking his head in defeat, Nano exhaled heavily, the rocks too much of a barrier. 'One day the two of you will be the death of me...' Nano muttered to himself as, resigned, he turned and headed back up alone to the village of Starry Cove.

# I

## Unrequited Love

*Present Day, Monday, 7th November*

'**M**iss?'
'Yes, Beth?'

'What does unrequited love mean?'

Terrific question. I take off my reading glasses and place them on my desk, blinking at my Year 7 English literature class.

'Does anyone want to have a go at answering?' I ask the sea of blank faces.

Not a clue. Good for them. No one should know a thing about it. But I happen to be an expert in this field. The unrequited bit, I mean. I don't know how many crushes I've had in my twenty-seven years of life, or how many times I've fallen desperately in love without any chance of success. None of my relationships have ever lasted beyond a month. The phrase 'It's not you, it's me,' was a dead cert in my case. But now I'm engaged to Stephen Stone, my headmaster at

Boynton Academy, the expression 'sleeping with the boss' assumes a whole new meaning.

Not that there had been much of that going on lately. Blame it on the stress of my job or the stress of his job, but since we got engaged, things have been getting a little stale. Let's just say that we never had been swinging from the chandeliers in the first place. But there's always hope, right?

Because at this particular moment in his career, Stephen and I are just like employer and employee. You'd think he'd make an effort to duck out of a meeting for just one minute to call and say hi, but no. He's one of those staunch workaholics who gladly spend all waking hours in their chair and have to be pried kicking and screaming from their desk.

I started out that way, too. There was nothing I loved more than teaching English literature to my students and working at Boynton. But lately—

'Miss?' Beth prompts me as the class's attention is now piqued by the fact that their English teacher is stumped by a simple question.

I clear my throat. 'Well, uhm, unrequited love means that they don't love you back, no matter what you do. That's what it means.' But as far as the word love on its own is concerned, I'm a bit confused myself.

Another blank look from my crowd. I should have stopped when their eyes glazed over and Joe nearly fell off his chair from chronic boredom. How can I get a man interested in talking about love when I can't even get a boy interested in *Much Ado About Nothing*, which is a comedy to boot?

As if on cue, a few ignoramus die-hards at the back

begin to snicker. What do these young lives know about the pains of humiliation and loneliness, of never being loved back? Of always being the first to call or the last to fall asleep? Or to bake his favourite cherry pies even if you're allergic to cherries?

And, just as I'm about to dive into a monologue of unrequited love and ask my students if they've ever felt the sorrow of such an experience, the bell rings, saving us all from further embarrassment. I watch them with a certain sense of defeat as they spill out of the classroom for their break. I once had high hopes that, by learning from the great works of literature, I could still spare them the existence of love pains. But now I seriously doubt it. Kids seem to grow up faster than we ever did.

I squeeze through my throng of escaping students, plunge upstream like a salmon into the hallowed corridors and head straight for the staffroom. Halloween decorations still linger on the walls, curling where the drawing pins or Blu-Tack had fallen off. The ghost-, pumpkin- and witch-shaped choccies in the sweet basket on the counter are already being replaced by much plumper Santa ones. Someone is willing the time to fly between now and the Christmas holidays.

Keeping an eye open for Maisie – one of the French teachers and my best friend – I grab a chocolate muffin from the box on the coffee table. Ignoring the din of the other desperate teachers, I sink into my chair and dig out yesterday's mail from my bag. What with marking and prepping, I've only remembered it this morning.

At the bottom of a useless pile of planet-killing flyers is a white envelope from Cornwall, no less. I don't know anyone in Cornwall, despite the fact that I was born there. The heading reads Lister & Associates (if he says so):

Dear Miss Weaver,

We regret to inform you that your grandfather, James Heatherton-Smythe, has recently passed away. His surviving wife, Mary Heatherton-Smythe, wishes to make your acquaintance at your earliest convenience to discuss your attendance at the service which will be held in All Saints' Church in Starry Cove, Cornwall, on Friday, 25 November.

The Heatherton-Smythe residence is 1 Rectory Lane, Starry Cove, TR17 0RS.

Please accept our condolences.

Sincerely,

Norman Lister & Associates

I sit back against my chair, reading the same lines over and over.

I have a *living relative*? In Cornwall? You'd think that my parents would have mentioned that I had two real people I shared DNA with. And now I've lost the only grandfather I could ever have known without having met him. I've spent my entire life as lonely as the poet Wordsworth's cloud thinking I was the last one standing while, in effect, I wasn't. What was wrong with my parents? Who would do such a thing? Why keep all this from me? And how did they even find me?

And what are the odds of the funeral service being on the same day as my engagement party?

All this news is too monumental for me to take on board in the space of a fifteen-minute break. I need time to think and right now, my heart is beating so erratically, I can barely hold the envelope, so I stuff it back in my bag just as Brad Day, one of the PE teachers, saunters by.

'Hey, Emmie, what are you hiding there, a love letter? Better make sure Headmaster Stone doesn't see it or he might decide not to marry you.'

Bettina, my German colleague who's swivelling round in her chair and munching on a Twix bar two stations down from mine, rolls her eyes.

'Dream on, Brad. When will you get it that she's not interested in you?'

I slide her a grateful look and shrug.

Undeterred, he leans over with his hands on my desk. 'Want to go for a few laps around the pool? I bet I'll beat you this time?'

I grin. I think the fact that I'm a stronger swimmer than our Phys. Ed. teacher is something that he can't get past. It's a freak thing, I don't know why. I just took swimming lessons at school as a kid and was very fast and strong. Not that you'd believe it, looking at my puny arms and pins. 'Thanks, Brad, but I think I'll take a rain check.'

'Come the day, Emmie, you'll know where to find me...'

And with that, thinking he's made a lasting impression on me, he winks and saunters off. You'd think that my being engaged to his headmaster would stop him from making a pass at me. It's a good thing that Brad is harmless. Not that Stephen is jealous at all.

When the bell signals the end of break, I furtively slip my hand back in my bag as if I were hiding a dirty secret. But it's my parents' secret and whatever it is, I've inherited it. Not being one who has any delicious secrets of her own, I have to make do with theirs, hoping it'll be a juicy one that'll spice up my life.

Because I need a break from the tedium. And I particularly need a break from dealing with the extravagances of the MIL – in other words, Audrey Stone, my mother-in-law – who is at present organising our engagement party by completely disregarding the list Stephen and I had put together.

With all the dramatics of a consumed West End actress, Audrey's a diva. Ever since her husband died, she's been treating my fiancé like her own, butting her nose into every aspect of our personal life. To an outsider – and Stephen – our exchanges seem pleasant enough as she professes that I'm the daughter she never had. But oh my goodness, what implications that entails! If you ask her, I'm the fractious child who doesn't understand that everything she does is for my own good, and that I should grow up and stop being so recalcitrant.

If you ask me, on the other hand, she's the kind of person who would have you think she's an all-giving martyr while I resist her motherly love with what I simply call free will. She's always trying to tell me what to do or judging what I've already done. But she's so masterful at her game that she comes off as being caring and kind while trying to manipulate me with the proverbial iron fist. Which makes it challenging for me to stand my ground without looking mean in Stephen's eyes. And which is one of the reasons we argue.

She already rules the roost over her son and I can't wait for him to move out of her mansion, even if he argues he has his own wing.

A widowed fashion designer, Audrey also resents my not belonging to a family of means. Or to any family at all. I can't tell you how many times she's asked me, just like Lady Bracknell in *The Importance of Being Earnest*, how I've actually managed to misplace the only living persons in my family. As if I had any say in life and death. I'm on my own and I've managed so far. But not in her eyes. I'm just not good enough, from the clothes I wear to the tiny flat in which I live.

Compared to all of her friends' daughters, who are watching Stephen like a hawk in case he dumps me, I'm the one who doesn't deserve her son's love. So yes, she is the main bane of my life. But maybe now that I've managed to produce at least one family member, she might stop frowning on me and get off my back.

I can't wait to meet my new grandmother! When do things like this ever happen to me?

I'd drive down there right now if I didn't have to go back to class. It would take me all of three minutes to pack a bag. It takes five hours to get there, granted, but that would be part of *the journey of discovery*.

Imagine showing up on her doorstep! She'd hug me and cry happy tears for having found me, but also sad ones because I've missed out on knowing her husband and my grandfather.

\*

The rest of the day is like watching paint dry and I find myself getting more and more internally frustrated with every student and I chide myself. It's not their fault for not falling in love with Shakespeare, poor kids. They're just used to faster, shorter stories. Who nowadays has the attention span to read such a long play? I honestly pity the poor kids who have only been fed a diet of Instagram and TikTok, who have never had to go to the library to do some good old honest research for a school project and fallen in love with the process of learning.

Stephen, on the other hand, is all about avant-garde teaching and everything technological. He believes that the more technology you can throw into a lesson, the better. Personally, I'm not a huge fan, as it takes me ages to set everything up and by the time I'm ready, half the period has gone. Just to teach my students about Elizabeth I's expertise in avoiding marriage, Stephen (who has a master's degree in technological science and applications, naturally) has suggested a digital dating game to explain why Henry VIII married so many times while his daughter never did.

You might be wondering how I could have fallen in love with someone so different from myself. But, with all of his faults and hang-ups, Stephen is a good man and he loves me. He is protective towards me, the way my parents never were. He is organised and gets things done and has solid principles. He wants a family. And children. I don't know how the hell I'm going to manage raising them between prepping my lessons and marking, while he calls me from his office to tell me that once again, he's working late or caught in a meeting. As a matter of fact, he already does that. It looks like I'll be raising any children we may have completely on my own. But I do want children. I want to cook for them as they wait for their dependable father to come home every night. I love how I can count on Stephen always to be steadfast. He loves what he does with a passion.

Personally, I don't feel the same passion anymore. It's not that I don't like my students – I love the little shits – but lately, it seems to me it's more about marketing our school as a business rather than actually teaching the children. I just can't get on board with all the craziness. I need to step away. Perhaps I could take a sabbatical. But I don't know how to do that without losing my financial independence.

Teaching seems to have become a losing battle where you can lead the proverbial horse to water, but... I even try to teach some of my students some proverbs, some clever, witty sayings. But apparently it's not the done thing, according to Stephen and all of my other colleagues. If it were up to him, English literature would be dropped completely from the curriculum, because it doesn't, er, serve any purpose.

How many of us can remember being much happier playing in the fields or, for the less fortunate such as I, in the cul-de-sac down the road, rather than clicking away like mad at a video game or social media apps? No wonder our poor youth, bar perhaps a couple per class, is almost brain-dead.

Luckily, the Christmas holidays are coming up. I need a break like my next breath. But I suspect two weeks isn't going to make much difference. I don't only need a break from teaching, I also need a break from London and my life.

I get off the Northern Line at my stop, Balham, and wrap

up against the cold winds lashing at my face as I miserably trudge home past endless rows of Victorian terraces to where my block of flats sticks out like a sore thumb. I've seen some lovely houses online for us, but the problem is that by the time I jump onto my phone to call the estate agent, it's already under offer. So much for the financial crunch; everyone seems to be buying a home these days except for us. But who am I kidding? It's not my area that's a problem, nor my pokey flat with the constant damp stains and dreary walls that seem to turn grey a month after I've painted them white.

No, it's more than that. It's my *life* that's grey.

In Audrey's eyes, I should be kissing the ground where her son walks, rather than try to keep the relationship on an even keel of mutual respect, which, lately, as you may have gathered, isn't working out very well.

No matter what she or Stephen says, it's just not normal for a future mother-in-law to decide about our wedding venue (in order not to disappoint her social circle), our honeymoon destination and even my wedding dress, because – apparently – I'm not tall or slender enough to wear what I want. I don't care if she's a fashion designer and is offended that I haven't chosen one of her creations. They're hideous and pretentious and scream of bad taste and money to burn. I'm a simple girl with simple tastes. I don't follow any fashion fads but wear what I like and believe suits me.

And now she wants to invite all of *her* friends to the engagement party instead of ours, because ours (meaning mine) aren't important enough. I don't *have* any MP or DDL –doctor/dentist/lawyer – friends. Well, at least now I'll have someone of my own to invite – my very own brand-new grandmother! Once again I slip my hand inside my bag and feel the envelope, which right now seems to me more like the lifeline I so desperately need.

## 2

*When a man is tired of London, he is tired of life,*
Samuel Johnson

Once inside, I dump the unbearable load of everything 'schoolish' (or ghoulish, in my case) on the kitchen worktop, turn on the kettle and put the solicitor's envelope on my tiny kitchen table. I don't wonder why Stephen hardly ever comes here; it's barely big enough for me and my mountain of books.

In my pyjamas, I make myself a cup of tea. Now I have no excuse not to tackle the letter that's been burning a hole in my mind. With trembling hands, I curl up on the settee and read it once again.

I have so many questions that have been bubbling inside me all these years, but now that my parents are dead and I'm getting married, it's suddenly become crucial to know my roots and why we never went back, not even for a brief visit. And I'll finally get to hear the truth from my grandmother, who will be a treasure chest of answers to all of my questions. Like, why were my parents so cold? Why did they never tell me about my grandparents?

My grandparents can't have been *that* bad.

What were the reasons for the estrangement? And then a barrage of possibilities flit through my head. Was my mother a female Heathcliff? Was she a Jane Eyre? What memories could she have possibly been escaping from?

I pull out my calendar to count the days. My engagement party day is looming – less than a month away but not so close that it can't be postponed. I mean, Stephen would understand that my newfound and lost grandfather's memorial service has priority, right? But the MIL? She's been planning this for weeks. If she were downright aggressive and mean, I could face her. But Audrey has this pretence that she's the closest thing I have to a mother and she uses it skilfully by overusing the word 'dear'.

I'll admit, having someone fawning over you when you never had anyone can be nice at times. She does things for us that only a mother (except mine) would do. Because my own mother couldn't be asked, Audrey had initially seemed like a breath of fresh air. The prepped dinners when I had no time to cook, the offer to run an errand when neither Stephen nor I could get away, the advice that made sense. But soon, once she'd secured her claws into what she thought was her new territory, aka my flesh, she became overbearing.

Soon the prepped dinners became mandatory, because it would be wrong to say no as, according to Stephen, she'd done it out of love. And seeing that Stephen was her only child, who else was she supposed to pour this thick molasses of motherly love over, if not on us? And was I so cold as to break such a fragile woman's heart? In truth, she was far from fragile. She was made of steel and ruled with an iron fist in a beguiling velvet glove. I need to get away from her and the two weeks during which she'll undoubtedly find a million excuses to invade the wing Stephen uses.

There are still seven weeks to the Christmas break. Maybe I can persuade Stephen to go to Cornwall instead. Writer Dr Samuel Johnson stated that when a man is tired of London, he is tired of life. *I* think that when a woman is tired of London, she wants a Cornish cottage.

'This entire deceased grandfather thing – got to be a scam,' Maisie says over the phone later that evening.

We've been talking for over an hour now. That's what it's like with us. But even when we don't talk, we know that something's going on. Call it telepathy or something, but we've got it.

Chirpy, coquettish and very *à la Française*, although she's actually from Grantham, Maisie – or as everyone calls her at school, Mademoiselle Lowry – is the closest thing I have to a family. She's my best friend and I love her like the sister I never had.

'I mean, people read obituaries and get all sorts of ideas, you know?' she insists.

'But it can't be. The letter was sent through a legal firm. I checked them out. They're legit.'

'Right. What does Stephen think?'

I hesitate. 'I… haven't told him yet…'

'And why is that?'

Here we go again. If Maisie were a judge, she'd have carted Stephen straight off to prison the first time he stood me up for a work thing. But she's right. I should have told him. He should have been the first to know. But he wasn't. Perhaps it's time to remedy that.

'I'll call him now,' I promise.

'Good girl.'

I ring off and dial Stephen's mobile. Luckily, it's on. You'd think that he'd always keep it on in case someone – I – needed him. And after ten o'clock he doesn't answer at all because he needs to catch up on his paperwork and go to bed early to be up at five.

'You're telling me you have grandparents in Cornwall?' Stephen asks as I pile my papers and shove them into the 'to be marked' tray.

'Looks like it. And my parents never told me.'

'That's strange, wouldn't you say?' he muses over the tapping of his keyboard.

He's good at multitasking, better than me. No wonder he's headmaster and I'm not. Not that I want to be, God forbid.

'Well, my parents never really cared for anyone.'

At the other end, his tapping speeds up as he snorts. 'I'll say, the way they've treated you. And judging by the fact that your grandparents couldn't be bothered to meet you, I'm guessing that they didn't care much for you, either.'

I baulk at his tone. Stephen isn't the most tolerant man on the planet, but even I have to admit he's right about that. Mum and Dad had never exactly been bursting with love and patience for me, the only accident they ever had, as mum had so lovingly put it.

At first I'd thought she was joking, but a second glance

in her direction had confirmed that not only had she been speaking in earnest, but also that she had no idea of the effect her words had always had on me at such a young age. To be unwanted. Simply to be tolerated as an inescapable fact. A done deal that must be accepted.

'In any case, it's just my grandmother now. My grandfather has just died.'

'Oh. Sorry to hear that.'

'Thank you. I've been invited to the funeral.'

'Really? The cheek.'

'Cheek or no cheek, I'm glad she's contacted me. Better late than never.'

The tapping stops. 'Wait a minute. Are you saying that you want to go?'

'Uhm, I guess that would be the right thing to do. For my grandmother, I mean. She's my only living relative.'

'Whom you don't even know.'

'Well, I have to go, Stephen.'

'Sod her, Emmie. She doesn't sound any better than your parents. Why would you want to put yourself through all that again? Besides, you already have a family – Mum and me.'

He means his mealy-mouthed mother who's gradually wheedled her way into our private life. She knows everything she shouldn't, like how much money he has in the bank, all of his passwords and even how old he was the first time he had sex. I hate to think what he tells her about us. Try as I might, and however sweet she tries to sound while manipulating me and telling me that she's the closest thing I'll ever have to a mother, it just doesn't *feel* right.

'If this woman cared about you, she'd have tried to meet you at least once but never did,' he adds.

'Oh, I don't know, Stephen,' I argue, eyeing my pile of work and feeling more and more depressed by the second. 'Who knows anything about others and why they do what they do? It's just too easy to judge, isn't it?'

'So you really do want to go?'

How can he even doubt it? 'Of course.'

'When is it?'

'Well, that's the thing, Stephen. It happens to fall on the same day as our engagement party…'

The tapping stops. 'Well, that's a moot point, then. You can't go.'

'What? No. It's my grandfather's funeral. I can't miss it.'

'Well, tell your grandmother to reschedule.'

'Are you serious? I can't ask the woman to reschedule the interment of her beloved husband just for me.'

'Why not? If you're so important then she should do just that.'

'But I can't, Stephen. Surely other mourners will already have made plans.'

'So have we! We've got an engagement party, remember?'

'Which can be rescheduled.'

'But what would everyone think? And do you know how much trouble my mum has gone to, to get that venue for the day?'

'A venue neither you nor I chose.'

'It was the only one available, Emmie.'

'I'm sure there are others.'

'I can't believe you want to postpone our party.'

'I don't want to, Stephen. I *have* to. This is about a family I didn't know I had. And it's important to me.'

'*We* are your family, Emmie. Not some old crone who never even bothered to meet you.'

'I'm sorry, Stephen, but it would be wrong not to go.'

'Mum won't be happy.'

'She'll get over it.'

He harrumphs as the typing once again resumes. 'So we're good?'

A long-drawn-out sigh. 'I'll talk to her. But she won't like it.'

*Too bad.* 'Thank you, Stephen. And another thing before I forget. I want to pop down there next weekend to meet my grandmother, just so we're not complete strangers at the funeral. How are you set next weekend?'

The tapping suddenly stops again. 'Set?'

'Yes, uhm, I mean, don't you want to come? With me?'

The tapping resumes, almost viciously now. 'Ah, Emmie, I wish I could, but I'm absolutely swamped with work.'

'I know. We work at the same school, remember?'

'Please don't start all that again, Emmie...'

'I'm not starting anything. But it's true that I need an appointment to see my own fiancé.'

'That's not true. In any case, it would be best if you went on your own. Meet this woman and find out why she never knew you from Eve. The cheek of her, expecting you just to abandon your life and rush to her side.'

If only Stephen weren't such a die-hard cynic about everything, including feelings. I can't even remember the last time he said something sweet to me or made a romantic gesture. While I'm always trying to create scenes and scenarios that'll get him in a romantic mood, he always finds a way out of it. And he does it so naturally, too, like a marathon runner avoiding all the potholes on a track.

He isn't someone who ever completely succumbs to instinct. At first I used to think that was because he was in total control of himself, but soon I began to realise that if anything, his mother controls him.

As he's determined not to join me on my Cornish blitz, I wonder if he's also set on not coming to the funeral either. I don't like the turn this conversation is taking.

'Can we change the subject or could you please at least change your tone?'

'There's nothing wrong with my tone. Don't be so thin-skinned all the time. And speaking of, Mum is now going to have to change the spa appointment she booked you both in for. She wants you to be perfect for our engagement party.'

'You mean *her* engagement party. I don't know half the people she's invited. Why can't we just invite our own friends?'

'They are my friends. I grew up with them.'

'They're not your friends, Stephen. When you broke your leg last year, the only people swarming through your door were the vultures wanting to become Mrs Stephen Stone.'

A long, protracted sigh. I wonder if it's the unborn germ of an acknowledgment that I may be right. Probably not.

'These are business relationships that my family has been building for decades,' he argues. 'I can't help it if she has an empire to uphold. We can't just ignore them on our engagement day.'

I want to point out that it is indeed ours, not hers. But with Stephen, I've often found that the less we speak of his mum, the better.

'Tell you what,' he says. 'If you go down there and meet your grandmother, she might be more inclined to postpone the service.'

My spirits sink somewhat at the prospect of having to go all the way down there on my own.

'And when you get back, things will be better, I promise.'

He's not budging on this one. In truth, he never does. I'm always the one making the sacrifices. It's a good thing that he finds ways to make it up to me.

'OK,' I reluctantly agree, curious to see how exactly he's going to manage that. Because things aren't looking too sparkly at the moment between us.

'Brilliant! And, oh! don't forget the fitting before you leave.'

I choke on my tea as I sit up from the settee. 'Fitting? What fitting?'

Another sigh. 'The fitting for your engagement gown.'

And there it is. Good old Audrey has sneaked all the way in again.

'I already have an engagement gown.'

'That may well be, but I'll bet you it's not a Stone design, is it?'

I flinch. 'No, but—'

'For Christ's sake, Emmie. You see? Everyone who counts will be there and you're showing up with something from Primark?'

'I am not!' I gasp. 'I have a beautiful dress, thank you very much!'

'But it's not one of Mum's.'

'I don't like your mum's clothes,' I blurt before I can stop myself.

An appalled silence follows.

I sigh. 'Look, I'm sorry. But they're just not me.'

'You mean they're classy and elegant.'

Ooh, how dare he! 'No, I mean ostentatious.'

'But that's the Stone look.'

'Exactly, Stephen. It's not *my* look. You're not marrying your mother, for Christ's sake. Not royalty who follows suffocating protocol. If I wanted that I'd have married a prince.'

'I resent your tone.'

'Now who's being thin-skinned?'

Another groan, followed by: 'Tell you what. If you promise to go easy on us, I promise to spend two entire weeks with you in Cornwall this summer, how's that?'

Now that catches me off guard. 'Really?'

'Of course. Anything for you, sweetie. You choose. Anywhere you want. Book the poshest hotel, everything you want. Deal?'

Now I recognise my man. 'Deal! And... thank you.'

'So we're good?'

'Yes. But I'm still not wearing your mum's gowns.'

'One day at a time. Just concentrate on the payback.'

'I am.'

Two entire weeks in Starry Cove! Stephen has come through again, and just in the nick of time, with a corner kick!

'Right. Listen, I've got to make a few calls to the governors, so I'm going to have to ring off now, but you let me know when you get back, OK?'

'Stephen, it's not for another week, I just told you that.'

'Right, yes. OK, then. Talk soon.'

And before I can get a word in edgeways, he rings off.

I sigh. The perks of sleeping with the boss.

# 3

*Madame Bovary*, Gustave Flaubert

*Tuesday, 8th November*

The next day I catch a glimpse of Stephen in the staff-room over lunch break as he ambles over and steals half of my sandwich.

'That's it?' I ask as he walks away, winking at me.

Not that I'm expecting a kiss in front of my colleagues, of course, but a *Hi, how are you? Would you like to have dinner tonight?* would have been nice.

'Saving the rest for later,' he promises with a ruffle of his eyebrows, and I know he's not referring to my lunch.

But that's Stephen for you. For every fault, he always finds a way to make it up to you. Most of the time.

With a glimmer of hope and some 'us' time to look forward to, I continue to chomp on what's left of my lunch.

'So, what's up with tight-arse?' Maisie whispers as she takes a seat on the teal velour settee in the staffroom next to me and nods to the door through which Stephen has just disappeared. 'I bet he said no to Cornwall.'

'Well, it's not really a no,' I defend, swallowing a piece of tomato. 'He promised to come with me in the summer.'

She faux-punches me in the arm. Or so she thinks. She's got the strength of a wrestler, Maisie.

'Cornwall in the summer! That's great, Emmie.'

'It is, although Stephen says I should refuse to go as they never wanted to meet me. But this woman is all the family in the world I have now. Apart from you, of course,' I add when she sticks out her bottom lip and gives me the spaniel eyes. 'Is asking him to come with me really too much? Shouldn't he actually be offering, without my asking?'

'Absolutely, he should,' Maisie agrees. 'Especially with his pretences of being a protector and all that. But he's all talk.'

I begin to fray the lettuce leaves protruding from my sandwich. 'I mean, he's got so many qualities and I love him, but I hate it when he plays the headmaster card to get out of something he's not keen on. I mean, shouldn't he be happy for me?'

'Stephen doesn't do family drama. He can't even see the mess his own family is. He'd amply deserve it if you left him.'

I roll my eyes. 'Maisie, stop. Why would I leave him if I love him?'

Maisie swallows the last of her sandwich, still piercing me with her eyes.

'I just don't understand, for the life of me, why you put up with him. You're young and beautiful. You could have anyone else.'

'Thanks, but I don't want anyone else. Stephen makes me feel—'

'Yeah, yeah, I know. Grounded. And unloved.'

I groan. 'No, stop it. He's... solid. Stable.'

'You're describing him like he's a kitchen table!'

'I mean, he's a good man. He's kind to me.'

'Is that enough to commit to a bloke nowadays?'

It is to me, considering my parents were totally indifferent to me. Kindness is everything. Even if Stephen has his days. But he's always there for me, and that's what I was looking for in a man. And now I've found it, perfect or not. 'It's much better than having your heart broken again,' I say, leaving it at that, because Maisie knows better than to dig up my past of unrequited love. 'So romance is now only about stability and nothing else? You see why I don't do relationships?'

If there were ever to be an official spokesperson for '*No love – we just have sex, thank you*', it would certainly be Maisie Lowry.

She sighs heavily. 'Forget about him. *I'll* come to Cornwall with you.'

You see why I love her so much? I didn't even have to ask.

'You would? Really? Thank you,' I whisper.

'Of course! I've never been. Plus I hear that the blokes down there are to die for. We'll both get what we want from this trip – you a family and me some good ol' Cornish lovin'.'

'As if you need more men,' I remind her.

For Maisie, a lonely week is one where she's only met one or two men, because it's her life mission to meet at least one handsome or interesting man every single day. And she even manages to do so. How, I swear I don't know, but I will tell you this: she's so charming, they all fall at her feet, while she always does all, and I mean *all*, the leaving.

Up until I met Stephen, my life was the opposite of hers. I did the loving and they did the leaving. But Stephen is different. Granted, he's not perfect, but, as opposed to all of the blokes I'd met, Stephen is the best. He's elegant. He's balanced. He's strong. Level-tempered, too, and, most of all, completely incapable of surprises, whether good or bad.

By Friday afternoon, I'm ready to set off for Cornwall straight from work, my suitcase in the back of my old Ford Focus and waiting for Maisie to appear. We're staying four nights and will be back to the grind on Tuesday the 15th as Monday is an Induction Day. As I'm waiting for her to come out, I catch sight of Stephen leaning against the main entrance, eyeing me.

'Are you sure you don't mind if I don't come, Emmie?' he asks as he approaches, hands in his pockets. 'I mean, you don't even know this woman.'

Exactly because I don't know her, I thought it would be nice if he accompanied me. Because that's what fiancés do, correct? Is not one of their main jobs to meet the family? Apparently, it had been convenient for him that I'd had none until now. All the holidays were spent at his family home – in other words, his mother's domain. Christmas, Guy Fawkes, May Day bank holiday, August bank holiday – you name it, we were there. And now I have to beg him to come and meet my only living and newly discovered relative?

'No, uhm, that's OK, Stephen. Maisie's coming with me.'

I can't even describe the relief that floods his face.

'Oh! Are you sure?'

And he asks me *now*, just as I'm getting into my car for a five-hour drive?

I sigh inwardly. 'No worries.'

'I'll make it up to you, Emmie,' he promises.

'I know.'

Stephen always keeps his promises. But all the same…

'I'm here, I'm here!' Maisie calls from the language block, waving her arms like she's on fire and dragging her own wheelie suitcase with the French flag embossed across the front.

Adorable, dependable Maisie. I can always trust her to save the day.

Stephen barely glances at her. It's no secret that there's no love lost between them and that if it weren't for me running to her defence all the time, she'd be working on the other side of the country. Maisie throws her suitcase in the back next to mine and salutes me in a horrible rendition of a Cornish accent.

'Cap'n Weaver, I'm proper ready!'

Stephen rolls his eyes as he checks that no one else is around to see, leans forwards and kisses me.

'And you're sure you don't mind?' he asks for the third time, for Maisie's benefit.

'I'm sure. Now go back to work.'

He grins. 'You're the best, Emmie.'

The best, I wonder as I wave goodbye, or the least demanding?

'Tosser,' Maisie coughs into her shoulder as she pulls her seat belt on.

'Maisie, do you want to get fired?' I moan as I pull out of the staff parking bay.

She pops a huge piece of purple bubble gum and starts to chew away like any old Daisy in a field. 'Has he at least agreed to couples therapy?'

'As if he'd admit there's a problem. He says he loves me but he's just not a fall-head-over-heels man. He likes to stay grounded.'

Maisie looks at me and I just have to laugh. Otherwise I'd cry and really don't want to go there.

'Can we change the subject?'

'Right, you win! So, are we going to be staying with your nan?' she asks.

'You must be joking. I can't spring up on her like that. Not this weekend. But I'll definitely get in touch with her before the funeral.'

She sits up. 'Then what the hell are we doing?'

I shrug as I turn onto the main road. 'I just want to get the lay of the land. I haven't confirmed I'm going.'

Maisie gasps. 'You little sneak! You just want to spy on her to see if she's worth meeting!'

'Of course she is! But I don't know that it'll be the same for her. Remember that she and my parents weren't on speaking terms.'

'But it'll soon be Christmas – isn't this the time to atone?'

'We're going to.'

'What if she's like your mum? You want to make sure she's nothing like your parents.'

'She won't be. No one is as bad as them.'

'OK by me. And in the meantime, I'll do some research for you,' Maisie informs me, waggling her eyebrows up and down.

More determined in matchmaking than Jane Austen's Emma, Maisie has her heart set on setting me up with someone who isn't Stephen, the cause being our three-year relationship that seems to be stalling (and staling) endlessly. But Headmaster Stone lives up to his name – hard as hell to crack and even more impossible to bend.

'In any case, I'll be looking for myself as well. One does not go to Cornwall and return without bedding a handsome young Cornishman!'

I sigh, shaking my head good-naturedly as I approach the M3. If it hadn't been for Alan, our music colleague who's Cornish, I'd have taken the M4, which my route planner had suggested. But Alan says that the M3 is much more scenic and who wants a long, hard slog with nothing to look at to distract you from the enormous amount of hours it takes to get there, right? And if you do the M3, A303 and A30 route, he says, you even get to see Stonehenge. What is there not to love?

'You should be looking forward to a quick weekend tryst, though,' Maisie insists.

I laugh. 'Maisie, is that all you can think of?'

'Of course, and so should you!'

'Technically, we're going to meet my estranged family.'

'Oh, so we *are* meeting the old biddy, then?'

'I'm still not sure.'

'So where are we staying while incognito?'

'I've booked a place overlooking the cliffs. It's called The Old Bell Inn.'

'Did you get me my own room? With a double bed? I'm feeling lucky!'

'Will you stop?' I laugh.

Not even ten minutes on the road and she's already cracking the innuendos. What would I do without her?

Five hours later, after a couple of bathroom breaks and with a pretzel-shaped spine, my satnav tells me that Starry Cove is well away from the next exit on the A394 south of Breage. Nearby villages include Wyllow Cove, Little Kettering, Penworth Ford, and Perrancoombe.

'Oh my God, are you serious?' Maisie screeches as she jumps out of the car outside our inn. 'Just bloody *look* at this place! Oh, Emmie, can we stay here forever, please, please, *please*?'

I laugh, hugging her. 'Thanks for coming, Maisie.'

'Are you joking? For the chance to ogle some prime Cornish beef!' she cackles, and I hug her even tighter. If there's anyone I'll always want to be with me, it's Maisie.

Once inside the inn, which according to a local tourist map is actually closer to Little Kettering than Starry Cove, the first thing we see is a huge Christmas tree dominating the area between the lobby and the check-in desk. It's still mid-November and contrary to what I'd thought, Cornwall is way ahead of London as far as the Christmas spirit is concerned. I instantly feel chirpier.

'Welcome to The Old Bell Inn! I'm Penny Fitzpatrick, the manager.'

Startled, I turn to see one of the most beautiful women I've ever seen walking towards us, hand outstretched. She has long flaming red hair, a cheeky but friendly face and a body I'd kill for.

'Hello, this is my friend, Maisie, and I'm—'

'Yes, Emily Weaver, welcome!' she says, shaking our hands. 'We've been expecting you. Pleased to meet you! You've got plenty of time to get sorted and relax before dinner. There's a bottle of champagne in your room, courtesy of Mr Stephen Stone.'

'Aww,' Maisie says, linking her arm through mine and resting her head on my shoulder. 'I might just change my mind about him. Not.'

'Maisie,' I plead softly, then turn to Penny. 'Thank you so much. We're knackered and famished and really appreciate your welcome. You've a gorgeous inn.'

'Thank you. It used to be my father's.'

'Oh,' I say, wanting to add I'm sorry he's passed, but she smiles just in time.

'He now runs Cove Cottages on the other end of town. Right, let's get you sorted.'

'Thank you. Is Starry Cove far from here?'

'Starry Cove? No, it's just down the coast. The villages are really all linked and everyone knows everyone around here.'

Ouch. Not good if I'm going to be incognito. Luckily, Penny doesn't ask and a young man shows up to carry our wheelie suitcases upstairs.

'I'd say probably late forties,' Maisie says as we follow the young man up the stairs.

'Who? Penny? She's much younger than that,' I assure her.

She rolls her eyes. 'Not her, her father!'

'Oh my God, Maisie, when will you stop recruiting and cataloguing men?'

'Hey,' she says, poking me in the arm as we reach the top of the stairs. 'I'm doing this for you as well. Come the day you come to your senses and dump The Stone, you'll be thanking me.'

'Room four,' the porter says, opening the door and stepping aside.

'Thank you,' I say, slipping him a tenner. I'm feeling generous today.

'Right!' Maisie says. 'Let's crack this baby open and then go to the pub! I'm dying for some proper Cornish pub grub!'

'You go ahead, Maisie,' I suggest. 'I need to sleep. I can barely keep my eyes open.'

'Poor love, you've been driving for hours. You must be knackered. OK, you have a nap while I scout around. You'll find me at that pub we passed on the way in.'

'Sounds good.'

Maisie is going to be OK. She'll have made friends by tonight. And by friends, I mean male.


I don't even bother to unpack but set my alarm for precisely one hour and collapse onto the bed closer to the window. What a truly gorgeous place. If only Stephen hadn't been so bent on getting his own way, he could be here enjoying all this with me.

When I wake all refreshed and ready to go, I find a text from Maisie:

This pub is seriously olde worlde! Except for the men, who are young! Get your arse down here pronto and wear something nice! M xxx

*Be there in half an hour*, I text back, grinning to myself. Maisie. You've just got to love her.

I take a quick shower and slip into my jeans and a simple white jumper, despite her style suggestion. I'm not on the hunt, but I'm glad she is. No man can resist her French vintage charm.

As I'm heading down the beautiful wooden staircase, the air already shamelessly filled with the scent of cinnamon and Christmas like a child who can't wait for the holidays, my mobile rings. It's Stephen. Hopefully in penitence mode.

'Hello,' I say, trying to keep the disappointment out of my voice. I always try not to hold a grudge for too long.

'Hi,' he says. 'How was the drive?'

How does he think it was?

'Well,' I reply, 'you know when you get into a car and drive for five hours? That's how it was.'

'Oh, come on, Emmie. Don't tell me you're angry. You seemed fine when you left.'

Perhaps I seemed fine on the outside. But after an ambush like that, five hours on the road is a long time to think, even with Maisie cheerfully chatting away in your ear.

'Well, as you can imagine, Mum is not best pleased about

you postponing our engagement party. But I've explained about this woman contacting you.'

'You mean my *grandmother*,' I correct him, already feeling the annoyance.

It must be that the Stephen effect decreases with the increase of the distance from London, which my maths colleagues would call an inverse proportion.

'I wouldn't get my hopes up too high, Emmie. We don't know this woman.'

'That's why I'm here, Stephen. To get to know her.'

'In any case, Mum has found a new date for the engagement party. December 24th. It'll be a Christmas Eve and engagement party all in one.'

Well, you can't fault Audrey's efficiency. I just wish I didn't resent her so much for running the show of my life. But I do realise it's mostly my fault for letting her. I'm going to have to address that when I get back.

'So a car will come and pick you up and take you to the venue,' Stephen says.

'I… wait, we're not going together?'

'I promised Mum I'd be there early to greet the guests.'

'You mean her clients.'

'Oh, come on, Emmie. It'll be just like a wedding! I'll be waiting for you, all gorgeous and in style in a Stone design. By the way, Mum says she loves the dress you chose for the engagement party, even if it's not one of hers. I hope you didn't mind me showing it to her.'

I do indeed, but let's not go there. I've just received a compliment from the MIL-to-be! Dare I hope that she might be slowly finding some respect for her poor, unconnected future daughter-in-law?

'Thank you, so do I.'

'But she thinks it doesn't suit you. She says you're too short.'

'Ah.' And here we go again with the fashion fascism. You'd think that by the way she goes on about it, someone's life depended on bloody couture. All I want is to get married. It doesn't matter what she thinks about my (lack of) style. 'Stephen, with all due respect—'

'Come on, Emmie. What difference does it make to you which dress she chooses for you? It'll be fun!'

Fun? I'm going to my engagement party on my own. And in a dress I haven't chosen…

'Hold on a moment. I never said she *could* choose my dress.'

'But think how awful it would look – her own daughter-in-law choosing someone else's design?'

'Stephen, I'm sorry, but our engagement party is a moment to share with our friends and family, not an invitation to the whole of the National Couture Guild.'

'But how would that look to her clientele?'

'That is of no concern to me. She should have thought of that before asking me to try on a dozen dresses, none of which I liked.'

They made me feel awkward and physically uncomfortable, like I'm being pulled in a hundred different directions at the same time.

'Emmie, you're being unreasonable as usual.'

'*I'm* being unreasonable? This is our engagement party, Stephen, not her showcase. And what do you mean by unreasonable as usual?'

'You never accept any of her suggestions.'

'That's because I don't like them.'

'But would it kill you for once to pretend?'

'Would you like me to pretend about other things, too, Stephen?' I ask, not really knowing where I'm going with it, but it suddenly feels good all the same.

He groans. 'I see that you're still in one of your moods.'

It's obvious that I've brought my problems with me to Cornwall, which was supposed to be my temporary bubble of peace. But at least I *have* moods. They don't call him Headmaster Stone Face (among other, er, endearments) for nothing.

'Look, can we talk about this when I return? I'm on my way out,' I explain.

'Where are you going?'

'To explore the town.'

'You mean you're meeting Maisie at the local pub of some godforsaken hamlet.'

Are we that predictable? 'Yes. And?'

He sighs impatiently, as if he'd like to say something but has thought better of it, luckily for me.

'Nothing. I'll call you tomorrow,' he says.

'Fine, talk tomorrow,' I agree, flicking my mobile off before he can add anything else.

Sometimes talking to him can truly aggravate me and ruin my mood. Oh, but not today, because it's time to explore this deliciously festive little village lying at my feet like an early Christmas present!

I literally skip out of the cosy inn and down the coastal path to Starry Cove, which offers me a bird's-eye view of the crescent-shaped inlet dotted with houses so colourful it could easily have been an island in the Mediterranean.

A pang of envy shoots through me as I gaze down on life by the sea. In the distance there are a few sailing boats drifting on the breeze and, further out, seagulls riding the thermals. Here, there are no buses ready to knock you down in the road, no fumes, no greyness ready to swallow you up. It's a completely different universe.

Grinning to myself with sheer delight, I wrap my scarf tighter around my throat and set out, teetering over high, grassy emerald cliffs that, in the absence of wind today, are literally kissed by the lapping cobalt waves. Despite the penguin weather, the air is clean and I can see for miles in every direction, including the other nearby villages dotting the coast that Penny had mentioned.

I soon discover that Starry Cove doesn't announce itself with a sign or anything so definite. Rather than a village, it seems more like a hamlet or a small settlement that starts haphazardly, almost by mistake. A farm here, another one at the top of the hill. Has a central flourish with a bounty of quirky old shops and houses huddled one atop another and then gradually eases off again to a farm or two, only to start over with the next hamlet. Utterly gorgeous.

'You're two rounds late,' Maisie greets me as I remove my coat and slide across the bench seat opposite. 'I'll choose for you,' she offers, getting up. 'We have to keep up with the locals.'

'OK, but I have to eat something or I won't make it to dinner alive.'

Angler's Rest, as it turns out, is a quaint olde worlde pub with authentic interiors and original features, judging by the hint of must that only an old place can have and that just can't be replicated. Not that you'd want to, of course. What comforts me is that there's no smell of cooking fat that usually permeates other eating places in cities across the country.

Maisie takes a sip from the overspilling pint glass as she returns from the bar, peering into the glass as if to fathom some deep secrets.

'A bit too strong for my taste, but I might get used to it!'

I take a draught from my own glass, smacking my lips and grimacing as I scan the menu. They actually have the gall to call this beer? This could strip paint off of a lamp post. And then I look up and freeze.

# 4

Opposite me, nursing his own half-empty pint, is the most handsome man I'll probably ever see in my entire life. He simply couldn't be any more beautiful if he tried, because not even a scrub-up or a shave could remove the patina of gorgeous ruggedness that clings to him. Worn black leather jacket, combat boots and an 'I don't give a shit what anybody thinks' air about him. He's the exact opposite of what Stephen represents with his designer suits, tailored shoes and expensive haircut.

Square jaw covered in stubble and ebony locks falling into his eyes, he's so sensual I can't help but sneak him another glance from under my fringe. But I needn't worry about being caught, because he seems to be completely absorbed in the contents of his pint. So I allow myself another illicit peak, noticing that he's smirking to himself as if he's enjoying some private joke. I have a feeling this must be his default expression. As if he's scorned everyone and everything.

And that's when he looks up straight into my eyes, unwavering. I try to look away, but my eyes are repeatedly drawn to his. Embarrassment kicks my heart into a pounding rhythm, like a sudden adrenaline rush when you sense you're in danger.

I look down at my hands to keep my eyes off him. They're sweating and shaking. My face is burning and my mouth has become parched as if I've spent the day in the desert.

What is wrong with me all of a sudden? For no reason whatsoever, I'm blushing until I'm practically purple in the face and looking for a place to run and hide like one of those damsels in distress. Who am I kidding? I *am* a damsel in distress, only no one knows besides Maisie, and I don't think even she knows the extent of my insecurities.

His eyes are still lingering on me, I can feel it, and when I can't stand it any longer and look up, he snickers to himself. I quickly avert my gaze again, realising he's laughing at me. Indeed, he must be sick and tired, if not overly amused, of women ogling him.

'OK, Emmie,' Maisie whispers. 'Don't look now, but at precisely twelve o'clock lies the hunkiest bloke I've ever seen.'

'Yes, I saw him,' I manage to croak as I put my glass to my lips to quench the sudden inexplicable thirst.

'He looks half-cut, though,' Maisie observes. 'Must be difficult to cope with, being so hot!'

And just like that, the man shakes his head at us and gets to his feet to amble unsteadily over to the bar. The barmaid leans over to caress his face, saying something to him lovingly before selling him another pint.

'Looks like he's the local pisshead,' Maisie wagers as he turns his back to the bar and totters back to his seat with a fresh pint.

A quick scan of the premises confirms that most of the females (and some of the males) are more than aware of his presence, some smiling, some lifting glasses, others giving him sultry looks. I swear, it's choose me, not her central in here. We observe the carousel of glances in amused silence for a moment or two. It's like watching a David Attenborough documentary on mating rituals.

'I wonder if...' Maisie murmurs to herself and slides out of her seat, aiming for him.

'Maisie?' I hiss. 'What are you doing? Come back here!'

You think I'd be used to her ease with men by now, but I'm always edgy when she talks to complete strangers. Like only she can, Maisie saunters up to his table and speaks to him briefly. He looks up at her, studying her, bursts out into a sonorous laugh, drains his glass and then heads towards the gents.

'Have you just gone mad?' I demand when she returns. 'You must need your brain tested. You don't just walk up to a stranger and—'

'But this is Cornwall,' she sing-songs. 'Anything is possible here.'

'Yes,' I snort as I take a sip of my beer. 'STDs from strangers, especially.'

'I'm not going to have sex with him.'

'Good.'

'You are.'

I splutter my mouthful all over the table. 'Me? You must be insane.'

Maisie reaches for the napkins and helps to mop up the mess I've made.

'Oh come on, Emmie. Why not? Do you really want to get married without sleeping with another man ever again? This is your one chance. Besides, what happens in Cornwall and all that, yes?'

'I would never, *ever* cheat on Stephen.'

'Not even if he cheated on you?' she insists.

I sit up. 'Why? What have you heard?'

'Shush, he's coming back.'

'Maisie...?'

'Nothing. I've heard absolutely nothing. The man is married to his work.'

That much is true. If Stephen can't find the time even to see his fiancée, how on earth is he going to find time for the... extras? Besides, Stephen isn't like that. Which is one of the reasons I love him.

The drunkard passes us on his way to his table and slides us what is more a sneer than a smile.

'Oh my God, just *look* at him!' she moans.

'I know, right?' I agree. 'What an unbelievable arse!'

'It's not just his arse – have you seen the width of his *shoulders*?'

I stop and stare at her. 'Are you serious? The man is an absolute jerk. Did you not see the look on his face of total disdain? Who the bloody hell does he think he is?'

'I don't know who he is, but we're going to find out and get you hooked up before you leave.'

I put my hands on my hips. 'Is that why you came down here with me? Just to try to get me to sleep with someone before my engagement party?'

Maisie shrugs. 'Someone has to, and as your maid of honour, the *honour* is all mine.'

'Yes, well, I can still fire you from that job.'

'Please do, then,' she begs. 'You know how against this wedding farce I've always been anyway.'

'It's not a farce, Maisie. Stephen and I love each other and we're getting married.'

'God Almighty, you sound just like one of those clueless damsels in one of those historical novels who pledge their eternal love to the wrong man.'

I bristle. She's never been in love, treating her one-night stands like sworn enemies the next morning. At this rate, she'll never find someone to love if she chucks them out the minute she's done.

'Maybe you should try him for yourself,' I urge.

She dismisses me with her hands. 'Please. I need a man who will be sober and *remember* me berating him the next morning. But you, my dear, could use a little rough and tumble before your big day. Your mother-in-law would freak at the sole idea.'

Maisie lets the thought sit there for a while and finally decides it's hilarious, suddenly cackling in delight. Despite myself, so do I. Oh, it feels so *good* to laugh! I can't remember the last time I laughed so hard.

'I need the loo,' I suddenly decide as I slide off the seat.

'Have fun,' Maisie says.

I steer clear of the man's table, relieved to see he's gone, and barely make it through the door, my bladder on the verge of bursting.

'You sure like to keep a man waitin',' comes a deep murmur from behind me.

I whirl round and there he is, the slosher, leaning against the sinks. In the mirror I can see the back of him, which is just as perfect as the front. Boozer or not, he is indeed a looker.

'I... uh...' I falter, but he just watches me like a hawk, assessing his prey. 'I only came in to, uhm...'

'Sure you did,' he drawls, but his eyes are telling me he doesn't believe me.

Up close, he's not as handsome. The quality of his features is still there, but he lacks in freshness, as if he's been pushed through a mangle, mauled by life itself. His eyes are red and rimmed, marks of a difficult life, and a scruffy beard hides a strong jaw.

But there's no fierce dignity you'd expect from a man who stands at least a head taller than the rest. To me it seems that there's little left of what may have been a young man with an entire life ahead of him.

He's obviously a bad boy who doesn't care to be accepted. Dangerous. The kind you avoid like the Black Death. I shouldn't even be anywhere near him. And yet, here I am, against all odds. And, against my better judgment, not running a mile. Or two. What am I still doing here (besides the fact that I need a wee), six inches away from him and those hungry eyes of his?

Maybe Maisie could tackle him, but there's absolutely no chance for me. I don't know what to do or how to deal with men like him. Which is just as well. Because he and I have absolutely no business in the same room, let alone a toilet.

'So, does yer friend always get you yer blokes?' he says in a Cornish accent so strong it takes me a moment to figure out what he's just said. 'Because, just for the record, you don't need her to.'

I blink. 'I beg your pardon?'

He grins, his white teeth stunning against his olive skin. 'Not everyone may go for your dainty looks, but every now and then, I quite like a lady, if only on the outside.'

A lady only on the... What is he talking about?

'Do you mind?' I snap, indicating with my chin that he's in my way.

'Go right ahead. I'll wait.'

I feel my eyes popping out of my head. 'I beg your pardon?'

He snorts. 'I thought you were a bit more amiable. Suits me. We don't have to do it in there,' he says, indicating the cubicle. 'Here's fine. I don't care if anyone sees us – and by the time I'm done with you, nor will you.'

I simply stare at him. He's winding me up, of course. That's what louts like him do. I'm absolutely going to kill Maisie for this.

'You're drunk,' I dismiss him.

He grins. 'Always. But that doesn't deter from the fact that I'm willin' and ready.'

For a moment, our gazes hold like earlier across the tables. He's waiting for a sign from me to go ahead. As if I were someone out looking for a good time and not worrying who with. All he needs is a nod or a smile or a sultry look like the ladies back in the bar. Well, he's going to have a long wait. I groan as I march past him, half expecting him to reach out and grab me. But he doesn't. He merely watches me with those liquid eyes, while I'm defying him with mine. If he gets any closer, I'll scream the house down.

Something must have flashed across my face, because he steps back as if I've slapped him.

'Women,' he says, his handsome face marred by a sneer as he turns on his heel and saunters out through the swinging doors.

'I swear I didn't tell him to jump your bones, Emmie!' Maisie pleads as she follows me, stumbling drunkenly, back to the inn.

It's dark outside, but the old-fashioned street lamps and sea of Christmas fairy lights illuminate our way. If I wasn't so furious with her, the walk back could have been a real winter's delight.

'All I asked him was where you could have some fun…'

I whirl round. 'You *what*? Maisie, what the hell is wrong with you? You're so worldly and then you go and do something so naïve like that? Don't you know how dangerous that is?'

'Dangerous, in this one-horse town? Please. I was only trying to make you have some fun…'

'I don't want to have fun!' I bellow.

'Don't I know it! All you do is pine for that overstuffed bore! You're much too nice to chain yourself to an arse like that. When are you going to act your age and be carefree?'

'What are you on about, Maisie?'

'I'm on about you dumping Stephen. God, it makes me so angry to see you wasted on him. You could do so much better. Why am I the only one who can see that?'

'Better?' I snort. 'Like that slosher in there?'

'I just don't want you to marry Stephen,' she whines.

And then I finally get it. How could I have been so obtuse?

'Maisie, you know that my marriage won't change anything between us. We'll still be the best of friends.'

Maisie snorts. 'My poor little innocent one. If you think that Stephen is going to let you live your own life, then you're sadly mistaken. He already tells you what to do.'

I stare at her. 'That's not true.' Mostly because it's Audrey who does the telling.

'You know it is, Emmie. You've changed so much since you came to the interview over three years ago. I almost wish I hadn't told you about this job. We used to see each other so much more before that.'

'Maisie…' is all I can say. Because deep in my heart, I know that, on some level, she's right. I have changed, and not in a good way. But I will sort myself out. I'll tell the MIL where to stick it and finally feel like my old self again. In other words, independent and free of family ties. Except for my new grandmother, that is. Because I just know that she's going to be a revelation.

But to blame Stephen isn't completely fair. Because I had been searching for stability when I'd applied for this job. And my relationship with Stephen had simply been a consequence of that search. In Stephen I'd found the solid rock to ground me in the storm.


Saturday, 12th November
After a night of tossing and turning despite the most comfortable bed I've ever slept in and the crashing of the waves against the cliffs below, at about 4 a.m., I finally give sleep up as a bad idea and quietly roll out of bed, careful

not to wake Maisie. I don't want to turn on any lights, so I curl up in the armchair in the corner and pull my Kindle reader out of my bag to finish my *Jane Eyre*, which I must have read a thousand times.

But it's no use. A million things are roiling around in my brain, but one sticks out particularly. The looming date of our engagement party forces me to think of how I'm going to be dealing with the MIL. I've done my best to try to make things light between us, but there's a not-so-underlying current of jealousy towards her own son. She tries to convince herself she loves me, too, and that we're all one happy family. And the pretence of actually caring for me? She only uses that angle when she needs to manipulate me for something or other.

But if I'm a mature woman – and I am – I'm going to have to solve this by myself rather than ask Stephen to dial his mum down. Because he, on the contrary, doesn't have the maturity to understand that I shouldn't even have to ask. He should be making sure that I feel at ease with the family rather than having to fight for a modicum of breathing space.

A couple of hours later, as I watch the sky brighten over the diamond-studded bay, I unfurl myself from the chair and my unread book. Having decided to let Maisie sleep off her hangover, I loop my bag over my shoulder, wind my blue-and-white scarf around my neck and softly close the door behind me. The inn offers breakfast, but I'm curious to try the delicacies of a shop we passed on our way back from the pub, The Rolling Scones.

The morning air is crisp and the damp sand on the south-west coastal path is as soft as sponge beneath my boots.

In the light of the rising sun, I squint as the fog is rapidly dispelling, just like my previous uncertainty on what to do. I've come here for a reason – to meet my grandmother. And that's what I'm going to do. If it becomes unpleasant and we don't get along, then Mum would simply have proven herself right about my grandparents all these years. No biggie, no major disappointment.

But I can't marry Stephen and start a family without knowing who I really am. Also, it would be nice to tell Lady Bracknell finally that yes, I did have a family, after all, despite my being so careless about misplacing it twice. In her own mealy-mouthed way, she never missed a chance to remind me of how my ancestry is, if not uncertain, very much broken, as it isn't proper to break ties with your family, acquired or not. You simply put up with them. Of course, she also means me. I know exactly how she feels about me, despite the false rhetoric of my being the daughter she never had. Make that the daughter she never had to kick around even if I've always been polite and patient in the face of a blatant offence that she claims is meant with motherly love.

On entering Starry Cove, the first thing I see again is fairy lights still visible in the early morning shadows, weaved among the bare branches of the trees, framing the shops, squirrelling up old iron lamp posts and even reflecting in the gently babbling water channels between the pavement and the cobbled streets. This is all so beautiful and I suddenly feel suspended in a bubble of happiness, or one of those glass Christmas snowstorms. All you have to do is shake it for the immediate Christmas spirit.

I pass a gate with a huge faded sign that says Moon River

Cruises, right under another reading Reclamation Yard: for nautical stuff, ask Jago Moon on the beach.

How positively, ridiculously quirky all this is! Almost too quirky to be true.

It's safe to say that in this holiday season, there are more Christmas lights than shops, the high street being aglow with a bakery, cafés, a butcher's and yes, an actual candlestick maker called At My Wicks' End. Next door there's a newsagent and a small variety post office next to the pub where I'd joined Maisie. And immediately the memory of that weird encounter flashes through my mind.

I hope I don't bump into *him* again!

# 5

*The Importance of Being Earnest,* Oscar Wilde

Once I reach The Rolling Scones, I hover outside to take in the beauty of it all. This isn't a bakery – this is an art gallery! The entire window is a miniature Starry Cove, complete with gingerbread houses and liquorice street lamps topped with yellow marshmallows plus tables and benches outside the pub made in KitKats. I can't get in fast enough.

'Hello. Name's Ralph, what can I get yeh?' an elderly man who looks like he's come straight off the set of *Poldark* waves from the counter when it's my turn.

'Hello, may I please have… uhm… I don't know – it all looks so good I'd have to live here a year just to begin sampling everything!'

He laughs. A loud, genuine belly laugh. 'Well, let's get you started on some Cornish gingery fairings, then.'

'Ooh, yes, please!'

'How about this one, topped with saffron icing?'

'Oh my God…'

'Start with a couple of these, on the house. What will you wash it down with?'

'Uhm, coffee, please.'

'Take a seat. I'll bring it over d'rectly,' he promises.

Happy as Larry, I sit by the window and look at the rear of the miniature cake village in the window. Even the backs of the buildings are perfect, from the Graham Cracker houses to the dark chocolate slate roofs. I've died and gone to Cornish cake heaven!

After the ginger fairings – OK, *and* a slice of carrot cake – I take a stroll through the village to walk it all off. The main road winding through the village eventually leads me down to the beach and harbour. Here, Georgian stone buildings act as a stepping stone for pastel-coloured cottages of confetti blue, apple green and candyfloss pink. They seem to climb atop one another on their ascent to the crest of the hill. An incredibly blue sky dwarfs the cove, where boats bob softly in the fresh morning air and the sky reflects in the clear waters.

I'm psyching myself to meet my grandmother. She won't be expecting me, so maybe I should call first. Or perhaps just sneak past there incognito, after all, just to get a feel of the place. But what's the rush? Why not buy myself a pasty for lunch and sit by the breakwater and watch this utterly lovely little world go by? So I do just that.

But at the counter, I'm at a loss. There are so many flavours to choose from that I can't make up my mind: cheese and onion, yummy yum yum. Venison, stilton and rosemary? Curried potato pasty? Scotch egg pasty? Cheese and Marmite? And shepherd's pie pasty? Have I died and gone to pasty heaven as well? As I'm contemplating my options, my mobile rings. I don't need the ringtone of the 'Monster Mash' to tell me it's my future mother-in-law. Nothing better to ruin my Christmas cheer.

'Emily? Stephen tells me that you're in Cornwall meeting your new relatives?'

Now why on earth had he thought it necessary to inform his mother?

'My grandmother, yes.'

'And she's the reason you want to postpone the engagement party?'

'Actually, the reason is my grandfather. He died.'

'And he *has* to be interred on the 25th?'

The cheek of this woman!

'I'm so sorry this inconveniences you, Audrey, but it can't be helped.'

Not that I was expecting her condolences. Those would have dutifully arrived only if the event hadn't clashed with her show.

'Yes, well, it figures. Back to square one in the family department. It's a good thing you have us.'

Audrey is fiercely protective of her family sphere and doesn't want anyone else to enter it, like an exclusive club you need a special pass to get into.

'My son also tells me you and your grandmother are currently estranged. Can you manage to keep it that way until after the engagement party? I have a perfect number and I don't want to ruin it.'

Can you honestly believe this woman?

Sensing my stupor, she adds, 'We can always invite her

to the wedding if you want to, but right now there's no room.'

No room for the bride's one family member? Surely you understand where I'm coming from when I say that she's a handful. I try to get along with her, truly I do. But how does one deal with someone like her?

'Er, Audrey? Seeing as the engagement party has been postponed, maybe you don't have to kill yourself organising it anymore. Stephen and I can do our own planning now.'

Regarding my gown, if I open my mouth, I might say something irreparable to the MIL for which Stephen will make me pay for tenfold with one of his oh-so-carefully-plotted guilt trips. But as far as my own (new) family is concerned, in her twisted mind they have no importance whatsoever. Different weights and different measures and all that. But this ends now. Because now—

A loud laugh rips through my ear.

'Nonsense. No one can plan their own engagement party, let alone wedding – at least not the way it should be. You're lucky I'm in charge.'

What actually makes her think that? I wonder. But then I answer my own silly question. Stephen and I are responsible for her attitude. And I'm even more responsible than him, truth be told. Because I hadn't nipped it all in the bud when it became obvious that she was going to be running the show. At first I thought she was just being overzealous and eager to please, and being new to the household, I didn't want to seem ungrateful. But then as time progressed, she gradually, and always with a smile, took over.

Stephen was absolutely ecstatic about it, while I was left

wondering how I'd ever got myself into such a situation. 'You can't let her mother you only when it's convenient for you,' Stephen had once said. I should have known better – and have only myself to blame.

'Oh, and by the way,' she adds. 'I need to pre-approve her wedding attire. We don't want any clashing colours for the wedding album.'

Do you still think I'm kidding? Yes, it's all true, and no, I'm not embellishing it in the least. That's authentic Audrey Stone for you. I don't know how I haven't managed to throttle her up until now.

'Audrey,' I say before she can catch her next breath. 'I'm going to have to call you back.'

And before she launches into her next tirade, I hang up, finding myself in front of a quaint little pottery shop called Bits 'n' Pieces. The window is packed with the colours of Christmas and fairy lights, resembling in many ways the cake replica of Starry Cove, decked out for Christmas, looking very much like a nativity scene. How positively adorable! It's all there, the breakwater, the bakery, the pub, the church – everything! Oh my goodness, could Starry Cove be any lovelier?

'*Nadelik Lowen!* Mother-in-law blues?' comes a voice at my elbow, making me jump.

I turn to see a very pretty blonde woman with a huge set of keys stepping up to open the pottery shop.

'Ugh, yes,' I admit instinctively. 'What's that you said, *Lowen*?'

She smiles. And it's such a pretty, natural smile.

'*Nadelik Lowen!* It's Cornish for Merry Christmas. We like to start early in Cornwall.'

'I'll say! And *Na-nadelik Lowen* to you, too, thank you.'

'It's cold out here – come inside for a cuppa,' she urges, using the largest of her keys to unlock the door as she jerks her head at me, beckoning me to follow.

And like Alice in Wonderland, I do.

'This Christmas dream shop... it's yours?' I marvel.

'It is, thank you. Come on in and browse. No need to buy. I'm happy for some company. Plus, I don't want to be guilty of eating all these by myself,' she whispers, producing a cake container.

Despite the fact that I've already eaten The Rolling Scones out of house and home, my mouth begins to water.

'It's pumpkin pie,' she whispers mischievously, her blue eyes bright with a childish excitement that I can't resist.

'Oh,' I laugh. 'Well in that case, gladly, thank you.'

She's so sweet and friendly I can't help but marvel. Can you imagine anyone in London inviting an absolute stranger for a hot drink and *cake*?

Once inside, I stop and look around me, slack-jawed. Every shelf is full of the most colourful Christmassy ornaments possible: angels, snowflakes, Santas and Rudolphs. It's like Christmas has exploded in here and I can't get enough of it.

'Are you visiting family?' she asks as she unwinds her scarf from her neck. 'Please, sit, sit. I'll put the kettle on.'

To tell or not to tell? I'm supposed to be incognito.

'Sort of.'

She smiles as she pulls out a tiny tablecloth and sets it over the small round table in the corner and selects a couple of chunky ceramic mugs, one in the shape of Rudolph and another of the Gingerbread Man, and I can't help but grin in anticipation.

'Do you make your wares yourself?' I ask.

'Oh, absolutely. No Chinese imports here. You can tell because it's all wonky. Look at the Gingerbread Man's legs. See? I'm no perfectionist.'

'You say that like you're apologising. I find everything in here absolutely charming.'

'Aww, thank you! My name's Rosie, by the way.'

'Emily. But everyone calls me Emmie.'

'Then welcome to Starry Cove, Emmie. I live on the edge of Little Kettering but practically spend my life here in Starry Cove. Everyone is so warm and friendly.'

'I just got here,' I admit.

Rosie looks up at me as she pours hot water into the humongous mugs and stirs in the hot cocoa.

'London?'

I nod.

'Me, too. I've been here for two years now, but it's like I was born here.'

'Lucky you. This place is so beautiful. It's like a Christmas fairy tale.'

'I know, isn't it? Christmas is a special time here. You do like pumpkin, right?'

'Like? Love,' I assure as she cuts a generous piece of the pie and places it on a red ceramic plate with snowflakes on it.

'Good. I made it myself. My husband says that it's the best he's ever tasted. But he doesn't count because he loves me.'

I take a bite and almost swoon as cinnamon and a hint of ginger wrap themselves around my tongue.

'Oh my God, this is amazing.'

Rosie laughs. 'Really? So he wasn't lying just to make me happy?'

'Definitely not,' I assure as I fork another piece into my mouth, my tongue thanking me for such a treat.

We eat and drink as Rosie chatters about the villages that are all 'strung together like Christmas lights', which is such an apt image. She tells me about the annual Christmas Day dunk, where everyone rushes into the water in their cossies and tea cosy hats at the stroke of noon, and how everyone complains about it, but every year the number of participants just gets higher and higher.

'But listen to me. I've gone and done it again. I talk a lot. Tell me about yourself – what about you?'

'Well, I'm staying in Little Kettering at The Old Bell Inn.'

She laughs – a cheerful laugh – and I get the impression that it's a relatively new thing for her, and that it hasn't always been this way.

'The inn is run by my step-daughter, Penny. Her father, Mitchell, used to run it. That's how we met two years ago this Christmas.'

'Oh, she's so lovely!'

'Thank you. She truly is. So young and already got her head screwed on tight.'

'So, how did you find yourself here? Were you visiting friends for the hols?' I ask, chomping on my pie.

She rolls her eyes while she pours me some more hot cocoa.

'That would have been nice. I was sent by my former company to, let's say observe and evaluate the inn. And Mitchell, who used to run it. And after a rocky start, we fell in love.'

'Now that is romantic,' I say, pointing my fork at her as if I've known her forever.

I don't know what it is, but here I feel I can let my London guard down. Everyone is so friendly and relaxed.

'And you?' she says as she spears a piece of pie with her fork. 'You said you were visiting family?'

'Uhm, well…' What the heck. She seems like a really nice woman and I know I can't stay incognito forever. 'I'm actually going to meet my grandmother.'

'And she lives here? Who is she?'

'Her name is Mary Heatherton-Smythe. Do you know her?'

'Oh, of course! Everyone knows her. So why is it that I've never seen you here before?'

'Well, I'm actually meeting her for the first time. I only found out recently that I had a living relative.'

Her eyes light up. 'Wow, that's amazing. Good for you, and just in time for Christmas. No one should be alone at this time of year especially.'

I want to tell her I'm not alone. That I have a fiancé.

'Actually, we're not spending Christmas here. Which is a shame, now that I see how beautiful this area is.'

She stops chewing and looks at me solemnly.

'Not here for Christmas? Oh, no! You're going to miss it. Christmas is incredible here in Starry Cove. On Christmas Eve they send a boat out full of fishermen to find Santa. You wouldn't believe the kiddies' faces when they come back with him. My son, Danny, absolutely loves it.'

'Aww, you have a son?'

'Yes. He's the love of my life,' she gushes. 'And of my parents. They moved down just to be with him.'

'That's so lovely,' I say, feeling the sudden warmth that the idea of family brings me.

My parents would never have done anything similar for me. It's such a shame that I can't bring myself to see the MIL as part of my loving family, try as I might. But hopefully, sooner rather than later, once Stephen and I are married, she might accept me as a done deal and stop weaselling her way into our private stuff. But for now, all bets are off.

'I'm assuming your family's in London?' she asks as she takes a sip of cocoa and I do the same before answering.

'Uhm, no, they've passed...'

Her face crumples in a sincere gesture of sympathy. 'Oh, I'm so sorry, Emmie. I keep putting my foot in it.'

'Oh, no, it's OK,' I hasten. 'I'm getting married next year, so...'

She covers her cheeks with her hands and gasps as if we've been friends for years.

'But that's sooo exciting. Congratulations! We need more than this – hang on a minute!'

And she jumps up and disappears into the back room. Something tells me she truly is a sweetheart and that she's in love with... love altogether.

'Here!' she cries, carrying two crystal flutes and a bottle of champagne. 'When we opened the shop, Mitchell went out and bought crates and crates of the stuff, but we never got round to drinking it all. Can you believe what a travesty?'

'Oh, Rosie, that's so kind of you, but you don't have to—'

*Pop!* goes the cap and she squeals in utter joy as she fills the two glasses, most of it landing on the table anyway. I laugh and try to mop some of it up. It appears I'm not the only one who can't not spill booze.

'Drink up, and congratulations to you and...'

'Stephen,' I say.

'To Emmie and Stephen!' she toasts, clinking glasses with me.

'Thank you. And to you and Mitchell and Danny and Penny.' How good am I at remembering names, eh?

'Oh!' she says. 'You have to meet my friends!'

'Sure, I'd love to, thank you, Rosie!' I could certainly use a friendly face right now.

'You'll love them! Nina is the famous Nina Conte, the scriptwriter.'

I feel my jaw dropping. 'Nina Conte? Are you kidding me? I love her!'

'We all do. And she'll love you, you just wait. And there's Natalia Amore, the—'

'Natalia? The one who wrote "That's Amore"?'

'Yes, just the one!'

'Oh my word. What is this? The secret haven of celebrities?'

Rosie giggles. 'More or less, yes. And then there's Faith Hudson, who's an interior designer. Oh, I can't wait for you to meet them.'

'To all of us, then, and to our new friendship,' I toast, thinking how I'd love to live such a simple life. And how I'd love to be as happy as Rosie.

The ceramic clock above the table suddenly chimes two, making me jump.

'Oh my God, is that the time? I'm so sorry – I have to go! But thanks so much for the company and the pie and all.'

'Ooh, good luck, then. And do pop in when you can. I'll always have cakes and a brew for you, Emmie.'

I stop at the door, grinning from ear to ear. 'Will do, Rosie.'

And as I close the jingling door behind me, I can't help but feel like I've just made a friend for life.

# 6

*The Unbearable Lightness of Being,* Milan Kundera

If the hot cocoa and pumpkin pie have warmed my heart and my body, the effect isn't going to last long out here in the biting cold. But despite the dropping temperatures, throngs of people are milling around, scurrying from shop to shop, saddled with huge bags full of wrapped presents and Christmas decorations that will make a home cosy and festive.

It's obvious that for some time the villagers of Starry Cove have been very busy with preparations. And it seems they'll be so up until Christmas Eve. But, with all the scurrying to and fro, they still find the time to stop and chat and laugh with their fellow villagers.

When was the last time I stopped to chat and laugh? I wonder. If it weren't for Maisie, I'd be completely on my own. My many acquaintances and colleagues is one thing, but true friendship I truly welcome and am glad to have met such a lovely girl as Rosie.

But Maisie isn't my favourite person right now after that

prank she pulled last night. Imagine, trying to get me and that lout together. He'd literally have to be the last man on earth and even then, I'd still say no.

I stand still in the stiff breeze, welcoming it, hoping it'll help me to clear my head of the cobwebs. As it whips my hair around my cooling face, I feel myself laugh. A real liberating, open-mouthed belly laugh. I can't remember the last time I've laughed. It must be all the chocolate and cakes and friendships, making me giddy with something akin to… levity of heart?

There's certainly something to be said about the great outdoors. For a brief moment, Stephen and Lady Bracknell seem more than five hours away. It's as if they're on another planet and I've just discovered an entire new world where they can't reach me with their everyday run-of-the-mill troubles and hassles. I'll be back to work and on fiancé duty soon enough, but for now, I'm a free agent.

I pull out my mobile in search of my grandmother's location. I've put it off long enough. Time to face the unknown.

As I breathe in the cool air to muster some courage, the wind whips at my scarf, which alights from my shoulders before I can grab it. In dismay, I watch as it soars beyond my reach and is caught by higher currents, which suck it upwards into the heavens, like a pixie spirit escaping its captor. I break into a run down the length of the coastal path as my scarf dives for the beach and at one point it looks as if it'll actually fall back down towards me. But soon another gust whips it away until all I can see is a thin line disappearing on the horizon.

'Oh, no,' I groan.

That was the last present from my mother before she died. One of the very few.

And then I spot him. The local drunk from yesterday. He's seen my every move and not made a single attempt to help. Perhaps because he looks unstable on his legs. I can't tell if he's still drunk from the other night or if this is a new bender he's gone off on.

'So *you're* the London lass everyone's talkin' about.'

I look back up at the sky in case the winds decide to surrender what is mine, but it doesn't look like that'll be happening anytime soon.

'What do you care who I am?' I bite off.

'Because I've never seen you before. And I know everybody.'

'Maybe I'm from the city of Truro and we've never met.'

'Trust me, you're not from Truro.'

'How do you know for sure?'

'First of all, because I know everybody and everybody knows me.'

'What are you, some kind of local celebrity?'

He guffaws. 'Oh, I'm infamous, alright. But you, you can't be from round here because you've got that Bambi look in your eyes. And no one here looks at me like you do.'

'And how exactly am I looking at you?' I straighten my head and close my slack jaw. He truly is beautiful. Such a shame he's damaged goods.

He tilts his head as if to assess me better.

'Without hatred or pity. A bit of impatience, maybe, but that's understandable. What are you, a teacher or somethin'?'

'That I am,' I answer, still straining my eyes on the horizon for my scarf. 'How did you guess?'

He shrugs. 'My parents, from what I can remember, were teachers. Like them, you have that sanctimonious air, like you ate bleddy books for breakfast, lunch and dinner.'

'You sound like you have a lot of disdain for education.'

'Of course not. I used the word sanctimonious, didn't I?'

'And what have you got against books?' Judging by his diction, he hasn't spent too much time anywhere near books – in other words a school, let alone a library.

'Me? Nothin'.'

'Good. Because I could recommend a few good ones.'

'I don't have much time to read.'

Too busy drinking your life away, probably.

'Well, maybe you could find the time and enrich your life with some proper words. Belonging to the English language. There are so many books you could read.'

He grins. That same arrogant grin he gave me while assessing me in the toilets.

'Yeah?'

'Yes.'

'What about?'

'Anything you like. There are books on practically everything.'

'Can you recommend one on how to disappear?'

I baulk. 'Well, that's rather rude. But I must assume you don't know any better. Goodbye.' I huff, turn my back and march away.

I don't know quite what it is, but I have to admit that his mere presence is somewhat unsettling. Or rather, unbelievable. It's a good thing he's a loner, as I can't see anyone wanting to spend time with him. Because beyond the physical presence – or, as Maisie had put it, the 'hunky looks' – he has literally nothing else going for him. And in a way, I feel sorry for him. But whatever he's done to alienate the rest of his fellow villagers, he's undoubtedly brought it upon himself.

'Stop,' comes his voice from behind me. 'I meant for me. I meant that *I* want to disappear.'

I turn. 'You?'

'Yes.'

'Why do you want to disappear?' I blurt before realising it's none of my business in the least. His passing comment on his parents belies the fact that he can't remember them. Did they fall out? Or did he lose them when he was young? Either way, he's not a happy camper and the root lies deep in his childhood. I recognise the engrained sadness in his eyes. I see it in the mirror every morning.

'It's what people do,' he says with a simple shrug, lingering, as if debating whether to strike up a personal conversation with a complete stranger or not.

My best bet is that he may have already exhausted his chances in this tiny village of any real friendships and that he must be lonely to talk just for the sake of it with someone he doesn't know. Or like, as a matter of fact.

'Abandonment is their favourite sport,' he says.

Ah. So he was left behind. Abandoned as a child, perhaps. I understand where he's coming from. But I can't ask, even if I recognise a kindred spirit. We abandonees do have that sixth sense.

'Isn't it simpler to move away?' What's the difference between being a bum here or in the next county comes to my lips, but I clamp my mouth shut.

He smirks. 'Moving away ain't gonna solve anythin'. It

never does, in case you were hopin'. Troubles have a habit of followin', wherever we go. And believe me, I'm trouble. So *I'm* gonna head this way and you do yourself a favour and head that way.'

And just like that, he lifts his collar against the stiff breeze, turns his back on me and stalks off back in the direction from which he came.

One hundred people in this village, if that, and I've already met the weirdest one.

And now to find my grandparents' home. It's so sad to think that I could have met my grandfather, had anyone bothered to tell me I had one. They certainly knew about me.

The Heatherton residence is at the opposite end of the village and, as it turns out, difficult to locate for one particular reason: it's not next to anything. Because it's not even *on* Rectory Lane but in a close of its own. I stop at the wrought-iron gates and peer through with a gasp. Beyond the bars lies a lavish, luxuriant park and a Tudor mansion. I check the address again from my Post-it note: Heatherton Hall, 1 Rectory Lane, Starry Cove.

It's the right address, but it doesn't make sense. There must be some mistake, because my mother's family aren't wealthy. I take a deep breath as I suddenly realise I've come here blindly, without so much as doing any research into the family. And now that I have this extra piece of information, I'm even more intimidated.

I can't just show up on her doorstep unannounced, can I? And say what, exactly? 'Hi. Sorry, got your letter but I thought I'd come and check you out in the meantime. And by the way, nice digs.' I should have found out beforehand what I was getting myself into. But who googles their own family, albeit an estranged one? I'd purposely not looked for anything about them because I'd wanted it all to be fresh, like starting over on a new slate. But this? Far from it. If Audrey makes me feel inadequate with her London home, you can imagine how tiny this historical mansion makes me feel.

No, I can't ring the doorbell. Not now. Not in this emotional state.

When I get back to our room at The Old Bell Inn, I find Maisie nursing a cup of coffee. Her eyes are shadowed as she looks up at me. Just one look at her and my heart melts. She puts her mug down and reaches up for a hug, which I readily give. I'm not good at holding a grudge where Maisie is concerned.

'I'm sorry, Emmie,' she whines. 'I came here to help, not to make your life more difficult. I promise I'll behave from now on.'

'Thank you. I don't mind you sleeping with someone in the village, of course, but don't expect me to do the same. I'm not cheating on Stephen.'

'OK, got it. But believe me, I never meant to intimate to that bloke that you were game.'

'I know. It's his fault for assuming so.'

She nods and wipes her eyes.

'But if you really want me to forgive you...'

'Yeah, anything for my mate!'

'Let's go eat. I'm always hungry down here. It must be the air.'

She laughs and wraps her arm around my neck.

'I saw this pasty shop that's going to blow your mind!' she promises and we head downstairs a little happier than before.

Who am I to refuse another pasty?


We sit on wooden benches outside the place I'd bought my first pasty earlier. The sun is setting as we happily munch away (I swear I'm going to put on a stone before we leave on Monday afternoon), I tell Maisie about my grandmother's house.

'Get out! It would be hilarious, wouldn't it, if you turned out to be of noble blood,' she chirps.

'I know!'

'The MIL would have kittens. And it would serve her right, too, calling you orphan Emmie all these years.'

'Yeah.'

'Oh, look!' Maisie says, shading her eyes. 'There's a scarf like yours…'

I sit up. 'Where?'

'There, around Pickled Loverboy's neck.'

It's true. There he is, standing at a drinks kiosk with a German shepherd the size of a small horse, and a beer in his hand, of course. And he's got my scarf around his neck! The nerve, especially when he saw how upset I was at losing it.

'I'll be right back,' I promise as I march in his direction.

Upon seeing me and my murderous gait, the dog's ears prick up and it begins to growl. If it bites me, I swear I'll bite back. I clear my throat, ready for battle.

'Erm, excuse me,' I say to his back. 'That's my scarf.'

He turns round to look at me, then down at his (my) scarf, then back at me with an attempt at making an innocent face.

'It is?'

I cross my hands in front of my chest. 'You know it is.'

'Prove it.'

'Prove it? You saw me lose it!'

'Nuh-uh. I saw that you lose *something*, but how do I know it's the very scarf I'm wearing?'

'Because it's not yours?' I suggest.

He considers, then shakes his head. 'Not enough. Use your imagination. Or your bookish words. They fascinate me.'

Is he serious? Just who the hell does he think he is?

'I'm sorry, but right now, of all the words coming to mind, none of them are bookish in the least.'

At that, there's a glint of amusement in his eyes. Eyes that are fanned by long dark lashes. It's such a shame he's elected to ruin his life when he could actually amount to something. I can tell he's bright. Perhaps he's lazy. Perhaps he needs a kick up the arse. He could easily enrol in college courses. I bet he'd ace them, seeing he seems to have a witty answer for everything.

'Sorry,' he finally says. 'But it's finders, keepers, especially when it literally falls into your hands.'

'It fell into your hands,' I repeat, unimpressed.

'Right out of the sky,' he assures with the face of an innocent four-year-old, the cad. 'Go figure...!'

'Right!' I rasp and, turning my back on him, march straight back to the bench.

'So much for showing him, huh,' Maisie says with a

giggle. 'He's still looking at you, by the way,' she informs as I scowl into the horizon.

'He's just hoping I'm going to break down and plead with him. Not happening. He can keep the damn scarf.'

'But your mother gave it to you…'

'So what?' I half barked, moistness already gathering behind my eyeballs. There's no way I'm going to show him how upset I actually am. 'It's not like it's that important to me, anyway.'

'Emmie…'

'Drop it, Maisie, please.'

'Do you want me to get it off him for you?'

'You think you'd have more luck?'

'Probably not. He seems to like you more than me.'

'Yeah,' I snort, taking a huge bite out of my pasty.

'Oh, I think so,' she insists. 'He can't seem to take his eyes off you, you know.'

'He's probably wondering what he can con me out of next.'

Maisie laughs and takes a swig of her beer. 'You know, this Cornish stuff, it's an acquired taste, but it's actually starting to grow on me. The same might happen with Jago Moon.'

I look at her. 'Who's Jago Moon?'

She swallows with a sigh of contentment and nods towards the monster with my scarf. 'Your scarf buddy over there.'

'And how do you know that?'

'I had a chat with Laura, the receptionist at the inn. She says he tried to drown himself in the sea, but they pulled him out just in time.'

Drown himself? My God, why? What could possibly induce a man to take his own life? What horrors have entered his heart? I'd seen the darkness in him from the beginning. The resignation to loneliness. That his life is worthless. No one should ever be made to feel like that. Someone should tell him that it doesn't go away with drink.

'She says he wasn't always like this. Laura loves a natter.'

'Sounds like it.'

Sensing we're talking about him, he turns and raises his pint glass to us. Then, to me, he points to his eyes with his index and middle finger in an I'm-watching-you gesture.

'My word, he's gorgeous,' Maisie swoons.

'Pfftt,' is all I can say. What are looks when inside you're a total mess? The man needs a therapist.

'There are rumours of him and the local GP.'

I turn in my seat. 'How is it that Laura is comfortable giving you all this information?'

She shrugs and takes another draught of her beer. 'Don't you know? People are lonely. They talk. But there's one thing they're not giving away...'

'And what's that?'

She points her pint at him. 'That man has a secret.'


I know time is running out and that I really should meet my grandmother on this trip rather than immediately before the funeral. And Rosie might mention it to someone. But I still can't bring myself to knock on her door again. As much as I'm dying to meet her, doubts have begun to seep in my mind.

Why has she never tried to contact me before? I couldn't bear it if she turned out to be as heartless as my own mother. What if she really is the harpy my mother always said? Come to think of it, she was a harpy in her own right, as well. Based on the philosophy that it takes one to know one, I'm not feeling all that confident anymore.

There's my fantasy version of her – a pretty little plump, round-faced dear who bakes cakes all day. Of course, I have nothing to back that notion up with, except for my subsumed desire of home and family. Mrs Heatherton doesn't sound like the kind of person who would spend her days baking cakes.

To keep me away from my grandparents, the feud must have been a horrid one. Perhaps then, just perhaps, I could go in, unarmed, and assure her that the past is in the past... I'm dying for a fresh start. Maybe she is, too. So perhaps a softer, less in-your-face approach would be better for the moment.

With a sigh of trepidation, I reach into my bag, pull out my agenda and my mobile phone to dial her landline number. She doesn't appear to have a mobile one.

I listen to the rings, thinking that this could either lead to absolutely nothing, or to everything.

'Heatherton residence...'

I almost drop my phone in surprise. 'Hello, my name is Emily Weaver and I—'

'Emily? Finally!'

I stop mid-sentence, thrown. She may be noble, but she's as affable as they come. I feel better already.

'It's so nice to hear from you. Thank you for getting in touch.'

'Oh! Well, yes, of course. I'm going to be in the area and I wanted to express my condolences.'

'Thank you. We're all pretty shaken up around here. Nano was much loved by all.'

Aww. I can hear the sadness in her voice despite the warm reaction. I only wish I'd been part of this life that I'll now never know about. An entire life, and I haven't got a single memory of the man who was my grandfather.

'... morning?'

'Oh, sorry, I didn't quite catch that.'

'I said would you like to pop in tomorrow morning?'

'Oh, I'd love to. Thank you so much.'

'Have you got the address?'

'I have, thank you.'

'Say about eleven?'

'Absolutely,' I promise and ring off.

She sounds absolutely lovely. What on earth was I afraid of?

I go into the bedroom expecting to find Maisie, but she's not there. My phone beeps with a message from her:

Just met a lovely bloke! See you tonight – or not, tee-hee! M xxx

If this were London, I'd be worried. But I think it's safe to say that in a village of a hundred souls, there's no danger. Should I call her? I don't want to bother her. Especially if she really has met a nice bloke.

On Sunday morning, I'm up, refreshed, showered and starving. I put on a grey wool dress and my favourite black boots. There – not too modern and not too flashy. I check there's no lip gloss on my teeth and make my way through Starry Cove, once again admiring the prettiness of it all.

The shop signs seem to smile out at me, beckoning me in, even to the ones that I might not need, such as The Cackling Fish, an angler's shop. All around me, like in a Christmas film, an abundance of fairy lights continue to point the way to the village church, behind which lies Rectory Lane. As I follow the plumes of my breath vaporising in the crisp air, I wonder if it's going to snow here this Christmas. Now that would make it even more picture-perfect. I imagine a thick layer of snow covering the lamps, the railings and the trees, almost expecting to see Mr. Tumnus from the Narnia books appear from across the way.

And soon enough, here I am again at my grandmother's gates, only this time I'm not surprised by the size of the house. But I'm still terrified. I know she sounds lovely and all, but what if she doesn't like me? What if I'm a disappointment to her, like my mother was? Or like I am to the MIL? But she's expecting me. What choice have I got? I don't want to be remiss and start off on the wrong foot. Not when there's so much at stake. A family! If I ever want the chance of having one, I have to ring the doorbell, right? So that's exactly what I do.

# 7

*Great Expectations*, Charles Dickens

Before I can panic and change my mind, the gates click open with a short buzz. With my heart pounding like a pneumatic drill, I push my weight against them and stop just inside, like Alice in Wonderland fallen through the rabbit hole. I can't seem to get used to it. Who would have known that at the end of a country lane lay vast green rolling grounds leading to a Tudor mansion, no less, with its steeply vaulted roofs, its many gables and the mullioned windows? How can my parents have kept all this information from me all of my life? And my God, what else do I not know?

Trying to breathe steadily, I make my way up the path to the ancient front doors. Before I can knock, one panel opens and a beautiful elderly woman with the kindest face I've ever seen appears. She's petite, in a blue dress with a neat bun and a pink rosebud of a smile. Instant relief floods through me.

'Emily! Come in, come in,' she chirps.

I smile and gingerly step into a bright, rich foyer, instantly dazzled by the copiousness and quality of the interiors. I'm no interior designer, but as far as I can see, a large part of the original features have been kept in pristine condition for many a century. Antique gold, silver and turquoise shades abound among the draperies, upholstery and carpeting.

'Your home is very beautiful, Mrs Heatherton,' is the safest thing I can think of saying. And yet, I botch that one, too.

She turns in surprise. 'Oh! I'm so sorry. I'm not your grandmother. I'm the maid. Nettie. We spoke on the phone?'

'Oh!' I cry, embarrassed, taking her outstretched hand. 'I'm so sorry, I just assumed—'

'No worries, no worries,' she sing-songs. 'Come, come. Let's get you in and sorted. Are you hungry?'

Now normally I would be. But once again, the panic has set in.

'No,' I whisper, sick to my stomach at the prospect of having to break the ice again with the real Mrs Heatherton-Smythe. 'Is… my grandmother in?'

'Lady Heatherton?' she says.

*Lady* Heatherton? So she has got a noble title, after all. Is this real? Audrey is definitely going to have kittens, then.

'Ah, now that. I'm afraid that Lady Heatherton isn't in at the moment,' she titters, embarrassed.

Not in? But… but… I was expected. It suddenly occurs to me that although my newfound relative is a noblewoman and the MIL-to-be isn't, they might have something in common, after all.

'She's gone to a book reading in Truro.'

A book reading? She preferred to go to a book reading, knowing I'd be here today? She'd rather read a book than meet her own granddaughter?

'I see,' I say feebly, feeling the heat creep up my cheeks and my heart sinking. My face says it all.

Nettie takes my arm and leads me into a luxurious drawing room with a huge neoclassical hearth. The walls are lined with books of every size and age. I spot several first editions of famous classics such as *Emma* by Jane Austen and *Vanity Fair* by William Thackeray. Well, it's obvious how much her books are important to her. So apparently we have at least one thing in common.

'Sit. Make yourself comfortable. You must be shattered.'

I haven't got the heart to tell this lovely woman that I haven't just arrived and catapulted myself over to see my long-lost grandmother. So I say nothing and let her do her hosting as I try not to take it too personally. Lady Heatherton must be one of those eccentric people who value many things before blood. Which is the last thing I need to hear. I've come all this way because she asked to meet me. And now I find she couldn't be bothered to cancel a book reading for her own blood.

I sit back, wondering about my next step. Why hasn't my own, albeit estranged, grandmother bothered to meet me? This doesn't bode well in the least. If I'm counting on Nettie to be of any help, it seems she knows her place all too well and is determined to keep it.

And she is a lovely friendly soul, chattering about the run of the house, Lady Heatherton's corgis, which she loves more than anything in the world (no doubt about that), and what a high standing she has not only in Starry Cove, but also in the entire county of Cornwall owing to her interest in culture and the arts.

We chat, or rather she chats and I supply the occasional question. My heart just isn't in it. Why can't my grandmother not bother to be here?

'… Emily? Don't be offended about your grandmother not being here to meet you. She was speaking at this literary benefit and couldn't stand to disappoint them at the last moment.'

Of course not. Why would she go out of her way to reschedule for someone she doesn't know from Eve?

'Would you like me to let you know when your grandmother returns so you could come and see us again?'

I want to tell her where my grandmother can put it. She's worse than Audrey, if possible. I get to my feet, feeling as if I were a thousand years old.

'Yes, Nettie, that would be lovely, thank you very much. And thank you for the refreshments and your lovely company.'

Nettie beams up at me when we reach the front door.

'Such a sweet girl you are, Emily.' Her face darkens for a brief moment, but then she smiles again.

My belly full of delicious scones and hot sweet tea, but my heart emptier and colder than when I'd arrived, I say my thanks again and dismally make my way through the extensive grounds and out into the streets. Back into pleb world where I belong – a mere speck on the crystalline, pristine world of Lady Mary Heatherton-Smythe.

But I also need to see the silver lining. Could the fact that my grandmother is a noblewoman somehow turn out to be a blessing in disguise? Because if the MIL-to-be finds out I come from blue blood, maybe she'll let off and ease up on me.

As expected, Maisie isn't there when I get back to the inn. There are no messages on my phone from anyone, let alone Stephen. You'd think he'd at least check to see how I got on.

Not knowing what to do with myself, I debate. I could go out and have a quick lunch at the local pub. But then I'd run the risk of having unpleasant encounters with the village slosher. Or I could sample the culinary delights of the restaurant of the inn, having heard wonders about it. Then again, I'm still full from all the scones Nettie has piled into me. In the end I choose to let myself go to dejection, stay in and feel sorry for myself.

It's still too early to give up for the day, but all the same, I slip into my pyjamas and into bed with the remote. But there's nothing on any channel that interests me. A documentary on the little blue penguin. Cute, but I can't concentrate. A spy thriller. No thanks. And, oh, look at that... teary romance. No thank you – I've got my own.

Settling on the penguins, I roll onto my side and snuggle up with a corner of the duvet under my chin. As it turns out, the little blue penguin is the cutest of all the species. Little baby blue furballs that you just want to cuddle forever. A group of penguins is called a waddle, but if they're in the sea, it's called a raft. Another interesting fact that I'd forgotten: the male penguins of some species give pebbles to their mate as a symbol of their undying love. Stephen uses diamonds. I look at the promise ring he gave me last year and know that Stephen has given it to me with the same determination as the dashing but cuddly male wearing a tuxedo on the screen.

I'm tempted to call him but already imagine how the conversation will go:

'What do you mean she wasn't there? Hadn't you told her that you blew off our engagement party for her? What kind of respect is that?'

'No, of course I didn't tell her. What do you want me to say?'

'There's nothing you can say, is there?'

To which I'd sigh and try to make up an excuse for all of us, which he'd see through.

Weary of this dialogue chess already, I turn off the penguins and give my pillow a good punch before I replace it under my head and pull out my Kindle to see what Jane Eyre is up to, as if I didn't know. The poor girl is currently being summoned to Gateshead by her rich aunt – Mrs Reed, who had never liked her enough to pull her out of poverty. And now I really know how she feels.

Of course, I could surprise Stephen with the news that I actually descend from nobility just to shut the MIL up, but that would ruin the joy of seeing the surprise when I tell her face to face.

When I look up again, my window has become a big black rectangle onto the night. I love The Old Bell Inn, because when you turn off the lights, there's no ambient light to disturb you except for the glow of the Milky Way. I turn over and scan the sky through the window, marvelling at how the stars look like diamonds that have literally been hand-tossed into the heavens. I don't know much about constellations, but I recognise a few here and there, such as Orion's Belt and Ursa Major. If I lived here, I'd definitely own a telescope. Much more fascinating than any film.

As I'm straining my eyes to follow a new pattern of stars I've never seen before, the door opens and in stumbles Maisie, whispering and giggling. She's with a man! How could she even think of bringing him back here, to the room we share? Just as I'm about to say something, there's a soft thud as they land on her bed.

I reach out an arm from under the duvet and feel for the light switch.

Lying diagonally across from the bed is Maisie, her arm trailing over the side of the mattress, and coming out of the bathroom – *our* bathroom – is a man with a wastepaper basket. Jago bloody what's-his-face!

He freezes as his eyes meet mine.

'What the hell are you doing here?' I rasp.

He puts the bin down and marches out of the suite, closing the door softly behind him without another glance in my direction.

Fuming, I want to wake Maisie and chew her out for bringing him back here. Drunk or not, she shouldn't be bringing anyone to our room. I'm going to have to have a chat with her tomorrow morning. Because if I wake her right now, as is my first instinct, we'll fall out for real this time.

The next morning when I awake, she's still in the same position, fully dressed and lightly snoring.

After a quick shower, I check the time – ten o'clock. Not too early to make that phone call to my grandmother. I'm hoping Nettie will answer as I'm not quite sure of how to speak to Lady Heatherton-Smythe. How do I address her? What do I say?

'Yes?' comes a soft voice.

Not Nettie's.

'Oh! Hello. This is Emily Weaver. May I speak with, er, Lady Heatherton-Smythe, please?'

'This is Lady Heatherton-Smythe.'

That's it? No 'Oh my goodness, I'm so pleased to speak with you.' Nothing.

'Good morning, Lady Heatherton-Smythe. This is your granddaughter, Emily.'

Silence, then: 'I assume you are staying at a hotel?'

'Yes, The Old Bell Inn.'

'I'll have someone contact you when I'm ready to see you.'

'I'm leaving early this afternoon.'

'Well, then we'll see you at the service in a few weeks.'

'Oh? Oh. Well…'

'Of course, you could have had the grace to let me know you were coming without leaving it to the last minute.'

'Oh, I, uhm…' I falter.

'That is all, Miss Weaver.'

I bite my lip, too stunned to reply as the line goes dead. And that's the end of that.


'Are you *kidding* me?' Maisie says, opening one eye. It's as much as she can handle this morning.

'I don't want to talk about it,' I tell her. 'Get dressed, have something to eat. We have a five-hour drive ahead of us.'

'I'm sorry about last night, Emmie.'

'I don't want to talk about that, either, Maisie. Just get ready, please.'

'Alright,' she agrees meekly, slinking off to the bathroom as I sit on the edge of my own bed.

What a crap thing to do to your only grandchild. What is wrong with this woman?

'Are you ready?' Maisie asks across the roof of the car as I hesitate to get in and take my place at the wheel for the longest slog ever back to Dreary Land and all the inhabitants of the Stone empire.

I finally nod. 'Ready.'

'You don't look too happy, and I don't blame you,' Maisie observes. 'Tell you what, I've an idea. Call Stephen and say we've both come down with food poisoning and can't travel.'

'As great as that sounds, we can't do that. We've got students waiting, remember? Plus I've got an engagement party to organise and a mother-in-law to face.'

'Ah, *quelle femme horrible*!' she tsk-tsks.

'You've got that right,' I sigh as I take my place behind the wheel. 'Come on – let's get this bloody ordeal over with.'

As I turn for one last look at the village that surely rivals the North Pole as far as the spirit of Christmas goes, a pang of regret shoots through me. Upon arrival, I'd been so full of hope at finally having my own family of origin, albeit only one member. I've missed out on my grandfather. I've tried to get over the fact that I'll never get to know him. I'll never be able to call upon memories of him. All of my hopes of even a dysfunctional family (better than nothing) have been dashed. And now I know that, promises or no promises, there's nothing for me here and that my grandmother isn't interested in meeting me in the least, despite her letter. Well, she never need worry about seeing my face again.

Cornwall has been an interesting break from my daily life. A breath of fresh air, and I'm truly sorry to leave so much of it undiscovered. But the next seven months are going to be very busy for me, what with a wedding, a move into a new house and perhaps even a promotion to Head of Year. Not that I am looking forward to that. In truth, I'm becoming more and more disenchanted with my job at school. With London. And, well, sometimes even with Stephen. Which is a momentary thing, I know. Once he moves out of his mother's house, we can finally live our own lives. Because every couple has its no moments and we're going through one right now.

But the fact that worries me is that I'm the only one who seems aware of it. Because Stephen is completely oblivious. To him it's normal that, as a couple, we don't do a lot of things, such as cook together or curl up on the sofa and watch an old film. All we do is work and argue about his mother's interfering in our lives, and I can't even remember the last time Stephen and I actually made love.

# 8

*The Passionate Shepherd to His Love,* Christopher Marlowe

After I've dropped Maisie off at her flat, my mobile rings. It's Stephen.

'Hi,' I chime, trying to inject a modicum of enthusiasm into my voice.

'Hi, Emmie. Where are you?'

'One minute away from home,' I answer. 'Please don't tell me you have to work.'

'Well…'

'Oh, Stephen…'

'Don't be mad. I got tied up.'

Is it normal for him to do this? Is it normal for me to be so upset I want to cry? I was looking forward to a good solid hug after all those emotions in Starry Cove.

'Right,' I sigh, resigned. 'See you tomorrow.'

But when I get in, dragging my wheelie suitcase behind me, Stephen is standing right there, in the middle of my flat, carrying a soup tureen to the table, all smiles.

'Welcome back, Emmie!' He takes my luggage from me and kisses me.

In total shock, I stare at him. 'What are you *doing* here?'

He shrugs, a warm smile on his face. 'Can't a man make his fiancée a welcome home dinner? I've missed you, Emmie.'

I swallow, suddenly moved by his demonstration of affection. 'Thank you.'

'How was Cornwall? Your grandmother?'

'Oh...' I breathe. 'I didn't get to meet her. She was, er, away.' *Reading a book in Truro.*

'You see – I told you that your family is here, with me,' he says, wrapping his arms around me as I lean against him.

'Yes.'

'Come, come, before it gets cold. I've made your favourite – beef stew.'

Actually, that's his favourite, but I'm not complaining. I wash my hands and face, slip off my shoes and sink into my chair as he passes me a smoking hot serving.

'Oh, I almost forgot,' he says. 'Speaking of family...'

I try not to groan. What has the MIL done now?

I paste a smile on my face. 'Yes?'

'Well, Mum's told me what our wedding gift is going to be.'

'Oh?' You'd figure she'd wait for me to get back to tell us at the same time. Or maybe even ask us if there's something we need. But no, I'm not going to go down that road. I'm not going to be bitchy about it like my newfound grandmother. I'm going to rise above the small stuff. 'So, what's the gift?'

He pours me some red wine, a huge smile on his face. 'She's paying for all the renovations – *and* the new furniture.'

'But we haven't even chosen a place yet. You can't buy furniture and... sorry, renovations?'

Stephen puts down his spoon and steeples his fingers together. 'Of the east wing.'

'I'm sorry, east wing?'

He rolls his eyes. 'The east wing of Mum's house, of course. Now it's ours. It's our wedding gift.'

Breathe, Emmie, breathe! It's just a terrible, terrible misunderstanding. Or perhaps simply a bad joke. Stephen never did have a great sense of humour.

'Uhm, Stephen?' I begin, putting down my own spoon. 'Don't you think it's a little too much? I mean, that's extremely generous of your mother, but we should really be choosing our own home, don't you think?'

Stephen's face falls. 'Emmie, what are you going on about? We've been talking about renos for months now.'

'Yes, but I thought you meant of our own find. When instead you meant... No, Stephen. I'm sorry, but I really don't want to live under the same roof as your mother. No offence intended, but—'

He suddenly stands up, throwing his napkin on the table.

'No offence intended? You literally refuse all she has to give us with a sorry, no offence intended?'

I look up at him. 'Stephen, you know your mother and I aren't exactly on the same page.'

He crosses his arms. 'Not being on the same page is one thing, Emmie, but outright refusing to accept such a gracious gift? This is the home I've lived in since I was *born*. I don't want to leave it. And I want our children to live in it. I want to continue the tradition.'

'The tradition of what? Living under Mother Stone?' I

throw at him. 'No, Stephen. I'm sorry, but I just can't. I value my privacy too much. She has a horrible habit of waltzing into any room without so much as announcing herself and I—'

'Announcing herself? Do you hear yourself? You want her to announce herself in her own home?'

'That's why I don't want to live with her, Stephen. I want our privacy.'

'You can have your privacy once you close the bedroom door. She's not going in there, is she now?'

I snort. 'I wouldn't put it past her. And besides, I don't want privacy only in my bedroom. I want to be free to walk around in my knickers and… and make love on the kitchen table if I so choose.'

Not that that had ever happened, and judging where this is going, it looks like it never will.

'You are unbelievably ungrateful!' he says as he reaches for his coat, heading for the door.

'What are you doing? I thought we were going to have a nice dinner and a chat.'

'You and I have absolutely nothing to talk about,' he says as he opens the door, stalks out and slams it behind him.

For a few moments I sit, waiting for him to return. But I know he's not going to.

'And then what? Did he call you back?' Maisie whispers, her sandwich forgotten in her hands.

Tuesday has started with a dreariness that has erased any remnants of the happy moments in Cornwall.

'No.'

'Jesus.'

I look around me at the staffroom still decorated with faded and forgotten paper pumpkins, ghouls and witches. Christmas, my favourite time of year, is only a few weeks away and already positively, irreparably ruined. There's no way on earth that I'm going to succumb to the MIL's will. And if Stephen cared about me the way he says, then he'll see the madness of his mother's ways and agree to live our own life.

I never said to cut ties with her completely, even if that's what would give me ultimate happiness. In my experience, it's better not to have anyone than a bad someone. It erases all the drama and the heartache. Look at me.

'So, what are you going to do?'

I shake my head. 'There's nothing I can do, Maisie.'

Maisie puts down her sandwich. 'Emmie, maybe this is the right moment to let go. I mean, we both know that he's not right for you. God knows I've told you time and again. Maybe this coming year will see a new life for you.'

I shrug. 'All I know is that I can't – I won't – fall to her whims.'

'Good for you, Emmie,' she says, patting me on the back. 'And whatever you need, I'm here.'

I hold back a sniff as the bell rings.

'Thanks, Maisie.'

Is this what I want? To end it with Stephen? Granted, things aren't going very well, but for this to happen, and so suddenly? Do I want to drag it out, or is it less painful like this? One thing's for sure: I'm not going to be spending Christmas with the MIL. Or Stephen, if this keeps up.

'Hey…' Stephen greets me as I'm making my way back

to my classroom as if he hadn't just stormed out of my flat the night before. 'You alright?'

I shrug, hefting my books, too angry to look him in the eye.

'Look,' he says, squeezing my shoulder. 'How about we have a chat about it tonight over dinner, your place? I'll cook. To make up for last night. We'll talk.'

I brighten somewhat. 'We will?'

'Of course. Just pop into Sainsbury's and fetch whatever you want and I'll cook it.'

Well, so much for making an effort.

'Don't bother. I'll just get something ready-made.'

'I said I'd cook and I'll cook, Emmie. Now be a good girl and cover for Allison, will you? She's off sick today.'

'Oh? Can't you get the cover supervisor to do it? I've got some marking to do for tomorrow.'

'You can do that later, if you wouldn't mind. Headmaster's orders.'

*Headmaster's orders.* Ah. Of course. Payback time for the postponed engagement party. Oh, how he's beginning to grate on my nerves – at school, in the car, whenever he's over for the night. For someone who seldom comes around, he's taken making himself at home to the next level, pushing my stuff around and sometimes even tossing it in the laundry bin when I was simply airing it for one more hour of wear in case I had to pop down to the corner store and didn't want to put on something new. His 'if it's dirty it goes in the laundry bin and if it's not, it goes back in the wardrobe' is something he's undoubtedly inherited from his mother.

Last week, he criticised the contents of my fridge by throwing some of my food away, even the yoghurt culture

I had going. My selection of veggies was met with a 'How long is this broccoli going to have to wait to be cooked?' Just like his mother.

'When I'm good and ready,' I'd snapped.

But at work, he's the boss, so I scoop up my belongings and head out for the science block, pulling my second favourite scarf closer around me. I don't know a thing about science and I know for a fact that Year 11 are a nightmare at the best of times. But what choice have I got?

I ask Tommy to pass the worksheets round and give them a five-minute start before I do my rounds. Verity is the brightest of the class and doesn't suffer fools gladly, but there are still too many weak students who need constant support, so I hover mainly in their area, giving the 'cool' end of the classroom my 'get your arse in gear before I come over and give you shit' expression on.

And that's when I notice that Joe Collins, the class bully, isn't working but drawing in his planner. Penises. Oodles of them. I have no choice but to ship him out and at three thirty, I'm sitting with him in the head's office.

Stephen leans forwards and looks into Joe's face.

'Why did you cover your planner in penises? Have you got a *problem*? Or is there something you're trying to tell us?'

*Oh my God!*

'Stephen… Mr Stone,' I counter, shaking my head in warning, but Stephen is on a roll.

'If you're trying to tell us you're gay, you've succeeded.'

This can't be happening! What the hell is wrong with him? Has he gone completely mad?

I clear my throat. 'Joe, you should go back to class now.'

Joe, who is still wide-eyed from being hauled into the headmaster's office only to be humiliated, nods and runs off, his tie flying over his shoulder and very probably tears in his eyes.

'Serves the bully right,' Stephen sentences as he straightens his own tie.

'Stephen, what the hell are you doing? You can't talk to people, let alone *children*, like that! So what if he's gay. He's entitled to his own life.'

'I have absolutely nothing against gay people. But I can't have my students drawing genitalia all over their planners. And by the way, I'm not having you contradict me ever again in front of one of my students.'

'Contradict you? I was trying to save you from yourself.'

'I also think that you should call me Mr Stone when we're not alone.'

I laugh. 'Are you serious?'

'Of course I'm serious. Look at the cock-up you just made in front of Joe. Now go and write your report.'

'*I* made a cock-up? You're the one who offended him and his presumed sexual orientation. I'll be surprised if you don't get a visit or an email from his parents tomorrow.'

'Ha! You'd love that, wouldn't you?' he seethes.

I sit up. 'Of course not. Why would you even think that, Stephen?'

He wipes his face with his hands, blowing air through his cheeks. 'No. I know. I'm sorry, I'm sorry. I've got meetings coming out of my ears for the whole of the next two weeks and I'm already exhausted.'

'Then why don't you take a day off?'

He snorts. 'Yeah, that's happening. Headmasters don't take days off.'

'They do if they're exhausted. Just one day will do you good.'

'One day? I'd need a month to sleep it all off. Can you believe that one of the governors called me at eleven o'clock last night? I had a mind to tell him off.'

'But you didn't.'

He snorts. 'Can you imagine me doing that? No. I'll just turn off my phone after work.'

'But what if I need you?'

'Just leave me a message. I'll be checking for them.'

I clamp my mouth shut. It's useless arguing. Stephen's going to do whatever he wants. Maybe I should start doing the same.

One period later, I'm back at my station in the staffroom. I sit and stare at a blank screen. I'm getting sick and tired of writing reports every single time a kid does something slightly out of the ordinary. OK, drawing penises in a planner isn't exactly someone being on their best behaviour, but why did he have to humiliate the kid? Where is the compassion, the dialogue?

Stephen's administration does little to ensure that there is any and I've heard rumours about some not being happy with him. Should I mention it to him, or would he take it the wrong way? He's not one to take positive criticism lightly. Even now, what with his stress levels and all, I can hardly talk to him. Better to wait until he's in a better, stronger place.

I look out of the window up to the bruised sky that looks as if it's about to burst into tears. I'd feel the same, having to look down at the mess of a modern city all day, with all its cement and grime and loneliness and violence. Everywhere I turn there's a weirdo talking to himself or eyeing someone strangely or even following them home. It's like a monster out of control.

After the longest bus ride in history, I finally get home to my flat and kick off my shoes.

I switch the kettle on, peel off my work dress and tights and slip into my leggings and an old T-shirt. I wind my hair up into my usual chill-time ponytail, which Stephen says makes me look like a syphilitic pineapple. Charming, I know.

I brew myself a cup of tea while searching for the biccies that will be the only thing to get me through this evening of marking and in the end I find a forgotten stash of my favourite chocolate digestives. Eyeing my marking pile and putting it off for just a little longer, I procrastinate by sharpening my pencils, re-stacking my stapler and even reorganising my desk drawers. What's the matter with me? Normally I'd have done it all by now, but I've been putting it off for days, since before Cornwall, and every day that goes by sees me deferring the work to yet another day.

I'm definitely not in the mood to deal with my students' weaknesses, wondering how on earth they're going to get on in their lives if they continue this way. I can barely deal with my own shortcomings and doubts, let alone theirs, and when I'm like this (hardly ever), I'm better off leaving them. When I'm in this mood I can't help but see the world at its darkest and gloomiest. And tomorrow I have another two batches on Shakespeare to mark. But tonight, not even the Bard can get me excited.

And then my wandering eyes spot my Cornwall wheelie

suitcase and I get up to open it wide, inhaling it as if any lingering scent could take me back. And it does. The scent of the inn lingers on the inside of the lining, as if the Cornish air has hopped in as a stowaway, just to follow me to London to see for itself why I'd even contemplate leaving Cornwall. Excellent question.

It's Friday night and I've prepared a conciliatory dinner for Stephen back at my flat. I watch him as he slips off his tie, opens the wine and begins to eat, obviously going through things in his head. I know this because he's actually talking to himself under his breath. The fact that we haven't spent a night in the same bed in months doesn't seem to be on his worry list, judging by the fact that he hasn't mentioned it. He always mentions the things that bother him.

'Stephen, why do you want to marry me?' I ask him out of the blue.

He looks up from his imaginary conversation with God knows who, almost as if surprised to find me there.

'What a ridiculous question. Why do you think?'

'You tell me. We have absolutely nothing in common except for work. You grew up with the Mayor of London, while I consider myself lucky if I manage to get through to a help desk on the phone.'

And as usual, he skips the sentimental stuff and goes straight for the practical side. 'Why didn't you say anything? All you have to do is tell me and I'll have my assistant take care of these things for you.'

'That's not the point. Besides, I can manage my own affairs, thank you.'

'No need to be snarky. I was just trying to help.'

'I'm not being snarky. I'm simply stating that I live in the real world while you're used to having everyone else do things for you.'

'Actually, I don't. You know I work round the clock. I hardly have time to breathe. And as a matter of fact, about Cornwall...'

I *knew* this was coming. I knew he'd find a way to get out of it some way or other.

I sigh. 'Forget it, Stephen.' And the sad thing is that I'm not even surprised.

'Emmie, that's not fair. You know how knackered I am and still you want to argue? I let the engagement party go. Even Mum has.'

'Well, seeing as you're not doing anything the night the party was supposed to be, I thought you'd come to the funeral with me.'

'Who says I'm not doing anything?'

'I don't want to argue, Stephen. In fact, I don't even want to talk.' And with that, I walk to the bedroom door, where I pause. 'I suggest you take the day off tomorrow before you do or say anything else you'll be sorry for.'

Not that he is sorry. If anything, he is completely convinced I'm the one who made a mistake. Like mother, like son.


The next day, Saturday, is Maisie's twenty-eighth birthday. As she hates surprises, she books a restaurant for her closest friends, just like every year. Tonight, the bloke of her choice is a rather dashing Mexican man named Pablo, whom she's dubbed Old El Paso, but he finds it adorable. He finds *her* adorable – and already I feel sorry for him because there's never any point in getting attached to Maisie if you're a bloke.

The party over, I head back to my flat, which is a short walk from Maisie's – literally three minutes, if that – so it's never been a cause for worry. Until tonight, because I'm particularly aware of the echo of someone's footsteps not far behind.

But when I turn, there's only a man on his mobile, quite far back and completely unaware of me. So I continue, although still somewhat wary. It's only when his shadow falls across mine that I whirl round in panic, but it's too late.

He reaches out and grabs me by the throat, nearly lifting me off the pavement, pinning me to the wall.

# 9

*Jane Eyre,* Charlotte Brontë

I don't know how long he's had me here for. Nor can I even describe him, because his face is in shadow and I'm beginning to black out from lack of oxygen. All I know is that I can't last much longer without taking another breath. And there's nothing I can do, because his other hand has immobilised both of my arms above my head and I'm completely paralysed with no means of escape. Before I lose consciousness, I become aware of a shrill sound – that of a girl laughing – and I pray that she's not on her own.

What seems like. the next morning, I come to, only to realise that I'm lying on the wet pavement with a group of youngsters around me, gently tapping my face and shouting, 'Hey! Are you OK?'

I try to sit up, aware of the rain pelting my face. Before I know it, a police car arrives and I'm put into the back of it. Bouncing around in the back seat despite the seat belt, I lace the fingers of my left hand with the ones on my right to ground myself emotionally. I've always done this. It feels like someone is actually holding my hand. Even looking down at it, for a brief moment one could believe that's the case. I do this often. Stephen isn't a hand-holder.

Which reminds me. I need to call him, tell him what's happened. He'll come running and take me home where it's safe. He's like that, Stephen. A protector. Which my own father never was, so it's nice to know I finally have someone who cares.

At the police station, they tell me I'm lucky nothing was stolen and ask me to describe my attacker. And is there anyone they could call? So I ring Stephen's phone, praying he hasn't turned it off as he always does in the evenings now to avoid work calls from people who don't know better. I'm lucky my phone was in my back pocket and that the kids scared him off, leaving my bag behind, after all. Much ado about nothing, in the end.

I wait a few moments and then, miraculously, he answers.

'Hello? This is Headmaster Stone's mobile phone. Who's calling at such a late hour, please?'

His *mother*? What the hell is she doing with his phone?

I clear my throat. 'Audrey? Is Stephen there, please?'

'Oh, hello, dear. Did you manage to go to the spa yet? I've already made three appointments for you and you never showed. That's rather embarrassing for me as I know these people, dear.'

I pinch the bridge of my nose. 'Sorry, Audrey, I forgot. I need to speak to Stephen, please.'

'He's not here. He left his phone at home.'

He never does that. Where the hell can he be? 'Can I leave a message?'

'You can if you want to, but if you leave him one yourself

on his phone, it's better. The minute he walks through the door, I'm giving him his phone, so…'

'Right,' I say, on the verge of screaming. 'Can you please tell him to call me back as soon as possible?'

'Why can't it wait until the morning? You know he needs his sleep, dear.'

'Because I've been attacked.'

'Attacked? By whom?'

'I don't know, Audrey. A stranger in the street.'

'What were you doing in the street at this hour? Honestly, you girls today… No wonder you get yourselves into all kinds of trouble. I bet you were wearing some skimpy outfit, as well. And now you were going to disturb Stephen so he could come to your rescue? Really, Emily! You should know much better than that, my dear.'

*What?* Is this woman for real?

'First of all, I don't own any skimpy outfits and even if I did, that doesn't give maniacs the right to… Why am I even explaining this to you? You're clearly against young women. I wonder why that is.'

'Don't be insolent, Emmie. It's not what I expect from my future daughter-in-law. You know we have an image to uphold and you're not doing very well, dear.'

'Well, you're not every bride's dream, either,' I snap before I can stop myself. Sometimes it's not always a good idea to suppress your words.

Stunned silence.

'I'll give my son your message when I see him.'

'Don't bother! Goodbye,' I snap and hang up. What a piece of work!

Immediately, my phone pings with seven messages from Maisie, the last one reading:

Where are you? Call me back. I don't care what time it is!!!

So as the police are driving me home I do, and she answers on the first ring.

'Finally! I was getting worried when you didn't answer my texts, so I waited for El Paso here to fall asleep. Crikey, the man is unstoppable. Did I wake you, love?'

'Not exactly,' I answer before the squawk of the police radio fills the car.

'What the hell was that? Where are you?'

'I'm in a p-police car. They're taking me home.'

'Police? Oh my God, Emmie, what happened? Are you alright?'

'I got a-attacked…'

'What? Oh my God! I knew I should have insisted on walking you home. Is Stephen with you yet? I'm on my way!'

'I tried calling him but he left his phone at his mum's.'

'I'll get a hold of him – you sit tight!'

'It's not necessary anymore, Maisie. I'm going home.'

But the line goes dead.

A winded Maisie bursts through my door five minutes later, El Paso on her heels. She eats up the ground between us and envelops me in her arms.

'Sweetheart, are you OK?' she cries, stepping back to check that I'm still in one piece. 'Why the hell didn't you call me? Oh my God, look at the bruises on your throat!'

'*¿Qué pasó?*' 'What happened?' the Mexican bloke asks.

You see? Even he seems more interested than my future family.

'I'm alright,' I assure them as they sink into the settee next to me.

'I've just called Pete McIntyre who's in a meeting with Stephen and a New York school. Stephen should be here any minute,' Maisie assures.

'Thank you,' I say, relief washing over me, when my mobile rings again.

It's Stephen.

'Emmie, are you alright? Pete told me that Maisie called him and said that you've been attacked.'

'Yes,' I breathe. 'Maisie's here.'

'Oh, is she? Good. Because we're in the middle of a Zoom meeting with a school in Texas.'

'Oh.'

'But I can ditch them if you need me. Just say the word.'

If I need him? What does he think? And I should even have to ask?

'N-no, that's OK. I'll be OK,' I assure, already envisaging his mum telling him about how I ran round the town naked in search of someone to 'pay attention' to me.

'Right, then. I'll give you a call tomorrow morning. Try to get some sleep.'

'Yep…' So much for being protective. That was one of the main things that had attracted me to him. But now, where has that gone?

'How long is he going to be?' Maisie asks when I hang up.

'He's… not coming.'

'What?'

'He's in a meeting. With Texas.'

Maisie's face reddens. 'What the hell is wrong with that bloke?'

I shrug as the tears finally come and I'm not even embarrassed that Pablo is here to witness it.

'I don't know, Maisie. I just don't know...'

I'd fallen in love with Stephen because he was stable. My rock, really. But now I see that I am, in effect, single and I didn't even know it. I only have myself and Maisie to depend on to see me through my darkest moments.

Stephen has given me everything I don't need. Gifts. Surprise trips or nights out. What he doesn't give me is sharing our deepest moments. But aside from the grand gestures and my efforts to bring us closer together, Stephen doesn't do emotions. Nor does he do female psychology, he tells me. According to him, as adults, we should already have sorted ourselves out *before* we engaged in a relationship. Coming from him, that's a mouthful.

It's going to be a very long night. El Paso is sleeping on the settee while Maisie tosses and turns in the double bed next to me, asking me every five minutes how I am, do I want something hot to drink, am I hungry and do I want to talk.

'No, I'm OK, thank you, Maisie,' I whisper so as not to wake the handsome man sleeping in the next room.

This is ridiculous. I don't know him from Adam and yet, knowing he's there manages to calm and reassure me. Somewhat. Because in truth, he, too, could have been some maniac or thief just waiting for us to fall asleep and rob us blind or murder us. Simply because he could.

The next morning, Maisie and I wake to the smell of bacon and eggs, buttered toast and steaming hot coffee. So much for our mysterious one-night stand murderer.

'*Buenos días!*' he chimes as we appear in his line of vision.

He's already fully dressed and has found the good plates, which he's set on the tiny bistro table for us. He's even managed to find my festive tablecloth (not that my three kitchen drawers presented an effort to go through).

'Morning,' I murmur as Maisie pounces on him, smacking a thorough kiss on his mouth.

I must admit, in the light of day he's particularly handsome. Good for Maisie. And he cooks. I make a mental note to suggest she make an effort to see him again. At least for our stomachs' sakes.

They chat amiably throughout breakfast as I contribute with my meagre Spanish – a couple of *gracias* and *muy buenos* (thank yous and very goods) – all the while thinking of Stephen.

We've known each other for three years now and have decided to get married and start a family. And yet, we have nowhere near the same amount of complicity Maisie and her *una sola noche* bloke here have. The mere thought is humiliating. And bears some serious thinking.

'… Emmie?'

I look up, suddenly aware of Maisie's voice and her hand on my shoulder. 'Hmm? Sorry?'

'I said are you going to be OK while we go home and change? I'll come right back.'

'Oh, of course. Go, go. I'm fine. And thanks so much for staying the night. But really, you didn't have to. *Gracias*, Pablo,' I say in his direction. 'For the amazing breakfast. And everything else.'

He smiles and takes a final swig of his coffee as he stands. He really is kind. And he makes a mean breakfast. I hope he and Maisie will continue to see each other.

'Pablo is a chef at the Cancun restaurant in Chelsea,' Maisie informs me as they shrug into their coats.

'Now I get the amazing meal,' I say with a smile.

'Come, both of you, whenever you like,' he says, throwing a sexy look at Maisie, who begins to gush.

Ah, the thrill of attraction. I truly miss those first furtive glances, waiting for the right moment for that first kiss to happen. All behind me now. Anyone who is engaged (if I still even am) should be happy to have left the uncertainty of romance behind them to welcome with open arms the maturity of a fully-fledged relationship – marriage. And yet, I can't bring myself to be cheery about it.

The rest of the day, with no sight or sound of Stephen, I lounge around, trying hard not to think about my attacker. I'd been lucky this time, but the next? Anyone living in a metropolis knows that there may well always be a next time. And I might not be this fortunate again. Where the hell has Stephen got to?

I look out of the window at the pre-Christmas buzz below me. Mums dragging children around or pushing them in their buggies, all the while ticking off lists. Why don't I feel the same buzz back here in London? Even before the attack, I felt nothing – no buzz, no rush. For the first time I have a real reason to be excited – my very own (which is debatable) engagement party. And yet, I can't seem to find any joy.

Perhaps the fact that my grandmother had been a disappointment is bothering me more than I thought. It looks as if, apart from the funeral, I won't have any reason to go back to Starry Cove. Because I feel that I owe my grandfather whom I've never met at least that much. He wasn't necessarily like his wife. For all I know he was a decent man. And it's a shame that she and I didn't hit it off, because I really like everyone I've met in Cornwall, from Rosie to Nettie to Penny and Laura at the inn. They seem to be the salt of the earth. I wonder what they're all doing...

I even wonder what bloody Jago Moon is up to. Probably taking the mickey out of his next conquest.

And speaking of conquest, it's as if Stephen has lost all interest in me. This is no way to be in a relationship. Granted, maybe I really am old-fashioned, but shouldn't a man drop everything if his fiancée gets attacked? This is ridiculous. Coming over the next morning, assuming he's going to, simply isn't good enough. Not anymore.

# 10

*The Bell Jar,* Sylvia Plath

About an hour later, as I'm huddled in my duvet on the sofa, trying to dispel the chill inside me, Stephen finally comes over, loaded with 'forgive me' flowers and food.

'Hi,' he says, eyeing me.

Whether it's to detect my emotional state or simply my mood regarding his absence is a conundrum of its own. As easy as Stephen is to read, sometimes I find it's best not to.

I nod out of mere courtesy. I thought I was going to rush into his arms, but now I find that I don't even want him in my flat. The nerve, to completely ignore what happened to me. I could have *died*.

'Oh, gosh,' he says when he spots my purple throat. 'Are you OK?'

'I am now,' I snap. 'He fled when a group of people came around the corner and scared him off.'

'What did he want? Money?'

'Does it matter? He certainly didn't want to buy me

dinner,' I snap as I wrap myself up further in my duvet, avoiding any eye contact.

He sighs. 'Look, I'm sorry. Maisie already chewed me out for not coming. I honestly thought—'

'You thought what? That I was exaggerating when I said a man had jumped me from behind?'

He lowers his head. 'Yes. I'm sorry.'

'What the hell made you think that I wasn't serious?'

'I just thought that you were doing it to attract my attention, is all.'

'Attract your attention? I can see you've spoken to your mother.'

'I left my phone at home, is all.'

'You could have found another way to call me to say goodnight.'

'I finished late and until the call I knew you were out having fun.'

'Not so much, as it turned out.'

'Is it my fault you were attacked?'

'If you'd come to the party, maybe this wouldn't have happened.'

He groans. 'Emmie, you know I'm a busy man.'

'I was attacked, Stephen!'

'But I didn't realise it was that serious.'

'Because you believed your mum rather than Maisie! Didn't you see all of her calls? Didn't you think that something was wrong? What the hell is wrong with you? What am I supposed to do to get your attention?'

'Look, I really am sorry.'

'Forget it. Just go home and leave me alone. I need to catch up on my sleep.'

He hesitates. 'I can stay. Watch over you.'

*Too little, too late.* 'I'm fine, Stephen. Go home. I'll see you at school.'

'Well… are you sure?'

'Will you just go, please?'

He jumps up as if I've cut his leash.

'Right. I'll give you a ring later, OK?'

I want to tell him not to bother, but instead I groan. 'Right.'


It isn't about the attack. Or perhaps not only that. Lately, I've been thinking about my parents. I have so few memories of them, or of a happy childhood. They never really loved me. But then I'd met Stephen at my job interview, with his proper manners and etiquette. He was kind and had a way with him. There had been three other equally qualified candidates. But perhaps that's just my innate insecurity playing up again. Because Stephen, with his social graces, impromptu dinners and Sunday brunches, had won me over immediately. I guess that I'm in a moment of my life when I not only want a man in my life, but also actually *need* him. What a rut to fall into.

I'd always thought of him as my rock. My knight in shining armour. The one who would ditch everything to help me if I needed. I thought I was his priority, or at least his second. I wanted to share this Cornish experience with him, tell him about my newly discovered grandmother and my dashed hopes for a real family. I wanted to provide some information on my family. I almost wanted to justify my existence to him and his mother.

Because not having met my grandmother despite having been to Cornwall, I'm still no closer to knowing what happened between my parents and my grandparents. Had they perhaps not approved of Mum's choice? I didn't see how that could have been even remotely possible. Dad had been a university professor with an impeccable reputation. And they'd been in love. Everyone around me was in love. Even Maisie, who didn't believe in love until yesterday. And now I sense that the entire world, fuelled by this Christmas spirit, is high on the feeling. Everyone is either in love or wants to fall in love. What is there for me?

That evening, I pick up the house phone and dial Stephen's mobile. The minute he says hello, I can tell he's harried.

'Oh, hello, Emily,' he says matter-of-factly. 'How are you feeling?'

*Lonely. Derelict. Abandoned.*

I sniff, rubbing my forehead. 'Can you come over, Stephen?' I whisper.

'What's happened? Are you OK?'

'Yeah. I'm just… uhm, feeling a little off.'

'Are you sick? Do we need to cover for you tomorrow?'

I huff. 'No, I just need to chat a bit.'

'It's late, Emmie, and I've still got to go through a mountain of paperwork for my 7 a.m. meeting tomorrow. We'll chat tomorrow, OK?'

When? I wonder. During break time?

'Are you sure everything's alright?'

I cough. Suddenly I've lost the will to speak. About anything.

'Yes. I'll see you tomorrow.'

'Emily, is this going to come back to haunt me during our next argument?'

Our next argument? I can't even bear the thought. I just don't have the energy or the will. Why does he always manage to make me feel like everything is my fault?

'No,' I assure.

'OK then, Emily. I'll see you tomorrow.'

'Right,' I say, a sudden weariness washing over me.

I ring off, curled up on the sofa, and think about my trip to Cornwall – the moment I'd first driven over the hill and had my first glimpse ever of paradise. I think about all the breathtaking views I'd seen and all the people I'd met. I think about every single moment, from beginning to end.

But it's no use. I can't relax either my body or my mind, just waiting for my attacker to grab my throat again. I need to get away from all this – my life, London, the MIL. And for now, Stephen's indifference. Maybe if he actually had a chance to miss me, he'd appreciate me. So I make up my mind. I'm going to call my doctor and tell him about my attack and take a leave of absence due to mental health problems. Not so much to put Stephen to the test as to sort myself out. I'll stay at The Old Bell Inn. I don't have to see my grandmother other than the funeral service. In fact, she doesn't know me, so she wouldn't even recognise me. Unless Nettie gives me away.

On Monday morning, during break, I tell Stephen of my decision.

'You're joking, right?' Stephen says, sitting back from his desk, eyes trained on me for the first time in months.

'I'm not joking. I am traumatised by the attack. My doctor has prescribed me some time by the sea.'

'The sea,' he repeats. 'As in the Cornish sea.'

I shrug. 'Might as well kill two birds with one stone.'

'We're having our engagement party on the 24th of December, Emmie.'

'I know – you already told me.'

'Well, don't look *too* happy. I mean, it's only our engagement party.'

'No, Stephen. I keep telling you, it's not our engagement party. It's yet another one of your mother's fêtes that doesn't take either of us into consideration. I'm constantly being monitored by her and her lackeys. Have I had highlights put in yet? Have I been to the tanning salon? Have I had my nails done yet, my elbows buffed and for God's sake, have I had a bikini wax?'

This causes him to snigger.

'Do you not realise how invading and invasive your mother is? This is my body, my life. None of it has anything to do with her. So, I'm taking a break. From both of you.'

'But you are coming back for the party, yes?'

I look up into his eyes. 'Do you actually care that I'm not happy right now, or are you more concerned about your social circle gossiping about you?'

His mouth turns into a grim line. 'Both. I have obligations, Emmie. I am a headmaster of a prestigious academy. I come from a solid background. My social circle already frown on me marrying a teacher. I can't afford any more faux pas.'

'They frown on you for marrying me?'

'I didn't say you as in you. In their opinion, a headmaster should aim—'

'Higher?' I volunteer, unable to believe my ears.

'I didn't say that, Emmie.'

'Tell me the truth, Stephen. Do you even love me anymore, or have you finally succumbed to your mother's way of thinking?'

He watches me in silence, then answers: 'You're the one who's been putting up a fuss with everything – the dress, the menu, the church – and now you're the one leaving. You do the maths, Emmie...'

'So it's easy for you just to let go? So *you* will appear to be the victim?'

'I'm tired, Emmie. I've had a long day and another equally long one ahead of me tomorrow. So I'm going to say goodnight. I'll speak to you tomorrow.'

'No, you won't, because I'm leaving tomorrow. I'll be back in time for the party. It's not like I'm needed for the wedding preparations, anyway.'

'Come on, Emmie, don't be like that. Tell you what. I'll come down to Cornwall with you. I can get away this time. Well, for a couple of days at least.'

'Uhm, no. I think I need to be alone for a bit.'

He laughs nervously. Somewhere between 'I can't believe you're doing this' and 'don't be silly'.

'What does that mean? Are you still angry with me?'

The truth is that I'm sick and tired of playing games of Stephen Says.

'I just need some time off.'

'Off... from me.'

'Just... off. I hope you'll understand.'

'Please tell me you're not still upset about me not coming to your rescue.'

Among other things.

'I just need to switch off from everything London right now.'

Silence, then: 'Right. That's fine. You can go if that's what you really need. I'm OK with it.'

'Gosh, thanks. I didn't know I needed your permission.'

'I never said you did.'

'It certainly didn't sound like that.'

'Emmie, you're tired and not thinking straight.'

'Yes, well, I'm certainly tired about a lot of things, Stephen.'

He sighs. 'Emmie, I know I've been a bit absent lately and I'm sorry.'

'It's fine, Stephen. I have to go now.'

'Yes, you go, while I wait for you to remember I exist.'

'No, Stephen. That's usually my role.'

Silence.

I huff. 'Look, I'll keep in touch.'

'I hope you know what you're doing, Emmie.'

'I've got to go, Stephen,' I repeat.

'OK, then. I love you, Emmie.'

I close my eyes and swallow. Why can't I answer in the same way? Of course I love Stephen. I've loved him for three years. We're planning a future together. So why am I feeling so estranged?

# 11

*'Tis Pity She's a Whore,* John Ford

## Tuesday, 22nd November

Some time in Cornwall can only be a good thing, as I can't think of a better place to chill. Nor, apparently, can anyone else, because the M3 is jam-packed with thousands of people who have had exactly the same idea, almost as if Cornwall were their only solution, their last resort.

Stuck in a bottleneck, my eyes roam to the other vehicles surrounding me, and all I can see is young families with 2.3 children champing at the bit to hit the coast and enjoy some freedom. Some have surfboards on roof racks, while others simply have those storage cases bursting at the seams. I slide a glance at my luggage and wonder if I'm under-packed.

As I drive deeper into the county along the coastline, turning and twisting down country bends, weaving in and out of the one-horse villages, I wonder whether I'm one of those who are only deluding themselves they'll find peace coming all the way down here. I mean, it's not where you are that should save you, but who you're with, right?

But in that case, I'm in trouble, because it suddenly hits me that I haven't thought about Stephen once in nearly five hours that it's taken me to get here. Which is a big no-no in a relationship. Then again, he's one of the reasons I've come down here – to get away from the sense of obligation and humiliation. And it suddenly occurs to me that for a few days, I'll no longer be under any obligation towards him, nor his mother, my future mother-in-law.

I won't have to go anywhere I don't want to or see anyone I don't want to – nor do I have to smile and make small talk with anyone in whom I've got absolutely no interest. I can be myself. Not wear any make-up or heels, or stupid, cruel shapewear or the latest in bangles or scents, or tote the best bag I can afford just so the MIL won't be ashamed of our future association. I've never been one to do so in the first place, but since she's appeared on my horizon, it's all about pleasing her so as not to displease him. It's all about appearances. Never mind what I'm feeling deep down, or what my true wants are. God forbid.

I can't even remember the last time I've let my hair down, or let Stephen see me in my leggings or without make-up. He's always in perfect order and can't understand why I could possibly need to let myself go.

'Next thing, you're going to start gaining weight,' he'd once said.

It was going to be a long life of restrictions if I couldn't bring him round to my way of seeing things. Or be myself in front of him.

★

When I arrive at The Old Bell Inn, it's like I never left. Penny and Laura are there, greeting me even more cheerfully. And if possible, there seem to be even more decorations and fairy lights. It's not even December and yet Starry Cove seems to have topped the charts of Festive Villages of England. It seems to be in its own bubble. Like a giant glass snowstorm with the miniature buildings and cobbled streets and lamp posts, all that's really missing is the snow.

For a moment I pause to wonder whether or not someone may be shooting a Christmas film, because it's absolutely perfect. They've also booked me the same room after I told them how ecstatic I'd been about the constellation views and the falling asleep to the sound of the waves. Tomorrow I'll call my grandmother and make arrangements to meet her. All I want is to pay my respects. What she thinks about me is irrelevant.

And before I know it, the joy of Christmas is dampened by what is both the day of my grandfather's memorial service, November 25th – and my original engagement party. Not in my engagement gown but a black mourning dress, and at precisely three o'clock, I'm once again at the gates of Heatherton Hall, feeling like a beggar. To her I must seem a beggar, seeing as I'm here even if she isn't interested in me. Just like she wasn't interested in seeing me when I last called. Ah, but since then, I've bounced back, ready to do my duty as a granddaughter. Just because.

There's a limousine ready to go with the driver, Calvin, who looks like Lurch from *The Addams Family*. But something tells me that he's awfully loyal. I wonder why, seeing as she seems to treat everyone like her personal slaves. Look at poor old Nettie, and yet she's still working her fingers to the bone to make things comfortable for her. And it's not just for the job. Nettie really does care.

Nettie answers the door with a grave face appropriate to the dark mood that permeates the house. But she winks at me and silently steers me towards the drawing room before she clears her throat.

'Miss Weaver has arrived, Lady Heatherton,' she announces from the door.

'It's about time,' says a soft voice I recognise from our previous call. 'Let her in.'

'Yes, Lady Heatherton,' Nettie says, giving me a gentle nudge.

Lady Heatherton-Smythe, my grandmother, is a tiny, elegant figure sitting at the piano, like a bird perching on its swing. Only she's not playing. She's studying all the silver-framed pictures resting on top. Dressed in a stiff black hat the size of a paddling pool and a very expensive outfit, Lady Mary Heatherton-Smythe is nothing but icy as she turns to assess me.

'Miss Weaver. You're late,' she says.

No warmth, no sign of recognition of my kindred DNA. If anything, her turquoise eyes scan me like a cold laser beam. I've fallen, I suddenly realise, from the frying pan of my MIL straight into the fire of my grandmother.

She studies me like you would a zit before popping it and I can literally see the disdain and the resignation of having to deal with the fact that I exist, despite her best efforts. I know that for a fact because my mother told me she wanted her to have an abortion. Who actually tells their kids that kind of stuff?

'Now get changed for the funeral or people will agree with me that you have absolutely no respect for the living or the dead.'

'Y-yes, ma'am,' I reply automatically. She may be petite but she's formidable. 'Only… I am changed.'

Observing her perfectly smooth face and pressed outfit, my hand steals to my own clothes. And scarf that hides my purple neck. She's still scanning me in utter silence. Then she sighs as she moves off into the hall.

'Someone get her a hat and a pair of gloves,' she says, and Nettie bounces into action.

'Thank you, Nettie,' I say as she places a pair of gloves and a hat in my hands. 'Are these my grandmother's?'

'Goodness, no. They're my niece's. She left them here from her last visit.'

'Oh, thank you, Nettie.'

She smiles. 'No worries. I'll see you when I return.'

'Return?'

'From Ireland. I'm leaving after the service.'

And then the impatient clatter of Grandma's cane announces it's time to go.


Starry Cove's church of St Piran is high above the sea, on an old grassy knoll, like in some old period drama, with windswept mourners struggling to walk upright – both for the weight of their losses and the wind against them. As I weave my way through the mourners, I adjust my scarf and raise my collar against the onslaught of the Cornish winter.

It's a closed-casket affair, so I can't see him in person. Not that I want any memory of him in death. But he must have been very loved, judging by the turnout and the fact that all the shops are closed.

All those I met on my first trip are here, including Penny and also Rosie, who's standing next to an astonishingly good-looking man. He could easily be related to Jago Moon, as they have the same kind of look. Only this man is sober, settled and serene, whereas Jago is like fury itself.

Not wanting to be noticed, I sit at the back, between two sobbing women. All around me is sadness, as is apt for a funeral. But there's also a pride, and even the vicar jokes about my grandfather's wicked sense of humour and love for the sea and boatbuilding. He tells of Nano's strong sense of community and wisdom, and how the villagers would always turn to him for advice. He was, the vicar continues, a man's man, but also a woman's man. (Snickering ensues.)

And then I spot him. Jago Moon, all solemn-faced, his head bowed. He certainly looks sad. I don't know why I'm even watching him. I'm not a stalker by any stretch of the imagination. But watching him without him seeing me gives me a sense of insight into his character. If anything, we have one thing in common: our parents hadn't been the best source of love and security.

Although mine had stuck around, I'm assuming that Jago's hadn't, abandoning him to his destiny. I know how he feels. The pain of knowing you're not good enough, not even for your parents. It makes you want to rise to every occasion and be the best person you can, almost as if to prove to yourself that it wasn't your fault you were abandoned. But our similarities end way before that, because Jago doesn't

seem interested in that kind of challenge. To me, he seems...
like he's completely given up on life.

After the eulogy, the casket is lowered into the ground as
my grandmother stands with her head held high, almost
as if challenging death to come and get her, too.

And that's when Jago materialises before me, his hands
in his coat pockets, looking out to sea. Not that I'd lost
sight of him, mind. I wasn't actually looking for him in the
crowd, but he just sticks out, at least a head taller than
the rest. Hard not to notice him. Or ignore him.

Considering he's the local slosher, he's scrubbed up
nicely. He's wearing a dark blue suit and tie. His shoes
are impeccable despite the blustery day and his coat looks
expensive. He looks up and, never taking his eyes off me,
weaves his way to where I've just stood up as the mourners
begin to disperse.

'Now I get it. *You're* the nuisance of a granddaughter. I
couldn't figure out why someone like you would want to be
in a place like this. But believe me, if you're looking for any
fuzzy, feel-good family warmth, you've wasted a trip.'

I huff under my breath, making sure no one can hear. 'I
was told to stay away from you,' I lie. 'Now I know why.'

'Oh, you don't know the half of it, sweetheart. The lady
doesn't do sentiment. Pity she's a whore.'

I can feel my eyes popping. 'I beg your pardon?'

'*'Tis Pity She's a Whore*,' he repeats. 'John Ford.'

'Yes, I got the reference, thank you. Do you always make
it a point to be so unpleasant to those you meet?'

He shrugs. 'I already told you – there's no one left here
to impress. I already know everybody and we pretty much
have formed our opinions on one another.'

'And now you've formed an opinion on me.'

He looks away from the horizon and back at me before he speaks. 'Pretty much.'

'And...? What would that be?'

He studies me, probably debating whether to give me the softer version or whether I can take the truth.

'If you're looking to be loved, you won't find it here. Your grandmother's got a heart of stone.'

'And so have you,' I reply before I can stop myself.

His eyes roam over my face. 'I certainly do now.'

'You!' comes my grandmother's voice, cracking sharp like a whip. 'How dare you show your face here! Go away before I have you carted off, you wastrel.'

And before I can take my next breath, it's pandemonium, poet S. T. Coleridge style, as she continues to scream a string of insults at him amid the mourners who are all craning their necks and migrating to the front rows for a better look.

At that, he straightens the lapels of his coat, runs a hand through his dark wavy hair and without even trying to defend himself or put her in her place, he stalks off as the entire village looks on in stunned silence. I watch in shock as he turns the church corner and as he snaps his head round for one last glare, the last thing I see is the flash of utter hurt in his eyes.

It's obvious that he had something to do with my grandfather's death. How? Obviously I don't know him, but the look on his face would be enough to move a stone giant. Whatever Jago's done, or what my grandmother thinks he's done, and no matter how wild he is, no one deserves that kind of public humiliation.

Before I know it, Lady Heatherton buckles and I barely

manage to break her fall as Nettie grabs her other arm to help. Out of the corner of my eye, I spot Calvin rushing from the verge of the road to our side as everyone crowds in to see.

'Clear, clear!' says a female voice from ahead, and the congregation parts like the Red Sea for a woman who bends over to feel her pulse.

Lady Heatherton is pale but trying to sit up, without much success.

'Let's get her to my office,' she orders Calvin, who immediately lifts her into his arms like the tiny weight that she is and heads for the car.

Nettie and I pile in with the doctor, who's measuring her pulse.

'Is she going to be OK?' I ask.

It would be horrible to see anything happen to her. Granted, she's not the nicest lady who ever lived, but I can think of worse. Besides, she's my only living relative. I can't lose her now that I've found her!

'Yes, she'll be OK,' she assures. 'She's just too highly strung and keeps having these episodes. They've worsened since Nano's death.'

Why did the encounter with Jago trigger this reaction? What's the story? I'm dying to know now.

In three minutes flat we're at a house on the high street that has a glass door with a tag reading Dr Janice Miller, GP.

'This way,' she beckons me, because Calvin knows exactly where to go.

I follow them into an entrance hall through to her examination room, where Calvin gently lays her down on the examination table.

'Has she been taking her medication regularly?' the doctor asks.

'All of it, religiously,' Calvin answers. 'And she does her morning exercises and takes her walks with the dogs. At least an hour a day.'

'Diet?'

'The one you prescribed, Doctor Miller.'

Obviously Calvin has worked for my grandmother for many years and seems very close to her. My eyes ping-pong back and forth between the two of them, hoping to glean some information. Is she ill? How ill? Am I going to lose her before I even get the chance to get to know her?

'It was to be expected today,' the doctor comments. 'Although I don't suppose Jago's appearance did her any favours.'

'No, Doctor. It certainly hasn't,' Calvin agrees.

'Why? What's Jago got to do with anything?' I ask them.

Calvin and the doctor exchange glances.

'Nano drowned in the sea,' the doctor says. 'Jago couldn't save him. Word is, he didn't even try.'

'But who would believe a thing like that? Why would he let him drown?'

Again, they glance at each other, but no answer comes.

What is going on here? I want to ask, but I have a feeling that, being an outsider, I won't be getting any joy.

My grandmother begins to stir and looks straight up at Dr Miller, confused.

'It's not Friday already, is it?' she asks as she eyes me, probably wondering what I'm doing here, before she looks back at the doctor. 'My medicals are usually on Friday…'

Dr Miller puts a gentle hand on her grandmother's arm.

'No, Lady Heatherton. You just had a little episode, is all. But you're fine now. How do you feel?'

'Episode?' she echoes. 'But I feel perfectly fine!'

'You just blacked out for a few seconds, Grandmother,' I offer. 'But you'll be fine.'

She stares at me with those huge turquoise eyes. 'I *am* fine.'

'Take her home, Calvin,' Dr Miller instructs. 'Keep her warm and feed her lots of liquids. In her emotional state and with her frail health, she'll need all the care she can get.'

'Nettie's leaving to visit family in Ireland tomorrow,' Calvin says, his eyes swinging to mine in hope.

'Oh, I'll stay!' Nettie assures us. 'I'm not leaving the lady on her own like this.'

Lady Heatherton waves a weak hand to dismiss her. 'I gave you some time off. I can't expect you to cater to my every need all the time.'

'I'll take care of her,' I offer.

'I don't need any taking care of,' she snaps.

Calvin, on the other hand, is so relieved he literally sags, losing about half a foot off his towering height.

'Thank you, miss.'

'Not a problem,' I assure.

After Lady Heatherton is brought upstairs and settled in and fussed over by a clinging Nettie, Dr Miller and I literally have to drag Nettie downstairs so that Calvin can take her to the train station.

'Her regime is written down by her bedside,' Dr Miller informs me as Nettie opens her mouth to restart her fretting. 'Any problems at all, you call me, not Nettie.'

I clear my throat, somewhat daunted by the task.

'Thank you, Doctor. I appreciate it.'

How long am I expected to do this? Plus, am I not here for my own health problems?

'Now don't you worry, Emmie,' Nettie says. 'Calvin is very competent. You ask him for anything you need.'

'Thank you,' I reply.

I wonder if he's got an extra dose of kindness and humility to lend the lady of the manor.


After a night spent in Heatherton Hall, the next day I'm preparing breakfast in the huge kitchen for my grandmother – two slices of buttered toast and one egg boiled for precisely four minutes, no more and no less – when Calvin appears at the kitchen door, clearing his throat politely.

'Miss? May I retrieve your belongings from the inn and put them in the guest room for you?'

I look up to see he seems relieved that he won't have to stay with the Beast of Heatherton Hall on his own. I know that she certainly doesn't want me here. What was I expecting – the beginning of the end of the permafrost era? In any case, he needs me and I can't say no.

'Absolutely, Calvin, please do.'

After all, how hard can taking care of her be?

# 12

*Little Dorrit,* Charles Dickens

## 2nd December

It's already December 2nd, meaning I've been here a week. The old servants' kitchen is the room I've come to know best, with its original scullery and butcher's block made of a slab of oak that must be over five hundred years old. This is where I'm spending most of my time, scrubbing and slogging. My fingernails are down to the quick, there are shadows under my eyes and my hair is a rat's nest because I don't have time to drag a brush through it before Lady Where's My Breakfast, Lunch, Tea, Dinner, Nail File, Book, Sherry gets wind of the fact that I'm still standing. How the hell does Nettie do it all? Well, at least the poor dear is getting some rest and enjoying her family.

I picture the streets of Starry Cove, the shops and the houses, the living room windows ablaze with Christmas trees and lights. I picture families gathered round the dining room table at Christmas, perhaps squished between old

Aunt Vera and distant cousin Norman whom they only see once a year. But still, they're happy. They have time off school and work, they're rested, warm, full of good old comfort food and tons of chocolate and cakes. Because at Christmas, all is calm, all is bright. Everything is easy (at least for the people not cooking and decorating).

And here I am, still trying to connect with my only living relative, who's far too absorbed in herself and her own sorrows to give a crap about me or Christmas. If only the MIL or Stephen could see me now. They'd have kittens.

Calvin is a dear – quiet and thoughtful. After his own duties, he comes in for a cup of tea and a slice of cake, asking me if I need any help. But more than anything, I value his company and his invaluable moral support. I like not having to talk all the time or raise my voice like I do in class to get someone to listen to me. It's pleasant adult company, where I don't have to impress or entertain. Calvin is calm and soothing, and the titbits he provides of Lady Mary Heatherton are priceless.

The room I know least of all is the bedroom I've been assigned. It's a large square room, all done in various shades of blue, and when the curtains are open – in other words, always – a beautiful quality of light bounces around the upholstery. The bed is huge, with a high mattress and very thick quilt with slightly frayed edges and a tarnished mirror. But I wouldn't change a thing. Especially the fact that it's a long way down the hall from hers, so every time she calls it's a mini-marathon. I swear I've never been so exhausted in my life.

'Emily! What's keeping you?' my grandmother calls from down the hall as I'm balancing her lunch on a tray.

Talk about juggling acts. From the day (a week ago) I volunteered to take care of her, I haven't stopped cooking and cleaning and doing the washing up and the laundry and the food shopping. If there's something we haven't got in the pantry, rest assured Lady Heatherton-Smythe wants it. And why (seeing that she's on Dr Miller's strict orders to stay in bed) she needs her silk dress and shoes dry-cleaned *this instant* is a mystery.

I'm so run off my feet I'm dizzy with fatigue. I barely have time to pee in the mornings, let alone do any proper grooming, than she's already calling me, demanding her breakfast. Are the oranges freshly squeezed? Has her egg boiled precisely four minutes? For someone who doesn't need me or even *like* me, she's certainly taking advantage. At this rate I'll be dead before Christmas.

'Emily, what took you so long?' she demands as I elbow the door open, my feet dragging as I bring her tray to rest on the dresser.

'Sorry, I dropped the toast and had to run back and make it again…'

'Did you clean the floor at least?' she says as she twiddles her fingers impatiently for her tray.

She's hungry this morning. Me, I'm starved and parched but I haven't got the strength even to open my mouth to speak, let alone eat.

'Please, no slouching, Emily! What is the matter with you?' she barks, and I stand to attention.

OK, she may be my rightful grandmother, but so far I'm only getting the MIL vibes.

'Well, Grandmother, to be perfectly honest—'

And that's when the doorbell rings.

'Ah,' she says. 'Dr Miller. Don't just stand there, Emily! She hasn't got the keys to the front door, you know.'

I stare at her, open-mouthed. This is not going well. Perhaps I should warn the doctor to keep her distance.

'Right!' I say as I turn and head for the hall.

I'm halfway there, when she calls after me: 'My breakfast, Emily! What is wrong with you this morning? And by the way, I thought I asked you to put up the Christmas decorations.'

She hasn't. But perhaps the festivities will mellow her somewhat. Christmas won't be coming soon enough.

I clomp down the stairs like a limping colt and throw the door open to warn the poor GP to run while she still can, but someone completely different is standing there. A very handsome man, in fact. It must be the Cornish air. Or maybe I'm so company-starved that everyone looks beautiful to me.

'Oh!' I gasp. 'I'm sorry. I was expecting Dr Miller...'

'And here he is,' he smiles amiably. 'Pleased to meet you, Emily.'

'How do you know my name?' I ask, and then roll my eyes. 'Scratch that. But you're not Dr Miller. She's a she.'

The man chuckles. 'You mean my sister, Janice. She's at a conference in London for a few days and has asked me to step in for her. I'm Dr Martin Miller.'

'Oh. Pleased to meet you.' I open the door wide for him to come in.

'How is the old battleaxe, by the way?' he asks as he takes off his coat and drapes it over the bannister.

'She... ah...' I falter, unable to hide my surprise and amusement.

He laughs and takes my elbow in a friendly gesture. 'I won't be long. You can wait here and take a breather.'

For which I'm grateful. The last thing I need is another mouthful or task from the great Lady Heatherton-Smythe. So, unsure what to do, I sit on the first step, my chin resting on my fist, trying not to nod off during my very narrow window of freedom. How much longer can I last like this? Perhaps I could sneak up to my room for a quick nap...

The telephone in the hall startles me awake and I jump as fast as my muscles will let me.

'Hello? Heatherton Hall,' I croak, sounding like the old battleaxe herself.

'Hi, Emmie, it's Rosie. How's your grandmother?'

At last, a friendly voice!

'Rosie, it's so good to hear from you. She's fine, thank you.'

'You sound exhausted.'

'I'm OK, thanks.'

'Listen, would you like to hook up with my Coastal Girls? They really want to meet you.'

The sole idea of speaking to someone friendly besides Calvin makes my heart sing.

'I'd so love to, Rosie, but Grandma's got me running on a schedule here. And now she's even asked me to decorate the house for Christmas.'

'Oh, that's too bad,' she says, disappointed. 'Hey! I've an idea.'

'What's that?' Anything, anything at all, at this point, would be better than this purgatory.

'It'll be a surprise,' she says. 'See you in an hour.'

'A surprise? Oh, I don't know. My grandmother doesn't like surprises... Rosie?' I call, but the line is dead.

'Your grandmother is going to live to be over a hundred,' Doctor Martin Miller assures me as he comes down the stairs.

'Yay me,' I can't help but blurt, and he grins.

'Chin up, Emmie. It'll be Christmas soon enough.'

'Not that you'd be able to tell in this mausoleum,' I quip.

'You think it's quiet now? You should have seen it when you weren't here. As silent as a tomb. Lady Heatherton does like her silence.'

'You're telling me. But now she wants the house to be decorated and in no time.'

He dips his head. 'That could be a sign that she wants to get on with life.'

'Or that she wants me under her feet,' I say with a laugh. 'If it weren't for your visits and the errands I run, I'd have become a hermit by now.'

'It'll get better, I promise,' he says as he pulls out his car keys. 'Gotta run. My patients aren't the most... patient, you know?'

'That's the oldest, and corniest, joke ever.'

'And yet, you smiled,' he replies. 'I'll see you next week, Emmie. Hang in there.'

'You too, Dr Miller!' I answer as I show him out.

Hang in there. Ha.

Precisely an hour later, a minivan with the logo Hudson Home Designs pulls up and out spill enough women and children to fill my reading room at school, all led by Rosie.

'Hi!' she chimes, prancing towards me and giving me

a huge hug. 'The cavalry is here! We've come to spread Christmas cheer. And who better than children, right?'

'Oh my word...' I swallow the sudden lump in my throat as I widen the front door.

The children are all between eight and fourteen, the teenagers carrying small boxes filled with Christmas decorations. It's a sight for sore eyes, especially my sleep-deprived ones.

'I don't know what to say, except for... thank you. Please come in, come in.'

'Everybody, this is my friend Emmie, Lady Heatherton-Smythe's granddaughter. Emmie, meet my Coastal Girls: Nina, Nat and Faith. You remember Penny. And these are a combination of nieces, nephews and offspring.'

It's like who's who central!

There's the famous scriptwriter Nina Conte. I knew she lived somewhere in Cornwall, but I can't believe we're sharing the same space. I've seen all of her films and loved them all, especially *Written in the Stars*. She's so lovely and down to earth.

And Nat Amore, the famous columnist, is the bubbliest after Rosie and is so sweet and caring. She's also the sister of Yolanda Amore, the celebrity chef.

And Faith Hudson – she looks like the happiest woman on earth.

'These are my nieces, Amy and Zoe,' Natalia says. 'They're ready to help decorate your tree, aren't you, girls?'

'Yeah!' answers one with an almost mischievous gusto, while the other rolls her eyes and groans emphatically, 'Give me strength!'

I laugh, welcoming them all.

'Just put everything down and come close to the fire – you must be freezing. I'm sure there's some hot cocoa and stuff somewhere.'

And I skip off, my heart flooding with gratitude at the sight of all these smiley faces coming to my rescue. It's a good thing that she can't hear anything from upstairs.

'So you'll be here for a few days?' Rosie asks.

'Oh yes. My grandmother had a spell, so…'

'No worries. We're here to help as much as we can.'

'Thank you so much. I so appreciate you all helping a complete stranger. What can I say except that I'm moved…'

Nina approaches with a toddler who looks like a cherub.

'Hi…' I coo, touching the baby's outstretched hand, which immediately wraps itself around my little finger. 'She's so beautiful. What's her name?'

'Maya,' she answers, looking at the beauty in her arms. 'And she really is a miracle. After Ben and Chloe, and my divorce, I really wasn't expecting a second chance. But there you go.'

'Aww, that's so heart-warming,' I say in earnest.

And it's also so lovely that she feels comfortable in telling me, a woman she only met five minutes ago.

'Thank you… Say hi to our new friend, Maya.'

'Ggggg…' says Maya, and I caress her cheek as my throat constricts.

'What a little miracle you are.'

'This is Emma – my forever bestie and wedding planner,' Rosie tells me, wrapping her arm around a beautiful blonde woman. 'And this is her daughter, Chanel, and that's Chloe, my little devil,' Nina supplies with a smile. 'And the other little devil you see running around is Ben, my youngest.'

It's an entire extended family I knew nothing of. And yet, they're here to help a perfect stranger decorate her old grandmother's home. It's so touching…

'Faith is our favourite designer,' Rosie says. 'She'll be directing the kids' work today.'

'I'll be right back with hot drinks and snacks,' I offer, moving towards the kitchen, where Calvin is busy pulling out trays and mugs, a shy smile on his face.

'Oh, wait, I almost forgot!' Nina calls after me, hefting a cardboard box. 'This is from Alfie and The Post of Ice Cream ladies.'

I stop halfway to the kettle. 'Post of Ice Cream? What's that?'

'Oh,' she laughs. 'It all started with the post office. The second 'f' was missing off the sign for the longest time, so we dubbed it the Post of Ice.'

'Quirky!'

'And opposite Alfie, three sisters run an ice cream shop, which they called The Post of Ice Cream just to take the mickey.'

'So is there a tiny feud going on?' I ask.

'Oh, no. They love him. They've been taking care of him since his wife died.'

'Aww…'

Nina smiles. 'Yeah. Alfie would be lost without them. They cook for him, do his laundry and sort out his paperwork.'

'That's so lovely.'

'Well, that's a small community for you,' she replies as she turns to look through the kitchen door at the buzz of activity in the living room. 'And so is this.'

She's absolutely right. When I first arrived in Cornwall

I'd seen nothing but kindness and open doors (except of course from my own grandmother, but that's another story). Complete strangers have invited me in, offered me hospitality, food, drink, a kind word and a laugh. They've opened their hearts and shared their own precious friendships with me as if they've known me for years. How can I not fall in love with these tiny villages strung together like pearls on a necklace? How can I ever forget these people? Going back to London isn't going to be a walk in the park.

Nina slides us a smile as the doorbell rings. 'That must be our Christmas tree,' she says and shuffles off as Nat pulls Alfie's cakes out of the box and I busy myself with the hot chocolates for the kids.

'I thought we had a Christmas tree,' I offer as an afterthought, but Nat rolls her eyes.

'That plastic thing? Please. Now take a look at that!'

I come out with the food and drinks and put them on the sideboard as the children gather round like bees on honey.

'Ho! Ho! Ho!' two voices in unison boom from the living room, and I look up to see a huge horizontal Christmas tree on four human legs.

And that's when with one almighty push from one of the men and an equally almighty shove from the other, the tree is righted to the ceiling and I almost drop my mug. Am I seeing things? Or rather, people?

Before me stand, flushed and happy, none other than the Hollywood actor Luke O'Hara and the British rock star Gabe York, side by side, like in a 'two for one' offer.

I turn to look at Nina. 'You are joking, right? Is this place some secret hideaway for celebrities? Or am I on *Candid Camera* or something?'

The two blond superstars laugh and remove their gloves to shake my hand as I, slack-jawed, let them, my gaze darting from Gabe to Luke then back again.

'No *Candid Camera*,' Luke O'Hara assures me, pointing to Nina. 'I'm with her.'

'You wish,' she says, winking at him.

'Oh my goodness! I've seen all of your films, Mr O'Hara. And, Mr York, I have all of your CDs and – oh, Jesus, do I sound like a stalker or what!'

Luke laughs. 'Not at all. But everyone on the coast here is so used to me they make me feel normal again. But if you want to make a big fuss over me, please do. I love it.'

'And I thought *I* was the ham!' Gabe laughs, clapping him on the back as his eyes swing to Faith, who's up the ladder, where she's adjusting some branches, completely oblivious.

'Dude,' Luke says, and when Gabe turns to look at him, Luke shakes his head firmly.

Gabe seems to have shrunk in the few minutes he's been here.

'Thanks for the tree, guys,' Nina says, nodding to Luke to get Gabe out of here asap.

'Right, well, we'd better get a move on,' Luke says.

Gabe's eyes dart back to Faith, who's now coming down the ladder, examining the result of her work.

He coughs. 'Right. Yeah. Let's go. Nice meeting you. See you soon, Nina.'

'Great meeting you,' I assure. 'And thank you so much for the tree.'

'Bye,' Faith says without a trace of animosity, but I can tell that there's something not quite right there.

'You know that second chance I told you about?' Nina says. 'They don't always come as often as we'd like, you know. And sometimes we don't deserve them.'

*Second chances. Sometimes we don't deserve them.*

'Hey! Time to leave Emmie to rest,' Rosie chimes from behind a pile of tinsel, waving everyone towards the door.

I take in the scene of easy friendship before me. It might be because of Christmas approaching, but I can't help but wonder why my moments of levity and laughter have become so few and far between. Apart from Maisie, why have I not surrounded myself with good friends like these lovely people, instead of people like Audrey Stone? What am I doing wrong?

'Thank you so much, guys,' I call after them as they bustle out into the night, still chirping like happy little birds. Children. I miss my students. But I don't miss work.

Later that evening, I sit alone in the darkened living room, sipping another cup of cocoa and absently munching on the last of the biscuits with only the Christmas tree lights to keep me company.

And trying not to let Gabe York's sadness and sense of loneliness seep in too much. If Faith ignores him, he must have done something serious. Rosie has told me that Faith is the kindest person she knows. So maybe Gabe doesn't deserve her. I think of Jago, who says he doesn't deserve anyone, either. Is this because he blames himself for not saving my grandfather?

And then I think of Stephen and how many second chances I've given him.

# 13

*A Christmas Carol*, Charles Dickens

'Emily!' comes a screech throughout the house, echoing in the hall. 'Emily, where are you?'

I pop the last bit of my sandwich in my mouth and rush out of the kitchen, down the main corridor and into the hall, where my grandmother is tottering over her cane, momentarily regaining her breath against the door frame of the drawing room, which is alight with Christmas. The incredulous look on her face says it all.

'What have you done to my drawing room? And the hall!'

'You mean the Christmas decorations?'

'My husband has just died. Do you really think that I want to celebrate Christmas, with him barely in the ground?'

I blink. Surely she remembers asking me to put them up. She's probably so frazzled that she's completely forgotten. Either that or I need to tell Dr Martin Miller. I feel for her, really.

'I'm sorry, Grandmother. I'll put everything away.'

'And you will no longer address me as Grandmother. I'm Lady Heatherton to you.'

I suppress a gasp. Is she really doing this? Is she really trying to push me away when all I want is to get closer to her? Why won't she accept me? What could I possibly have done to offend her? It's not about the Christmas decorations. They've only acted as a catalyst for her rage towards me. At first I thought it was merely indifference, but now I realise I'm a true imposition on her. Well, we can fix that immediately.

'I'll pack everything up. And then I'll go.'

I'd better call Penny at The Old Bell Inn to see if I can get my room back. Or any room. Even the cellar would be more welcoming than this pile of rage.

'That is not necessary, although I'm sure you must have a life elsewhere.'

'Oh, I do have a life, Lady Heatherton. I have a job and a fiancé. You needn't worry about me.' The fact that I need time away from both is none of her business.

'I don't. Now, clear up this mess. Later, I'd like to discuss a few things with you.'

I groan. 'Like what?'

'The grocery list for next week.'

Don't you just want to strangle her! I can already see the headlines in the local rag: London School Teacher Throttles Long-lost Grandmother with Fairy Lights. Oh, yeah…

The sudden ring of my phone jerks me out of my thoughts. I look down at the screen, which is bright in the twinkling room. It's Maisie, my lifeline.

'Excuse me, I'll be right back,' I say as I move into the next room for some privacy.

'Enjoying the manor life?' she quips. 'The old harridan warmed up to you yet?'

'Not exactly.'

'Then why don't you come home?'

Why don't I, indeed? 'I just want to make sure she's OK.'

She snorts. 'Women like that are always OK. They drive other people into their graves.'

Which is exactly what I'm thinking. Lady Heatherton is aloof, insensitive and distant.

'So, when *are* you coming home?' she asks.

'I don't know, Maisie. I need some time to think. Plus, my grandmother's housekeeper is away and all she has is Calvin.' I don't mention my tiff with the grand lady.

'Who?'

'The driver. He can make a good cup of tea and polish her cars, but he can't do Nettie's duties.'

A silence on the other end, then: 'Emmie, please come home for Christmas. I can't bear the festivities without you, you know that. Tell the harpy to hire more help. It's not right that you spend the holidays as her captive down there.'

'Oh, but I'm not her captive,' I defend. 'She wants me to believe she's this tower of strength, but between her nagging and her sudden silences, I can tell she's aching for her husband. And yes, I'll be home just in time for our engagement party on the 24th.'

'Oh, *that*. Have you seen Jago Moon?'

'Jago Moon? What's that got to do with anything?'

'No reason – just curious. I think he's a real character. And maybe that's the real reason you're staying.'

'Maisie, you've got it all wrong. I barely know the bloke. Besides, apparently he's the family enemy number one.'

'Oh?'

'Yeah. My grandma kicked him out of the funeral service. In front of everyone.'

'You're joking! The poor, poor bloke.'

The image of his hurt face as he turned the corner comes back to me.

'You sound fond of him,' I observe. 'But then you were going to spend the night with him at the inn, had I not been there.'

'Oh, Emmie, it wasn't like that. I've already explained it to you. He was a complete gentleman with me that night. All he wanted was to get me home safe. Besides, you know I always side with the outsiders.'

'Well, you're right about that. There are lots of people who seem to hold a grudge against him. And yet others, not so much.'

'I wonder why. What could he possibly have done to divide the village like that?'

'Haven't got a clue. No one actually says anything round here. They'll gossip about silly stuff, as they do in small communities. But I have a feeling that when it comes to the serious stuff, they come together.'

'So you think it was something serious?'

'Well, for my grandmother to have seen him off, it can't just have been a fight for a parking spot.'

'Guess not,' Maisie agrees. 'Why don't you ask him? Go straight to the source.'

'Why would I? It's none of my business.'

'But you're dying to know. Why don't you ask that girl you were telling me about, the one with the pottery shop?'

'Rosie? I don't know. I wouldn't want to seem that I'm

prying into his life. Besides, why would I want to know, anyway?'

'I don't know, Emmie. Why would you want to know?' Maisie quizzes.

I sigh. Maisie and her mind games.

'Look, I've got to go. My grandmother will be up any minute wanting her tea.'

'OK, Little Dorrit, off you go.'

'Thanks for that. And no one is in prison, by the way.'

'Think of what I said.'

'You said a lot of silly things, which I'm trying to forget.'

'Yeah, well don't forget my advice. If you're going to stay in Starry Cove a few more days, you should make it worthwhile, if you know what I mean.'

'Will you stop? I'm not staying. I'll be back… in time for everything.'

Just the thought makes me want to hurl. The holiday season isn't going to last forever and, come the new year, I'll have no excuse to stay.

As if I wasn't physically strained enough by my house duties, I've now got into the habit of taking lovely walks across the coastal path during my breaks. But this is a good kind of exertion – a breath of fresh air to throw Heatherton Hall behind me.

Call it what you want – paranoia, PTSD or simply wimpiness – but after my attack only two weeks ago, I haven't felt safe in London. I was hoping I'd feel safe here, but now a sense of panic is welling inside me. Oh my God, isn't there a safe spot anywhere?

I turn to look over my shoulder, but of course there's no one behind me. All the same, for no reason, I feel compelled to break into a run to shake off this uneasiness. What's happening to me? I used to be so brave. A streetwise girl, living on her own in a metropolis. And now, because of a lowlife mugger, I'm frightened by the mere rustle of the marram grass above an idyllic village… Is this what I've become?

But it's not only the rustle of grass – someone *is* following me!

The wind up here is so loud that I can't discern any specific sounds, but I sense someone is there. I can't even hear my own breathing soughing in and out of me, and before I can stop myself, I break into a run against the wind, too afraid to look over my shoulder.

And soon I hear someone pounding the ground behind me, closer and closer. Any second and he'll have caught up with me!

Before I know it, a loud explosion erupts behind me and I instinctively throw myself on the ground and protect my head, listening as the noise gets louder and louder. Any second now he'll reach me – and there's not a thing I can do but cower in fear.

A rasping sound suddenly fills my ears as someone yanks me and throws me around on my back and I'm faced with a huge dog. Jago Moon's dog. And then bloody Jago, who's staring down at me in fury.

'What the hell is *wrong* with you?' he shouts, shaking me. 'Never, ever run from a dog!'

I try to sit up as he pulls the beast back.

'Max!' he shouts. 'Heel!'

'He was chasing me...' I pant, trying to pull myself together.

'Of course he was. He's a dog!'

'You should put him on a leash.'

'They should put *you* on a leash. Don't you know better than to traipse around the countryside all alone if you're afraid of dogs?'

I get to my knees, noticing how he doesn't even offer to help me up, the monster.

'I'm not afraid of dogs. I just wasn't expecting to be ambushed by one.'

'Ambushed? This isn't London, you know. Or a war.'

'Yeah, well it is to me,' I mutter, rolling over until I can find a way to get to my feet without looking ridiculous. 'Why does my grandmother hate you?' I blurt.

He stares at me for a moment, then laughs. 'She hates everyone.'

'But you in particular. Why were you not fit to attend my grandfather's funeral?'

His mouth turns into a grim line. 'Go home, city slicker. You'll only get hurt if you stay.'

'I want to know the truth.'

'The truth is none of your business. You think you're special, just because you're the granddaughter of Lady Mary? She doesn't give a crap about you. She never has and never will. No one wants you here. So save yourself the heartache and get out while you still can.'

He's right. No one gives a crap about me. Neither here nor in London. I don't belong anywhere. I'll never fit in anywhere. If a metropolis hasn't got room for me, how can a one-horse town like Starry Cove welcome me? I'm an outsider wherever I go. Not even my own blood loved me. My parents never did, and now my only living relative doesn't, either. What was I expecting? For blood ties to open doors to me?

And Stephen – how much can I count on his love? Where is he now? Why doesn't he call? Why doesn't absolutely anyone care about me?

'Wait a minute, what's *that*?' Jago demands, his eyes widening at the sight of my throat.

'Oh,' I croak in surprise, covering it up. 'It's nothing…'

'The hell it is,' he snaps. 'Let me see that. That didn't happen just now.'

'No, it's nothing,' I say, backing away.

He's so big, much bigger than my mugger, and could easily snap me in half if he wanted. Only his stance isn't ominous in the least. If anything, he looks… *concerned*? Could it be that he's actually got a drop of warm blood in him?

'Who did this to you? Was it your boyfriend?'

'What, Stephen? Of course not,' I bite off.

I can't even remember the last time Stephen had been anywhere near me. As a matter of fact, right now, Jago is standing much closer to me than Stephen has in weeks, and his eyes are delving into mine in search of the truth. Aren't we all?

'Well then, who?'

'I was a-attacked, just outside my flat.'

His mouth falls open. 'Jesus Christ! No wonder you bolted back there.'

'It's OK. I'm OK now,' I assure, my lower lip suddenly doing this ridiculous wobbly thing.

I guess I hadn't been expecting any concern from anyone except Maisie and Stephen, and the latter was a no-show. How I'd wanted him to drop everything, just for me, and come running to console me, if not save me from the evils of the world. Because I'd amply proved it to myself – I can't save myself. And God knows I've tried.

As I feel my eyes burning, I whirl round to run away before the tears come.

'Hey!' he calls after me. 'Emmie!'

'And put that dog on a leash!' I shout over my shoulder before I break into a new sprint up a hill, my legs and lungs burning one minute in. But I can't afford to show anyone my weakness.

'His name is Max!' he calls back.

Is it so very wrong, in this day and age, for an independent although not single woman to resent her partner for not running to her rescue? Is it not unacceptable that Stephen didn't come over immediately? Was I not important enough, or am I really acting like a damsel in distress by expecting my partner to be there for me, and possibly protect me against any physical harm? Am I living in the wrong century?

I like being independent and supporting myself and all, but I also like to get a phone call from Stephen every once in a while to make sure I'm OK. After all, it was his total indifference to my well-being that drove me out here.

Originally, coming from a somewhat cold family, I'd always thought that I didn't deserve to have anyone being concerned or watching out for me. But then I'd discovered that that's what people who love you naturally do. Even Maisie and her one-night stand Pablo had come running to me.

So why was it that with Stephen, I always feel that I shouldn't be asking or expecting anything? He's my fiancé, for goodness' sake. When is he going to start acting like one? A visit from him the next morning is simply not enough. Why do I let him treat me like a second thought, when I was ready to blend my life with his and even put up with the monster-in-law? Something just doesn't compute.

The next morning, there's a message for me under the door:

Miss Weaver,

Please be prepared at 10 o'clock this morning for a meeting in the dining room.

Lady Mary Heatherton-Smythe

*Miss Weaver.* Like there's no relation between us whatsoever, and I haven't been on my knees scrubbing her personal commode. And if that's not enough, I'm still waiting not only for an acknowledgment of the beautiful Christmas tree in the drawing room, but also every other festive touch strewn over the house.

I had wanted to reconnect with my only living relative, despite the fact that she hasn't shown any interest in me whatsoever. It serves me right for practically begging her to belong.

She's beginning to seem a lot like Stephen with his taking me for granted. And what about the fact that I've extended my stay in Cornwall to take care of her, when she could have hired anyone else to do the job? Why do people think that they can just take advantage of me? Let her source out her own bloody carer until Nettie comes back! Come to think of it, where would she find someone else – www. mindlessmartyrs.gov.uk?

And this morning's meeting? I can already glean what kind of meeting it's going to be. In fact, the note should read:

Miss Weaver,

You've done your duty attending the funeral of your estranged grandfather. But as I'm not on my own deathbed yet, your presence is no longer required. So off you pop.

Lady Mary Heatherton-Smythe

Tomorrow I'm going to make some calls to see if I can find someone else to put up with the old bat. But for today, all she has is me and unfortunately for me, I still have a heart.

Sighing, I slip into my boots and prepare for the dreaded slog ahead, starting with Dr Martin Miller's early morning visit.

'So, how are you doing?' he asks. 'You look pale. Are you alright?'

'Oh… yes. Thank you, Martin.'

'And you've lost a bit of weight.'

'I don't wonder at it,' I joke. 'The lady's got me flitting around the place like mad.'

'You need to take more care of yourself, Emmie,' he says gently. 'Eat more, sleep more. And smile more. It's all good for you, you know.'

'I know,' I concede. 'But it'll only be until I go back home.'

'Your grandmother will miss you.'

'Ha! Very funny.'

'Of course she will. Don't let the stony face and British stiff upper lip fool you.'

'Well, I really don't think she'll miss me much. I'll miss her, funnily enough. To have come so close to a family and then, poof! Gone. But I will miss my new friends. And you, Martin.'

'Likewise, Emmie, likewise…'

'Just in time, Emily, I'm glad to see,' *Lady* Mary Heatherton-Smythe addresses me as she indicates a seat opposite at the dining table where a team of suits is sitting.

They're armed with briefcases and gold pens, gaping at me, probably wondering what a pleb like me is even doing here in the first place. Which is exactly what I'm wondering. Because you don't have to be a rocket scientist to figure out that these are Lady Mary Heatherton-Smythe's solicitors, *Esq.*, and that they've lost no time in determining the estate of my poor Nano.

And it soon becomes clear, by the look on their faces, especially my grandmother's, that they want to dot all their i's and cross all their t's – in other words, assure me that I'm not getting a penny. Funny, all this, because I don't even want any of it – not from a family who refused to have anything to do with me or my parents my entire life. I mean really, if not come and visit from time to time, would it have hurt them to pick up the phone to speak to me – check how I was coming along? But no. They just couldn't be bothered and now I've been summoned here this morning for the ultimate humiliation.

'Actually, Mrs Heatherton... I refuse to call her Lady '... er, I've got to be somewhere,' I lie.

Or is it a lie? I should be somewhere – anywhere – else rather than here.

The nitrogen turquoise eyes swivel to me, freezing me on the spot.

'Sit down, Miss Weaver...'

'Uhm, right,' is all I can say.

My grandmother is certainly a force to be reckoned with. Judging by the way people scurry to her beckoning, she always gets what she wants, when she wants it. Especially with a squadron of solicitors behind her. And yet, somewhere in there is a trace of vulnerability that reminds me of my own. Despite her piercing cold eyes, there's a chink in her armour, I just know it. There has to be. No one can be that cold.

Groaning inwardly, I square my shoulders, ready to counter with maximum dignity their fobbing me off.

'These are my solicitors. They are here to read my husband's will.'

'Yes, I gathered as much, but, if you'll pardon my question – what has any of this got to do with me?'

'You are a family member, at least on paper,' she replies as if she were sucking on a lemon. 'Now sit, and do not delay us any longer.'

Delay? She just said I was on time. Something tells me that

she's worse than the MIL. Because for some unfathomable reason, I can't quite talk back to this old harpy. Not that I'd be rude to anyone, but with her I can't even seem to defend my own rights. There's simply something about her that scares the bejesus out of me.

As one of the old crones at the table begins to drone on and on in monotone, I'm trying to understand as much as I can, but being in legalese, they pretty much lose me ten minutes in. If it had been written in Elizabethan iambic pentameter, it would have been much more comprehensible to me.

'In a nutshell,' concludes one of the solicitors, 'your grandfather has left you the sum of two million pounds, plus a 50 per cent share in a river barge – *The Miranda* – a small cottage plus a general store – Bend or Bump – with one Mr Jago Moon.'

I start. Jago Moon? How is that even possible? If Mary reacted like that at his presence at the memorial service, she's going to have an absolute blinder of a fit now!

I look around at all the impassive faces that haven't so much as blinked once since I sat down. Utter silence reigns, as all of them are waiting for me to speak. Even my grandmother doesn't look surprised in the least; nor does she say anything. In fact, if it wasn't for a nervous twitch in her eye, she'd look like a wax figure. I open my mouth and close it again.

'M-me?'

They all nod in unison.

'But why me? I never knew him... Mum always used to say that Nano was the cause of the rift between you two.'

'Oh, for goodness' sake, Emily. He was a sentimental old sod. Just accept it gracefully, if you can.'

Gracefully? I'm nothing but confused. Why would someone who never took the time to meet me, not even once, actually leave me anything at all? It just doesn't make sense. And what the hell has Jago Moon got to do with my grandfather? Judging by the scene at the graveyard, Jago was the last person Lady Mary wanted around her husband.

# 14

*The Million Pound Bank Note,* Mark Twain

'Two million pounds?' Maisie screeches. 'Bloody hell! For that kind of dosh, *I'll* marry you.'

'And a cottage and a boat. Why would he leave all that to me when he didn't even know me?'

'Because you're his only living blood relative?'

'He could have remembered that a bit earlier, don't you think?'

'Emmie, are you kidding me? You've just inherited a fortune and you're playing the pride card?'

'I just think that he could have been there for me while I was growing up. They both could have, him and that harridan. And besides, most of it's going in inheritance taxes.'

'Ungrateful, much,' she quips.

'Not in the least. I'm extremely grateful but overwhelmed. The upkeep of a house and a boat cost a lot. What am I going to do when it runs out?'

'Emmie, may I suggest the obvious? You sell everything and put it in a safe place where Stephen can't get to it.'

'Stephen doesn't need my money, Maisie.'

'No, but there's a huge difference between need and greed.'

'But I can't sell up. It was my grandfather's gift to me.'

'His gift to you was your financial freedom. Why else would he leave you all that money if not to do anything you like with it?'

I hesitate.

'Emmie, you've been handed the chance of a lifetime. Why don't you take this stroke of luck as a sign to start over – *without* Stephen...'

'Maisie, I'm not with him because of the money.'

'I know that. And now you can buy yourself a nice flat and maybe even apply to another school where you won't have to see him every day. I'll tell you what – I'll quit, too, and we can apply to schools together! It'll be just like when we were students.'

I laugh. 'Easy, Maisie. I can't make a decision just like that. I need to find my feet first.'

'So what kind of shop is it?'

'It's a shop that sells everything but the kitchen sink.'

'Quirky! So you're going to let your new business partner run it? Have you met them yet?'

I hesitate. Here she goes, Maisie on her field trip.

'That I have.'

'Are they nice?'

'It's a he, and actually, he's not anybody's ideal partner. So can you guess who it is?'

A gasp. 'No! Jago Moon, the slosher?'

'In the flesh.'

'Oh my bloody God, I can't believe it! It's a *sign*!' she squeals.

'Yeah, that my grandfather had bad taste in friends.'

'So, what are you going to do?'

'Not a clue. Possibly ask him to buy me out so I can do my own thing. Or perhaps I could buy him out…'

'What are you talking about, Emmie? You sound like you've a mind to stay.'

I *am* thinking about it. A brand-new start in life in a gorgeous place, with money behind me… Who wouldn't think about it? But how can I justify staying in Cornwall when I've promised myself that I'll sort out my relationship with Stephen, who has no interest in moving down here? I know it isn't just his fault – I have a few things to address, as well. So perhaps running off to Cornwall isn't the best solution, after all. But… it feels so right! Still, I need a strong excuse, besides my grandmother not being able to cope without me, which is a huge lie, of course.

'Emmie? When are you going to admit Jago Moon intrigues you?'

'Don't be silly. I'm just annoyed that I'll have to be dealing with him.'

'Then let *him* buy you out.'

'You think he can? It's more probable that I'll have to buy him out.'

'Emmie, you're not seriously thinking of staying in Starry Cove, are you? I mean, it's gorgeous and all, I'll give you that. But what are you going to do on the weekends when the shop closes?'

I don't need to think about my answer.

'Live! Be happy. In any case, I don't even know that he'll want me as a partner. We didn't really get off on the right foot, as you remember.'

'Do you realise we've been talking non-stop about Jago for a while now? My advice? You dump Stephen now, because the clock's ticking. Your engagement party is only a few weeks away.'

In a few weeks I'll be drinking champagne at a party organised by my future mother-in-law. Surrounded mostly by people I don't know. Her and Stephen's people. But after that, once I convince him to move out, we can start living in our own home. If I can convince him to move out, that is.

But what if he doesn't want to? That's a huge stumbling block, and a shaky start to a marriage, to say the least. We have a lot to talk about. But our conversations, or rather, arguments, never seem to reach that depth. It seems to me that it's all more about the actual engagement party and the wedding ceremony that matter to him, as he wants to give his mother answers.

But he never seems to be interested in actual married life. Is it because he thinks nothing is going to change? That I'll just slot into his and his mother's home and lifestyle, rather than build a new life? Does he think he's still going to be leading the bachelor life?

'Emmie…? You still there?'

'Mmh? Yeah. I've got to go now. I've… got stuff to do.'

'Liar,' she says, but I can hear the smile in her voice. 'You go get him.'

'Who?'

'The man who would smile the knickers off you, that's who!'

I sigh. Her and her sexual fantasies. Intrigue me? Jago Moon? What a crazy notion to entertain, even remotely.

If anything, I loathe him – the one with the arrogant stance of one who thinks the world owes him a living. OK, maybe I don't actually *loathe* him. Maybe I feel a smidgen of pity for someone who can't seem to form any kind of successful attachment to anyone. There's got to be a reason why someone becomes a loner. And a drinker.

Not that the locals, as friendly as they've become over the weeks, are volunteering any gossip, mind. I know absolutely nothing about him. Just like I know nothing about my family, save the fact that I'm a part of something irreparably broken.

'What did Stephen say when you told him?'

Just the fly in my champagne. 'I haven't told him yet.'

'Ah.'

*Ah* is right.

'Are you afraid of his reaction? Or the MIL's?'

'I'm not afraid of anyone, Maisie. I'll tell him tonight.'

'That'll make him one happy camper.'


Maisie's absolutely right. I've never heard such enthusiasm in his voice since I met him.

'That's incredible, Emmie! How is that even possible?'

'Well, apparently my grandfather was a sentimental man. As opposed to her.'

'Sounds like you hit the jackpot. Do you need me to come down and sort out your affairs for you?'

*Now* he wants to come down?

'Uhm, no, thank you, Stephen. I'm perfectly capable of doing it myself.'

'But you shouldn't have to. From now on, I'll take care of your finances and when we're married—'

'Stephen…? Would you mind if I come home the day before our party? I need some time to sort things out.'

'Yes, yes, of course, you sort everything out there. But call me if you change your mind and need me to come down before then. Maybe we can spend the Christmas holidays together in Cornwall!'

Together? If Stephen was coming down over the Christmas hols, he certainly wasn't going to leave his mother on her own, was he? Meaning that Audrey would come down, too. That's all I need – the bane of my life following me into my new life. No, thank you.

'Uh, how about I just pop back to London for the 24th and then come back here?' I offer.

'That sounds like a lot of driving, Emmie. Why don't you just come back for Christmas and let that be the end of it?'

'The end of it? This sick leave I'm on is a real one. Because I literally am sick of everything, so it *counts*.'

'I know. I'm sorry. We'll do it your way, then, OK?'

'Thank you, Stephen. I'll talk to you soon,' I promise and end the call.

Life is strange. Its possibilities are endless. One day you're a complete orphan and the next you discover you have at least one breathing relative. I wonder how they felt when they discovered I existed. They must have felt cheated out of many years with me. Well, I'm hoping that at least Nano did. He sounds like a lovely man. His wife, not so much.

And now, perhaps fate is trying to recompense me by giving me a relative and an inheritance. A legacy. My own home and perhaps family memories I'm dying to learn about. Every milk jug, every picture will be connected to a story. I'll finally have a connection to something! And I've even got a 50 per cent stake in a business, no less. And a boat!

Time to go and have a look at the shop and have a row with my brand-new partner.

At first glance, the shop looks like a hole in the wall, or an entrance to a cave. Nothing more, except for the sign, Bend or Bump. What could a shop like that possibly sell?

I have absolutely no idea what I'm going to find in there, if anything, as I've never stumbled down this backstreet before. Why would I? It looks like God Himself has forgotten all about the place. And again, there could be literally anything (or nothing) in there.

I push the door inwards and nearly drop to my knees as it's yanked open from the inside.

'Easy...' comes a familiar voice as someone grabs me by my elbows, saving me from a ruinous fall down a set of steps.

I look up into, you guessed it, Jagodrinker Moon's eyes. Laughing eyes. I almost didn't recognise him but for the leather jacket.

'You really must learn to walk, Emmie,' he drawls as he pulls me up.

'I'm sorry. I would have called, but I don't know your mobile number.'

'I don't have a mobile phone. Don't need one. People know where to find me, assuming they want to.'

'I came to discuss business.'

'Oh?'

'I've inherited my grandfather's share of this shop.'

'That's old sentimental Nano for you.'

'I wanted to have a chat with you, if it's convenient?'

And that's when I spot her – a completely naked woman sitting in the semi-darkness at the back of the shop.

'Oh!' I exclaim and turn to run as my ears catch fire.

But I've forgotten about the low door and bang my head, staggering back helplessly, grasping the air for purchase. Finding none, I crash to the floor in a doubly humiliated heap.

'Jesus! You alright?' he calls as he lurches forwards to drag me to my feet again.

'I'm… I'm… f-fine,' I manage as the entire hole in the wall expands and contracts, going through a myriad of colours.

This is what Samuel Taylor Coleridge must have seen while writing about the lavish palace Xanadu. Only there was no pleasure in my pleasure dome. Just unadulterated, throbbing pain. And, oh – did I mention the humiliation?

Out of the corner of my eye, I see the naked woman coming my way and I cringe. Why does she have to flaunt her sexuality like that in a public space? What about the prudes like me?

'Here,' she whispers, giving him a cold cloth, which he applies to my head while he gently nudges me down onto a chair.

Now standing in the only ray of light in the room, I see she's put on a wrap and is leaning towards me, mirroring

Jago's stance. Before me are four quivering rainbow-coloured heads.

'Better?' asks one of Jago's heads.

'That was quite a bump,' says one of the woman's heads.

'I'm s-sorry, I must have the wrong place...' I stammer.

Jago pulls a wad of pound notes out of his pocket. 'Here, Sally, see you tomorrow.'

Sally pushes his hand away with a smile. 'It's on me, hun. See you tomorrow.' And with that, she slips into her dress, coat and boots and heads for the door.

'Hope you feel better,' she says to me as I try to pin down her image from flipping upside down in a topsy-turvy movement. I must have really banged it good.

'And don't wear a bra next time,' he calls after her.

At the door, she turns and smiles a naughty smile. 'Anything for you, Jago...'

Are they really having this conversation in front of me? Seriously? I can't stand here in this madhouse-cum-brothel a moment longer. I struggle to my feet.

'Where are you going? You can barely stand,' he protests.

'I'll come back to inspect the premises another time,' I assure as I fight to walk steadily past the swaying walls. 'And I'll be looking at the accounts.'

And with that, I head out back onto the street on wobbly legs. How am I even going to make it across the street?

'I have nothing to hide,' he calls after me.

I turn, bracing my hand against the wall. 'Nor does your friend,' I shoot over my shoulder as everything begins to spin.

'Aww, c'mon, Emmie. Get back here, will you? You don't

want our business to start off on the wrong foot, do you? Besides, you can't even stand.'

That much is true. I've got up too soon.

Jago covers the distance between us, taking my elbow.

'Come on in the back. Let's have a cup of tea and that chat.'

I sigh. Even if he's a misogynistic bastard, he's making an effort. And he's right. If we're going to be partners, wherever I am, it's best to be on good terms.

'OK, then,' I agree as he leads me back inside.

I look around, unable to see anything.

'Sorry, why is it so dark in here?' Stupid question, I figure as I remember the lady in the nude. 'I know you don't have any respect for society, but I didn't think you'd go as far as conducting your personal affairs on a premises of a business. Then again, you're always one to surprise me.'

At that, he grins one of his rare beauties. 'You don't look like the kind of girl who likes to be surprised... in any way.'

'What's that supposed to mean?' I challenge weakly. I'm really not up for another tiff.

He shrugs. 'Dunno. Not sure yet. I'm still studying you.'

'Well, I've got you all figured out, actually. Finding you with a naked woman isn't very original, even for you.'

He grins. 'I promise to try harder in future, then. Maybe you'll find me with two. Or perhaps even three.'

'Ha-ha. And what a cheek, to pay her in front of me.'

'What difference does it make?'

'If I were you, I'd try to keep it private.'

'It was private – until you barged in.'

'And then, to top it off, you holler to her not to wear a

bra next time. In front of me. My first impression of you was right – you really are a chauvinist pig, do you know that?'

'Glad I haven't disappointed your expectations, after all,' he says with a strange look on his face.

I haven't seen this expression yet. It's a new one.

'Just so you know,' he adds, 'Sally is the model for my new painting, not my lover. And I asked her not to wear a bra because it leaves marks on her skin.'

His model? I look back and as he turns the lights on, the entire table behind him is illuminated with jars of paints and brushes, and off to one side, a half-finished painting of a woman sitting by a darkening window.


Audrey rings me as I'm rushing out of the door.

'Emmie, dearest, it's your mother-in-law!' she ta-dahs over the phone.

Mother-in-law. I guess word of Emmie Weaver being an heiress is out. Why else would MIL practically be fawning over me, let alone calling me, when the last time she did it was to tell me not to invite my grandmother to the wedding and how I was embarrassing her? But now things have changed. She can smell money from across the nation and will do everything she can to be related to it. You'd think her own would be enough, but no.

'Hello, Audrey.'

'I heard about your newfound fortune,' she sings. 'Congratulations are in order.'

She congratulates me for my money, but nothing about having both lost and found a relative? Do you see what I mean?

'Thank you, Audrey.'

'So, when are Stephen and I meeting them, dear?'

'I'm sorry... who?'

'Lord and Lady Heatherton-Smythe, of course. We can come down end of this week. How does that work for them?'

I clear my throat. 'Sorry, Audrey, but perhaps you were distracted. I came down here for my grandfather's funeral. He's passed away...'

Silence. 'Oh, I'm so sorry. Condolences are in order, then.'

Oh, dear God, how can she be so out of touch? She's completely forgotten.

'Thank you, Audrey.'

'I'll send a floral arrangement. What flowers did your grandfather like, dear?'

I sigh inwardly, a migraine already forming behind my eyes.

'Oh, to have inherited from a lord and not even know him,' she continues. 'How fortunate are you?'

Are you hearing this? Because I don't think anyone outside Maisie and the Coastal Girls would believe me.


'Don't mind her, Emmie. She means well,' Stephen assures when I call to tell him that even if he and his mother did threaten to come down for the holidays, Lady Heatherton-Smythe is *far* from wanting to meet any of my acquaintances, let alone put them up in her own home. And can he please pull the reigns on his mother...

'I can't tell her that, Emmie,' he regrets. 'It'll hurt her

feelings. She's already told her friends that your grandmother is going to be the guest of honour at our engagement party.'

'I'm sorry, but... What? My grandmother? Guest of honour? At *our* engagement party? Not happening.'

'Oh, come on, Emmie. It's the best way to introduce your family to our society.'

'But it's not my, or her, society. She'll never come, not in a million years. And by the way, with what gall does your mother tell her friends that my grandmother is going to be there?'

Stephen sighs. 'She didn't know that your grandmother would refuse, Emmie. What does that say about her as a grandmother?'

I can feel my heart racing, my head about to explode.

'OK, so a) you missed the memo that we don't exactly get along, and b) you don't assume someone's coming to your party just because... Oh my God, Stephen, when is this going to stop?'

'Emmie, she's just a little, you know, overwhelmed, what with the wedding and all.'

'Overwhelmed because we're getting married.' That's the MIL for you.

'Well, you know, all she has is me. She's just being affectionate.'

'So it's OK for her to be affectionate with you, but it's not OK for you to be affectionate with me. I get it now.'

'Oh, come on, Emmie. I'm really getting tired of all this, you know? You ditch me before the engagement party and take off for the funeral of someone you've never met, to a place you've never been, and then you say you need time away from me. What am I supposed to think? You don't even like your grandmother, so who are you spending all this time with, hmm?'

'No one special,' I whisper. 'Just my new friends.'

He snorts. 'Your new friends! And I'll bet they're crawling all over you since your newfound fortune, aren't they?'

Like his own mother, he means, but I hold my tongue. About that tiny bit. The rest, I can't suffer.

'That's unfair. They're lovely people – much wealthier than I, in any case.'

'Oh, really? So Starry Cove is the hub of millionaires now, Emmie? Give me strength...'

'Listen, Stephen. I only called to tell you that I'm considering a business option.'

'What business option?'

'The shop I inherited 50 per cent of – I'm figuring out what to do with it.'

'What to *do* with it? Sell it, Emmie. Sell it all and come home!'

'But that's the thing. I don't feel like I'm away from home, Stephen. Starry Cove... it's growing on me. There's a business for me to run. A cottage to live in. And then there's the boat. I was wondering where you stand on all that?'

'What do you mean, where do I stand?'

'I mean, what do you think about living here? You could always apply to a school in Truro...'

Silence, and then: 'Emmie, Emmie, Emmie... what am I going to do with you? You can't keep living your life putting everything in question. You live in London. You're an English teacher. We're getting married.'

'But why don't you come down here and see for yourself how lovely it is here?' I suggest.

Perhaps we *may* be able to sort things out between us. Perhaps all I need is to be able to believe in him again. In *us*. See him as he used to be when we were happier. Or, perhaps I need something more than he's giving me. I'm always on trial with him and it's making me miserable.

'Emmie, we don't have that kind of time. We have obligations here in London. And as far as your business partner is concerned, get him to buy you out.'

That's a good one. I can't even get my own fiancé to move elsewhere with me and he wants me to sort out other people?

'It's not all that easy, Stephen. I can't just go up to him and tell him what to do.'

'Of course you can. Some people need to be spoken to in a certain manner, you know.'

I suppress a sigh. Some people do, indeed.

The next day, Martin (or as I've dubbed him, Doc Martin) is back to check on the lady of the manor. I keep out of her way, God forbid, but Martin and I have fallen into the habit of sharing a cup of coffee and a biscuit or two afterwards as he fills me in on her condition and gives me advice on how to avoid throttling her.

'You're a trooper, the way you're handling all this,' Martin says, holding a porcelain cup up to me in a form of salute.

I laugh. 'She just takes getting used to, I guess.'

'True. Mary's like that. She doesn't leave anyone any space to breathe. And speaking of, would you like to come out to dinner with me tonight?'

'Dinner?' I repeat. An evening away from the harpy? 'I'd love to, but... I don't know if I can.'

'I'm sure Calvin can cope for the evening. And if there's an emergency, the doctor is always on call,' he says with a kind smile.

'True,' I agree. 'Dinner it is, then. Thank you, Martin.'

'Tonight, then. I'll pick you up.'

'This is nice,' Martin says as we dig into our steaks. We're at Persephone's Inn, a lovely pub with a jetty, but as it's freezing cold, we're sitting inside at a table by the open fire.

Christmas is in every corner, from the stockings hanging from the mantelpiece to the mistletoe under the main entrance, to Michael Bublé's old Christmas album playing in the background.

'Yes, I love fires,' I muse. 'I've never had one in my home.'

'And now your grandmother has at least ten of them,' he chuckles. 'Strange, life, isn't it?'

'This is so nice, Martin, thank you. I feel like I've known you forever, you know?'

'Me, too,' he chimes as I shove a succulent bite in my mouth.

'Oh my God, this is amazing! Who's the chef? Jesus?'

Martin laughs, his huge blue eyes twinkling and wrinkling at the corners. He's actually quite good-looking, Martin. In a way, he and Jago have something in common, beneath their extreme behaviours – Martin being the proper village doctor who cares and Jago the village badass who doesn't.

'Don't let the vicar hear your blasphemy,' he warns me.

'Would that be the same vicar who celebrated my grandfather's memorial service?'

'That's the one. Blimey, that was quite the spectacle, wasn't it?'

'You mean my grandmother, yelling at Jago Moon? Yeah. What's the issue there?'

Martin swallows his wine, eyes on me. 'You don't know?'

'Not a thing, except that Jago was abandoned.'

'Ah. That. Yes. And how is working with him?' he asks, his eyes studying me above the rim of his glass.

'Interesting,' I say, not wanting to give anything away. In a tiny village like this, the less people know, the better.

'I'd be very careful around him, in any case. He is a bit of a womaniser.'

'I can't see how,' I reply as I take a sip of wine. 'He's not exactly loquacious, is he?'

Martin dips his head. 'Men like Jago don't need to talk, Emmie. They crook their little finger and the women go running after him. It's an alchemy I'll never understand.'

Nor can I, I think to myself. Who wants to be with someone so arrogant and uncouth?

'Have you seen him lately?' I find myself asking.

Martin shrugs. 'He's probably off on one of his suicidal benders. Maybe this time he'll actually succeed.'

I gasp. 'How can you say that? You're a *doctor*… '

He sighs, eyeing me. 'Listen, Emmie. Jago's not the man he used to be. We've all told you that. The nice bloke that once was is no longer. And besides, what do you even care? You never knew him back then. For all you know he could always have been bad.'

'No.' I swallow. 'I know he's not.'

'Oh? And what have you got – a crystal ball or a time machine?'

'No. Just empathy.'

Martin sighs sadly. 'He's right. You really are a sweet girl.'

My jaw drops. 'He said that about me?'

He grunts. 'Wake up, Emmie. A man like him will eat you for breakfast. Destroy you completely.'

I've learned a couple of lessons since I've arrived here in Starry Cove. One, never to go blind into a place of business you share with someone else, particularly one Jago Moon. Lord knows what he'll be doing on the premises and who with. And two, never go walking in the Cornish countryside or on the coastal path where I currently find myself without a stick. So now I always take an umbrella with me, just to fend off any other feral animals, Jago included.

And like clockwork, as if he's expecting me, Jago's dog comes bounding over the horizon, his huge tongue flapping in the wind. Instinctively, I brace myself as he tries to launch himself at me like the other day, but he only skids to a halt right before me, as if awaiting my orders. He, too, must have learned a lesson.

'Hi,' I coo, bending down to pat it, albeit with trepidation. This thing could take my hand off. But instead he licks it, the big lump of fuzz that he is.

'I swear that if I didn't know you better, I'd think you're stalking me,' I blurt as Jago saunters up the hill towards me, hands in his pockets.

'Hard not to bump into the same people in Starry Cove.'

'I was talking to your dog,' I quip.

'Got me,' he says, scanning the horizon, just like he did at the funeral.

It's like he's always looking for something. I wonder what he thinks is out there.

'So, why are you so adamant about staying in Starry Cove?' he asks. 'Can't resist the village charm? Or is London worse than I remember?'

It's because I don't want to go back to London. To the soullessness. To the indifference of those who are supposed to love you. Like Stephen. And my future mother-in-law. But who am I kidding? Cornwall is no better. My own grandmother doesn't even want me. She's made it abundantly clear. But now I'm committed to staying at least until this inheritance ordeal is sorted.

I shrug. 'My grandmother needs me here.'

'Is that what she told you? Your grandmother doesn't need anything except for slaves in chains. She reigns with an iron fist, that one.'

'Is that why you don't get along?'

He snorts. 'Now that's an understatement if ever I heard one.'

'I know we don't know each other, but... what is it with the two of you and all this anger?'

'You mean mine... or hers?'

'Both.' I shrug. 'I mean, what do you know about my grandmother?'

'That she doesn't know her arse from her elbow, for starters. And just in case you were hoping, she's never going to accept you. She doesn't like giving away any of her money.'

I bristle. 'I'm not here for her money.'

'Well then don't even try to fit in. You don't belong here. Trust me, you're never gonna be accepted. Your grandmother won't permit it.'

'I don't need to be accepted,' I lie. 'I just came here to do my duty.'

'It's not your duty to take care of that old battleaxe.'

'I'm just keeping her company. Her doctor can't be with her 24/7.'

'And Martin has taken Janice's place on watch.'

'Yes.'

'Well, it sounds like he's sure making an effort with her.'

'Yes, he is.'

'He rarely makes house calls.'

'Oh?'

'But he does for your bloody Granny *grootmother*. I wonder why that is?' he drawls, eyeing me quizzically.

'How am I supposed to know?'

'Rumour has it he's besotted with you.'

So he knows I went out to dinner with him. What a tiny world we live in.

'That's ridiculous,' I protest. 'He's simply a good bloke.'

'Unlike me?'

'What has any of this got to do with you?'

He shrugs. 'He was a good friend of mine once. I'd hate to see him suffer.'

'And what makes you think I'd make him suffer?'

'The fact that you're not even remotely interested in him.'

'That's not for you to say.'

'No. It's for you to tell him. You should explain that you're madly in love with your fiancé. The one you should be getting back to by now, rather than leading that poor sod on.'

'And when did you become so worried about a former friend?'

He shrugs. 'It's you I'm actually more worried about. Why put yourself in yet another relationship that's doomed from the start?'

Doomed? Is that what he thinks about my relationship with Stephen?

And... can I blame him? If I have to be honest and put a hand on my heart, can I say that we're solid?

'Enough about me, Jago. What I'd like to know is how did you come to be my grandfather's friend?' I venture.

He looks at me and then his eyes shoot out to sea as if projecting himself there again. As if he's still scanning the horizon for his friend who's no longer there. He exhales heavily, unsteadily. Not a groan, but a way to flush out the emotions overwhelming him.

I'm beginning to notice things about him – his gazes, his reactions. I can tell when he's impatient by the puffs of air that escape his lips when they're set in a tight line. But now they're not tight. They're drooping at the corners. This is a truth that's hurting him, that he doesn't like to talk about. The guilt is etched in his features.

His eyes return to my face and they're solemn.

'When I was a kid, he took me with him on his fishing boat.'

'That sounds like fun,' I offer.

He pauses and then looks out to sea again.

'We'd be gone for weeks at a time. I loved it, out at sea. He taught me everything there is to know, from tying knots to weaving fishing nets, and rigging and trigonometry and cartography. He raised me, loved me like a son.'

There is, for a brief moment, a new light in his eyes that resembles the opposite of his habitual resignation and self-deprecation. And then he swallows as his voice deepens again.

'I was nothing before he found me. I was a bloody outcast. I had no one and nothing. And when he died in my arms, I was nothing all over again...'

The unspoken thought, *I am still nothing*, hangs in the space between us, along with the misery that he hides under a layer of sarcasm and arrogance.

My heart aches for him. 'Oh, Jago, you know that's so not true. You're smart. You could do so much with your life.'

He snorts and then mumbles, 'Yeah, I could do so much more damage.'

'Jago? Can I ask you something?'

'Uh-oh...'

'Why does my grandmother blame you for Nano's death?' I ask.

He snorts. 'Well, she's right. I am to blame. Completely.'

'How did he die? My grandmother isn't exactly helpful information-wise.'

He sighs.

'I'm sorry,' I say. 'I understand if—'

'No, it's OK. At least someone wants to hear my version besides the police. We were out at sea. He wasn't feeling very well, so I suggested we go back, but he didn't want to. That night, I was asleep below deck. A moan woke me, followed by a splash. I raced to the deck. Nano had had a heart attack and fallen into the water. It was dark and I jumped in blindly. But I wasn't fast enough. By the time I got hold of him and tried to bring him back, he was already dead.'

I can picture Jago trying to resuscitate him, once, twice, even three times. He's not one to let things go so easily, I've learned. But it was too late. There was nothing more he could do. Poor Grandfather James. Poor Nano...

# 15

After dreaming of a family, my second fantasy was to live in a typical village by the sea. It would have a quirky name and Narnia lamps in the street and an old Anglo-Saxon church with a backdrop of green countryside. It would become snowy white in the winter, especially in time for Christmas Eve. If I could have called that place my home instead of busy London, I'd have been the happiest child on earth.

And today, by some strange twist of fate, here I am, in the little village I dreamed of without knowing it really existed. It's like a living Christmas card.

Leaving Starry Cove at my back, I pick my way down a private lane to a fence with one of those old-fashioned country stiles. I gingerly climb the three steps leading up and then down the other three on the other side, careful my wellies don't slide in the mud. Another full five minutes of walking, or rather, skidding and hopping to the grassy patches for purchase, takes me to a clearing by the sea.

I saunter up to the double-fronted building, frowning. If ever a name was apt for a home, certainly Stormy Cottage was befitting for this abandoned Cornish property. But it could also have been Windowless Abode, Hole in the Roof, Leaking Walls or, why not, perhaps even Barely Standing.

Placing the large iron key in its lock, I try to turn it, but nothing happens. I try again, but still nothing. I look around me, seeing if maybe I could use a rock to smash it open.

'Need a hand?' comes a voice at my elbow.

I whirl round to see a man walking his dog, a beautiful Border collie. The man is a dead-ringer for the actor Sam Elliott, with the same shock of white hair and black eyebrows. You know how they say that dogs resemble their owners? Well, in this case they had the same colours. And both had very kind faces.

'Oh! Thank you. I just can't seem to—'

'Here, let me,' he volunteers, twisting the key while pulling the door to him and then pushing it.

It gives like a puppy heeling.

'Thank you, sir.'

'Bill. Just call me Bill. You the Weavers' daughter?'

I guess that the funeral was my unwilling debut into this society. 'Yes.'

'Condolences on your loss.'

'Oh. Thank you.'

'But also, congratulations on the inheritance. It might not look like it right now, but it's a solid house.'

*If you say so…*

'Survived thousands of storms, it has. In any case, if you need help, you can call my boss. She's based in Truro but lives up the coast. She truly is the best.'

'Oh, thank you, I will,' I promise, about to ask for a name, when he whips out a card.

'Here – Faith Hudson, interior designer. I'm sure we can sort you out.'

'Oh, I know Faith. Would you like to… come in? Are you busy?'

Bill rubs his collie's head. 'Daphne doesn't mind if we come in for a spot, do you, sweetheart? But if you don't mind, I'll go first. You never know what kind of stuff can fall from the ceiling. Technically, we'd need hard hats.'

'I'll be careful,' I promise as I follow him and once inside, I immediately wish I hadn't.

There's a heap of seagull poo all over the floor, as if all the seagulls in Cornwall have designated this very entrance for their bodily functions. And the stench is unbelievable!

I skirt round the heap and make my way into what looks like a living room to my right. I blame the presence of a torn settee for my audacious assumption. There's also a green felt-covered card table that stands (barely) in the corner, surrounded by odd chairs.

To the left is another huge reception room, but completely bare except for a fireplace and a broken curtain rod dangling to the ground. At the back there's a large kitchen the width of the entire cottage, but it's falling apart under the weight of its years.

Upstairs it's even worse. There are four bedrooms, all in a shambles. The furniture has practically rotted, alongside something else that I dare not investigate.

'Don't worry,' Bill says. 'Beneath all this rubbish, the house is solid. It just needs a little love.'

Don't we all, I almost say. 'Why did they let it fall apart like this, Bill?'

He shrugs. 'Many reasons. Come on – let's go and look at the garden.'

Outside, in truth, is no better. Weeds have literally turned into bushes and the picket fence has joined the family of rot. There are remnants of African lilies in the pots just outside the door and I can almost picture an ancient scene of the previous tenants watering them lovingly. I wonder where they are now, but it's not Bill I should be asking.

A loud bark makes us turn our heads to see a huge German shepherd bounding towards us, its huge red tongue lolling.

'Max!' Bill calls, getting down on his haunches as it careens into him, licking him all over. 'Where's Jago?'

'Never far behind,' calls a deep voice through the thicket as my skin prickles.

Does he have to be *everywhere* I go?

'Hiya, partner,' he greets me quizzically. 'Bill – what's up? Why are you here?'

'The lady's come to see her house,' Bill replies, ruffling Max's fur.

'Her house? This is my property.'

Bill's mouth falls open as he turns to look at me. 'You didn't inherit it?'

I nod. 'Yes, I did. My grandfather left it to me. Well, 50 per cent of it. I didn't realise Jago was the other shareholder. I thought that was just the shop…'

'The hell he left it to you,' Jago snorts. 'He can't give what isn't his, now can he? A 50 per cent share in the business is one thing, but this cottage belongs to me.'

Bill lifts his hands. 'I assumed—'

'No worries, Bill. A lot of people round here seem to be assuming a lot lately.'

And with that, Jago shoots me an annoyed glance as if I were some pestiferous insect ruining his day. Just about now I'd like to clock him. Right in the middle of that self-satisfied face of his.

'I'd best be off, then. Miss, I'm sorry for the misunderstanding,' Bill says. 'If you need anything else, please don't hesitate to call us. You have our card.'

I glare at Jago, then turn to Bill. 'I... thank you, Bill. You're very kind.'

Bill gently pulls on the leash. 'Jago, no hard feelings?'

'Of course not. See you, Bill,' he says.

'Come on, Daphne, let's go home,' Bill says, heading back to the entrance of the clearing.

'This is too rich. Just what makes you think that it's all yours?' I demand as soon as Bill and Daphne are gone. 'My grandfather was the rightful owner and now he's left half of it to me.'

'Not happening. This cottage is mine.'

'There's a will that states otherwise.'

'A will I wasn't summoned to.'

'Well, at your convenience, maybe we could sit down like two civilised people and discuss it. All I want is what's rightfully mine.'

Jago shakes his head. 'And so it begins, the schooling of the next Lady Heatherton.'

'My surname is Weaver.'

'Poor, poor Miss Weaver. You've no idea what kind of mess you've just walked into.'

'Then why don't you tell me?'

He studies me for a moment, then shakes his head. 'Naw. I'd rather you heard it from the horse's mouth.'

And with that, he walks into the cottage, followed by Max, and shuts the door in my face.

# 16

*Nostromo,* Joseph Conrad

When I get back to Heatherton Hall, angry and humiliated, my head and heart full of questions and doubts that only she can solve, I find my grandmother sitting in the dark drawing room with the curtains drawn and only the fire and the Christmas tree lights on. I'd decided not to take them down when she'd snapped at me. And since she hasn't asked me to remove them again, I boldly left them up. I'm sure that Nano would have wanted her to celebrate Christmas even without him.

As I near her, she seems to be crying. I honestly didn't think she was capable of such a simple human gesture. But I guess I was wrong. She may just have a heart, after all.

'Grandm... Mrs Heatherton, are you alright? What's wrong?'

'Oh! Emily, you frightened me. One usually knocks upon entering a room.'

Fooled you, didn't she? You and me both. With a

suppressed sigh, I sit opposite her fragile form that harbours a heart and mind of steel.

I wish I'd met her years ago. I wish we'd had a relationship to speak of, rather than this strange stalemate situation where I don't know where I stand. She doesn't seem even remotely interested in the fact that we share the same DNA.

Is she simply tolerating me for the love of her late husband? Why is it so difficult for her to accept me as her own flesh and blood? Why can't she put her tumultuous relationship with her daughter behind her, especially now as she's no longer with us? I'd forgiven my mother a plethora of misgivings.

But now I find it hard to forgive my mother for never telling me any of this. I lost out on having a grandfather watching me grow up. I never had the chance to show him the poems I wrote in Year 3 or to hold his hand during an autumnal walk through the park. Or to cry on his shoulder about Joe Hawkins who bullied me (undisturbed by my parents) all the way through primary school.

I know he'd have been a better father than my own. Most people say that grandparents love their grandchildren even more than they love their own children. Which wouldn't be a hard record for anyone to beat where my parents were concerned. With Nano, I feel like I've lost him twice, and now I'm struggling to connect with my distant grandmother.

'What's upset you? Has Jago got anything to do with this?' I ask.

She dabs at her nose daintily with a lace handkerchief and looks up at me, her voice trembling. 'So you've spoken to him.'

I shrug. 'I'm trying to get him to reason about the inheritance. He says that I have no claim over what wasn't Nano's to give in the first place. What does that mean?'

'It means that he's a liar and a thief, among other things.'

'He seems like a lonely man. The drinking—'

'The drinking is the least of his problems.'

'It's like he's got a beef with the world. I wonder what it is.'

She sits up, alarmed. 'You stay away from that man, Emily! Do you hear me?'

'I... Of course. I was just wondering—'

'No, no wondering! He is trouble in capital letters and never brought anyone any good.'

'Alright, please don't get upset. I don't intend to speak to him outside of business anyway.'

'Excellent. Maybe you do have slightly more salt in that head of yours than your mother did. I meant what I said. If you see him socially, I will see to it that you are disinherited. Do you understand?'

I sigh. 'Please don't take this the wrong way, but when I came here to Cornwall to meet you, I had no idea you had means. I only came to meet my grandmother. So please understand that you can't bully me into doing what you want by threatening me with losing something that I don't actually care about. I've always had to work hard for everything in life, so not inheriting a penny doesn't scare me.'

At that, her face changes. I don't know her well enough to understand this expression I've never seen before, but I can tell she's not pleased. As she says nothing, I'm assuming

I'm not on her black list quite yet, so I sit a while in silence, watching as the fire spits and hisses, an occasional crack reverberating in the room like a distant gunshot.

Having established that, the other elephant – Jago's claim to my inheritance – is still looming largely in the room. Jago isn't someone who can be ignored easily. Whether you like it or not, he gets under your skin and tests your limits the way no one else can. He's a force to be reckoned with.

'Please, make an effort,' I whisper after a few moments.

She turns and studies me with those beautiful yet cold eyes but says nothing.

'Does my existence mean absolutely nothing to you?' I insist. 'Talk to me. Tell me what you're *thinking*…'

She grips her armrests and closes her eyes.

'Why am I here if you don't want me?' I press her.

'Because your grandfather did. And I keep my promises…' she sighs.

'I know you miss Nano…'

She looks at me quizzically. 'He talked about you all the time. He wondered what you were like, what you were doing, which traits you'd inherited. Sentimental old sod that he was.'

'It's so sad, what my parents did. I missed out on my family. My own blood. Years and years of stolen memories. I don't know that I can forgive my mother for this as well.'

Her eyes open and she turns her head towards me. 'As well? What do you mean?'

I shrug. 'She and my father, they were absorbed in their own lives. They never cared much about me.'

'I'm not surprised. They were very selfish, self-centred people.'

Says the Lady Mary Heatherton-Smythe of Heatherton Hall and snob extraordinaire.

'And they never kept in touch with you?' I ask.

She shakes her head. 'Never. We'd send birthday cards and gifts for you, but never got an acknowledgment. Nano was heartbroken. And so was I...'

'I'm so sorry this happened to you.'

'Yes, well, it can't be helped anymore,' she says with a trembling voice. 'They're all gone. Every single one of them.'

I'd like to tell her that they're not all gone. *I'm* still here. But I don't think it's much consolation. Simply looking my way must remind her of her daughter. But apart from that, I'm still a stranger. I only wish she'd open up to me. I'm not a gold digger. I didn't even know they existed before the letter. How can she not see that? Why does she resent my presence so much now? Will I ever be able to penetrate that vault that is her heart? But perhaps, rather than pressing her more, I should start with the simple things. Get to know her.

'Shall I make us a cup of tea?' I offer after a few minutes of her unbearable silence.

She slowly turns to me again as if she's already forgotten I'm there.

'Yes, that would be nice, thank you, Emily.'

'I'll only be a minute, then.'

I get to my feet and go into the kitchen, and as I fill the kettle, I wonder how I ever got myself into this mess in the first place. I was perfectly unhappy and confused in London without having to come all the way here to be even more unhappy and confused. Now here, so far away from everything I know (and don't love), I still feel somewhat at a loss. I was better off when I didn't have an inheritance to worry about. I was better off when my path was already clear and cut for me. Marriage to Stephen, my work as a teacher and maybe some children. End of. Now, I find that there are too many ways to turn and I don't know what to do with myself.

When I return to the drawing room with a tray of tea and her favourite shortbread, she's looking frail and paler than usual. Perhaps I should call Dr Martin Miller.

'Ah! shortbread. Lovely. Thank you, Emily.'

Dare I hope that one day we can be a real family? But for now, because I don't want her to think that I'm only interested in my inheritance, I'll keep quiet. It does worry me, however. I have to sort Jago out once and for all and try to come to an agreement of sorts with him. Maybe he could buy me out. In any case, tomorrow I'll go and check out the third and last asset I've inherited, my grandfather's boat.

*The Miranda*, as I've been told, was Nano's fishing barge. I don't know anything about barges, except that they float on water. But I've inherited half of it and it would have seemed ungrateful on my part not to come down to the cove and inspect the wretched thing. Apparently, this was his prized possession.

But if it's anything like Stormy Cottage, it'll be another utter wreck. And, like all things, any form of repairs will inevitably be costly. Hardly worth the work. And all that to do what, exactly? I can't fish and nor would I want to. As lovely and picturesque as the idea of a barge floating down a river is, I have to be practical. Perhaps I can convince Jago to buy me out of that, too. Although he doesn't seem to have any means.

Why would my grandfather leave half of his assets to me and half to Jago? What does he expect me to do with it if not sell it? And if Jago won't buy me out, I'm stuck with the stuff. Why hasn't he left me any indications in his will?

And my grandmother? What does she expect me to do with it? Is she laughing herself silly at me for inheriting it? Or is she angry at Nano for leaving me a 50 per cent share of a business? Even if it may not be profitable.

The barge is moored in a quiet, practically deserted inlet. I cross the dock and the plank leading to the front door and once on deck, I put my key in the lock, hoping I'll be a bit luckier this time. The key turns like a dream and in I go, stopping on the threshold in surprise at the excellent state of the barge. It's been converted into a home to a very high level. Very nice, Nano!

The inside has simple but quality furnishings. There's a beautiful oak coffee table next to a reading chair and off to one side, a unit full of books with many classics. The place is absolutely beautiful, with soft rugs and gorgeous lamps scattered here and there. Faith Hudson herself would gush.

'Well, if it isn't Lady Weaver of Heatherton Hall!' comes a voice from behind.

'Oh, not you again!' I cry as I whirl round to see Jago coming out of what I can only presume is the bedroom, dressed only in a pair of black hip-hugging boxers. Very distracting boxers, if I may say.

I try to keep my eyes on his face, but his lean yet muscular body is difficult to ignore, starting from the wide shoulders and six-pack. Let's stop there. Do not look any further, Emmie.

'The feeling's mutual,' he drawls in a low, sleepy voice.

His hair is a silky mess and his jaw is covered in morning stubble. He sits down and runs his hands over his face.

'Sorry, if I'd known you were coming, I'd have brushed my hair and baked some biscuits!' he smirks.

'What are you *doing* here?' I demand. 'You're practically everywhere!'

'Actually,' he says slowly and pointedly, 'I live here.'

'Oh, come on! I thought you said the cottage was your home.'

'No,' he says, 'the cottage is my property. *This* is my home.'

Oh my God in heaven. Is there no getting rid of him?

I clench my teeth. 'Have you got proof?'

'I don't need proof. I've been living here forever.'

'Well, not anymore, you won't be. It's mine, too.'

'What?' he groans. 'Impossible!'

'Check with Lister & Ass!' I hiss.

He rubs his face. 'No, no, no, there's been a huge misunderstanding. Someone somewhere has made a massive mistake.'

'No mistake,' I assure. 'It's all very clear – I get 50 per cent of the barge *and* the cottage.' He doesn't need to know about the money, does he? 'It's all in my grandfather's will.'

'Very difficult to believe, seeing as he'd already left it to me.'

I cross my arms. 'Well, then it looks like we have a huge problem on our hands.'

'Yeah – you.'

'I beg your pardon?'

'You heard. Before you arrived, everything was tickety-boo.'

'It doesn't look like that to me, seeing your reputation. There's no way I'm sharing my inheritance with some... some... confidence trickster who bamboozled my grandfather into a false friendship just to get something off him.'

'We were friends!' he suddenly roars, raking a hand through his unruly black locks. 'What part of that did you not get? I've lost someone I actually loved, while you – you didn't even know he existed.'

I'm sorry for him, truly I am. But it's not up to me to sort out the misunderstanding. I have enough problems of my own. So I channel my inner Mary.

'You are kindly requested to meet me at the shop tomorrow to talk about this. Where hopefully everyone present will be dressed!'

'Oh, come on, Emmie,' he drawls. 'Lighten up. It was just a naked woman, you know?'

'And I'm sure you've had your share of them,' I blurt before I can stop myself.

His expression changes to one of surprise.

'Look,' I say, trying to windmill myself back to the higher road. 'It's obvious that we won't be getting rid of each other soon, so we need to come to some sort of agreement.'

'Highly unlikely,' he concludes distractedly. 'Unless you want to do tradesies? I give you the house and you leave me the barge.'

'That's not happening,' I assure, crossing my arms over my chest as my face begins to heat.

The cheek, offering me the ruin while he gets the cool place!

'Why not?' he insists. 'It's not like you're going to move to Cornwall. Let me buy you out and we can go our own separate, independent ways.'

That's just the point. I don't want to go anywhere. And this shop of which I'm a 50 per cent sharer is already, and surprisingly, doing very well. Why would I want to give it up?

'Is having me as a partner really so bad?' I ask.

He looks at me with those dark, soulful eyes. 'It's a bloody disaster.'

'Why?'

'There yeh go again, askin' questions that you don't want answers to. I'm not your type, Emmie. Accept it and move on.'

'Not my type? What exactly are you on?' I bite off. 'I'm not interested in you in the least! I'm getting engaged in eleven days! Eleven days! I'm going to be married to a headmaster – a man of means and culture. And he's as solid as a rock.'

'So solid he couldn't keep you out of harm's way!' he bites back. 'You're just kidding yourself, Emmie. He's no good for you.'

'What do you know what's good for me?' I hurl in his direction before turning on my heels.

I stomp down the steel plank and, fuming, make my way up the hill leading back into Starry Cove. Here, I turn into the first café I find and plop myself on the hard cushion-less benches for a shot of caffeine.

That arse! I can't believe he's everywhere and has his fingers in every pie. Maybe that's why my grandmother can't stand him. I'm sure Nano's left him something else that she's not too happy about, either. I wonder what it is. And I wonder why Jago was important enough to Nano to inherit any of his assets. It's not like he was his son or anything, right?

As the sound of loud music batters the insides of my ears, I look around me. Rather than the cosy café I was told it used to be, hipsters are standing around the GloLite bar or perched on chrome stools, hanging on to their lattes as if they're the latest accessory. Abstract paintings of eyes, ears and mouths literally run across the four walls, interrupted only by the door to the kitchen. And nowhere is there any sign of Christmas. It could be any day of the year.

Upon closer inspection, I realise I'm actually the oldest person in this place, which is more appropriate for my students. They have newer and stronger eardrums.

What a shame. At one point this place must have been cosy and quaint, but the modernisation has stripped it of its original authenticity and feel. And if their business goal here is to make the customer drink their coffee and shoot off in a hurry just to get off the hard seats, they've got it spot on, because I'm the only one actually sitting with a book in my lap. What a naïve choice.

As I sip and read, I think about how nice it would be if I could just sit in peace and quiet, maybe exchange a few words with someone at the next table, pat someone's dog on the head or smile at someone's child whose mouth is slathered with chocolate. Or perhaps it would be nice simply to look out of the window and see water rather than the shops opposite.

And that's when a brainstorm hits me. Perhaps I won't be selling the barge, after all. I could start my own business. But what kind of business? you may ask. What is the one thing that I'd be good at – one thing that I know very well? Why, books, of course! I could open a library-cum-bookstore. With a café. I could bring in all of my old books and also serve refreshments.

People could come in, sit and read. Have a hot drink. I could call it Books on the Barge! Yes! I can already see it. I'd need a steady income to afford to set it up and I wouldn't even need a nautical licence, seeing as it would be moored. I'd have to look into that. Maybe talk to a few people down at the town hall. I'm sure I can manage to get all the necessary paperwork. Congratulations to me! I've just come up with the idea of the century (well, of the day, really) and think it might just work, if I can get Jago Moon on, or rather, *off* board, if you'll pardon the pun. All this, however, would entail one thing. I'd have to move to Cornwall lock, stock and barrel.

I can already imagine Stephen. He's much too attached to his desk at Boynton Academy, London, and his mother. Still, if he had a choice between all that and me, could I depend on him choosing me? Are we strong enough?

Personally, I have no ties in London except to Maisie and although she doesn't approve of my living in Starry Cove indefinitely, she's still my one safe port. My grandmother, on the other hand, can't wait to get rid of me.

'Why was Jago Moon Nano's partner at the Bend or

Bump?' I ask when I get back to Heatherton Hall. 'He says he and Nano were friends. *Good* friends.'

My grandmother looks up from her book – a collection of poems by Emily Dickinson.

'I thought I told you not to talk to Jago Moon.'

'Pretty difficult not to in a town of ninety-nine souls.'

'When are you going to stop asking questions and go back to London?'

'Why are you in such a hurry for me to leave Starry Cove, Grandmother? If you don't want me in the house, I can always go back to that beautiful, beautiful inn where they always have a kind word for me.'

She turns to spear me with those icy eyes of hers.

'If you're determined to stay, I'd rather you remained under my roof where I can keep an eye on you.'

'I'm touched by your affection, Grandmother.'

'Good Lord, Emily! You have your grandfather's inheritance. What more do you want? Why don't you sell everything and go back to where you came from?'

Why, she asks. She just doesn't get it. I want a family. An inconvenient, annoying, binding blood tie with someone who has my same origins. I want to recognise my eyes in someone else's face. I want someone to feel bound to me instinctively. To stick with me no matter what. Just like families do. But she doesn't understand. And she never will. Because to her I'm a nuisance. An afterthought that she'd actually forgotten about.

'I only asked you to come to Cornwall because my solicitors had informed me that you were inheriting. They found you, not I. Nor did I care to.'

What else do I need to hear? That I'm a mistake she'd gladly be rid of? That my mother should have, indeed, had that abortion? Because they all knew they'd never love me, no matter how cute I was as a kid, or how decent I am as an adult. They just didn't want me – none of them ever did and still don't. Without a word, I whirl round and leave the room before she can see the tears burning my eyes.

# 17

*Mansfield Park*, Jane Austen

The only place I can be alone now is at my new secret spot – a tiny bridge over a brook at the other end of the village, just before it widens into the river. Here I sit, contemplating how badly everything is going. My grandmother, whom I'd half expected to love me despite being strangers, has decided that it's not going to happen. The past that I was so desperately trying to piece together is nowhere to be found. My parents had made it literally impossible for me to have any good memories whatsoever and if I was hoping for a happier future upon finding my grandmother, well, tough luck for me.

Interrupting my thoughts, my mobile rings as Stephen's picture appears on my screen. I sigh, wondering if he's going to make my mood even worse, if that's at all possible.

'Hi,' I say simply.

'Uh-oh. What's happened now?'

'Nothing. But seeing as you called, can I run something by you?'

'I've only got a couple of minutes,' he warns. 'Is it going to be long?'

Is it? How long does it take to give up on your future or kill a dream?

'I was thinking about my inheritance...'

'Yes? Have you found any buyers yet?'

Here's another one who wants me to sell up. 'Buyers?'

'For your assets. The sooner you find buyers, the sooner you can leave that dreaded shithole and come back.'

I snort. If he only knew. If I could only bring myself to tell him that part of me would actually like to give it a go, that I want to ask him to consider it seriously.

'What is it, Emmie? You sound miserable.'

I huff. 'My grandmother isn't very well disposed towards me. I thought she'd mellow, but—'

'I told you she was trouble,' Stephen scolds me. 'I told you from the start, Emmie.'

'Stephen, this isn't a good time for I told you sos. If you're not in the mood to be nice, call me back when you are.'

'Emmie, it's not going to be getting any better, you know. I think you made a huge mistake even entertaining the idea of meeting her. You want to think long and hard about your next step. Even Mum has her reservations.'

'Your mum?' I sigh, suddenly weary – *weary* of it all. Weary of him, weary of Audrey. Of everything. 'Stephen, I was hoping to speak with *you*. That you could help me to clear my head and cheer me up. But I see I'm always hoping and coming up empty-handed. I'm hanging up now. Goodbye.'

'Emmie, come on, I'm—'

As I ring off, the sound of silence is pure bliss. How

much longer am I going to let people treat me like rubbish? How much longer am I going to put off making my own decisions? There isn't one thing that Stephen doesn't push his nose into, from what I wear to how I speak. When is he ever going to let me be me? I'm a woman chained to a rocket that's about to shoot off into the sky of his mother's London high fashion society and I can't seem to break free without hurting anyone but myself. I can't go on like this. Something somewhere has to give.

Because there's no use in hiding it from myself anymore. It's time to stop teetering and tottering over the brink of a new life. I should just dive in. Would Stephen be able to change in order for us to enjoy our new life together, or am I going to have to make the decision to leave him and my life in London, once and for all?

And that's when, sitting on the dock, my feet swinging over the water, I come to a decision I thought I'd never make. I pull the SIM card out of my phone and flick it into the sea.

'That classifies as littering, you know,' comes a familiar voice at my back.

I turn and who else could it be but my leper buddy-cum-business partner-cum-opponent Jago Moon. I shrug and redirect my attention to the moving waters before me.

'Call the police, call your solicitor. I don't care...' I say.

'Is it that bad that you don't want to be connected to the world anymore?' he asks, dropping to his haunches and sitting next to me on the wooden dock.

'Look who's talking – the village hermit,' I mumble.

Village hermit dripping with women, apparently.

'That's different,' he argues.

'Why? Why is it different?' I challenge. 'Why is it OK for you not to be accepted but the minute *I* pull away, it's not OK?'

'Because you're a sociable girl, Emmie. You have so much to give.'

'And you? Apparently you used to have lots of friends.'

'*Used to* being the operative word.'

'Would you like to tell me what happened?' I ask.

'Not really.'

'Would you like to hear what happened to me?'

'I have a funny feeling you're going to tell me anyway.'

'Ha! No one says that anymore.'

He snorts. 'No one does a lot of things anymore, either.'

'Such as?'

He sighs. 'Living. Loving. Being happy.'

'Wow! That's profound even for you.'

'Just tell me what happened to you, Emmie.'

And so I do. I tell him about my grandmother not giving a toss about me. I tell him about Audrey who was only kind to me when she heard of the inheritance. And finally I tell him about Stephen. Because sometimes, the person who cares about you least is the one to give you a right kick up the arse.

In the space of one day, I've definitely lost my only family member and at the same time realised that my dream with Stephen was only mine. I have absolutely nothing left to lose now. The money comes and goes.

'Maybe you should do nothing. About any of it,' he suggests.

'What do you mean?'

He shrugs. 'Think about all the hours we waste worrying

about things that we can't control. Is it worth it? Maybe your grandmother and your fiancé should make the next move. Maybe you've done enough. See what they do.'

Hmm. Such a simple idea. And yet, genius.

'Like President Kennedy ignoring Khrushchev's ultimatum?'

He grins, his eyes crinkling at the corners. 'Exactly.'

'I will, thank you, Jago.'

He grins wryly. 'It's nothin'.'

I get to my feet. 'I have some errands to run for my grandmother,' I explain.

'Careful she doesn't run you into the ground,' he warns as I head towards the village.


In effect, my entire afternoon is spent running rings around the village taking care of errands for the lady of the manor. She's got it down to a fine art, indeed, making sure every aspect of her life is taken care of. I've got a long list of things to do, which takes me around Starry Cove at least four times as her medical prescriptions need filling out as well as sorting her particular shopping list, which includes food that I'll never be able to afford. Who the hell buys caviar by the crate? And oceans of champagne? Is she for real?

As I slog past The Rolling Scones, I can see the soft glow of the Christmas lights from within. Outside, the cold bites at my skin. But inside, there are young families with their children and hot cups of coffee and tea and cake. There are also young couples holding hands and elderly ones chatting quietly. Not a single person in there is on their own. What I wouldn't do to park my own arse there, with a huge, noisy, dysfunctional family to call my own, and wash down a slice of cake with a cup of their celestial coffee. And listen to the recorded carols playing on a loop. I wouldn't ask for more. But instead I've got a quasi-fiancé who pooh-poohs every idea that crosses my mind, a nana who can't bear the sight of me and an empty, un-festive London flat.

With one last longing look at the shop window, I wonder how my life here is any better than in London.

When I get in later that day, I hear shouting in the drawing room. I put my bag down, wondering who would have the gall to come into my grandmother's home and treat her like that. Surely no one on the entire coast would dare to. I'm about to knock, when I recognise Jago's voice.

'You know damn well that boat was left to me – and the cottage! If you want to give your granddaughter something, why don't you give it to her out of your immense assets and leave mine alone?'

'You know that had absolutely nothing to do with me,' she answers calmly. 'If I'd had my way, she'd never have inherited a penny. We were perfectly happy without her and now she's come to ruin my peace of mind. Every time I see her, I think of all I've suffered.'

'And when you see me?' he asks. 'What do you see?'

'What do I see? I see the face of my dead husband,' she replies calmly.

I suppress a gasp as tiny shreds of logic begin to coalesce, like metal filings to a lodestone. Jago's inheritance... Oh my God! Could Jago be my grandfather's love child?

Oh, come on, I tell myself. This isn't the Middle Ages. Why would that be a secret nowadays? Unless… it wasn't. And perhaps… Mary knew. Was that why she hated him so much and why she resented him inheriting from Nano?

Jago snorts. 'How disappointed you must be, Mary. Don't say that we're complete opposites. We have a lot more in common than you like to admit. And you know it.'

Silence, then: 'Get out of my house, Jago.'

'Your house? Not for long, old Mary. When you croak, half of this goes to me. And you know what I'm gonna do with it, *Grandmother*? I'm gonna donate it all to an orphanage. You know what those are, Mary? It's where they take care of *unwanted* children. Your comeuppance is nigh.'

He called her grandmother? What the hell is going on? Is he really her grandson? But if he is… what does that make Jago and me? Cousins? Oh my God! Why did she never tell me something so monumental? Now I understand why she was so adamant that we never became close. Not that that's ever happening.

I hide in the wings until he stalks out of the house and then creep into the drawing room.

'Grandmother, what was that all about? I thought he was *persona non grata* at Heatherton Hall?'

She looks up and spears me with an accusatory look, one eyelid flinching, a telltale sign that she's hiding something from me.

'It's not proper to spy on people, Emily.'

'I wasn't spying. I just happened to see him.'

'And hear him.'

I shrug. 'Hard not to. The two of you aren't exactly friends.'

And that's when Lady Mary Heatherton harrumphs. Like you and me, mere mortals.

'Grandmother, what did he do to upset you so much?'

'Pah! Forget him. He's just a flea – a useless fly.'

'But why was he here? What does he want, apart from my inheritance?'

She closes her book. 'You said you weren't spying.'

'I wasn't. I had a run-in with him the other day about assets. I think he might contest Grandfather Nano's will.'

'Impossible! He has no right to anything,' she spits, her face reddening.

'Grandma,' I warn. 'Please don't get upset. I shouldn't have said anything. I'm sorry. I'll sort it.'

'Pass me my little phone book, Emily, and let me deal with this. The nerve of that lowlife scumbag, thinking he can come in here and dictate…'

There are several options here. Either he's blackmailing her about something or has a hold over her of a different kind. But what? What ace could he possibly have up his sleeve? Unless… I need to know.

'Please tell me, Grandmother. Are Jago and I related?'

'*What?*'

'Are we from the same bloodline?'

'Related? In a way, unfortunately. Do you have the same blood? No. So don't worry your pretty little head over things like that. You won't go to hell for your wanton thoughts. At least not just yet.'

*Ha, ha. Isn't she just charming?*

So we're not related! What's the story, then? How can I get her to share her life and feelings with me, and how are we ever going to grow close if she keeps shutting me out?

★

A few hours later, Calvin appears at the kitchen door, where I'm peeling potatoes like a proper Demelza from *Poldark*.

'Emmie? I forgot. There was a delivery for you a few days ago. It's on the console by the front doors.'

'For me? Thank you, Calvin,' I reply as I go out into the hall and reach for the small brown paper packet on the table.

Who could it be from? The only people who know I'm here are Maisie and Stephen. And the MIL, of course, but I can't see her sending me a gift of any sort. I turn it over, but there's nothing except my name on it, scrawled in a masculine hand I don't recognise. This is exciting!

Inside is the scarf I lost to Jago, with a note:

Seeing as we're in this fifty-fifty until we find a solution, I thought we'd have joint custody of the scarf. You might want to hang on a bit tighter next time.

No signature, of course. As if I didn't know who sent it. But why the sudden change of tack? Did he think that this unexpected kindness would make me change my mind about my inheritance? In that case, he's got another thing coming.

We meet the next day in Starry Cove, on the breakwater – the perfect place in case I need to chuck him in and get rid of the body. But he doesn't seem as aggressive as I expected. Still, we have come to a stalemate. He won't budge and nor will I. It's December 15th and I'm nine days away from leaving for London for my engagement party on the 24th to start a new life and I can't even get my assets straight because of him.

As we walk side by side, I'm aware of people throwing curious glances at us, and possibly already making up scenarios between the duelling owners of Bend or Bump. Yes, well, I'd gladly bend him into a million pieces. Or bump him off.

'Need a hand?' he says as I falter on the flagstones. 'The first ice is always the slippiest.'

I move away from him purposely. 'No, thank you, I don't need your help. I can actually walk by myseee...!'

And before I know it, I slip, do a frantic dance to right myself and end up flat on my back, hitting my head on the flagstones.

He'd been watching me amused, but when I hit the ground, he lurches forwards in concern, skidding to my side, checking me for broken bones, his hand sliding behind the back of my head, which is bleeding.

'Judas, are you alright?'

I lie completely still, waiting for my brain to stop rocking inside my skull. It hurts like hell. Oh! how it *hurts*...

'What do you care?' I bite off to fight back tears of pain.

Without a word, he peels me off the ground, lifts me into his arms and crosses the breakwater to the shore as if he were carrying a child.

'I can walk,' I suggest, but even the sole idea makes me want to hurl.

'And you sure proved that,' he remarks grimly as he carries me into the village, where people turn to stare at us.

Not a few weeks in and I'm already the centre of attention. Grandmother will be rightly pleased.

'Where are you taking me?' I manage as I rest my head against his chest, grateful that he's decided to carry me despite my resistance.

'To the doctor's office. Where else?'

'She slipped and banged her head on the ice,' he explains to Dr Janice Miller as he gently lays me on the examination table before her.

Her hands immediately circle my head, feeling her way around.

'No swelling – good sign,' she assures. 'Are you dizzy?'

'Not as much,' I admit.

She gently rubs a cold gel into my scalp.

'This is for the bruising. It's just a bump. You were lucky. You could have done yourself some serious damage.'

'Great,' I whoosh, relieved. 'Thank you, Doctor Miller.'

'You're very welcome, Emily.'

She slips off her gloves and grins at me, sliding Jago a glance. She is, I can tell, totally, utterly enamoured with him. What is it with women and Jago Moon? Although I'm not getting the impression that he reciprocates. Ah, the usual unrequited love has reared its ugly head once again. And I feel for her. Gosh, do I feel for her. Because I know what it's like to be unable to hide the longing looks, to not be able to breathe naturally when he's around. The object of your love, I mean. Not Jago, of course. He's not the object of my love. Pftt! what a thought.

And she's evidently still smarting from whatever had happened between them.

'Jago was right to bring you in, though.' And she looks at him again, blushing. 'It's good that you did that.'

But why is she saying it like he's done some humongous act of bravery? Is he usually a heel?

Jago shrugs. 'I didn't want anyone on my conscience, least of all a city slicker who doesn't know how to use her legs.'

My mouth falls open, but Dr Miller chuckles.

'Still, you did well. Emily, you'll be alright. Just stay put for a bit. No more dangerous walks, OK?'

'OK, Dr Miller. Thanks again.'

At a closer look, she's rather pretty, with shiny brown hair and an oval face. Not glamorous or fake, but a true, deep beauty based on good genes and a healthy lifestyle. And, I suspect, a good heart. You'd have to have a good – and a strong – heart to work as a GP with characters like Jago Moon, for starters.

'I've got another patient in the other room. Jago, can I leave her in your capable hands to get her home?'

'Yeah, sure, Doc.'

'OK, then. I'll come and check on you and your grandmother tomorrow at Heatherton Hall,' she promises before she closes the door behind her with one last smile for me and another furtive glance at Jago.

'Nice doctor,' I comment as the door closes.

Jago shrugs. 'Yeah, I guess. She's always on my case.'

'And why is that?' I ask, trying to avoid the obvious.

We both know it's about his drinking, but we elect not to go there.

'Because people around here can't mind their own bleddy business.'

'Then if you're so bothered about it, why don't you get away?' I suggest before I can stop myself. It's not like it's any of my business either, is it?

He thinks about it, his eyes lost somewhere between the past and the future, I can't tell which. Does he want to escape the mysterious memories of his past, and is he afraid of a future elsewhere, where people might not be so willing to tolerate him? Do people know his secret? And has it got anything to do with my grandmother's attitude towards him?

'I just might,' he answers, sliding me a glance. 'Then again, maybe I won't.'

And then silence falls. What does that mean, maybe he won't? Why wouldn't he?

'Do you expect me to thank you for returning my scarf?'

'I don't remember doing anything like that.'

I mentally roll my eyes. 'You sent me my scarf.'

His eye twitches. It's his tell.

'Doesn't sound like something I'd do.'

'Oh, come on, you can't have been that drunk,' I contest, then bite my lip.

'Maybe I was, maybe I wasn't.'

'Listen, thank you for taking care of me. I can walk home now.'

'I'll walk you back. You never know. We'll talk business another time.'

'OK,' I agree, wondering what the grandmother is going to say when she sees him. 'Listen, I'm sorry about barging into the... barge like that... the other day.'

'You were a bit presumptuous, in fact,' he agrees. 'But I forgive you.'

'Thank you. That's very gracious of you. A bit uncharacteristic, but gracious all the same. So, how are we going to solve this?' I ask. 'Are we going to involve lawyers, or are we going to come to an agreement of our own?'

'It's simple,' he answers. 'You leave me the barge.'

'In exchange for what?'

'The cottage.'

'Again. You'd rather have the barge, as cool as it is, rather than bricks and mortar that will increase in value as opposed to a boat?'

'Yes.'

'But why? You already have a house. And a business.'

'The barge is my home.'

'Well, you can't have it all.'

'So, you're not willing to compromise?'

'I don't know if I can trust you. Why do you want the barge? Is it lined with gold?'

He laughs bitterly. 'On the contrary. It's a renovated wreck.'

'Then why is it so important to you?'

He sighs, rubbing his thighs. He wants to tell me. But at the same time he doesn't. Luckily for him, we're at the gates of Heatherton Hall.

I stop and turn. 'I think it's best that you don't show your face around here for now.'

He nods, looking out over the expansive emerald grounds. 'You do realise where this is going, yes?'

'Hopefully towards an agreement.'

'Oh, there'll be an agreement alright. Because eventually, you're going to succumb to my lack of charm.'

I laugh. 'You are funny. I didn't think you were, but you are.'

He grins back. 'Glad to have surprised you once again.'

# 18

*Middlemarch,* George Eliot

When I get in, I find Nettie, like an apparition, at the kitchen table, peeling potatoes.

'Nettie!' I cry and instantly move to her for a hug.

'Hello, pet.' She greets me with a fierce squeeze. 'I hear the lady's been puttin' you through your paces.'

'Oh my God, only you can imagine! When did you get back?'

'Just now. Calvin picked me up at the station. Ooh, it's so good to be back. My sister is a pain in the arse.'

As if my grandmother wasn't. We laugh at our new private joke.

'Need a hand?' I ask.

'No, no. You just relax. Shall I get you a cup of tea?'

I jump up before she does, as it's the only way to stop her. 'I'll make it. Fancy one?'

'Please.'

I lean against the worktop as I wait for the kettle to boil, watching her from behind. She's so thin – worked to the

214

bone, poor woman. Grandmother should hire someone to help her. Someone to do all the harder work. How old is she, anyway? She doesn't seem to have any children. And yet... she looks familiar, in a way. The eyes... where have I seen them before?

'I saw you and... Jago,' she begins, nodding through the window.

'How well do you know him, Nettie?'

She baulks. 'Me? Why do you ask?'

'I just need to know who my business partner really is. I feel that there's more to him than meets the eye,' I explain with a groan as I put her cup of tea before her on the table.

She places her knife down and wipes her hands on a tea towel. 'Thanks, love. Well, you're right about that. He... used to be a lovely boy when he was young. There was never anything he wouldn't do for you. But then all that changed.'

'When?'

She turns to look at me, pity in her eyes.

'I think you should ask him that, pet. Or, better yet, stay away from him. His life's a right mess.'

'I see that. But why does everybody gang up on him like that? And why does my grandmother seem to hate him so much?'

Nettie studies my face.

'Oh dear! You haven't already fallen for him, have you? Be careful, Emmie. Sooner or later, everyone does – at their own expense.'

Brilliant. Just brilliant.

She smiles and pats my hand.

'You want a word of advice, pet?'

I look up into her eyes. 'Please.'

'You stay away from Jago Moon. He's not right for you. He'll break you if you let him.' She gives me a knowing look. 'And trust me, you'll let him.'

It seems that no one is willing to reveal anything about Jago. Who is he, really? What's in his past? What made him start drinking like that? Is it something he absolutely can't get over? And if not, what makes him wake in the morning nowadays? And why is everyone trying to protect me from him? Or protect him from himself... I realise that Starry Cove, more than a close-knit village, is a den of secrets and that if I want to know anything at all about him, I'll have to find out for myself.

'What was I supposed to say to that?' I ask Maisie over the landline that evening, seeing that I'd thrown my SIM card into the sea. 'No one wants to give me any info apart from the fact that he's bad for me. Why does everyone assume I have any interest in Jago besides him being my new partner?'

'Whoa! Slow down,' Maisie laughs. 'Why are you getting so hot under the collar?'

I groan. 'Because I'm frustrated. I want to know who I'm dealing with so I can understand what to do with this business, but I can't seem to get anywhere with anyone.'

'Here's a thought, Emmie. If you're so intrigued by all the mystery, why don't you ask him directly?'

'What? You mean Jago? I can't do that!' At least, not again, seeing as he'd skirted my question the first time.

'Of course you can. It's done all the time between business partners. It's called getting to know each other.'

'You laugh, Maisie, but I—'

'Emmie? Can we finally have that chat now? The one where you finally admit that you're unhappy and I tell you I'll be there for you?'

I bite my lip. Here we go...

'You're attracted to Jago Moon. You'd easily call off your engagement to Stephen, but you feel bad about it because you have a heart of gold and would never hurt anyone.'

'Er...'

'That's your only worry, because deep down you know you'll be fine without him. You can always find a job in another school.'

This woman knows me better than I do.

'But that's the thing, Maisie. It's not just the difficulties with Stephen. It's my life in London. Apart from you, there's nothing keeping me there. I just wake up bloody miserable even at the thought of having to go into work.'

She sighs. 'I know, Emmie, I know. And if you want to leave Stephen, I'm with you all the way. There's still time left. Well, sort of. The engagement isn't for quite a few days. I'll back you up. But to move to Cornwall? How do you know that you'll be happy there?'

'Oh, I will be,' I assure.

'So, does that mean that you really are going to leave Stephen?'

'I... guess so,' I reply.

Who am I kidding? I *know* so. Because even if I offered him the choice to move down here with me, he'd say I was mad. But I'm already going mad. This countdown to the party... I've been dreading it as a countdown to the end of my freedom. When did I start feeling chained to him? When did I start feeling more oppressed than protected? And is it simply the distance that is making me see things more clearly than ever before? There are so many questions and emotions whizzing around in my mind. I don't know what's right or what's wrong right now. But I do know that I can't get engaged to Stephen now.

I have to think about what I want, too, and with Stephen, there's no room for me. I'm the afterthought. The appendix that never quite fits into his life. I won't settle for second or even third best. Because I come after his mother and his job. He's proven it to me time and again. Never, not once for the sake of argument, put me first. We always had to do things his way. Or Audrey's, lest she had a sulk.

We always had to live where she wanted, eat what she wanted, wear what she wanted. We even had to get engaged where and when she wanted. And the last straw… my attack. When he didn't come, he broke my heart. He cut the last thinning thread binding me to him. He cut it loose. And now I can't go back. I don't want to. I know that now. All I have to do now is tell him.

'Will you do me a favour?' Maisie asks.

'Of course.'

'Don't make any decisions based on a man. Jago Moon might not be the one you hope he is.'

I laugh. 'OK, first of all, you're absolutely mad if you think Jago has anything to do with any of this. Even if you were the one badgering me to sleep with him.'

'Sleep, yes. Love? No. Emmie, you know my opinion about men.'

'But what about El Paso? You really liked him.'

She sighs. 'I did. I do.'

'So then why don't you give him a call?'

'Because… Because I made a promise to myself never to be the needy one who calls a bloke. How would it look?'

'Like you fancied him?'

'Exactly! No. Better this way. If he liked me enough, he'd have called. But he didn't. So there. I move on.'

'But he was so nice,' I insist. 'What if he really was the one and you let him go?'

'No,' she insists back. 'If he had been the one, he wouldn't have let *me* go.'

Could she be right? Will he really let go without a fight?

On Friday, 16 December, I'm still here in Cornwall, my mind in turmoil, trying to think of a way to end this without hurting him and looking like an absolute heel. I know that the longer I leave it, the worse it'll be. He'll be furious, naturally, and the MIL will be all over him, telling him that it's a good thing he still has her.

I'm sitting in The Rolling Scones with the Coastal Girls. Just being in their lovely presence, knowing that I'm in the process of making real, long-lasting friendships, is heart-warming.

'So what we need to do is get Jago Moon to accept Emmie's business plan,' Rosie says as if it were the easiest thing in the world.

If she can pull that off, I might just ask her to sort Stephen out for me!

'How are you planning to do that?' I ask.

Nina pats my hand, winking. 'We have ways, my dear. Ways no one even knows…'

'You sound spooky,' Nat laughs, and then stops.

'We could do an anti-Scrooge operation on him. Have the Ghost of Christmas Past scare the almighty crap out of him,' Nina suggests.

'No, that's too cruel,' Rosie agrees. 'I don't want to scare him when he's vulnerable. Maybe I could scare him when he's sober.'

'Good luck finding that narrow window,' Nat laughs, then slumps in her chair for a moment. 'Oh, he used to be so sweet. It's such a shame none of you knew him back in the day.'

'My husband went to school with him,' Nina says. 'He was top of the class in everything from maths to physical education to English.'

'English? Really?' I say, making an impressed face. 'He certainly fooled me.'

'Oh yes,' Faith replies. 'Even my husband speaks the world of him. He says Jago should have continued his career.'

'As what, the town drunk?' Nat says.

Rosie rolls her eyes. 'As you can see, the jury is still out. Nina and Faith are con Jago. Nat and I are the more forgiving ones.'

'Ha, ha. Or the smarter ones,' Faith says. 'I know what it's like to fall into drink. But I pulled myself out of it and so should he. Let's let Emmie make her own decisions, yes?'

Which is probably what I should be doing about Stephen. But here I am, talking about my assets and the slosher. And yet, there's so much more to Jago than an angry hangover. You can see it in his eyes. They're pained. Soulful. There are so many unspoken words on his lips that dare not fall. I wonder why that is. In a sense, we are similar – both the village outsiders. Or I would be, if it wasn't for my new friends.

I feel like I've been part of their group for ages, even if we've only just met. There's something about each and every one of them that exudes kindness, and I can tell by their understanding looks that they've been where I am now – tottering on the edge of a new life. Wanting so badly to change and yet so afraid to make the jump. I *want* to change my life. Truly, I do. But dare I take the steps to get there? What do they imply? What have I got to gain, and what have I got to lose?

I turn to look at Faith, the most recent survivor of heartbreak.

'One of my crew told me about a run-in at Stormy Cottage between Jago and a girl,' she says out of nowhere. 'It all makes sense now.'

I shake my head. 'Yes. I don't know what's worse – him or the state of the cottage. Bill mentioned you might be able to help, but now I don't know, because Jago claims it's all his.'

'Then get a lawyer involved.'

'Oh, I don't know…'

'Things like this will mushroom very quickly. And if you don't sort it out sooner rather than later, they may take your procrastinating as indecision. You need to go in all guns blazing with Jago Moon. No backing down.'

Rosie nods. 'I expect he'll be determined to keep the barge.'

'Well, once you sort it out, let me know if you'd be

looking to renovate the place for yourself, or you'd want the neutral scheme to sell it.'

All eyes focus on me. They want to know if they'll ever see me after this.

'Oh, you have to keep it, Emmie!' Rosie exclaims. 'Stay with us in Cornwall – you'll love living here.'

'Oh, I already do, believe me.'

'And you'll be so much happier!' she adds.

I laugh. 'Is that a promise?'

Nina shrugs. 'Look at us. We left London for the good life here. If you're not happy where you are…'

'Well, my fiancé loves London…'

'And you? What do you love? What do you want?' Nat asks.

I sit back with my cappuccino and study the swirls of chocolate. What do I want?

'Peace. Love. Hope,' I say.

'And… forgive me for asking,' Nina says. 'But I've been there and I recognise the look on your face. Is your fiancé going to be part of this new life?'

Is he? No. But if I gave him an ultimatum, would he follow me? Give up his cushy job and settle for a smaller school down here? And what about Audrey? Would he be willing to leave her behind, or would she follow? Just the thought gives me the shudders.

'No, I don't think so. I'm… thinking about a lot of things,' I admit.

Nat leans forwards and, in a gesture as kind and natural as friendship, touches my wrist.

'May I make a suggestion, Emmie? My husband was a pompous arse who tried to erase me. And when I found out he was cheating on me, I kicked him out, coat of arms and all. But it was a tough time. I was feeling guilty about my mother who lived in Wyllow Cove while I pined to live in the village, too, rather than in the old mausoleum on a clifftop. I was always putting everyone else first.'

I nod.

'We've had our Phils and Neils and Marks and Gabes. But after all the heartache, we finally decided that *we* came first. Because we owed it to ourselves. If you're not happy, you have to find the answer in your own heart. No one else can tell you what to do.'

'We know it's tough,' Nina says, 'starting all over somewhere new, and already having these problems. I wish we could do something more to help.'

'You are…' I assure her. 'Back home, I only have Maisie, my best friend. But here, I have a squadron.' I shake my head in grateful disbelief.

'Well, it's not all a bed of roses,' Faith assures. 'You're going to have to put up with parties and dinners and all the kids running around…'

'Sounds good to me. I love kids. I do miss my students.'

'But not the job, I'll bet,' Rosie says.

'Not the job,' I agree. 'Maisie says it's because Stephen is also our headmaster. But also, he's career-minded. He wants children, but not yet. He says we're too young.'

Nina snorts. 'So you'll just start popping them out in your fifties when he's comfortable?'

'I know,' I admit. 'But I'd have one today if I could. I mean, does life have to be perfectly settled in order to have kids?'

Faith laughs. 'There's no such thing as a settled life.'

'You should meet Stephen,' I say. 'He won't do anything until he has all his ducks in a row.'

'That kind of man will never be happy,' Nina says. 'I get the five-year plan and all – we've all had them. But they don't always work out and in the meantime, they've wasted the best years of their girlfriend's life.'

'Don't let that happen to you, Emmie,' Rosie says softly. 'Listen to me. I was in a similar situation, only I already had the kid. Mark was never there for me. I raised Danny on my own, until Mitchell came into my life. So don't wait for the dream. Make it yourself. Grab what you want. Now. And if Stephen doesn't want to share your dreams…'

'Then he shouldn't share your life,' Nina says.

'Maybe we're being too pushy,' Faith says. 'You need time to think, time to heal, without being pushed in any direction.'

I look around the table at my new friends. 'I do need time to think, yes. But seeing how happy you all are, I want that for myself, too. I haven't been happy in…' I swallow.

'Oh, Emmie, you will be, very soon,' Rosie promises. 'All you need is to take that leap of faith.'

'Maybe that's what I'm lacking. Faith. Confidence. My engagement is in a few days and I still haven't had the talk with him. He has no idea I want out. And what if I sell my flat, leave my job, move down here and start my own business, and it's a complete flop?'

'It won't be,' Nina says. 'But just to stay on the safe side, don't sell your flat just yet. Let it out. Be cautious. Take a sabbatical and try living here before you decide.'

'And live where, in the meantime? My grandmother isn't the easiest to get along with. The cottage I inherited is being contested by that dreadful Jago Moon, alongside the barge that I wanted to be my business. And I have to put up with him as my business partner.'

'Sounds like a recipe for disaster,' Nina says.

'Or a love potion,' Rosie titters.

'Oh, that's not happening,' I assure. 'I can barely stand the bloke.'

'Well, you never know. Stranger things have happened...'

I sigh. 'I've got to get back to my grandmother.'

'How is Lady Mary?' Nina asks.

'Oh, you know – same old pain in the arse. *Get me this, get me that, where's my tea, what do you think you're wearing.*'

They laugh.

'That's old Mary for you,' Nina says.

I nod. 'That's what Jago calls her – old Mary.'

'To her face?' Faith asks. 'That man has more balls than I thought.'

'Poor Jago...' Rosie sighs. 'I feel so sorry for him.'

'Me, too, in a way,' I confess. 'I mean, he has to have a reason for being that much of an arse, right? It's like he thinks the world owes him a living or something.'

Silence around the table.

'OK. So all of you know what happened with him, as well? I can't get the truth out of anybody around here. Come on, then, fess up.'

'We can't, Emmie, I'm so sorry,' Rosie apologised. 'We swore we never would. But we can only say one thing – if you're leaving your boyfriend and moving to Cornwall, don't do it for Jago.'

'Wha-at?' I laugh. 'Of course not! I told you – I can barely stand him. In any case, if I'm going to become a Cornish citizen—'

'Then you'll find out soon enough,' Nina says. 'Or he'll eventually tell you himself.'

'That's not happening,' Faith says. 'You know what he's like.'

'Forget about it,' I say. 'I'm not interested in his secrets, just as long as they don't involve me.'

'Emmie,' Nat says, 'from Jago Moon, expect anything, anytime.'

They're right. Jago isn't going to be letting go of his claims anytime soon.

It's not going to be a 'let's talk it through' thing, after all, apparently. Jago is an unreasonable man and is going to be a tough nut to crack.


I've tortured myself enough. Sleepless nights and days of worry. I know what Stephen's reaction will be about Cornwall. He simply doesn't love me enough to put his job after us. And quite frankly, if I'm going to be happy, I need to do things *my* way, and now. Rip the bandage off quickly and all that. And soon enough, this will all be an unhappy, distant memory. I know I'm making the right decision, albeit a tardy one.

Something inside me is changing and I can't say I don't like it. After so many years of doing what Stephen said I had to, now I'm going to do what *I* want.

I phone him from the telephone in the study. Grandmother never comes in here for some reason. His phone only rings once before he picks it up.

'Stephen Stone,' he says mechanically, and I can already picture him surrounded by piles of documents that need his attention.

'Stephen, it's me. I need to talk to you. It's important.'

Silence, then: 'I'm listening.'

I swallow. How do you get something so monumental off your chest without hurting someone?

'Well, it's about us.'

'Ri-ight...?'

'I, uhm, think I'll be staying here in Cornwall.'

He sighs loudly. 'Jesus, Emmie, I've listened to all your malarkey about detoxing from London and all, but we're getting married in a few months' time. How do you imagine that happening if you don't get your arse back here?'

Of course he's angry. I would be, too, if my fiancé took off on me. But I'd be even more angry if my fiancé was never there, just as he's never there for me. The main reason that had attracted me to him was his dependability, but now, the one thing I'd counted on was sorely lacking.

The proof, apart from the fact that he waited until the day after the attack to come by and see how I was doing, is in the fact that he hasn't come down to Cornwall once to see me, or even made a romantic call to tell me how much he's missed me. Nothing. And the sad thing is that I wasn't even expecting one.

'That's just it, Stephen. Forgive me, but I think I'm going to be staying here indefinitely.'

'What the hell is that supposed to mean, Emmie? Is this a ruse to get me to move to Cornwall? Or are you telling me that you want to postpone the wedding? What are we supposed to do with all the summer-themed invitations, the summery menus? Even your dress is sleeveless, for Christ's sake!'

'I... how did you know that, Stephen?' I ask, the huge yellow cartoon balloon letters in my mind's eye: his mother's told him.

'I... uh, figured it would be sleeveless,' he mumbles.

'Did you really, Stephen? Or did your mother tell you? Please don't lie to me.'

'No, she didn't mention a thing about your dress, I promise.'

'Then who did?'

'No one.'

I sigh. 'Stephen, you always were a terrible liar.'

'I'm not lying when I say I want to marry you.'

'Oh, Stephen, please forgive me, but... I don't. Not anymore.'

'Jesus Christ...'

'I'm sorry. I really didn't want to do this over the phone, but—'

'Then don't say another word. We'll talk about it when you come back for the engagement party.'

I clear my throat. 'That's what I'm trying to tell you, Stephen. I'm not coming back and there is not going to be an engagement party because there is not going to be a wedding.'

'Why the hell are you doing this to me, now, only a few days before?'

'I know, I should have told you earlier, you're absolutely right. And I hate having to do this over the phone, but you weren't interested in coming to see me, so—'

'May I remind you that you were the one who needed time from me?'

'Maybe it should have been clear to me then, but I was just—'

'What, Emmie? You were psyching yourself up to become my wife?'

'No, Stephen, please don't take it that way.'

'You're dumping me over the goddamn phone, and just a few days before our engagement party! How do you expect me to take it, exactly?'

'Not well, of course. I'm sorry – you're absolutely right. I'll come up and apologise to you and your people in person.'

'And do you really think they'll want to see you after I tell them?'

'I guess not. I'm sorry. I can't seem to win either way. If I don't face everyone, I'm a coward, but if I do, I won't be welcome. Why don't we just call it a day and peg it down to a narrow escape from a huge mistake, then?'

'A narrow escape? You're leaving me practically at the altar and you call it a narrow escape?'

'I'm not leaving you at the altar, Stephen. Come on – it's months away. You can tell everyone you left me, if it makes you feel better.'

'No, it won't, but thanks for the offer,' he snaps.

What did I expect? Forgiveness and forever friendship? Perhaps not, but what I didn't expect was to feel this sad. And... empty. For months I'd been feeling less and less involved, less convinced of my decision to marry Stephen until I could no longer deny it to myself. When had I stopped loving him? And why had he not even asked me that same question? Was it not one of the first things you asked when your significant other ends the relationship? And on my part, it simply isn't wise to go ahead with such a huge decision, when everything inside me is screaming for it not to go ahead. But still, even if I know I'm doing the right thing, it's not easy.

And I know my new life is going to have a rough start, with a grandmother who barely tolerates me in the memory of her husband, no business of my own as of yet, no real home if you don't count the crumbling cottage. And no one to share my dreams with. It serves me right for being what I call brave. And now comes the hardest part – following up on the great act of courage, because after the brave gesture, anything can happen now.

'I'll pay for the cancellations,' I offer.

A flicker of panic makes his voice rise.

'So you really are doing this. You're really leaving me...'

'I'm sorry, Stephen, but you know it isn't working out. It hasn't been for months now.'

'Nonsense,' he snaps, then reverses. 'We're just going through a rough patch.'

'A rough patch is temporary. You've been like this for most of our time together.'

'But you can't leave me – what am I supposed to tell everybody?'

'Is that really what's bothering you?'

'You're being silly, Emmie. You know we'd be perfect together.'

'No, we wouldn't. For once, your mum was right.'

'My mum adores you...'

'Ha! You know damn well that she hated me from the moment she laid eyes on me. I'm not good enough for her precious son.'

'Don't be like this, Emmie. Yes, my mum's a bit of a snob, but who cares? I chose you.'

'You could have fooled me!'

'Why? Why did you choose me?'

'Because I love you.'

I shake my head as if he could see me. 'Maybe you did, a long time ago. Now, I'm just the prize that you put on the shelf. You have to keep cherishing the woman you love, not treat her like she's a big nuisance who scuppers your plans.'

'But you *are* scuppering my plans! All I wanted was a nice easy-going woman to have my kids and live in my house. What's wrong with that?'

*My* house. And there he is. The stable, boring man has finally come full circle. He's become what he was destined to be. While the nice easy-going woman he once met is no longer. Now, I'm no longer content to do as he wishes, just to be along for the ride. Now, I have my own will, my own plans, and I'm not going to let them go because he thinks he rules the roost.

'You'll quit your job, obviously,' he says.

'Obviously.'

'Then make sure it's on my desk by Monday,' he snaps and hangs up.


Of course, it's not long before I get a call from the MIL to give me a good, solid rollocking, and just as I'm opening up the shop.

'Really, Emily! I'm so disappointed in you – a person of your lineage doing something so shameful.'

Here she goes – on one of her beauties... 'I beg your pardon, Audrey?'

'How could you do that to him?'

'Audrey, I'm sorry, but you are *not* interfering in our lives anymore.' Or at least not mine. 'Your son is a grown man now. When are you both going to accept that it's over, or do I need to break up with you officially, too?'

'All I know is that you broke his heart.'

And then just like that, after three entire years of bowing my head for the sake of peace, I lose it. Completely.

'What about *my* heart?' I challenge. 'I wanted to keep it civilised between you and me, but now I've had enough. For three years I've been at his beck and call, both at school and at home. I've been at your beck and call, too, Audrey. I've bent over backwards in the hope of being accepted into your family. But all you do is try to manipulate me and make me look like I'm the difficult one.

'And when I called because I'd been attacked? You said it was my fault for the way I dress! Really, Audrey! And you call yourself a philanthropist – a woman on the side of women? I don't think so! I'm never going to be your daughter-in-law. And by the way, now I have a grandmother, a blood relation, I don't need you to keep telling me you're the closest thing I'll ever have to a mother. So I'll kindly ask you to refrain from contacting me ever again. Goodbye, and have a great life!'

And I hang up with a wild growl. The woman is unbelievable!

A loud clapping sound comes from behind and I whirl

round to see none other than the omnipresent yet elusive Jago Moon, a huge grin on his face.

'You tell her! I wish I'd seen her face. So you finally bit the bullet and sent him packing. Good for you.'

'Are you stalking me?' I blurt.

He snorts. 'What…?'

'I asked if you were stalking me. Every time I turn round, you're there.'

He shrugs. 'What do you expect for a village of a hundred souls?'

'I expect a modicum of privacy.'

'A celebrity are yeh, then?' he scoffs.

I cross my arms. Any minute I'm going to start tapping my foot, too.

'No, I'm not a celebrity. All I want is to be left alone.'

'Kinda hard, you hob-nobbin' with the high-flyin' ladies,' he observes.

He means the Coastal Girls.

'People with lots a money and clout. You don't fit in with them.'

'I beg your pardon?'

'Yer grandmother may well be a rich harridan, but you're different.'

'As in I'm not rich or I'm not a harridan?' I find myself saying.

He surprises me with a smile. It's a nice smile and I'm surprised to see he has very straight teeth. I don't know why it strikes me. Perhaps I truly am a stereotype kind of person. But my entire subject is based on stereotypes. Literature is so full of tropes and themes and arrogant lords and damsels in distress. I spend so much more time in that world than in reality that it's difficult not to expect the same in the real world. Oh, if someone saw the inside of my head, they'd back away in horror.

Yes, I am that kind of girl – old-fashioned and romantic, in case you haven't figured it out by now. I don't know why, but I think, apart from some of my students, I'm the only romantic person I know. I mean, mealy-mouthed, shamelessly romantic. The kind who *wants* the fairy tale.

'So that didn't last long,' he says, nodding to my new phone.

'No, it didn't,' I huff.

'Is it over? With your beau?'

I hesitate. What does he care? 'Yes.'

'For good?'

'Yes.'

'Good for you. But let me tell you now, if you did it for some bloke, you'll come up empty-handed.'

I gawp. 'What the hell is that supposed to mean?'

And that's when he turns to look at me, leaning in, his face solemn.

'Aww, Emmie,' he murmurs as his hand rises to my face. 'You and me... it's a mess...'

Without any warning, my heart begins to hammer as his fingertips near my cheek and even before he touches me, I realise I'm breathless. And waiting for his touch. And when his fingers caress my face with a gentleness that I could never have imagined, it's a revelation.

Never in a million years would I ever have thought that Jago Moon could be anything more than contemptuous, sarcastic or sardonic. Never would I have thought that he was able to stop his endless deprecation of himself and others, and that we'd be standing here, face to face, talking about feelings. Weaknesses. Anything at all deep. And yet, here he is, gazing into my eyes with a strange kindness. Almost resignation.

'I suggest you go back to London,' he says out of the blue. 'Starry Cove is too small for you. You'll never meet a man here.'

'What makes you think I need a man?'

'Everyone needs someone. Except for me, of course.'

'Of course.'

'For me, relationships are too draining. You always have to be on the ball, attentive, never make a mistake, never lie. You have to be patient, and also a good listener. I'm none of the above.'

The magical moment has dissolved, even if my heart is still hammering away with… I don't know what. I'm probably just tired and vulnerable right now.

'I'm no good for you or anyone,' he says.

Now I recognise him again.

'You must be very lonely,' I reply.

'You'd say that, Emmie. You're absolutely in love with the idea of love, aren't you, you poor misguided soul. Now, a one-nighter, that's worth expending all of your energy for. For that, you give your best like there's no tomorrow. Which there isn't. You treat her right, like there's no one else in the world like her. You make her feel like a queen. And then the next morning you go your separate ways. Absolutely brilliant.'

'But what if your lady friend doesn't agree with you? What if *she* wants more?' I ask.

'A whole night is plenty. Besides, I can't give any more than that. I don't fall in love.'

'So you're incapable of feelings?'

'Of course not,' he grins. 'It's called unadulterated, mindless lust. But I understand people like you. It must be nice to live in la-la land. To believe in things that just aren't there. You think everything is about love and that love is perfect. Well, baby girl, it's neither.'

I step back as if he'd slapped me across the face. 'Why are you doing this? Why are you being such an—'

He laughs. 'An arsehole? I told you to keep away from me from the start. I'm not a good man.'

My throat constricts as I struggle to breathe past the huge boulder forming.

'I have to agree with you,' I retort.

What else can I say? He has, in effect, warned me. Told me he was no gentleman, or boyfriend material. It's not much of an effort to be perfect for one night only, whereas relationships prove to be more difficult. They last too long and sap too much of his energy. Too much tension.

And besides, what makes him think I'm even remotely interested in him? Not one to run away and give him the satisfaction that he's hurt my feelings, I stay and do my fill of work in the shop. But I'm on tenterhooks. And in a foul mood now. To distract myself, I rearrange the entire shop, Christmas decorations and all. They suddenly seem offensive to me, all these lights and laughing Santas. Everyone is so in love with the holidays and completely oblivious to the real world, albeit for a few days. But me? When is it ever going to be Christmas for me?

When I can't take it anymore, I find an excuse to leave

and go for a walk. The sky is as bruised as my ego. It's not every day that someone tells you they are not interested in you. I guess I had it coming. So Jago isn't interested in a relationship. Not with me, not with anyone. As if I care, right? I can't say he hadn't warned me. But it's not like I broke up with Stephen for Jago, is it? I mean, look at the two of us. We couldn't possibly be any more different. We have nothing in common. And yet, when he touched my face, I thought I was going to shake myself apart. What would you call that sensation? I've never felt it in my entire life. And I don't think I ever will again.

The cobbled streets of Starry Cove welcome me with a warm embrace despite the bitter temperatures. I breathe out and watch the air condense before my face. Why doesn't it just give up and snow? Why the resistance? Even if it hardly ever snows in the south, that's what Christmas is for – lots and lots of beautiful snow. And tobogganing, sleigh-riding, making snow angels. And snowball fights. Snow is the main character in the show. Without snow, what kind of Christmas is it? It's like the icing on the cake, the kiss under the mistletoe. Without snow, where is the promise of love? Where is the happy ever after?

Jago is like the snow. He won't give himself up and do what he should – let himself go to life and whatever it may bring. Look at me – I've done it. But is he going to admit what he needs, what he wants? No. He's going to stand there and not let it snow. It's going to be a cold, grey Christmas despite all of my greatest expectations.

And speaking of expectations, I've come to a financial decision. Not that I understand much about numbers, but it's obvious that Jago is actually making a good living through his general store. Imagine if we increased the floor space or opened another venue… Or even diversified. But as long as we're at loggerheads with the inheritance, we'll be stuck in the mud. It would be so easy if we could just come to an agreement.

So I head back and patiently wait for him to wrap some presents that a young couple are hoarding into their basket. They look happy, excited. And from the twinkle in their eyes when they grin at each other, I bet this is their first Christmas together as a couple. Good for them. May it last forever and not come crashing down on their innocent little heads.

'I have a business proposition for you,' I offer over the clanging of the bell on the door as they leave.

His eyes widen and then narrow. 'OK, my little viper's nest. Shoot.'

'I'll leave you the business if you leave me the barge.'

He laughs. 'Again? You do know that the barge is worth absolutely nothing. But a business—'

'I'm aware. But I have an idea for a business on the barge.'

His eyes narrow even more. 'What kind of business?'

'I don't know. Perhaps a floating café with books, or a picnic boat.'

'You want to turn my barge into a café?' he asks, his face reddening.

'*Our* barge. And that's the idea, yes.'

'Not happening. And even if it was yours, you haven't got a nautical licence.'

'No, but I can get one.'

'It's not that easy.'

'But possible.'

'You don't know the first thing about navigating. Coordinates. How are you at maths, geometry, trigonometry?'

'Oh, come on, Jago! You mean to tell me that every single boat owner is versed in numbers?'

His lips tighten. 'Only the ones who want to live. Everyone here with a boat knows how to pilot one. And you don't.'

'I'll learn.'

'Why?'

'Because I've decided I'm staying.'

At that, his mouth tightens. Goodness, he really does want to get rid of me.

'You must need your head tested. What are you going to do here in Cornwall? Your home is London.'

'Actually, I've got plenty of things I want to do here.'

'Fine. Then go find something else. I'm not letting you take my barge anywhere near the water.'

'Well, first of all, you can't stop me. I can do whatever I want.'

'What did you just say?'

'Are you deaf? You can't stop me.'

At that, he stands to his full height, his dark eyes burning, his mouth firmly set.

'Oh, I'll stop you alright! Just you watch. I'll fight you at every turn.'

'Who do you think you are? I didn't move here to let another man tell me what I can or can't do.'

'Well, maybe someone needs to. This barge is never going out again, d'you hear?'

'But why? What do you care?'

He takes a deep breath. 'I do care, because this is my home. Nano gave it to me.'

'Which you still have to prove, by the way. And if that's the case, for argument's sake, I'm offering a switch…'

'Not happening, Emmie.'

'Oh, come on, Jago. There's plenty of cottages you could rent if you wanted to.'

He groans impatiently. 'OK, so a) that's not true. This is Starry Cove, not London. And b) I don't want to live anywhere else.'

'Well, I'm sorry, but unless your solicitor comes up with any valid proof, it's my barge too.'

'Why the hell do you want it so much? A week ago you didn't even know it existed and now you want to turn it into a business. You don't know the first thing about cruising a barge.'

'I intend to learn.'

'You are an English teacher, for Christ's sake. You know absolutely nothing about business. Go back to your books. In fact, go back to London, Emmie.'

'I resent that. I have a right to do anything I want and I don't need your permission, either.'

'You're delusional, Emmie. You know how many city slickers I've seen come and go, wanting to move to Cornwall? It's a trend, nothing else.'

'It's a lifestyle change.'

'It's a game. A few sandwiches and a little bunting doesn't a riverboat business make. And besides, it'll never tide you over for the rest of the year.'

'Look who's talking – wasn't Moon River Cruises yours?'

His face darkens. 'That was a long time ago, and it was a huge mistake.'

'I don't think so. I've spoken to the community and they'd love Nano's boat to come back in a new guise.'

'You mean you've spoken to your new girlfriends. Are *they* gonna pay your bills, then? People come here in the summer, they see blue skies and blue sea and move here. But when winter settles in and they can't afford to turn the heating on… that's reality, Emmie. Who's going to help you when the money runs out? Your grandmother?'

My mouth snaps shut. I know he's right, of course.

'But riverboat cruises are feasible. I've done my homework. There are companies that run all year round…'

'And how many tourists do you actually think will come down in the winter, exactly? And besides, it's my boat and you're not getting it just so you can put it back in the water.'

'But why?' I insist. 'It's a great idea and you know it. What are you afraid of – a little competition?'

'Competition? Is that what you think this is all about? Hasn't it occurred to you that it's moored here for a reason? That barge is not safe for navigating.'

'Well then I'll *make* it safe.'

'Emmie, listen to me and listen good. You are never going to get that boat in the water while I'm alive.'

'Are you sure about that?'

'Absolutely!'

'Well then maybe I'll see you in court, after all,' I threaten.

He stares at me, incredulous, then throws his hands in the air. 'Bring it on!'

Fuming, I go back to my grandmother's home. I need to sleep. I'm so tired and angry. I'd left London for the good life, but ever since I got here it's been nothing but a battle against Lady Mary and Jago Moon. I swear they're both killjoys.

Strolling on the beach in the mornings is probably the only thing that soothes me nowadays, so I'm grateful to have it practically on my doorstep. Just being here, breathing in the freezing salt air, watching the seagulls swirl over my head, the dolphins floating in the distance... wait. Dolphins *floating*?

I shield my eyes and look out to sea. At least a hundred yards out, there's definitely something. Only it's not a dolphin. Is it a child? I squint. Are there two of them? And they seem to be struggling to stay above the surface.

Instinctively, I kick my boots off and throw my coat down on the sand, running as fast as I can into the water and finally diving in.

The water isn't icy – it's past that. But there's not a moment to waste. I don't know how long these people have been in the water and by the lack of thrashing around, either they're close to passing out, or... I can't even bear to think of it!

I wish someone had seen me go in. I wish I'd called for help. Helping one person is difficult enough, but how am I going to handle two?

As I near them, I can see it's a man and a child, almost motionless now.

'It's OK!' I call while spitting out seawater. 'You're OK. I'm coming to get you.'

The man whips his head round.

'Jago?' I cry.

'Emmie! Go back! It's the Hendersons' boy. Call an ambulance.'

Not having to be told twice as in these situations every second counts, I whirl round and swim as fast as I can back to shore, the cold air freezing my lungs and limbs. But I keep going through the pain, hoping I can make it back before the cold paralyses me completely.

Even if Jago's saved the boy from drowning, the danger of hypothermia is just as serious. For both of them.

On the shore, several people have gathered as Max, Jago's dog, arrives with more help as two big men run out to help me.

'It's the Henderson boy!' I gasp in between breaths. 'Jago's got him, but he needs an ambulance!'

Their response is immediate. They swim out, while a bystander calls for an ambulance.

Now on dry land but still heaving for my next breath, I watch as the two men go in, stroke after strong stroke, reaching Jago. One of them takes the boy from him, while the other makes sure that Jago is OK.

Thank God for Max being such a smart dog! He must have realised that something was wrong with Jago not coming back, and called for help. Are they going to be OK? Up until now, I always thought of Jago as a strong man, physically. What if they've been out there too long and—? Of course they'll be OK. They have to! I know that Jago has this self-destructive streak, but I know that deep down he truly wants to save himself. And know that someone else cares as well. I care. Who wouldn't, right? Because the thought of something happening to him... and Starry Cove being without him... it just wouldn't be the same around here!

The sound of a siren reaches the beach, just as the rescuers touch dry land. Jago and the other rescuers hand the boy over to the paramedics spilling out of the ambulance. It all happens so fast I've hardly time to register what's going on.

But the boy is safe. Jago Moon is safe. There really couldn't be a better start to this day. I want to rush to Jago and throw my arms around him, but I don't. Instead, I turn away and burst into tears.

'Hey,' comes Jago's soft drawl. He is wrapped in a foil blanket, his hair plastered to his head, his eyes red from the sea salt and exhaustion, but he's otherwise unharmed. He could have died! The boy could have died…

'You saved his life!' I cry as I lose my poise and throw my arms around him, too late to remember I'm supposed to hate him. 'Are you OK?'

His own arms envelop me in his blanket. 'Are *you* OK?' he echoes. 'You should never, ever have done that!'

'I thought I could help…'

'Sam! We need to check her, too.'

'I'm fine,' I say as Jago hauls me into the other ambulance, where the paramedic puts a blood pressure cuff around my arm and a clip on my thumb to check my oxygen levels.

'Fit as a fiddle,' the paramedic reports back. 'Your turn, Jago.'

Someone pushes a hot drink into my hand. It's Ralph, the owner of The Rolling Scones.

Jago turns back to the paramedic. 'The boy's vitals?'

'Stable. He's halfway to the hospital. Now it's your turn, Jago.'

'I'm fine,' he barks, swatting the man's hand away and

then turning to me with a slow grin. 'Not bad for a Sunday outing, is it? Where the hell did you learn to swim like that?'

I shrug to deflect the attention on me. 'Swimming lessons, of course. Why is it that you have so few friends and yet every time I see you, you're doing something nice for someone else?' I ask.

He shrugs. 'Maybe I'm doing it for your benefit.'

'My benefit?'

'Yeah. I see you and go and do something nice just to prove that everyone is wrong about me.'

'I thought you didn't give a hoot about everyone's opinion on you?'

'Maybe I do, maybe I don't. Why do you care so much about what people think about you? Because in all honesty, I can see the weight of the world on your pretty little shoulders.'

Pretty little shoulders – the nicest thing he's said to me so far, and still I'm not convinced he meant it as a compliment. *Au contraire.*

'What's any of this got to do with me?' I ask, already regretting it. 'And for someone who doesn't read, you have a lot of opinions.'

'I don't need to read to have my own opinion on what's right and wrong in life.'

'Oh? Then what do you believe, Jago Moon?'

'I believe that people are fundamentally good but weak-minded and actually blind to the truth. And I don't need a book to tell me that.'

'Right.'

'Plus, I have my own experiences to go by. I know what

I've done wrong and I know that no amount of grovelling will fix any of it.'

'Are you sure? Many still believe in you, if only you showed a bit of remorse for whatever it is you did or didn't do.'

'Aren't you just dying to know?' he says, suddenly smarmy. 'Why is it that you care so much, Emmie Nightingale?'

'I-I don't know,' I falter, biting my lip.

'Oh, for Christ's sake, just stay away, Emmie...' he groans. 'Let me tell you – you'll *never* be able to fix me.'

I stare at him. 'I'm not trying to fix anybody. I'm merely trying to understand what kind of hold you have over the people in this village. You're like Marmite – either they adore you or they loathe you, and I'm literally fascin...' I bite my lip as his mouth curls into a smile that doesn't reach his eyes.

'Yes, that's it. You're fascinated by the village monster. You want to understand what goes on in a mind like mine. You're wondering how I can have done so much wrong to my people, yet still they talk to me.' He leans in. 'It's called entrapment, Emmie. And whether you know it yet or not, you're going to get caught, too. Because I can't help reeling people in and spitting them out like chewed gum.'

'Don't talk to me like that!' I say, moving away from his beautiful face.

He's like Dorian Gray in Oscar Wilde's novel. Beautiful beyond belief on the outside, while inside he's rotten to the core. Or at least, that's what he wants people to think.

Because although he's an utter arse, I just know that beyond his looks, there has to be some good in him. You simply don't act kindly only when you think no one's looking. You don't care for animals or help the elderly to cross the road or defend kids if you don't give a hoot.

And most of all, you don't push the new girl away unless you're absolutely not interested in her and you find her completely unattractive. Oh my God! Was that why he was pushing me away all the time? Is that what this was all about? And here's me, trying to become his friend. Does he actually think I'm chasing him around because I'm interested in him? In that case, he must be truly delirious.

# 19

*The Secret Garden,* Frances Burnett

The next morning, Maisie calls me.

'Hi...!' I breathe, jamming the phone between my jaw and my shoulder.

'Hey, girl!' she chimes. 'OK, either you did something you shouldn't have done or it's fate.'

'What *are* you talking about?'

'Well, you'll never guess who called me, so I'll just tell you: Pablo!'

'Old El Paso? That's fantastic, Maisie.'

'Is it? I dunno. I think about him all the time and that's not good.'

'Why isn't it good?'

'Because you know what happens when I start caring for someone,' she wails.

'You dump them.'

'Exactly. And I never see them again. But Pablo... he says he misses me. I met him for coffee and he had the saddest spaniel eyes when he said he doesn't want to lose me.'

'I'm sure he doesn't. Why don't you give the poor sod a chance?'

'Because... if things go well—'

'You might be happy...?'

'No, not that. *Au contraire*. If I fall in love and he falls out of love – then what do I do?'

'Oh, Maisie, you can't live your life in fear of what might or might not happen. You have to go for it and *que será, será*.'

She chuckles. 'It's amazing how you always have such good advice on relationships and never follow it yourself. Now why doesn't that apply to you and Jago?'

'Me and...? You've got it all wrong, Maisie. I can't stand the bloke.'

'You mean you *think* you can't stand him. Ah, Emmie, you and I are much more similar than you think.'

'No, you don't know what he's done. He's after my inheritance.'

'What? The shitbag!'

'I know!'

'How can he even do that?'

'He claims that Nano left it all to him, except for half the shop that's mine.'

'So what are you going to do?'

'I don't know. But I have to act soon. There's no telling what he's capable of.'


I have to thank Rosie and the new friends I've made who have actually made me feel welcome in Starry Cove. Because between a grandmother who still doesn't want me here and a business partner who's trying to get me disinherited, I can't really say I've done very well so far. What was supposed to have been a new start in life is looking pretty grim at the moment. I'm sincerely wondering whether I should have stayed in London, after all. At least there, I have a job, a flat and a friend. Here, it seems that I have to fight just to keep what should rightfully be mine. And I don't mean the inheritance but my grandmother's affection. How can she not feel the instinctive blood bond? Why is she always pushing me away? Whatever happened in my family, why is she so bent on making me pay for it?

'Morning, partner!' Jago salutes as I push through the door of the shop the next morning.

I nod and slam my bag down.

'Ouch! Don't tell me. The old battleaxe is giving you a hard time. Bossing you around with the excuse you're family but never actually letting you in.'

I swallow. If anyone can understand my anger towards her, it's Jago.

'My grandmother has made it very clear that she doesn't want me here. To her, I'm just one huge problem that won't go away.'

'That's what she's like.'

'She hasn't been affectionate towards me once since I've been here. I was doing her laundry, for Christ's sake, and she couldn't even find the decency to say thank you. As if the entire world owes her a living.'

'Textbook Lady Mary, alright.'

'She's told me that I'm a nuisance and that my birth was a huge burden on everyone. As if I actually asked to be born into this *shitty* life...'

'That's not like you to say things like that, Emmie.'

'What do you know about me and what I'm like?'

He shrugs. 'I just know that you're kind and caring and optimistic.'

'Yeah, well, it's not like I've had any reason to be lately. I wish I'd never inherited anything and never heard of Lady Mary Heatherton of Heatherton Hall.'

'Hang in there, Emmie.'

'How can I?' I bite off. 'Even you are giving me a hard time and I don't know why.'

He shrugs. 'I'm just not used to being around someone like you, is all.'

'What's that supposed to mean?'

He looks at me as if trying to decide for himself.

'It's just that… you're *teg* through and through…'

'*Teg?* What does that mean? Daft?'

He laughs. 'No, it's a word we use to describe… several things: a sunset, a newborn, a flower.'

'Is there no English equivalent?'

He nods. 'There is. But the word beautiful just doesn't seem to do you justice. It's lost its depth.'

I can feel myself blushing. 'You just called me beautiful.'

'More than that. You're *teg*. Inside and out…'

'Thank you,' I whisper, at a loss for words.

An argument I can expect from Jago. A smirk, or why not a challenge. But a kind word? That throws me completely.

'Listen,' he says. 'About the court thing… I'm willing to hash it out privately, if you like. Because I really, really hate lawyers.'

'Me, too,' I confess.

In any case, congratulations to myself are in order.

Despite my grandmother's several attempts to convince me otherwise, I'm slowly managing to crack the nut that is Jago Moon. I'm The Nutcracker extraordinaire.

'I'm handling my business partner with due caution, you'll be pleased to know,' I tell my grandmother. 'I'm imposing some decisions on him.'

She sits back and studies me as her thin eyebrows shoot up. I swear that she almost looks amused.

'Well, I am glad to see that despite being the spitting image of your mother, you are nothing like her. You are intelligent and kind. I have been observing you.'

'Thank you, Grandmother,' I say softly. 'We are, in fact, very different.'

'Nano hoped you would be. But then, he was always a dreamer. But I valued his opinion very much, even if I sometimes didn't agree with his choices.'

'Oh? Such as, if I may?'

She shrugs. 'The shop. He didn't need to run a business, not with our financial and social position. But I couldn't stop him, because it made him happy and, in his words, kept him grounded, in constant contact with his fellow villagers.'

'That's nice,' I say. 'It would have been lovely to meet him.'

'Well, you didn't. And now, what was his, is yours.'

As she takes a sip of her tea, she happens to look out of the window.

I follow her gaze, only to see Jago, in the flesh, strolling across the grounds to the front door as if he owned the place. This man seems to be everywhere. I understand that

Starry Cove only has a population of a hundred, but he's the bad card that keeps coming up.

'Speak of the devil,' she mumbles, scrunching up her little pink mouth. 'May I give you some advice?' Grandmother asks as the doorbell rings. 'Don't commit to anything yet. Say you'll speak to your business advisor first. I know a good one.'

Nettie knocks on the door. 'Milady, Jago Moon to see you, if you please…'

My grandmother turns to her. 'I don't actually please, Nettie, but we'd better get it over with. Let him in.'

'Yes, milady.'

She leaves, only to return with her unwanted charge.

'Good afternoon, ladies! I hope I'm not intruding.'

'You could have called, Jago,' Grandma says. 'Then again, you'd still be intruding.'

Jago pauses before us and, sliding me an ironic glance, bows theatrically before her as a jester would to his queen. As he does so, he turns and winks at me.

'I wager thirty seconds before she kicks me out this time. The last time I didn't even make it to the grand hall.'

'To what do we owe the ordeal of your visit?' she prompts, although she already knows.

My God, Grandma could make a killing at poker.

'Aww, c'mon, Mary, don't be so contrary. After all, your old man and me were great friends.'

'And the reason is still beyond me,' she drawls, rolling her eyes.

'Anyway,' he says, taking a seat without being invited. 'Down to brass tacks. I'm here to buy Emmie out.' He grins, his white teeth flashing, his eyes crinkling at the corners like a man who's smiled all his life, but I can't see it. 'Not that you need the money, of course…'

Grandma glances at me and I swear I can almost see pride in her eyes.

'Whatever my granddaughter chooses to do with her assets is her own business. Rest assured, should she want to, I'll be very happy in giving you an extremely hard time and making your life more miserable than it already is.'

His eyes, which have been darting back and forth between the two of us, now rest on mine.

'Well, my new business partner and I have every intention of getting as much as we both can from this situation,' he says.

But if I was expecting him to want to shake on it, I'd have been left disappointed. Not that I'd want to be in any way associated with someone like him. And yet, if Grandma found him contemptible, then that meant there was more to him than the mere nuisance. There was something else going on, I can feel it in my bones.

'And in any case, I like hard times,' he says. 'It's the only way to live!'

'Well, then you are in for a treat,' she replies, eyeing me. 'My lawyers will rip you apart. By the time they are done with you, you will be living in the shack on Tempest Island at the fishermen's mercy. You already have no friends. We will drive you out of Starry Cove. You don't belong here. Your presence was a mistake from the start!'

'Grandmother, please calm down,' I say for her sake as her face begins to turn red. 'Remember what happened last time you got so upset…'

'Yes, Grootmother,' Jago snorts. 'Remember? You almost kicked the fish pail last time. And many more times before that.' He looks at me. 'She used to fake illnesses all the time when she and Nano disagreed on something, which was practically always. The poor sod didn't have the heart to see her like that, so she'd always win. It must have run in the family. But it doesn't work like that anymore, Mary. Nano's gone.'

My grandmother stands up, panting, furious, but perfectly in control.

'Get out. You will be hearing from my lawyers promptly.'

'Well, it's about time someone pulled their finger out,' he says, then turns to me. 'I'll see you at work tomorrow. Bring an accountant. You never know, I could be fixing the books to supplement my luxurious lifestyle.'

I stare at him as he turns to her with a huge grin.

'I've been kicked out of here enough times to know my way, so don't bother. Ladies…'

And with that, he tips his imaginary hat to us, turns and marches off.

'Lout,' Grandma sentences as she picks up her tea and takes a sip with shaky fingers. 'Do you see what I meant about him, Emily?'

'Grandmother… leave it. Don't call a lawyer. Jago and I will hash it out between ourselves.'

'And leave you to the mercy of that wastrel? He is smarter than you think, Emily and he will eat you for breakfast. You mark my words. There will be nothing left of you when he is done.'

## 20

*Home Truths,* David Lodge

It's early Thursday morning, two days until Christmas Eve, and I've used my own keys to let myself into Bend or Bump. I switch on the lights and take a good look around. This place really should be called Everything and the Kitchen Sink, as any object you can think of is for sale here, stashed away in the many low alcoves off the main room. Do you need candles, soap, oil? No need to go to the chandlers. Rope? Tools? Lamps? Cookery? Rain macs? No fear, it's all here.

Despite the blustery day, I open the door wide and put out the portable sign. Then I write in bold chalk letters: Come in – we're open for business!

There.

I pick up a cloth and begin dusting the few clear surfaces, but who am I kidding? This place needs a total rehaul. I wonder if I could ask Faith if she does business premises as well. What we need is more storage. Preferably working in vertical, using the walls. What customer is literally going to want to dive through this stack of textiles here, for example? And the smell! I pick up the shop phone and dial Calvin's mobile.

'Yes, miss?'

'Calvin, I hate to trouble you. Do you think that maybe you could run an errand for me when you have a moment?'

'I am just finishing picking up some dry cleaning and will be right with you. Where are you?'

'I'm at Jago Moon's shop.' I still can't bring myself to say *my* shop.

'Very well. I'll be there in a few minutes.'

'Thank you, Calvin.'

And he's true to his word as always, Calvin. By the time he gets here, I've already formed bundles from the textiles based on their colour and texture.

'Could you please take these back to the dry cleaner and have them redelivered in separate packets? Thank you.'

'My pleasure, miss.'

After, much to his horror, I help him load the boot, I go back inside, ready to tackle my next job. Definitely the windows. I don't know why Jago keeps it so dark in here. Probably to make it more comfortable for all of his demons piled up inside. I push the shutters open – demons begone! – to change the air and then start looking for a mop and bucket in the back room. Which is as neat as can be, with all the cleaning products and utensils.

As I'm finishing my first window, the shop phone (which I had installed, much to Jago's dismay) rings.

'Hello? Bend or Bump,' I say into the mouthpiece.

'My, you do sound grand, Emmie!'

It's the ex-MIL. Just what I need. What part of 'don't ever contact me again' does she not understand?

'Hello, *Audrey*...'

'Hello, my dearest.'

Here we go again. I was always her dearest when she needed to manipulate me with her false offerings of motherly love.

'Why are you calling me?' I ask. 'I thought I had made it clear.'

'Oh, Emmie, please reconsider and call my son. He's extremely upset that you've abandoned him practically at the altar.'

Straight to her dramatic point as usual.

'Audrey, again – I have abandoned no one at the altar. And I'll thank you for not interfering. *Again.*'

'Interfering? This is my son's life we're talking about. I am his *mother*. You don't know what that means to love unconditionally. When you have a child of your own, you'll love it no matter its faults. A husband doesn't always enjoy the same privilege. Luckily, I'm here to love him, no matter what.'

And on she goes about sacrifice and duty and responsibility. But not a single word about love. I can't listen to another breath.

'Audrey, I'm sorry, but we're done here. I have to go now.'

She sighs. 'Just think of what I said. Don't deprive yourself of a good man, Emily.'

Argh. 'Goodbye, Audrey,' I growl.

'So, the mother-in-law is taking it harder than the fiancé, huh?' Jago says at my back.

'When are you going to stop sneaking up on me like that?' I cry as I jump.

'Sorry, the door was open. And so are all the windows. No wonder it's so frigging cold in here. So, what's up with the monster-in-law?'

'What do you care? All you want is to get me out of here.'

'That's not true. I don't like to see you unhappy. C'mon, talk to me. We can still be civil with each other, right?'

I huff, then eye him. Can we? 'OK, then. What if your girlfriend told you she wanted some time off? Would you respect that?'

He grins. 'I don't have a specific girlfriend.'

'Play my *What If* game.'

He purses his lips. 'Of course I'd respect it. But if I got the inkling that I was losing her, I'd certainly make sure she knew how much I loved her. What's the matter? Still confused, are you?'

'About?'

'About what you want. I can see it in your eyes that you're completely lost.'

'I'm not lost, Jago.'

'Sure y'are. How long are you going to keep denying it? You don't know what to do. You don't know if you should go back to him or stay here with us. Funny how he's nowhere to be seen. If you were mine and I was losing you, I'd make damn sure you didn't love me anymore before I let someone like you go.'

*Someone like you...* I wonder what he means exactly. Certainly, it's a compliment, but I can't help but wonder whether or not he means anything more by it. Because it comes as a surprise that he thinks someone like me worth keeping. 'If you were mine,' he'd said…

I close my eyes, imagining what it would be like if we were an item. Would we bicker as we do now, or would the certainty of an attachment mellow us both? Because, if I was as bitter as a spinster but with a fiancé, he was the portrait of a relationship gone derelict.

Would love make him happier, or would he still be his old cynical self? I've seen the way Grandmother treats him and he seemed so used to being treated that way, as if it were the norm and all he had to do was shrug his shoulders to shake off the venom. Whereas I'm unable to think of anything else but the hurt.

'Is that what you think?' I say.

'I think, Little City Slicker, that you don't even know what you want. You'd like to come out of your shell and from under the shadow of your previous love story – or your dysfunctional relationship gone sour – but you haven't got the guts.'

I feel my eyes widen in disbelief. 'I beg your pardon?'

'You'd like to live a life larger than your own, but you wouldn't know what to do with it.'

'What a ridiculous thing to say,' I counter. 'Of course I know what I want.'

'Then why are you here? Why are you not in London, at your job, in your pokey little flat ordering a takeaway with your boyfriend who falls asleep halfway through your Netflix film?'

How does he even know that? But then, to be honest, isn't that how most of us live? Day in, day out, over and over, like Groundhog Day?

'I'm... just taking some time off.'

'From work, or from your fiancé?'

'Why is it so important for you to know anything at all about me?'

He shrugs. 'I don't need to. You girls are all the same old, same old.'

I laugh. 'And you are the usual pathetic man who thinks that life owes him a living.'

He dips his head. 'Perhaps. But at least I live my life my way, like the song.'

'So do I.'

To which he laughs. A mirthless laugh.

'Say what you want. You're getting very close to discovering that you have the power to change your life, without ever having to ask anyone for permission. And yet, you don't have the guts to jump. To get on with your own life.'

'Like you?' I blurt.

He looks over at me. 'Me? Emmie, I'm a completely different animal to you. I don't crave for anything that everyone else wants.'

'What do you crave for, then?'

He thinks about it. 'Nothing. Just... oblivion.'

'Is that why you drink?'

He shrugs. 'It helps, but not as much as you'd think, because the minute I wake, nothing's changed.' He grins. 'But I do enjoy the trying part.'

He truly is an original creature, Jago Moon, in such a strange, twisted way. He's soulful when you least expect him to be and yet you wouldn't consider him anywhere near shallow. He has that air about him of the damned and dejected, and yet when he looks into your eyes, you know that there's so much more there behind the sadness. An entire parallel world of unspoken thoughts and hidden emotions and...

Suddenly, like giant balloons, Nettie's words flash through my mind: *Sooner or later, everyone falls for him at their own cost...*

'And what do you do, to keep from falling apart?' he asks, interrupting my epiphany.

'I have no idea what you're talking about.'

'Don't you?'

I watch in stupor as he leans in close enough to touch me, his eyes reaching inside mine as if to pull up the blinds that hide my most naked self. This realisation that has just struck me is at the same time fascinating and terrifying. I'm not used to feeling like this. I *can't* be feeling like this!

'You do realise that acting like one of those introspective and tormented heroes from the twentieth century while at the same time pretending to understand women isn't going to solve your issues,' I comment, hoping to get the focus off my own newfound weakness.

His smirk widens. 'Then we're making progress. I'm pleased you see me as a hero of sorts. Not many do around here.'

'I don't wonder at it,' I bite off like a drowning man grabbing a lifeline, 'seeing the reputation you have.'

'My reputation? What about you? You're exactly like one of those lost little girls who have never taken their nose out of a book, who don't know left from right. Who want everything – adventure, excitement, breaking the rules and all – but are too afraid even to poke their nose out of their own front door.'

I shake my head. 'From what you're saying, I think you need to read some more modern books. The days of *Madame Bovary* are over. Women today, like it or not, have the power of their own freedom and their own minds.'

He laughs as if he knew some magic secret that I didn't.

'Oh, I'm all for female empowerment,' he assures.

'You are?'

'Hell, yes. But you? Are you in charge of your own life? Does your boyfriend know that he's not the boss of you? Have you actually told him that you don't love him anymore? Have you actually called it off?'

'I...'

'Of course you haven't. You don't have the balls to reach out of your own comfort zone and maybe, God forbid, live a little and actually be happy.'

Who is he to talk? He's a recluse with a million demons of his own.

'I'll be fine,' I lie.

He shakes his head in what seems a gesture of pity.

'You? Are you really convinced of that? You poor, poor girl. You've seen none of the joys of life. Pah! A new job, a new car, a new dress? Is that what makes you happy? That's just palliative care for a dying soul. Society's blinkers. You might be comfortable, wedged in as you are in your little life, but are you happy? Or just convincing yourself that you are, just so you don't blow your brains out? Or does even the smallest part of you resent your fiancé for keeping you back, for not sharing even your silliest, most insignificant little joys? For not making up to you what life has taken away from you.

'He hasn't given you what that little girl wanted. If anything, you're having to work harder than you thought at merely being content, for want of a better word. There's no being content, Emmie. Not from a man who's put himself at the centre of your life so that there's no room left for you.

'People like that don't even care that you might not love them as much as you used to. They simply want you to feel obligated just enough so that you actually stay in the web they've weaved for you. They just want a victim to feed on for as long as they need.'

And just like that, he's touched my very core. Grazed my thinnest veneer of self-acceptance and pulled the skin off my very bones.

'Why does everything have to be so dramatic with you? Why are you black and white? And in any case, look who's talking. Are *you* happy, Mr Bloody Miserable Boat Fixer-upper? Because if you want to talk about the truth, *you're* the one who isn't living. Half the village hates you. The other half fear you for God knows what you did. And how do you react but with that constant fake 'who gives a crap' smirk, while deep inside something is seriously bothering you.'

He grins. 'I knew you wouldn't appreciate me stripping you down to the bone. You're not used to being so exposed. Hurts, doesn't it?'

I shrug. 'Not really.'

'How about a truce of sorts?'

I eye him. 'A truce?'

'Yeah,' he assures with a smile. 'How about we don't let money get in the way of becoming… friends.'

'You… want to be friends?'

'Sure.'

Hmm. 'What do you mean, exactly, by friends?' Just so I know.

He shrugs. 'People who chat. Who have coffee together. Who don't tear each other apart every time they meet.'

I shrug back. 'OK…'

'OK!'

'Good,' I conclude.

'Good indeed.'

'Oh my God, he *so* wants to get into your pants!' Maisie squeals as I'm letting myself into Bend or Bump.

I roll my eyes. 'He does not…'

'Trust me – all the signs are there. This is going to be one hell of a rollercoaster ride.'

I certainly hope not. I've got too much on my plate.

'My only goal is getting this whole inheritance thing sorted. I wouldn't put it past him trying to chat me up just for that,' I snap, knowing how crude, and wrong, that sounds.

There are a million men like that, of course, but somehow Jago Moon, despite his claim against my inheritance, isn't like that. He is upfront and honest. He wouldn't go behind my back. I do understand that he wants what's his. Only no one is willing to tell me *why* he thinks it's his in the first place.

As I'm bustling down the central aisle, I catch sight of Jago emerging from the back room.

'Speak of the devil, gotta go,' I whisper into my phone and hang up.

'Hey,' he greets me. He looks quite chipper, today. Perhaps this could work to my advantage.

'Hey,' I say back. 'So, uhm, after all your talk about being adventurous, would you agree to be adventurous yourself?'

'Meaning?'

'Would you agree to let Faith Hudson in and refresh this place? I've got some ideas that I'd like to share with you to make it look nicer and attract more customers. We could start with a Christmas theme.'

'*Christmas?* Have you looked around? Starry Cove is exploding with Christmas every bleddy day of the year! I don't need it in my shop. My customers are mainly tradespeople who need bits and pieces. They don't need to be slowed down by fairy lights and plastic Santas. They want to come in, get what they need and get out. I'm a boatbuilder. I don't deal in festivities. Here, people actually come to me to get *away* from Christmas.'

Oh, brilliant. An authentic Cornish Scrooge. If this is any indication of our work relationship, we're already dead. Jago isn't one to compromise so easily.

'But it's not just your shop,' I correct him. 'And I get 50 per cent of the say.'

He looks at me as it begins to dawn on him that whatever I decide to do with my life, *I'm* his business partner now, not my grandfather anymore, and that he's going to have to deal with me, either on the phone and through emails or in the flesh. I suspect he prefers the former, so he can fob me off at his leisure.

'Well, then you can do what you like in your 50 per cent of the shop.'

'What?' I laugh.

'There! That half at the back,' he says, jerking his thumb over his shoulder to the darkest corner of the already cave-like ambience. 'Knock yourself out.'

I put my hands on my hips and glare down at him as he pretends to go through some paperwork. When he realises I'm not going away, he looks up with a huff.

'Are we playing teapots?' he says, nodding at my stance. 'Maybe you could put a Santa hat on and—'

'Are you deliberately trying to piss me off?'

He sits back and grins, locking his hands behind his head. 'Now why would I want to do that, partner?'

'I'm not going anywhere.'

'I noticed.'

'Good. I'll be having a friend in to see what can be done.'

'That's coming out of your expenses.'

'I have no doubt.'

'And I don't want to see anything Christmassy at the entrance. I don't want to drive my customers away with any of this childish nonsense.'

'Fine by me,' I agree just to shut him up.

What I haven't told him is that I'm looking for an expert opinion to make sure this dive doesn't actually cave in on my festive mood – or my brand-new customers.

But can Jago and I actually live in the same village now, work side by side every day without ending up arguing over absolutely everything, and enjoying every moment of it?

## 21

*Decline and Fall*, Evelyn Waugh

'It's actually got quite good bones, Emmie,' Faith says as she looks around the shop.

'You think so?' I ask.

'Absolutely. I'll bring in a structural engineer just to check, but it's just a reno job.'

'That's great. When would I be able to decorate? I want to make it Christmassy.'

'Oh dear,' she winces. 'Jago won't like that. He hates anything festive.'

'Oh no – he's agreed to let me do what I want with my half of the shop.'

She makes an impressed face. '*Really?* That's a first. Well done, then. We'll come and give you a hand with the other girls. They love spreading Christmas cheer, as you've seen.'

'But you've already helped me so much…'

She shrugs. 'It's a tradition among the Coastal Girls. Most of us come from screwed-up families, so we've sort of pooled our resources, you know?'

I know. Rosie has told me a bit about how Faith and her sister were adopted, and how the need for a loving home made her become an interior designer. And also how her hopes of a happy home had later been dashed by her fiancé.

'Well, I… thank you, but are you sure?'

She smiles. 'Absolutely. You're in.'

It's too late. I can't stop them. The tears, I mean.

'Hey,' she says, hugging me. 'What did Rosie tell you? We take care of one another down here. Now, don't you go worrying about anything, understand? You have friends here, Emmie.'

'I… thank you. I don't know what to say. Ever since I got here I've been met with nothing but kindness from everyone…'

'Well, almost everyone,' she says with a laugh.

I dry my eyes. 'Do you mean my grandmother, or my new partner?'

'Both. They'll come round. They just need time.'

Time to what? I wonder. Ruin my life more than it already is?


Having matured the decision to resign from my old job, I'm now taking care of the paperwork and also listing my flat, as I'm no longer prepared to let anything stop me from living my own life the way I want to. So the next day I go down to the town hall to speak to someone about getting a mooring licence for the barge business.

'First, you'll have to present a report detailing the state of the boat, and then take it to a boatbuilder and have it adapted. He'd then have to write his own report about the feasibility of the barge as a business concern. He's in a meeting now, if you want to wait?'

So I wait. And plan. And budget. And jot down some ideas and sketches in a little blue booklet that never leaves my bag. I put everything in there – phone numbers, happy memories, to-do lists and even my favourite scraps of poetry. It looks more like a Mexican piñata than a notebook.

When it's my turn, I take a huge breath and knock on the massive oak door. I can do this!

'Come if you want,' the muffled voice beckons, and in I go, unable to contain my happiness.

For about two seconds. Because there, behind the massive desk, like a king on a throne, is Jago bloody Moon!

'Oh, come on! Really?'

He grins up at me sheepishly, then sits back and nods for me to sit down.

'Emmie! So nice to see you. Come in. What can I do for you today?'

But I hang back. This is too rich.

'What? You're everywhere, like God?'

He dips his head. 'If you believe in such things. But it's too early in the day to start delving into people's souls, don't you think?'

'I thought you said you didn't have one.'

His eyes search mine and he grins back. 'You're right about that, maid.'

I roll my eyes. 'Have you ever tried speaking in real English?'

'English is boring. We make our own language.'

'Oh, God, here we go again…'

As it turns out, moving to Cornwall and changing my

life around isn't going to be as easy as I'd envisaged, what with Jago blocking me at every turn. First, I'm going to have to sell my flat in London. My estate agent had several viewings lined up and is very optimistic. Not that that will be a problem, by any means, but it means a huge upheaval. Once I'm out of London, I'll be out for good. And never one to make decisions lightly, I have to think long and hard before I make a decision – any decision – from which there's no going back.

'How did your meeting go?' Martin asks as he comes down from my grandmother's bedroom.

It's the day before Christmas Eve – and the day before my former engagement party, but I don't want to think about that. Everyone has been scurrying around like mad for last-minute purchases, despite having been at it for more than a month now, but Martin seems like he's not in any hurry to go anywhere. Which is good, because I have a gift for him – an ancient rod of Asclepius, the symbol for the medical practice.

'Thank you,' he grins. 'I have something for you, too.' He pulls a small packet out of his pocket. 'It's just a simple thing. A history of Cornwall...'

'Oh, wow. Thank you so much, Martin. It'll be my bible guide to getting around.'

He smiles. 'I hope you'll ask me if you need anything.'

'I will, Martin. Thank you for being so kind.'

He shrugs. 'So, how's the debacle with Jago Moon going?'

I huff. 'Moral of the story? He's not signing off on it. He insists that the barge is a death trap.'

'It is. No lie there.'

'So you two can actually agree on something, then?' I quip.

He shrugs. 'I realise I may have sounded harsh. I don't want him dead, of course. If you ever needed something, Jago was always the first to be there. He was my best friend in the whole world. But when he stole my girlfriend, he was dead to me.'

'He stole your girlfriend?'

'He says he had nothing to do with it and that he'd never have done anything like that to me, but I knew I'd lost her, on Christmas Eve, to boot, and it was because of him.'

'Well, it doesn't sound like he set out to hurt you, Martin,' I defend. 'Could you not ever be friends again?'

'It's never going to happen, Emmie. Not while I live and breathe.'

'Oh come on, Martin. I'm sure he cares about you?'

'Who knows? Jago loves only himself nowadays. But let me tell you honestly, Emmie. If you're thinking of him in that way, forget it.'

'What? Of course not. He's just a business partner – we were practically thrown together.'

'Ah, but Jago grows on women. At first they find him appallingly rude and say they absolutely hate him. And then, like magic, they suddenly change their minds…'


'The cad!' Nina huffs as she stirs her hot chocolate across the table from me.

Faith and Rosie are shaking their heads in sympathy.

'Who does he think he is, stopping you from using the barge? It's yours, too!' she adds.

'Well, you've got to admit that Martin's right – Jago is an authority in manners of the harbour,' Faith says.

'Who does he think he is!' I seethe.

'He does have the authority to stop you,' Rosie says. 'He's the town councillor for all things sea and safety.'

'Well, then I'll find another way,' I assure as I take a sip of my coffee.

I need to be vigilant and ready to bounce back at a moment's notice. I can't be lulled into the festive season too much. After all, I've got a job to do, a life to make.

'Emmie,' Nat intervenes. 'There's a lot about Jago Moon that you don't know. We think it's best if you stay away from him. For your own sake. It's bad enough you're partners. I'd run a mile.'

'But why?'

'We can't tell you why,' Faith regrets. 'We promised never to talk about it again. The entire village did. But please believe us when we say that Jago isn't the same person he used to be. He'll pull you down with him and destroy you.'

'Oh, this is all so sad,' Rosie sniffs. 'I don't believe he's all bad, you know?'

Nina rolls her eyes. 'There goes old waterworks again. In fairness, Rosie, you're too soft-hearted for your own good.'

'You need someone who will take care of you. Jago can't even take care of himself right now,' Nat says.

I'm getting tired of hearing the same thing over and over. And repeating the same thing.

'There's nothing between Jago and me. He already has a hundred girlfriends and whatnots. He's *just* my business partner.'

'OK,' Faith soothes. 'You know, I was in love with a bad

boy. And in the end, I paid for it. We don't want you to have to go through the same.'

'Is there nothing you can do to get rid of him?' Rosie suggests. 'Like maybe buy him out?'

I huff. I don't want to get rid of him. I want to run this business with him and make a success out of it.

'He's got what it takes. I need his knowledge,' I say.

'Maybe you should take a few days off, Emmie,' Nina suggests. 'Clear your head.'

I laugh bitterly. 'From the pan to the fire. I left London because I couldn't stand another single day there. And now, what do I do? I go and put myself into yet another mess. Brilliant. Stonking brilliant...'

'Hey...' Rosie says, patting my back. 'Chin up. You've made huge progress since then. When I met you, you were miserable and didn't have any idea what you wanted to do. At least now you've found your real family and have a business.'

'Well, that's one way of looking at it.'

'Come on – I mean it. You're your own boss,' Rosie says. 'I can't tell you how horrible my supervisor was. Susan the Sacker, we used to call her. Ugh, just the thought of her...'

'Rosie's right, you know,' Faith says. 'The freedom of working for yourself is priceless.'

Priceless. Like my own freedom. The option to choose what I want to do, where I want to live. I need to find a way to support myself, and it's true that occupation rates in Cornwall outside the summer season aren't exactly the highest in the country. I could apply to the local school, Northwood Academy in Little Kettering, which services all the villages and is apparently one of the best in the country. I could actually do that.

But I won't. I don't want to move to Cornwall just to find another teaching job. There's no way I'm returning to teaching, what with all its stress and hierarchies of every kind you could possibly think of. Head of Year, Head of Department, Head Ache. What's the point of leaving a lifestyle I hate just to start all over again elsewhere in exactly the same job?

No, I need a fresh start. Something that will inspire me. Like, perhaps, something that will put me in contact with the locals rather than smart working. Like this boat licence thing. I haven't really thought it over so much as desired it with all of my heart. In the end, if I can't get a nautical licence for whatever reason, be it Jago or the town hall's opposition, there's absolutely nothing stopping me from living in it, just like Jago is.

As I turn the corner into Blackberry Lane, I spot my grandmother leaving Bend or Bump and getting into her limousine, her face fierce. What's she doing there? She hates Jago. What more could she possibly have to say to him?

By the time I've picked up the few things I need at the stationer's, Jago has locked up and left without so much as leaving me a note. He doesn't have a mobile phone, so I can't call him. As I'm unlocking the shop for any possible last-minute Christmas shoppers and debating how to contact him, it becomes a moot point as a sudden barrage of Christmas shoppers pour in, flooding the shop, asking me questions of all sorts. Have I got this item in blue. When will it be in. Can they get a discount.

As I work my way into the afternoon, my eyes dart to the door every time the bell goes. But it's never Jago. Where the hell has he gone?

Later that evening after work, as I'm walking back to my grandmother's in a downpour – without my umbrella – I spot a couple of kids hunched over something in the street. There's also the sound of a dog barking.

At a closer look, I see that it's a man, looking very much like he's been knocked down by a hit-and-run. I quicken my step, ready to call someone for help, only to see that it's Jago Moon, arm twisted under him, dead pale and eyes closed.

## 22

*Ulysses*, James Joyce

'Jago!' I call as I fall to his side. 'Jago!'

'He's only drunk again, miss,' the kids dismiss him with a laugh. 'He'll get up when he's slept it off.'

And with that, they run off.

A couple of others walk by, completely unmoved by seeing a man down. I call to them, but they shake their heads and walk on. What the hell kind of community *is* this? Wasn't Starry Cove supposed to be a magical village where dreams come true?

Max is nudging him, but Jago is still.

'Jago!' I cry again, pulling at him by his jacket. 'Open your eyes! Talk to me!'

But he groans and turns over as if the cold and hardness of the cobbled streets have become his second home. Max barks to wake him, pulling on his sleeve with his teeth, but Jago is oblivious.

I wipe my eyes with my sleeve. 'Please! Get up! You can't lie here like a heap of rubbish.'

'I *am* a h-heap o' r-rubbish,' he corrects me in a broken voice.

I continue to pull at him.

'Jago, please! I can't lift you and I'm not leaving you in the road to get run over.'

'Leave me here... save the trouble of a proper send-off... Undrownable, anyway.'

'Oh, Jago, please don't say things like that.'

The thought that he'd actually tried to kill himself and might have been trying again tore through my heart. How desperate would he have been even to think such a thing, let alone say it?

'Jago, come on. Pull yourself up. We can't stay here.'

'Hmm...' he groans. 'Go home, Emmie.'

'Come on, Jago. We have to get you home.'

'Go,' he repeats. 'I'm no good for you.'

I've been getting a lot of that lately, but that's another story.

I crane my neck and catch the attention of a man crossing the road. He stops when he sees me waving my arms, meeting me halfway.

'Please, can you help me? There's a man in the street...'

He shakes his head. 'If it's Jago Moon stone drunk again, just leave him there.'

'What? Why? How can you *say* that? How can you just leave someone like that?'

In response, he looks at me and snorts, shaking his head.

'My advice, miss? You go on home and forget you ever saw him. He's no good for the likes of you.'

What is it with everyone in this village? Why will no one

help? I whirl round, muttering every foul word I know. If only my students could see me now.

I flag a teenager with a mobile phone down and ask him to call Dr Miller's office to explain the situation. In five minutes, both Janice and Martin are there, and Max follows us into the car. We drive Jago to his barge, where we manage to carry him inside onto the sofa. As they set him face down, I grab a wastepaper basket and put it by him.

Martin glances at his watch and then at his sister.

'It's alright, you can both go. I'll stay with him,' I inform them.

There's no way I'm leaving Jago to drown in his own sick.

'The bleddy old bag...' Janice mutters to herself, biting her lip, shooting me an apologetic glance.

'You mean my grandmother, don't you? I saw her limousine earlier. I know she went to see him. She's the cause of this, isn't she? She was heard shouting at him. What did she say to him to upset him so much?'

'He won't say,' Janice answers. 'All I know is that Ralph from The Rolling Scones says she drove by the Bend or Bump. And when she left, he closed up shop and went for a walk. The rest, you know.'

'Oh my God. What the hell could she have possibly said to hurt him so much? I know she doesn't think much of him, but to lay into him like that?'

'Emmie,' Martin says. 'There's really no reason for you to get caught up in this.'

'If you want to stay and take care of Jago, fine,' Janice interrupts her brother, 'thank you. But for your own good, just... stay out of everything else, OK?'

'I'm getting sick and tired!' I shout. 'I need to know what all this cloak-and-dagger business is about. What's going on between my grandmother and Jago Moon? How are they even connected?'

The two glance at each other.

'He'll have to tell you himself, if he wants to, Emmie,' Janice says. 'All you can do is be there for him if he needs you.'

My eyes swing to Martin, who nods.

'It's not for us to say anything, Emmie. We're sorry…'

'Fine. *I'll* take care of him. Thank you for helping me.' *Not.*

'I'll call in later, OK?' Janice promises.

I wipe my face in anger and nod.

'Thank you, Janice.'

'Hang in there,' she says, squeezing my arm. 'It's worth it.'

Whatever that means.

When they're gone, I rush into the bathroom and get some facecloths to wipe his face. Then I remove his shoes and belt and cover him with a soft blue throw. Should he wake in the night, I'll give him a couple of aspirins and get him to drink some coffee, maybe even eat something.

Poor Max. He hasn't left Jago's side for a moment. He must be exhausted. The sheer loyalty of this beautiful creature brings tears to my eyes. I freshen his water bowl and open a can of dog food from the pantry, sitting on the floor next to him as he polishes it off in one minute flat, his intelligent eyes scanning me. He knows I mean him no harm. He knows I'm here to help.

I go into the kitchen to make something to eat, but his pantry has few items besides sliced bread and Marmite. This man doesn't eat. Instead, there's a full-blown collection of dog food, plus booze of every kind and price. I stand back, my eyes travelling over all the bottles. It's like a suicidal mission. Why, oh why, is he doing this to himself?

As I'm making some Marmite sandwiches, through the door I see him stir. I wipe my hands on a tea towel and bring in a strong cup of coffee and the sandwiches, which I set on the coffee table before him.

'Hey...' I whisper as he opens his eyes and turns to look at me in surprise.

'What are you doing here?' he rasps, scratching the stubble on his throat.

'You're OK,' I say. 'You're home. Janice and Martin have been and say that you just need some sleep. And some food.'

He suppresses a moan.

'You shouldn't be here,' he admonishes. 'Your grootmother will have a fit.'

'I don't care about that,' I assure him. 'I just want to make sure you're OK.'

'Why?'

'Because we're partners. And I don't believe you're as bad as she depicts you.'

He grunts. 'Worse. I'm worse. I'm absolute scum.'

'Stop *saying* that. We all know you're not.'

He smirks. 'What the hell do you know about me, Emmie?'

'I know you're not a bad person. I know something happened that hurt you.'

He's silent, his eyes lost on the ceiling.

'Let me help you, Jago. Let everyone help you to get back on your feet.'

He snorts. 'Help? No, Emmie. There's no help for the likes of me. I'm dead inside, and out.'

'But, Jago…'

'Emmie, stop. You've seen how I drink. I reckon I've got a few good years left in me before my liver packs up, but I'm going to live them my way. Not expecting anything from life.'

'But why? You're still young, Jago. Please. Please let me help you.' Without realising, I've migrated into his personal space, my face inches from his. 'Please let me do this.'

His eyes shift from the ceiling to mine. Lying here like this, he still looks formidable, only his huge dark eyes betraying his vulnerability as they peer almost hopefully at me. If I can get him to hope, I can get him to live.

'That's sweet of you, Emmie, but no. Not gonna happen. Bums like me just don't put themselves back together again because they have a couple of friends. It doesn't work like that. For your own sake, just stay away from me. Go home.'

In the past, I'd have fled a mile from someone like him. The bad boy, the tough one on the street. But there's something about Jago that I can't define or describe. He's not the bad man he portrays himself to be. I've seen him perform selfless acts. Heard about the brave things he's done. Of how everyone loved him and protected him out of the memory of the man he used to be.

There has to be something of that man somewhere inside him still. A man with integrity doesn't simply disappear into thin air, no matter what happens to him. There has to be a reason for someone to go through such a drastic change. And there's only one person who can explain.

After Janice arrives and settles herself, I leave Jago and march all the way into Starry Cove, up Rectory Lane and through the gates across the grounds of Heatherton Hall.

She's sitting in her drawing room, calm and composed, as usual, in one of her elegant suits. I'm aware that I'm a mess, stomping through the house like an enraged bull, that my bag is falling off my shoulder, that my hair is in my face and that I look like I'm about to crown someone. That someone being Lady Mary Heatherton-Smythe.

'Oh, Emily,' she greets me as I barge in on her and a group of elderly women. 'Come and meet—'

'What the *hell* did you say to him?' I demand, heedless of all the ladies in haute couture sitting around sipping their tea.

She looks around the gathering, wide-eyed and innocent.

'I beg your pardon? Are you alright, Emily? You seem upset.'

'You think *I'm* upset? You ought to see Jago Moon! What the hell are you up to, Grandmother?'

'Dear Emily, you are not thinking straight and are being rude to me. What could *I* possibly say to Jago Moon that would make him any more of a mess than he already is? The man is a lowlife. And you would be wise to stay away from him, as I have instructed you to do so many times in the past.'

'Instructed? You don't instruct me, Grandmother!' I roar. 'Nor will you continue to intimidate people into avoiding him. Because of you and your stupid influence, a lot of people have turned their backs on him, and I want to know why. And I want to know what you did to him.'

'Me? My dear girl, you must be out of your mind. Or perhaps,' she titters, turning to her appalled friends for support, 'seeing the company you keep, you must be drunk, too.'

'I'm not drunk, Grandmother,' I assure. 'But there is a man who's lost the will to live and I know that *you* have something to do with it. So tell me, what exactly did you say to him? Did you threaten him with your lawyers even when I asked you not to? Why can't you just leave him be? You have so much money already, and if Nano perceived it a good idea to leave him some of his assets, I don't see why it should bother you.'

'I beg your pardon?'

'No! No *pardon*, Grandmother. You've treated me with indifference at best ever since I got here. Remember that I didn't ask for anything. You had your solicitor write to me. Because it was actually too difficult for you to pick up the phone or write me a line or two welcoming me to the family.'

She stares at me as if I've gone mad. Maybe I have. But I'm no longer willing to be pushed around by anyone, be it Audrey, Stephen or my grandmother. Because I don't know anyone who's been ignored by her entire family without ever having done anything to deserve it.

'First of all,' she says calmly, 'this has nothing to do with you. You are an outsider. You don't, and will never, belong here.'

I stare at her, unable to speak for a few beats, but then I find my voice.

'D'you know what I find funny, Grandmother? That a perfect stranger, my former future mother-in-law, albeit for her own reasons, was willing to be associated with me. Just because her son loved me. While you, my own flesh and blood, for some crazy reason, refuse me.

'I've racked my brains as to why that is and you know what? I've finally come up with an explanation. You're so wrapped up in yourself and your estate and your memories and your narrow-minded ways that you can't for one single minute actually think about someone else besides yourself.

'You think that people are always after your money. Is that really all you have to offer? And you don't for one minute think that Jago Moon might be interested in me for me. He, as opposed to you and Stephen, sees something more in me. He respects me. He's put me before himself. He always has. And you – you should be ashamed of yourself for all you've said and done. In fact, you're no better than my almost mother-in-law. Gosh, two bullets dodged in one month. How lucky am I!'

'Emily,' she says. 'If you even entertain the idea of having a tryst with him, I *will* disinherit you. Do you understand me?'

I nod. 'I do. I understand that you're a very sad woman with no room left in your heart for love and forgiveness.'

'How dare you speak to me like that!' she scolds, but I continue nonetheless.

'I don't know what it was that my mother did to you – or didn't do, for that matter. We never talked much. But I can assure you that I am my own person and had things been reversed I would be ready to wipe the slate clean and start over. So if and when you're ever ready, you just let me know. Because that's how I personally do things.'

She stands up with the support of her cane.

'You want to know why I can't let him be? Because he is a murderer, that is why! A cold-blooded killer who should have rotted in jail for years rather than a few months!'

Jail? Oh, Judas! How can that be? He told me he was bad news when we met, but… murder?

No. Impossible. Jago isn't like that. He is a little on the rough side, but underneath that iron crust lies a mushy filling. He can't be capable of such a heinous crime. And yet, Mary wouldn't say so if it weren't true. Even she knows the consequences of slander.

'I've got to pack,' I snap as I turn on my heels and march out of her grand drawing room, leaving her as still as the ornate Anaglypta wallpaper behind her.

It takes me all of five minutes to slam my few belongings into my wheelie suitcase. For *weeks* I've slaved for her – taken care of her and her home while getting to know the lovely people of Starry Cove. While not only dreaming, but actually working towards a new life here. And she simply dismisses me by saying that I'll never belong? Is this what family love is all about? All my life I've dreamed of it, fantasised about it, and this is it? This is how she treats people? How soul-destroying can she be?

The next day, Christmas Eve, I wake up with a sense of oppression in my chest so great that I can't seem to contain myself. I need air. I need to get out of here and go somewhere. But I don't want to see anyone. Jago Moon, in jail…! He never told me that. Then again, why would he? It's none of my business what he does. He's told me that several times.

I've had enough of it. I never indicated I was interested in him, so where does he get all that *I'm no good for you* from, anyway? And what does he know what's good for me? Who is he, my keeper?

Without realising, I find myself at the harbour. There is a sign reading Christmas Eve Cruises. What a great idea! There are small motorboats for hire that don't need a nautical licence to be piloted. After a brief explanation by the owner regarding the dashboard and a few simple rules dictated by common sense, I'm given the keys with a nod and a *bon voyage*.

As if driving a car, I turn the key in the ignition, pull in the anchor and manoeuvre out of the harbour and down the river towards the open sea for a bit of coast-hugging. So far, so good. I'm so glad I did this! From the sea, the Cornish coast is even more stunning, with a mixture of gentle grassy slopes stooping to the majesty of the sea, whereas other portions of the coast resist it by presenting high, impervious granite cliffs. I pass a few boats every now and then, and the passengers all have that same look on their faces – sheer bliss.

It is a glorious day for December, and the fact that today is Christmas Eve makes it all the more special and memorable for me. I first piloted my own boat on Christmas Eve! I have a funny feeling that down here, in gorgeous Cornwall, I'm going to have many, many firsts and I'm damned if I won't enjoy each and every one! I intend to be less fearful, less careful and just live in the moment because... life is much too short. I might not have survived that attack in London and be dead by now. But I am alive! And free!

Straining my eyes for the horizon, I soon become aware of the fact that it's not as clear as it was a moment ago. In fact, in the space of a few minutes, or at least I think so, the skies have darkened and I now have hardly any vision ahead of me other than dark swirling clouds and a blurry grey smudge that's my visual limit a few yards ahead. And just as I'm manoeuvring to turn round, a rain bomb hits the boat, pummelling it with all the water it can.

The boat rocks from the pressure of the falling rain and from the choppy waves underneath. A quick glance tells me I'm no longer hugging the coast but have somehow drifted out to the open sea. And there's no one else around to see that I'm already in trouble, fighting to stay upright as this monster of a storm bounces the boat around. And every time it lands with a thud and a screech back on the crest of the wave, another one replaces it with even more force, sending me higher and higher. At every bounce, I wonder if it's going to be my last, because now I've lost all control of the boat, its little engine is nothing against the fury of the waves. How did this happen in the space of a brief moment?

As I ramp up the speed to try to get out of the rain bomb, I realise it's a losing battle. At every new strike from under the boat, I grip the wheel, clenching my eyes shut, praying that I won't be thrown overboard and into the sea. But who am I kidding? It's a miracle I've lasted this long. And once in the freezing water, how long am I going to last out here, on my own?

And now it's only a matter of *when* and not *if* it's going to happen. And that's when an almighty heave tosses me into the air, boat and all, only to crash back down through the surface of the icy waters below.

# 23

*'Death by Water',* T. S. Eliot

Under the surface of the sea, time seems to stand still. Everything is slow. My limbs don't move as fast as I command them – my arms are as if paralysed and my brain is muddled.

Only instinct allows me to fight my way back up to the surface gradually, where the howling winds whip my hair into my eyes, stinging my face. I can't open my eyes against the force of the wind and rain pummelling them shut. Having made it back to the surface is not enough. Every wave that hits pushes me under, over and again, and every time it takes me longer to resurface – and when I eventually do, I'm weaker and weaker. I can't do it anymore...

I can't believe I've left the safety of dry land to come here to die!

And no one except Maisie would actually care. Which scares me more than death itself. Not to have anyone cry for you, ache for losing you. Only to have *been* for a fleeting moment and then be gone, like a drop of water in the ocean, never to be found again, if not lifeless. It's unbearable – more than death itself.

I try to shut out the invading images of the remains of my grey dead body, washed ashore one day in the distant future. No one will know who I am. No one will fall to their knees in anguish and cry my name. Not Stephen, not even my grandmother.

My mind begins to wander, so I know I'm rapidly losing my core heat. My body is beginning to shut down. My mind is whirring – I'm going off the rails. For some crazy reason, I can see myself when I was born, tiny and helpless. I can hear myself crying, keening. And I suddenly realise that I'm still in the same position after all these years. Tiny and helpless. Crying and keening for an embrace that will simply not arrive. And the rest of it? Besides becoming an English teacher, what have I managed to do with my life? What mark have I made? Who will remember me?

And it hits me. I never really counted for anyone. No one really loves me. No one will really miss me. And so this is it. The end of my short, dreary life. And it's meant nothing to anyone, not even my own parents. I begin to bawl. Helplessly, hopelessly bawl, my cries lost in this immense ocean, along with the cries of the wailing wind…

But wait – it's not just me. There's another sound on the wind. Another keening sound. Or is it the wind itself, ringing in my ears? I can't tell.

I try to listen beyond my own gasps for air, but there's nothing. My mind is playing more tricks on me. I'm wondering what my last thought will be. Certainly not a family or a husband or children. Now, I'll never have children. I'll never be able to have a family and live to tell them about the horrifying moment I faced death.

Because I can't keep fighting for every breath much longer. My mind is numb. I can't think anymore, I can't stay awake. I make an effort even to remember to breathe. It's so much easier just to stop fighting and let go, surrender to the cold darkness enveloping me.

I think of Joe, Tommy, Verity and Beth and all of my students. They'll grow up, live and love...

My mind is completely lost now, and it's so sorrowful, to know you're letting go and unable to do a thing about it, like a spectator. You see it all but can't intervene because it's much too late.

'Emmie!' comes the wind again.

From zero perception, I'm suddenly aware of my surroundings. I can now again feel the cold, the fear, the helplessness of my situation. And then steel arms envelop me, pulling me, but I don't know which way. Someone is in the water – coming towards me? How is that even possible? My mind is playing tricks on me.

And in one irrational, instinctive moment, I *know*.

*Jago!* I want to call out, but I have no voice. I want to reach out to him, but I have no body.

He shouts in my ear, but it's barely a whisper, carried off by the raging sea, followed by something else.

I cry out as his grip on me tightens. It's the only way I know he's still there, because I can't see him, but I can feel his hand around my wrist, like a lifeline. In this defining moment, all I know and all I am depend on his determination and ability to hang on to me despite the waves that continue to crash into us as if they had a personal reason to pound us to the bottom of the sea.

All around us is hell. I can't tell up from down. Nor can I see an inch from my nose. I hang on to him like a rock. But he's just a man – practically nothing against the fury of nature. I can't believe that he's going to drown in this storm while trying to save me. Foolish, foolish man!

'I've got you!' he shouts over the roaring in my ears.

And I can do nothing – not even hang on for dear life anymore, because I have no strength left in my body, not a single drop. But I can feel sorrow. Sorrow for Jago, who's out here in this madness, with nothing to hang on to. Where is his boat? Surely he didn't swim out in this weather... That would be madness. He must have fallen in, in an attempt to save me.

*Save me. No, save yourself, Jago. I'm too far gone now. Too far gone to come back. Save yourself...*

# 24

*Othello*, William Shakespeare

Why are there flames in my bedroom? Is my flat on fire? I try to jump up, to reach for my phone to call for the firefighters, but I can't move. I'm bruised and torn and every inch of my body feels like I've been dragged through a hedge backwards.

And like a huge flash of lightning, it comes back to me. The storm... I was drowning. Am I... dead? I don't feel dead. Is this...? What *is* this? If I'm alive, where am I?

'Welcome back,' comes a deep voice from somewhere above me.

For a split moment, I think it's actually God, telling me I'm dead. It's a voice I know but can't quite place.

Stephen? No. Someone else. Someone strong. Dependable. But who...?

And then the mist clears. Cornwall. Jago Moon. I can trust him. Because he's blunt and sincere, no matter what. The barge. The speedboat. The storm. Jago yelling my name over the pandemonium around us. In my darkest, most perilous moment ever, he's come to my rescue, risking his own life. When no one else has.

'We're alive?' I rasp, trying to sit up, but every bone in my body hurts. 'How?'

He's grinning, moving through the shadows, carrying a lamp, which he sets on a bedside table. I'm in a bed, covered with thick, heavy blankets up to my chin.

'You forget I'm a seaman. It was a big one, but we made it to here.'

'Here? Where is here?'

'Tempest Island. It's a tiny rock a few miles off the coast of Starry Cove.'

Images come to me of monolithic, biblical waves towering over me, invading my lungs. Fear of blacking out completely. Fatally.

'You… saved my life…' is all I can say.

He shakes his head. 'Honestly, I don't think I had any say in it. Someone up there wants you alive. But yes, it was a close call.'

'But h-how did you even know where I was?'

He shrugs. 'I asked myself where a silly city slicker who doesn't know a thing about boats could be in this kind of weather, and I knew.'

'The storm…' I try to swallow, but my throat is burning.

He pours some water from a bottle into a cup.

'Here, drink up,' he says, holding it to my mouth.

I cough, but at least the burning sensation has subsided. 'Better?'

I want to tell Jago how the storm caught me unaware, but suddenly I'm exhausted and try as I might, I can't stop my eyes from welling with silent tears. I dash a hand across them, refusing to bawl.

'It's OK,' he whispers, wrapping an arm around me so that I'm leaning against his side. 'Let it all out, Emmie. It's good to cry.'

'I'm not crying,' I deny as more tears come. 'I don't understand what's happening...'

'You're in shock. It happens to the best of sailors when they have a close brush with death. It's OK, Emmie.'

Is it? Is crying going to rid me of this utter feeling of helplessness, of how tiny and insignificant my life is compared to the force of nature? I know I'm supposed to feel relieved to be alive. The overwhelming force of it has hit me like a high-speed train.

'You're exhausted. You need to eat,' he says, moving away from me.

I fight the effort to reach for his hand in a silent prayer for him to stay. This is ridiculous. I'm a grown woman. The danger is over. What am I afraid of?

I look around but can barely see beyond the halo of light that the lamp is casting around the bed. There's a table and two chairs. And what looks like a sea chest. In the far corner, there's another source of light – a hearth. And in the hearth is a crackling fire. Next to the fire is a pile of wood.

'Thank you, Jago, for saving my life.'

'Yeah, well, Saint Piran owes me big time.'

Jago rises to poke at the fire and in the semi-darkness, I can clearly see the sinews in his lean, muscular body. He turns to look at me.

'You alright?'

'I'm fine,' I assure.

Well, maybe a tiny bit exhausted, but much better than I thought I'd be, lying at the bottom of the sea.

'You may well be now, but in a few minutes the shock is going to set in,' he says as he pulls out a pot with a chain for a handle and some cans of food, which he unceremoniously empties into a pot with a plop.

He places it on the fire, off to one side, next to his soaking jeans, rubbing his hands on his naked thighs. I look away as my own thighs begin to tremble.

'Here,' he says softly, moving close and wrapping another blanket around me.

'Tha-thank you,' I whisper as my teeth begin to chatter. And not just from the cold.

'Sit up,' he orders as, kneeling at my feet, he begins to rub my calves briskly. 'I'm not being fresh – it's just to get your circulation going again,' he assures, as if the idea of him touching me for any other reason was out of this world.

Just imagine, Jago Moon, lifetime seadog and playboy, actually being interested in boring, burned-out but chilled-to-the-bone secondary school teacher Emmie Weaver. As if. He's already covered that part. He's not into relationships. Sex, yes, and loads of, thank you very much. But relationships? Pass.

Not that I'm attracted to him, of course. We have absolutely nothing in common, from our backgrounds to our ambitions to our lifestyles. Absolutely zilch. I mean, really, after we're done with all the sparring and brownie-point scoring, what will the two of us possibly talk about? Well, it looks like I'm finally about to find out. Because it seems we'll be stuck together now for a while. At least until the storm is over.

'What is this place?'

'It's just a fisherman's shack,' he says as he bends to tend to the fire. 'We all keep it stocked with cans of food and firewood, so we'll be OK.'

'But how are we going to get back? We've lost our boats…'

He looks up at me from the pile of logs as slow, shy flames lick at the twigs.

'The boats are gone. But the shack is strong. It's withstood many a storm like this one. I think it'll endure one more.'

I wish I had his confidence. The wind has died, but the rain is still beating down on the slate roof like it wants to take it apart stone by stone.

'Emmie,' he whispers, 'you're shaking. Come here…'

'I'm OK,' I mumble before a violent shudder takes me and he returns to my side to wrap an arm around me.

I clear my dry throat. 'How, uhm, long do you think until the storm is over?'

He looks up at me, the firelight reflected in his eyes. And not only that. For a moment, I could swear I saw a flicker of… something in there. Tenderness? Kindness? Or is he just exhausted like me, with no will to bicker?

'Come the morning, they'll be here for us. This is the first place they'll try before they give us up for dead and start checking for our bodies in the various inlets.'

I swallow. 'Does… does it happen often?'

'That people drown in a storm? Yeah. Mostly stupid tourists who don't know any better.'

I flinch and pull back.

'I didn't mean you. You're kind of one of us now,' he says, looking up at me again.

From here I can see the top of his bare shoulders – something you don't see often for a man this height. Numb with stupor, I watch as his large, powerful fingers rub my skin briskly again, and ask myself had circumstances been different, would he be touching me at all? Would he have been gentle? At times, although rare, he does seem to slip into a softer, quieter mode. I often wondered about him. What his past as a neglected child had been like and how he was before that major but mysterious event that ruined his life had occurred. Had he been a happy youngster, with lots of friends and laughs?

Maisie always says that if you find yourself wondering what a bloke was like as a boy, then it's too late, because you're already in too deep. Not that I am, of course. Mine is simply a passing curiosity about this strange man who appears neither to have nor desire any friends.

So what did happen to him to change him and those around him so completely? I'd thought and thought about it and all sorts of scenarios had flashed through my mind, but none seemed to be the case. He is, I believe, still loved by many of his fellow villagers. The men speak of him as a living legend and yet they resent him, while others merely seem to pity him. The women, on the other hand, seem to be... almost mesmerised by him.

But it isn't a question of his looks or his reputation for being a heartbreaker. I believe it goes much deeper than that, at least for most. There's a soulfulness to him that I can't describe. A depth that he tries to hide. But even I, as a stranger here, had instantly felt that there was something different about Jago. He isn't your ordinary run-of-the-mill bloke from next door.

There's something about him that I just can't put my finger on. Because he isn't just one man. There are so many others inside him, so many facets to him, different shades that you can never freeze and capture. Because by the time you think you've understood him, out comes another side that completely contradicts all of your theories. The man simply throws me.

He gives me a glass of liquor and grins. 'What a time for me to quit, huh?'

I can see his thirst. I can feel it. But he moves away from the bottle, his body and essence visibly pulsing, quivering, alive with that pure, banked strength that he keeps at bay by the sole force of willpower. The effort and strength it must be costing him to stay dry, especially under these circumstances. One slip – one nanosecond of weakness – and it would all be blown to smithereens, just like the boats in the storm.

I glance at the glass and then at him. 'Thank you,' I whisper.

'Merry Christmas,' he murmurs, never taking his eyes off me.

'Merry Christmas, indeed.'

Who knew I'd end up on a desert island on Christmas Eve with the village bad boy? I take a small sip and splutter.

He laughs.

'What is this?' I cry.

'Rum, of course.'

'From when? The eighteenth century?'

'Yep,' he replies. 'A good batch at that.'

A wave of nausea hits me.

'Urgh, I'm not feeling very well,' I admit, my ringing ears playing a concerto of their own, my head spinning atop my wobbly neck.

'It's OK,' he assures in a whisper that seems so much more real than the howling wind outside. 'Here, take another sip. It'll warm you from the inside out.'

I do as he says and shudder as the horrid taste burns its way down to my insides. But he's right. A radiant, slow-burning heat begins to spread from the bottom of my stomach to the rest of me.

'Another,' he urges me. 'A nice slow gulp.'

I take another sip. Not that bad anymore, actually, considering I could be dead instead.

'Good girl,' he says, and all too soon, he stands to turn and tend to the fire again.

With a wooden spoon, he stirs the contents of the pot and I can see the chiaroscuro of light and shade from the muscles on his back undulate in the firelight. I take another sip. Definitely better than being dead.

With only the crackling of the lively fire and the smell of soup filling the air, I watch him as he studies the fire without a further word.

After a moment, he looks up at me. 'We'll be fine. We'll eat and get a good night's sleep.'

'So you're not worried about the storm? I've heard that a few years ago this very island disappeared underwater.'

He kneels in front of me again, looking up into my eyes.

'Listen to me, Emmie. I'm not going to let anything happen to you. That I can promise you, OK?'

'But the forces of nature...' I babble, feeling another irrational surge of panic welling inside me. 'You can't—'

His hands cup my face. 'Anything at all. Do you understand me?'

I study his face in the firelight, his eyebrows knitted in earnest solemnity. He's risked his life to save my miserable arse and all I can do is doubt him?

He, too, is shivering from fatigue and the cold. And from the effort of not helping himself to alcohol, I suspect. His face is so close to mine, I can see where his pores should be. I'd always considered his face to be hard, his profile almost sculpted by the sea winds. But at this distance, I realise that what were supposed to be the deep shadows of his eyes were actually the darkness of his lashes.

There are crinkly laughter lines at the corners of his eyes. And yet he seldom smiles. The harsh, unforgiving lines of his mouth are now soft, relaxed, his lips parted as if in surprise at our proximity. Up close, Jago seems like a completely different man. The width of his shoulders is no longer hunched in anger or defeat but wide, wide plains for me to rest my hands on should I ever have the courage. I know that if I did, his body would be hot to the touch.

'You're staring at me,' he breathes, the heat from his mouth beckoning me closer.

My eyes roam over his face once again and drop to his mouth.

'So are you,' I answer, just as breathless.

And then I pull back the covers to make room for him in the bed. 'Jago?'

He looks at me. 'I've told you before – I'm bad news,' he warns as if afraid of turning into a werewolf before my eyes.

'Come to bed,' I whisper, not knowing what I mean by it.

He takes me by my elbows. 'Emmie, run while you still can.'

'I don't want to run, Jago.'

'But you can't be with me. I'm bad for you.'

'Jago, what are you talking about?'

'I'm not worthy of someone as clean and honest as you,' he says, his voice cracking. 'So just… ignore me.'

'Pretty difficult at the moment, wouldn't you say?' I wryly observe.

'I'm nothing but instinct, Emmie. An animal. So protect yourself.'

'I don't want to,' I whisper, craning my neck to be closer to his lips.

And then he moistens them with his tongue and I pull him to me, more than aware of the sound of our lips gently sucking.

Instinct. Something I'd suppressed for years. In my profession, years of self-discipline and control had been my saving grace. But now, who needs control? *I kissed him, reader!* You bet your little Cornish pasty I did.

We both know that it's an instinctive reaction. I can scarcely keep my own breathing normal as my heart is hammering in my ears, begging me to let go. We both know what we're on the brink of doing and in this moment, my engaged self from x months and y miles away feels like a completely different person. A stranger with whom I have nothing in common anymore. The once prim and proper, buttoned-up Miss Weaver with nary a hair out of place is no more.

Whatever life I've had, at my school, and with Stephen

and my daily routine, is gone. I know that now. No matter what happens with Jago here, tonight, I'll never be the same person again. I can't go back to who I was. Every cell inside me screams at the mere thought of going back.

'Emmie,' Jago breathes, sending shivers down my spine. 'Scootch over a little, for your own sake.'

'Shh,' I whisper, sealing his lips with my fingers. 'I don't understand how this can be happening between us, but let's just lie here for a while, frozen in time.'

'Frozen?' he chuckles softly. 'Can you feel my body?'

'Yes. It's burning hot. Can you feel mine?'

'Oh, yeah. It's speaking volumes.'

'And what is it saying?'

'It's screaming that you want me almost as much as I want you.'

'Almost?'

'I can feel your body humming like a power line, Emmie. You're about to snap. But not quite. You're not ready yet.'

I'm beyond snapping, beyond ready. I'm already in a million pieces that have shot in a million different directions like bomb particles.

What do I want now? It's obvious in my breathing and if Jago could read my mind, he'd be entertained at the scene playing therein. In technicolour, so vivid, it's difficult to tell them apart from reality, so vivid it frightens me. Because if I can fantasise as much as I want, there's no turning back from the real thing. Because if Stephen made me feel grounded, with Jago I'm lost at sea, with nothing to hang on to but the waves of our emotions.

'You're determined to make me misbehave, aren't you?' he murmurs as I reach up to pull him closer.

As if plunged into a world of our own, made of Jago and me, I have no choice but to let go to the greater force of instinct. I *want* him. Like I've never wanted anyone in my life. I know it'll never lead to anything, but desire doesn't stop to think about the whys and wherefores –least of all the afterwards. Desire is an overwhelming force of nature, like the storm that we've just survived, and I'm right in the midst of it.

Like in a daze, my eyes barely register my dark surroundings as Jago, lying above me while resting his upper body on his elbows so as not to crush me, pushes back my hair to cradle my head in his strong hands. With a slowness that frustrates me beyond belief, he studies my face for what seems years before he takes my mouth in a kiss that completely undoes me, his mouth claiming me with an intimacy I'd never felt before with anyone.

With Jago, no words are needed. He speaks to me with his body. And I know he wants me as much as I want him. I don't need to be reassured of anything but the heat in his body against mine and the desire that it emanates. I don't know how it happened, but this man, whom I've known for the best part of five minutes, is suddenly the centre of my universe, the only thing my body craves or cares about.

When I wake, I find myself still wrapped in his arms. From his steady breathing and relaxed muscles, I know he's asleep. And yet his arms still protect me. How many times had I lain next to Stephen, wide-eyed and staring at his back? How many times have I been led to believe that that's all there is to it?

But Jago… holding Jago is like touching lightning bolts with your bare hands.

And just as I think I'll pass out if he ever touches me again, he reaches out and pulls me back against his chest, wrapping his arms around me once again.

'You warm enough?' he whispers into my ear and I nod, shivering in delight at the contact.

How have I managed to live until now without feeling this way? But I haven't lived. I've only existed. Because *this* Jago – who after a night of wild sex is now tenderly kissing the side of my face while making sure not an inch of my body is exposed to the night air – *this* is the Jago to remember.

I rest my head against his chest, listening to the reassuring sound of his heartbeat.

'Emmie?' he whispers above the sound of the crackling fire.

'Hmm…?'

'We've got a bit of a problem…'

I turn my head to look up at him. His stubble is growing back and I gently run the side of my finger over it. He pulls me up to stand, blankets sliding to my feet as he clears his throat.

'I've tried my best, Emmie, but I think I've gone and fallen in love with you…'

Love. He *loves* me.

This is it. The defining moment when the damsel and the knight pledge their eternal love to one another and live happily ever after. The moment that poems, plays, books, music and every form of art are based on. *Love.* The thing that everyone throughout history and fiction has striven for. The ultimate goal.

I rise to my tiptoes to kiss him. 'And I love you, Jago Moon,' I whisper. 'More than I've ever loved anyone in my life…'

'Oh, Emmie…' he breathes as his mouth crashes down on mine.

The air is indeed cold against my naked skin, but I don't care. All I want is to feel Jago against me, from head to foot. I want to feel his muscles and sinews and the blood pulsing through his veins as his breath catches in his throat.

I lift my legs and literally wrap myself around him, and his hands come up to support me as he takes my mouth again.

'I don't want to screw it all up, Emmie,' he breathes between our kisses.

'You won't,' I assure as I grab his head in my hands to make sure he stays close.

'Oh, but I will. I always do.'

'It'll be OK. I promise you, Jago.'

But Jago isn't listening to me anymore. Back are his demons, haunting him with a vengeance. He lets go of me.

'Jago?'

He groans and turns away. 'Go back to sleep, Emmie. It'll be a few hours before they come looking for us.'

'I don't want to sleep. I want you—'

'To ruin your life, I know. But one of us has to stop while we're ahead of the game.'

'Come on, Jago. Please don't be like this. You just said you loved me.'

He turns to look at me with those soulful eyes that bear all of the world's sorrows and my heart turns in my chest as he groans and pulls me to him for what feels like a last searing kiss. I clutch at him, not wanting to ever let go, but he gently takes my wrists and pushes me from him again, shaking his head sadly.

'Get away from me while you still can, Emmie. I've told you before – I'll only end up hurting you.'

'You won't.'

'Listen to me,' he says softly, his usual scowling eyebrows now raised in a plea as he gently takes my hands in his, caressing my fingers. 'You think you know me, but I really am bad news, Emmie. Trust me on this.'

'No, Jago. I know you. You act all hard and big, but you couldn't hurt a fly if you wanted to.'

'Go back to bed, Emmie, and dream your dreams of a fairy-tale love. Because I can't love you the way you want me to. I'm broken and I can't be fixed.'

'So just like that, we're done?'

'Emmie,' he moans, his hands on both sides of my face. 'You think that I don't *want* to be with you?'

'I-I don't know...' I falter. 'You're never the same from one day to another. I never know where you stand.'

'There's no way that it's ever going to work between you and me.'

'Why?'

'Look at us! You're magnificent. Luminous. Respected. While I'm considered to be dodgy at the best of times.'

'But that's just it. People consider you like that because you never give them the chance to get to know the real you.'

'And you think you know the real me?'

I swallow. 'Yes. Or at least some of you.'

He shakes his head as his eyes hold mine. 'Oh, to be the

man you think I am – the man you so desperately want me to be... You poor, poor girl. You have no idea. You have no idea what I've done. What I'm capable of.'

'Then why don't you tell me?'

He groans. 'Let it go, Emmie, for your own sake.'

'My sake?'

'I'm trying to protect you.'

'I'm not a child, Jago. I don't need protecting.'

'Sure you do. Every woman does. You might be all independent and stuff, and I respect and admire a strong woman. But look at you – a stiff wind could knock you over. This world is full of nutters who would happily harm someone smaller. And I will hurt you. I'm like the scorpion on the frog's back. It's my nature to kill, however good my intentions may be. That's me – an animal.'

And so, cold and refused, I return to bed, stifling my sobs in the pillows as he sits by the fire, still and silent. How could he refuse me right after telling me he loves me? On what planet does any of this make sense?

Only, in a way, his own prophecy has come true. He did hurt me. Like no one else ever has. When had I given him this power?

The morning after, Christmas morning, is worse than I'd feared. Rising from the profundity of a restless night, I hear the distant sound of a motorboat, then a whistle with a response whistle back. I sit up, still confused, but it doesn't take me long to return to reality. I've slept the last leg of the night by myself, my heart stone cold and devoid of the warmth that Jago's presence gave me.

From what I can hear, he's outside, hauling in a boat, the sound of a keel on pebbles grating in my mind and heart as I overhear an exchange outside.

'Figured you'd be here. You got the lass safe?'

'Yeah.'

'Folk think you've had a Miranda repeat. They reckoned you'd managed to top this one off, too.'

I sit up, straining my ears. A Miranda repeat? Top off?

'Shush…' comes Jago's voice.

'She doesn't know you were married? You didn't tell her?'

'No. I told you, no one knows, besides you, your wife and the vicar who married us.'

*Married?* Jago was secretly married to this Miranda? Is she the same woman whom my grandfather's barge was named after? And did Jago really top her?

Silence.

'Christ, Jago, what game are you playing? You have to tell her.'

Silence, then: 'I'm going in to wake her up.'

Reality is back knocking on the door. Not that I care.

But now? All I wanted was to be with Jago. Who, as luck has it, doesn't want me. How could I have been so blind? How could I have not put two and two together? All the facts were there, right in my face, and yet, I'd completely bungled it.

'Hey… you're awake,' he whispers. 'The cavalry has arrived. Come on – get dressed. We're heading back.'

I sit up, looking him square in the face.

'Who is Miranda and what did you do to her?'

# 25

*The End of the Affair,* Graham Greene

As the speedboat bounces through the choppy waves that still seem to reach for the black clouds above, my mind is in just as much turmoil. The three fishermen who have come to our rescue are, apparently, Jago's closest friends. Whom I've never met. As a matter of fact, I haven't met *any* of his friends. And it's true that I know absolutely nothing about him. Or his past. Or his present.

He himself said he was a bad person, and I didn't want to believe it. Everyone warned me about him, from my grandmother to the Coastal Girls to Jago himself. And I hadn't listened.

Why had no one, not even Rosie and the girls, bothered to tell me about any of this? It was one thing to give me a vague warning to stay away from him, but this? Murder? Have I really made love to a murderer? I can't believe it. And yet, the facts are all here.

The three sun-bleached, hard-set faces around me are as hermetic as a bank vault, avoiding even glancing my way.

I swing my gaze towards Jago, who's tried to give me a blanket I won't take, a cup of hot coffee I've turned away and his arm around me that I've flinched from, even if only to keep me warm. For an island that's barely a few miles off the Cornish coast, it's taking forever to reach mainland.

'I've gone and fallen in love with you,' he'd said last night. And not in the proverbial throes of passion, but afterwards, in a moment of tenderness. So he couldn't have meant he loved me as one loves a friend. He'd specifically said 'fallen in love'. But how can you say that to someone you hardly know and, most of all, who doesn't know you? Shouldn't love be all about honesty? Shouldn't he have told me about this Miranda?

And now, what am I supposed to do with his feeble excuses and explanations that don't stick? They married in secret, against Grandmother's wishes. No one knew. Then she died. I'm sorry for that, but he should have told me everything before he slept with me.

As the boat finally reaches the shore, Jago hops out into the freezing water and reaches for me. But I ignore him and jump out on my own, my legs recognising the sting of freezing water, nearly paralysing me again. I trudge on, chin up, eyes focused ahead on a crowd of people huddled in coats and scarves. My grandmother is the first person I see, along with Rosie, Faith, Nina and Nat.

'Dear God, Emmie!' my grandmother bawls, taking me in her arms, where she whispers, 'I was so afraid I'd lost you for good.'

'I'm alright, Grandmother,' I assure as I hug her back, somewhat surprised by her emotional outburst.

She truly is shaking and her breath is uneven in my ear.

My eyes swing to the Coastal Girls, who seem so relieved to see me again that they're in tears, hugging each other because they can't get to me quite yet.

'Jago, you're the hero of the day!' someone cries.

'Or the villain of the night,' someone snickers.

Or a cold-blooded murderer? He could have killed me, too. Once a murderer… But he didn't. He said he loved me. What am I supposed to do with all this new information now?

I look at him. He's clearly heard the comments, but he seems determined not to let it bother him. What has he done exactly? Has he really killed this Miranda? What do I really know about him, after all? He could have duped me royally. He seems to have tricked many of his fellow villagers who have known him for years, and I'm blaming myself for falling for his charms? And am I going to hang around long enough to find out that I'm the odd one out of some torrid love affair? I seem to have a knack for trouble.

'You're shivering like a scared kitten. Let's get you home,' Grandmother sentences, nodding to Calvin. 'Nettie's made a nice hot stew to warm you up. You must be starved. When was the last time you ate?'

Last night. I had a bowl of steaming canned beef stew. By a blaring fire. In a hot bed. Hot in so many ways I can't tell you about, Grandmother. And he said he loved me. But he was lying. Because he's keeping secrets from me about another woman. His wife! Whom he may have killed! And if it hadn't been for a complete stranger with a big mouth, I'd be going back to his place now to finish where we left off last night. And possibly for him to finish me off, seeing as I'm the only thing standing between him and a, if you'll pardon the pun, boatload of money.

'There, there, eat up,' Grandmother soothes from her chair next to my bed. 'What a horrid experience it must have been for you with that nasty, nasty man! Did he say anything untoward to you?'

Untoward? Absolutely not. Naughty? Yes, utterly! And now? Now what do I do? He'll never come here to speak to me, and I won't be let out of Grandmother's sight until I'm up and running again. Which, judging by the way every inch of my body hurts, isn't going to be tomorrow. Or the day after. But I can't wait another day to find out the truth.

'Grandmother, he saved my life.'

She spears me with a suspicious glance. 'And for that, I will always be grateful. But, Emmie, that man is the devil himself. Please promise me you'll stay away from him.'

I groan. 'Grandmother, I need you to be honest with me. Anyone who seems to know anything won't breathe a word about it. What did he do? This can't just be about Nano, right? They were good friends.'

'Ha! Good friends – ridiculous. Everyone knows that my husband died because Jago didn't call an ambulance in time. If I had proof, he'd still be in jail. And not only that, but he also killed my granddaughter Miranda.'

An invisible fist grabs my throat and squeezes, making it hard to breathe. So Miranda was my grandmother's granddaughter? My cousin? One I never knew I had.

It seems that there are more ghosts in my family than I thought. In my own muddled head, picturing Jago as a bad boy sounds almost feasible. But these accusations from my grandmother's lips? I don't know what to think. One minute they seem absurd, but then the very next they seem plausible.

'Your granddaughter?' I manage.

'He could have saved her. He's an excellent swimmer. He saved *you*, didn't he? And now I know why. You're his next path to our family fortune. But I'm not going to let it happen. You and Jago Moon will never see each other again. Do you hear me?'

No need to tell me that. Not anymore. 'But certainly you don't think that Jago cares for money.'

She raises her eyebrow.

'I mean, he only wants what he claims is his. Why is he claiming it's his? He—'

She suddenly takes the bowl of stew from me and slams it on the bedside table as she bursts into tears. I slowly ease myself out of the high bed until my feet are touching the plush carpeting and wobble towards her, my hand on her shoulder.

'Grandmother… Please tell me – what has Jago Moon got to do with her? And did you know that they were married?'

# 26

*The Age of Innocence,* Edith Wharton

'Married?' Grandmother apes, incredulous. 'Impossible.'

'The vicar secretly married them.'

'That sounds just like something Miranda would do, alright. That's why he was so adamant in insisting the inheritance was all his. She was his road to riches. And he killed her. If you're not careful, you'll be next.'

As if I care about my inheritance now. Jago Moon is not the man I thought he was. That night was all a sham.

'I never told you that Miranda was your cousin.'

My heart jumps. My head spins. My throat tightens. 'Cousin?'

'She was my granddaughter from my first marriage. Your mother was jealous of her. Half-sister.'

'And we were kept apart all these years… because of sibling rivalry?'

'Your mother had everything. She was young and healthy and beautiful. But her sister, Maura, Miranda's mother, wasn't so lucky. While you got more and more beautiful each day, Miranda became more and more fragile. She hardly ever left the house. Eventually, when your mother mellowed towards us, she sent pictures of you and while we were happy for you, I couldn't stand the sight of you, so pretty and healthy, while Maura – my first daughter – was trying to cope with a sick child. It just wasn't fair.'

'I understand that, Grandmother. Truly I do. But how was it any of my mother's fault?'

'She could have had some sympathy. Telephoned or even visited once a year. But she never did. But trouble started when Miranda was ten years old and laid eyes on *him*... the wretched, *blasted* Jago Moon. And it was the beginning of the end.'

The sound of his name makes my blood rush. He *lied* to me. He knew who I was and he *lied* to me. He reeled me in, with his 'I'm no good for you' ruse. He made me fall in love with him, all the while knowing I was the only heir left in the family. How could I have been so stupid to fall for someone like him?

At least when Stephen had asked me out, I didn't have a penny to my name. But Jago? He knew. He knew all along. And he played me.

My grandmother's words reach me as if travelling through treacle, in slow motion, distorted.

'Jago was only after her money. Everyone knew it. Even Miranda knew it, but she didn't care. She loved him too much. He even went so far as to get her pregnant. Yes, she was expecting a baby from that lout when she drowned.'

A baby? He's been mourning the death of his *child*?

My head swims as it all clicks together. This is why he

tried to kill himself, why he's been off the rails for all these years. He's been seriously suffering from a huge loss – not simply a sense of uneasiness or unhappiness caused by a few bad decisions or a breakup. This weight has been on his shoulders all this time, without any possibility of a solution. How do you get over something so monumental by yourself?

'So you can see why I didn't want you involved with someone like that.'

'I'm so tired,' I moan, falling back into bed, my head spinning as if I were still in the storm.

Like the waves pushing me under and tossing me up, I'm riding a rollercoaster of emotions and being yanked every which way. Who is Jago Moon? How much can he be trusted? If I do trust him, will I be forever destroyed, as he himself once told me? Or is he a kind but desperate man who's had the worst of life thrown at him?

I want to believe him. *Need* to believe him. But every time I feel myself letting go to thoughts of being with him, something pulls me back.

She steps towards the bed and pulls the covers up to my chin, her hand lingering on my forehead.

'Rest, Emmie. You'll never have to see Jago Moon again. I'll make sure of that.'

And this is how I spend Christmas Day after looking forward to it an entire year.

The next morning I wake to a low grey sky and not even the Christmas decorations strewn throughout the grounds manage to spread any festive cheer. After having touched the heavens with Jago on Christmas Eve, by Boxing Day I'm already dead inside. Is that how short happiness is? Just a quick preview, a flash of things that'll never be?

There's a taste of cotton wool in my mouth, as if I've been trying to poison myself. My head is so sore I can barely lift it off the mattress. But I have to, because my stomach is practically in my throat.

With the room spinning, I gingerly push one foot out of bed, hanging on to the bedside table. My bones can barely support my weight and only a massive effort to stay strong keeps me from tumbling to the floor.

I look out of the window to the grounds. Acres and acres of wet grass, topiary, fountains and artificial rivulets. Who needs to own this much money, and why? What's it all for? Has it brought my grandmother any happiness? Her daughters? Miranda? Me? If anything, it's brought me misery. If I hadn't been half Heatherton-Smythe, Jago would never have accosted me. When I arrived in Starry Cove, he already knew who I was. Had he not known, he'd have completely ignored me. But instead, he played that hard-to-get game, and I fell for him, hook, line and sinker. I should have stayed in London. It's safer there.

'So, how are you recovering?' Nat asks as they all pile into my bedroom, announced by Nettie, dropping their coats and Christmas gifts in a heap in the corner.

They're like a Christmas float, bright, beautiful and cheerful. I wish I could be like my new friends, happy and hopeful, but now I know I never will be.

'I'm fine,' I insist. 'It's my grandmother who won't let me get up.'

'And she well shouldn't after what you've been through,' Nina sentences.

'So! *That* was an adventure to tell the grandchildren,' Rosie chimes as they gather around me on the huge bed, ready for some juicy details.

'Did you...?' Rosie asks.

'Stop!' Nat warns. 'You can't ask her that! Unless you want to tell, Emmie?'

Did I want to tell? I want to shout it from the rooftops. I'm in *love* with Jago Moon! And the night we spent together was... life-changing. I discovered things about myself – and him – that I never knew.

I look up to see their huge eyes. They're literally hanging from my lips. Did Jago and I make love? I nod, gushing despite myself.

Rosie squeals. 'I knew it! How was it? Tell!'

How was it? Surreal. But he had to go and ruin it all by lying to me.

I shrug. 'I found out... about Miranda.'

At the mention of that name, they all glance at each other in sudden panic.

'What?' Nina barks. 'He didn't tell you before?'

I sigh. 'No, he didn't.'

'What an arse!' Nina sentences.

'Oh my God, Emmie!' Rosie exclaims, folding her legs under her. 'We thought he had in the end, seeing as you'd grown so close. I'm so sorry!'

I shrug. 'It's not your fault – nor your job to protect me.'

'Not our job?' Nat growls. 'He's going to have to deal with us now, that big oaf.'

Rosie taps my shoulder with a cheeky, questioning smile. 'You still haven't told us how *it* was.'

I sigh miserably. 'It was bloody phenomenal.'

Rosie squeals in delight as Nina wraps an arm around her.

'Calm down, Cupid. But I'm curious: are you going to forgive him for not telling you?' Nat asks.

I groan. 'How can I? This is not an "I forgot to buy the milk" lie. This is epic. To not tell me he and my cousin—' I cough, my throat tightening.

'But he's been through so much, Emmie,' Nat says. 'Give him a second chance.'

I shake my head, fighting back the tears. 'No. I just ended a rotten relationship. I can't... I haven't got the strength to do it all over again. Plus, he never told me he went to jail for murder.'

'But he was acquitted,' Nat says.

'I have to agree with Emmie,' Nina admits. 'I mean, it's a mess. Why would she want to get involved?'

The trouble is, I already *am* involved.

'Whatever you decide, Emmie, we're here for you,' Rosie reassures as the others nod.

'Hell, yes,' Nina says.

'Thanks, girls.'

'Come on – open your pressies!' Rosie chimes, shoving a colourful box under my nose.

Christmas. I'd had such high hopes. A new family. A new place to live and a business. But now, I have less than what

I started with. Because I've lost any hope of being able to trust Jago Moon ever again.

As I'm finishing my lunch the next day, Grandmother comes into my room, bright-eyed.

'There's someone here to see you!' she chirps.

I sit up, brushing the crumbs from my lip, my heart lifting.

'Who? Is it Maisie?'

'No, better,' she assures as the door opens.

At first I don't recognise him, dressed in jeans and a sports jacket. He's lost weight – a stone at least.

'Hello, Emmie.'

'Stephen! What are you *doing* here?'

'I came to take you back home.'

I sit back, pulling the covers up to my chin. I feel absolutely nothing for him, if not perhaps a little bitterness for the years I've lost on him. If I think of all the times he and Audrey had tried to dominate me. And that I'd almost succumbed. But not anymore. That sweet, malleable Emmie who would do anything for love is dead. And Stephen has no idea how dead. Drowned, perhaps off the coast of Tempest Island.

I lift my chin and look him in the eye. I'm no longer afraid of ruining that fragile balance between us, where I walk on eggshells so as not to upset his karma – or his mother's – usually quelling my own will just to avoid yet another argument. To think he hadn't even come to comfort me after I was attacked. What boyfriend actually does that? Could his priorities have been any clearer?

Sod it. Sod him and his silly vacuous, garment-venerating mother.

'I told you – this is my home now.'

He watches me in silence for a moment, running his hand through his hair like when confronted with a problem he doesn't know how to solve. That's what I've always been to him – a problem to solve.

'Oh, come on, Emmie – I miss you. We all do.'

'Who, you mean you and your mother?'

'Emmie, that's not fair. Audrey has a soft spot for you, only she doesn't know how to show it.'

'If I had stitches, they'd have popped out with my inner laughter,' I quip, suddenly finding the scenario amusing.

Audrey – fond of me? What next? I'm the perfect match for her son? To think she was so right. Stephen and I are like chalk and cheese. We couldn't be more different. And now I know.

Like a cautious animal, he sidles closer to my bed.

'How are you? Your grandmother told me about your incident.'

Has she told him I spent Christmas Eve alone with a man in a cabin on an island? I almost hope as much, so he'll get the idea. I'm not going back. Anytime.

'I'm perfectly fine, thank you. But you really shouldn't have come all the way down here to hear me say what I already told you.'

'Yes, you told me on the phone. On the phone, Emmie? Really? Don't I deserve more than that? Don't I deserve your respect?'

'My respect? What about me, then, lying on a cold pavement and then sitting in a police station, waiting for my fiancé to come and take me home? You were much too busy, weren't you?'

'Ah. I knew that would come back to haunt me.'

'By "that", you mean the night I was attacked and your schedule was too hectic to rush to my side?'

But I have no desire to start another argument when I'm well and truly done arguing with him. I never thought that I couldn't care less for Stephen. But here we are. I couldn't care less.

'Emmie…' he says, shifting from one foot to the other.

His eyes dart in every direction and finally out of the window. It's almost as if he's been sent by his mother to patch things up. Which makes me laugh.

'I still love you, Emmie.'

He loves me? His impatience. His curt tones. Never spending any time with me. Expecting me to do his bidding in my own home. My own life. Always putting me last.

*Then there's Jago. Jago…*

Giving up his feelings for me. For my own good. I still don't know the story behind it all, but I'd seen the pain in his eyes during our goodbye. I'd seen how much it had cost him. The tenderness in his eyes, in his touch. His sad, resigned smile. I'd never seen a man suffer for love before. Certainly not Stephen.

But Jago? Jago's moist eyes had broken my heart. Jago could finally feel. He'd got over his fears of letting go, whereas Stephen had never felt anything akin to Jago's love in his life. Jago had suffered in the past because of someone else. Stephen never suffered – he made others do that.

Jago… I've lost him… And I'll never get him back.

He's a man of honour. A man capable of the deepest

feelings, albeit afraid to show it. Capable of huge sacrifices for those he loves. Stephen only loves himself.

I shake my head, tears springing. 'It's too late, Stephen. I'm sorry.'

Stephen leaps up, taking my elbows, the most intimate contact we've had in months.

'Aww, Emmie, you're crying, see? That means you feel something for me, too.'

I wipe my eyes. 'No, Stephen. I'm crying because of all the time I've wasted with you.'

His jaw opens, then shuts as his eyes flash. And finally, like the curtains closing on a play, it dawns on him. We're past over. We need a new word for it.

'Who the hell is *that*?' he suddenly demands, changing tack as he walks to the window and looks straight down.

My muscles freeze. I can't see from where I'm lying, but instinctively, I know.

'And why is he looking up at your window?'

I turn on my side and bury myself deeper under the covers. Everyone is under the strictest orders to keep Jago away and for once, I'm grateful.

'What does he want from you, *Emmie*?' Stephen insists.

'What makes you think he's here for me?' I throw over my shoulder. 'I'm tired now. I need to sleep. Don't bother coming back.'

Behind me comes his tsk-tsk. How obvious it is that it doesn't touch his heart but only his pride. How annoying for him, to be surpassed in your efforts by another man who isn't even trying. Only Jago doesn't surpass him in the least, because I never want to see him again, either.

I can hear Stephen, still standing there, debating with himself for longer than I'm prepared to stand. Finally, he turns on his heels and leaves my room. And quite frankly, I think he's actually just as relieved as I am.

# 27

*Romeo and Juliet,* William Shakespeare

The next day I'm ready to get up. I pad downstairs into Grandmother's drawing room.

'Oh, hello, Emmie. I didn't hear you come in. Are you alright?'

'I'm fine, thank you, Grandmother. And thank you. For taking care of me. And for sending Jago away. I saw him from my window.'

She looks at me with those huge turquoise eyes.

'About Stephen,' I begin. 'We broke up some time ago. But he won't let it go. If he ever comes back...'

'I'll know what to do,' she says with a nod. 'Funny, what love makes people do.'

She looks a little strange and then, glancing down at the coffee table, I understand. Her eyes follow mine.

'My wedding album. Daft, I know, but I really miss the old man.'

'Oh, Grandmother, that's not daft at all.'

'I don't want to bore you,' she says, closing the album.

'Please, Grandmother. I want to look with you, if that's OK?'

'You want to see your grandmother when she was still unwrinkled, then?'

I laugh. 'Please.'

'Well, don't say I didn't warn you.'

Her puny beringed fingers reach for the corner of the album and almost reverently open it from the beginning. There are so many pictures of them going back at least sixty years. And in each and every picture, Nano has his arms around her. You can almost touch the love. So much love, and now it's all gone.

I look up at her and I want to hold her in my arms and tell her I understand how she feels. To have loved so much and lost… there is no remedy, no antidote. You can never be the same, after having lost true love, can you?

'You must be exhausted – and starving. Let me call for something to eat.'

I still her with my hand. 'I'll do it, Grandmother. You just relax. What would you like?'

'Whatever you choose. I am not really hungry, Emmie.'

'Had a cracker yesterday, did you?' I quip, grinning at her over my shoulder.

'There is some good cheese and a fresh loaf of bread in the pantry. And some fresh coffee beans, if you are making.'

'Coming right up,' I reply.

A few minutes later, I've brewed the coffee and made several rolls, which I put on a tray on the coffee table before I slip off my shoes and tuck my feet under me. Her eyes flicker over my casual, unladylike position but says nothing. She's slowly warming to me – I can feel it.

'So, Grandmother, how are you really doing?'

'Me? I'm well, Emily. What I would really like to know is why you broke your engagement off.'

And so I tell her everything about Stephen, about the mugging, and about Audrey and her lack of respect for me, as Grandmother sits there, her knowing eyes studying me.

'Well?' I prompt. 'What do you think?'

'I think that you were brave to follow your instincts. Many women don't have that kind of courage.'

'Was it like that with you and Nano?'

She laughs, almost as if to herself.

'I married him out of spite. Because my parents wouldn't agree to my marrying the man I really loved.'

'Grandma!'

'Oh, yes! So I went down to the cove and chose the roughest, toughest-looking fisherman I could find.'

'Nano,' I say, nodding.

'Nano. Only I didn't know he was actually from the Heatherton-Smythe family. He had been abroad most of his life. You can imagine my surprise when I found out who he really was. He had a heart of gold and I had fallen head over heels for him.'

'You just know when it's right. And when it isn't, I guess,' I observe.

'In any case, I sincerely hope that you left Stephen for yourself and your own happiness, and not because of Jago Moon. He can only bring you sorrow upon sorrow. Believe me – I know what I am talking about.'

'Oh, Grandmother – it's not like that. I was thinking about leaving Stephen for so long, only I couldn't bring myself to do it. But then, when I came to Starry Cove—'

She groans and I take her hand gently.

'Please, Grandmother, stop. Starry Cove has given me something that I never had before.'

'And what is that?'

'A sense of belonging. I know, it's crazy. I've only been here for a short time, but I know that this is the place I want to be. This is the place I now *need* to be.'

But Jago – being without him, not speaking to him, not seeing him, knowing he's less than a quarter of a mile away from me, is killing me. How am I supposed to get over him, ever? How does one mend a shattered heart?

I haven't seen him for two days now. Since Christmas morning, to be exact, but it seems like years. Years of not looking into his eyes, hearing the deep sound of his voice. How am I going to avoid him? We own a business together. And how am I ever going to be able to look at him without falling apart all over again?

# 28

*Rebecca*, Daphne du Maurier

'Emmie?' Faith calls from the top floor of Stormy Cottage. 'Can you come up a minute?'

We're having a look at the contended cottage. In the new year, we'll start work on it. Jago has finally agreed to let me buy him out. I know that because I got a letter from a lawyer. It was never a home to him anyway, he wrote me in a note. Along with many other things. Such as he loves me. That he wants me to give him a chance. That I make him whole again.

I want to believe all this. Truly I do. But every time I think about him, all I can think of is how he'd not told me about Miranda. How could he, what with all that was blossoming between us? No one makes love like that, unless there's truly something there.

I drop my broom and climb the stairs to find Faith and Bill on their knees, hunched by the hearth. There's a pool of soot between them and, on top of that, what looks like a leather pouch.

'This fell out. It was your Nano's pouch – I recognise it,' Bill says. 'Used to carry it round his waist all the time.'

'And it was hidden in the chimney breast?'

'I guess he didn't want anyone to find it but you, Emmie,' Faith says.

I look back and forth between them as the two of them get to their feet.

'We'll leave you to it. We're downstairs if you need us,' Bill says.

I nod, not taking my eyes off the pouch. How can they be so sure it's for me? It looks old enough to have been forgotten there forever. And if it really was left there for me, why not give it to the solicitors? Why hide it from my grandmother?

With trembling hands, I pluck at the buckle across the front. I half expect it to fall apart in my hands, but it's of a good quality – the kind they don't make anymore. Inside is a first edition of no less than *Jane Eyre* and a letter, which I slowly open and unfold. It's written in a neat scrawl:

Dearest Emily,

I don't know where to start. I don't know if you will even find this letter. If you have, it means you have found your way to Starry Cove, despite all odds.

You, of course, don't know me. My name is James Heatherton-Smythe, but everyone calls me Nano. And I am your grandfather. Unfortunately, your mother took you away from Cornwall when you were a baby. This is partly for what I did, but I am glad I did it and would do it all over again.

I want you to know that I have always wanted to be a part of your life, but circumstances have always prohibited it. You might believe this is just an excuse, but once you learn the truth of how things were back then, you will begin to understand.

You must know that many years ago our daughter, your aunt Maura, adopted a little boy. His name was Jago Moon. But he was a wild little thing and your aunt was afraid of having him around their own little girl, Miranda.

Jago? Jago? My heart skips beats, running around my ribcage as if looking for a way out of my chest. With shaky hands, I grip the letter further:

As it turned out, Miranda became besotted with him at a very young age, so her mother decided to return him to the orphanage. Which broke my heart. He was such a clever little boy! I missed him so much. He was the grandson I never had.

We had so much in common. We had the same interests. I so missed sitting with him in the fishing boat and talking for days and nights on end, waiting for fish to swim into our nets. We had literally become like father and son. I so desperately wanted him back, while your grandmother was relieved to get rid of the poor boy, whose only fault was to fall in love with Miranda.

And then one day, he showed up on my boat with those sad, beseeching eyes. He didn't want to leave Starry Cove, which he considered his home.

So, much to everyone's dismay, I took him on to work with me on my boat and continued to teach him everything I knew about the sea, thus theoretically and spiritually adopting him all over again. I also sent him to good schools.

When he turned eighteen, I sent him to Oxford University, where he obtained a law degree. I had very high hopes for Jago. But after all that, he ended up living with Miranda in Truro. And she made his life a misery. He was her slave in every way.

I am almost certain that my wife will have already contested my will, as she loathes Jago Moon. She blames him for Miranda's death. But I was there, too. We tried to save her but couldn't. What is worse is that she was carrying his child.

When they died, Jago was completely lost. The hopes of having his own family to love the way he never had been loved… well, they were all gone in an instant. He began to spiral downwards and drink, not caring about himself or anyone else anymore. He was dead inside. The world no longer held any interest for him. He had lost that spark that had defined him. That curiosity and zest for life. The ability to laugh at the simplest, silliest things.

I have a very fragile heart. My doctor told me that I don't have much time left. So that is why I am writing to you. I am too weak to travel to see you. But I have instructed my solicitors to find you.

And now you, his only rival for the inheritance, need to make sure that Jago gets what is rightfully his, although they were never married and nor had they lived under the same roof long enough to be common law. But Jago would have a child of his own now, if it hadn't been for Miranda's reckless attempts to dominate him. I am aware that there is no sum that can repay him for losing their baby, but somehow I have to make amends to him.

I have provided for you financially, Emily, so you never need to worry about that. You are my beloved granddaughter whom I never met because your mother was vindictive. Just like Miranda. Please let all that end here. Please let it end with love.

Please seek out Jago, if you haven't already met him. Who knows? You might even see in him the great man that I see.

Your loving grandfather,

James Heatherton-Smythe

I reread the letter. Twice. My grandfather's affection for me, although we'd never met, is palpable. As is his love for Jago Moon, the son he never had. And Jago was Miranda's man, technically entitled to all of her assets. And yet, he didn't involve a lawyer to claim what was his. He'd left it to my discretion. And I hadn't listened. He would have let me take what was rightfully his.

'Jago called by for the umpteenth time today,' Grandmother says when I invite her to sit down, her keen eyes trained on mine.

I pour her a cup of tea.

'I swear, the more I send him away, the harder he bounces back. But I suppose he always did.'

I sit up as my heart begins to jump around in my ribcage.

'Jago Moon? What f-for?'

'He wanted to see you, of course,' she says as if it's the most natural thing in the world. 'But I told him he could sling his hook.'

'Grandmother!'

Her eyes twinkle with mischief.

'But I must tell you, Emily – I am beginning to think he actually does care about you.'

'Why would you say that?'

She puts her cup down and stares straight at me.

'Because I have never seen him so miserable – not since... since Miranda died.' She sighs, sitting back, her arms encircling a scatter cushion as her eyes dart back to the past. 'We have made so many mistakes with him. Or rather, I have. And Maura.'

But then she looks at me again.

'If he and Miranda were married, then that means that he doesn't need your half of the inheritance. All that was hers, and I can assure you that her assets are immense, is now his. I genuinely think he has formed an attachment to you, for who you are and not what you own,' she says.

'What makes you think that he has actually formed an attachment to me?'

'Well, first of all, he didn't try to dispose of you.'

'Am I supposed to feel flattered?'

She leans forwards. 'All I know is that he saved your life, when instead he could have left you to drown so he could inherit it all. Which means that I was wrong about him.'

'Grandmother?'

She shakes a finger at me. 'You, my dear, did what Miranda couldn't.'

Something that Miranda couldn't do? I find this highly unlikely.

'You make him happy, Emmie, and I was blind not to see it. And you, my granddaughter, are infinitely better than Miranda was, or could ever be. You are right for him. And he is right for you. It took me a long time to come to this conclusion, but now I finally see things as they truly are.'

She's serious. I look for traces of jest, but there are none.

She sighs. 'All these years, I could never understand what the two of them had in common. Miranda was so elegant and poised and dignified, while Jago Moon was never one to keep his opinions to himself, to use an understatement.'

That, I had to agree with.

'But,' she admits, 'I now realise I was wrong about him

all along, and Nano was right. Jago is a good man and he does have a heart. And I think it's been broken again.'

'Does that mean that you won't come between him and his inheritance?'

She hangs her head. 'Yes. First Maura, and then I, had been trying to get rid of him for years. But once kicked out of the front door, he came back in through the window. He may not have any right as Maura's once-adopted son, but as Miranda's companion, it would be illegal to deprive him of what was hers. I understand that now. I will talk to my solicitors.'

'Thank you, Grandmother.'

I try to think of something else to say, but nothing rational comes to mind. This turnaround is jarring, to say the least.

'And,' she adds, 'knowing me, I am surprised he even dared show his face around here, knowing how we all feel about him. Am I correct in assuming that you love him, Emmie?'

I look up at her. 'I-I'm afraid so. But I don't know what to do, Grandmother.'

'Far from me giving you any advice – the Lord knows I have provided more advice than ever required – but...' She leans forwards and places a hand on my knee, looking me straight in the eyes, as is her trademark. 'I believe that if you listen to an old harridan such as myself, you might wind up losing everything that is most dear to you. Don't make the same mistakes I have made. At the end of the day, monetary fortune is nothing compared to having someone you love next to you.'

'But if you were happy, why wouldn't you let Miranda and Jago be?'

She shrugs and sighs. 'I guess that I just want to rectify

the course that the Heatherton-Smythe women were taking. I wanted for Miranda someone who could love her.'

'Better than Jago?' I suggest.

She's silent for a moment, her eyes lost on the intricate pattern of the rug at her feet.

'I thought that she deserved more. As it turns out, she was the one who didn't deserve him.'

Like me, he's reneged on the life that had been laid out before him. He's been honest enough with himself to admit that he wasn't happy doing what he'd worked so hard for. And he's had the courage to change his path, no matter how many might have tried to dissuade him from giving up a cushy life for the sake of his own freedom. A kindred spirit, indeed! Because Jago Moon adores what he does. He lives on the sea, free of any constraints. If only his heart and mind were free, too.

'So you can see how Jago has always been one to do as he pleased. The only person who tried to change him was Miranda. She threatened to leave him if he left his lucrative profession. She never understood he was a free spirit and, in all honesty, I never advised her against that, in the hope he would tire of her. Conniving of me, I know...'

'And did it work? Did he? Tire of her?'

Grandmother shakes her head. 'The more they argued, the more they seemed to want to thrive and hang on to each other. It was a toxic relationship that could only end in tragedy.'

Now *that* was something I knew about. Stephen was never happier than when I was miserable or he'd scored brownie points against me just to prove he was more intelligent than me. I can't even begin to count the number of times he said

'I told you so' or 'you should have listened to me'. How he loved to pontificate for the sake of it, just so he could tell himself he had one over everyone else. Frankly, I'm not surprised half of his staff fear him and that the other half hate him.

'I guess there was only one way it could end,' she observes, resigned.

'How did it end? Between them, I mean?'

'After the umpteenth argument, she stormed out of the house. Probably hoping he would go after her. But he didn't. He was too angry, too hurt. So Miranda got in her grandfather's river barge, *The Miranda*, and took it downriver and out to sea, just to worry Jago enough so he would go and retrieve her. And when he found out she was out there, it was already too late. She had already drowned.' She covers her mouth to stop the horror, but her voice spills out in agony. 'My Miranda!'

I slide from my chair to embrace her tiny form. 'Oh, Grandmother...'

'Come back home, Emmie,' she whispers, tears in her eyes as she holds my hands. 'I need to have my family with me.'

I open my mouth to speak, but there's a ring coming from her bag.

'Have you finally got a mobile phone, Grandmother?' I ask.

She rolls her eyes as she digs into her bag. 'And I haven't had a moment's peace yet.' She squints at the number. 'Oh, God, not her again...'

'Who?'

'Your former-slash-future mother-in-law.'

'Audrey Stone?'

'And she's like a dog with a bone,' she informs me as she pushes a button on her screen. 'Just give me a minute, Emmie. Mrs Stone!' she booms.

How can such a tiny woman make so much noise?

'I don't know why you keep calling me to intervene on behalf of your son. That certainly says a lot about both you and your son, and I don't mean that as a compliment.'

I stifle a giggle, but she raises a finger so that I may listen.

'Mrs Stone, a man who can't keep a fiancée is highly unlikely to keep a wife. If Emmie doesn't want to marry him anymore, there is certainly a good reason. My granddaughter is an intelligent young woman and she has the patience of Job. But she's no fool. And besides, I wouldn't want my granddaughter to be mingling with the likes of your son. She is a lady and my ancestry would be appalled. Good day.' And with that, she puts the phone down and beams.

'Grandmother!'

'Come and give an old crone a hug, Emmie. You have brought me back to life. How can I ever thank you?'

She reaches out for me and I don't have to think before I throw myself into her arms.

# 29

*The Remains of the Day,* Kazuo Ishiguro

The village is abuzz with villagers making their way through the high street with their electric candles like a fluorescent river in song. It's a tradition of Starry Cove that the end of the year is welcomed by a festival of lights. Like a river of fire, people flow through the streets bearing candles and chatting among themselves.

We're making our way down the coast, from village to village, the path lit by torches as the chatter rises skywards like an earnest prayer. I've never been overly religious, but tonight I realise that where there's peace and unity, there's love – the greatest of powers. Whether love between a couple, or a mother and her child, that between siblings or for a friend – as long as it's love, the world is right. It's beautiful beyond surreal and I've never felt so connected to every single person as if I were one with them.

When we finally reach the end of our journey, The Old Bell Inn, we all gather in the dining hall and pitch in to set the tables and dish up the delicious food prepared by not only the chefs Yolanda Amore and Hope Hudson, Faith's sister, but also the deliciousness by the local bakeries.

Alex, head *pâtissier* (baker), and Ralph's son at The Rolling Scones, wraps his arm around Laura and kisses her smack on the lips with all the love he's capable of. It's so genuine and catches me by surprise. She's a lovely girl and deserves her happily ever after.

All around me are happy couples, from Nina to Nat, Rosie and Faith, surrounded by their husbands and babies and nieces and nephews. There are also others I don't know. Faith is talking to a woman with a tattoo on her neck, cuddling her baby. The woman looks like a wild child but seems to have found peace with the baby in her arms. There are also some celebrities, such as Luke O'Hara, laughing and dancing with Nina while her husband pretends to be annoyed. But between the two men there's a genuine affection. Even Gabe York is there, albeit on his own, his eyes following Faith's every move as she's dancing with her niece and nephew, Verity and Jowen, and step-son Orson. Gabe, on his part, seems to be taking in the scene philosophically.

Snippets of happy conversations float towards me, filling me with as much joy as I can muster nowadays.

Faith's twin sister, Hope, is speaking with celebrity chef Yolanda, eyebrows raised while she says 'You want *me*? Head chef at your restaurant? Oh my God! This is the best news ever.'

Faith is talking to the wild child with the baby, sneaking glances at Gabe.

'Did you talk to him?' Faith says.

'Yes. I've agreed to let him see Grace every other week.'

'That's great, Vanessa. I'm so happy for you both.'

'And you? Have you forgiven him?'

Faith shrugs. 'It's easier when you love someone.'

'Forgiving is easier when you love someone...' I murmur to myself. It should be true.

Rosie sidles up to me and puts an arm around my shoulders. 'So much love around, you see?'

I nod, sniffing, and she pulls me closer for a proper hug.

'This cold... it's stinging my face,' I offer in way of explanation for the moist eyes.

But Rosie looks at me with her eyebrow raised. She isn't buying it.

'When are you going to forgive him? You were one of the few who saw the good in him when he was at his lowest. You should see him now. He hasn't touched a drop since Christmas, which doesn't sound like much, I know, but it is for him. He opens the shop on time and makes an effort to smile at his customers. But on the inside, he's dying for you, Emmie.'

My throat constricts. I can't. I just can't. For so many reasons. How can I ever compare to the woman he loved enough to marry? *That* is true love. However it ended, it had been real. I don't know that I'll ever be able to take her place. I don't think I even want to. He'll always be comparing me to her and I just can't bear to love him more than he could ever love me.

Stephen, I had dealt with and got over. I'd put up with the heartache and the disappointed expectations throughout our relationship, but not any longer. I was done with the making up of excuses for his shortcomings. But an ending with Jago, I'd definitely not survive.

I shake my head as tears fall.

'Oh, Emmie. You came all this way to learn about your family and in the meantime, you've discovered that you didn't want to marry Stephen. Now, you can't keep your mind off Jago. What's it going to take for you to understand that the two of you are in love? What's the man supposed to do – jump through hoops?'

I miss him so much, it hurts. How can I have fallen so deeply and badly in love with someone I've only known a few weeks? It must be just an infatuation, I've told myself repeatedly. It's what I tell myself over and over before finally passing out to sleep. If it were real love and not just an obsession, I'd be able to think about anything else for a mere minute or two. But I can't.

He's with me in my mind, speaking to me, smiling at me, holding me, kissing me, yanking me from the clutches of the storm, or lifting me after my fall. Everything I hated about him, I now love, from his mocking eyes to the sexy curve of his lip, the deep voice, the stubble on his jaw. Everything.

I have to stop. I can't go on thinking about him like this. And I can't go on living here in Starry Cove, where everything reminds me of him. Jago Moon *is* Starry Cove. He's all the good and the kindness of this little village.

New Year's Eve. The noisy celebrations, the countdown, the fire crackers. And no one to kiss at midnight. Even Martin has got the message and turned elsewhere. I'm surrounded by lovely, lovely people and yet I've never felt so alone.

The next morning, everyone has gathered on the breakwater for the New Year's Day plunge. If I'm going to be one of them, I have to have the same stamina. It's like an initiation rite or being baptised. Besides, after my close call with death, nothing scares me anymore.

And that's when I see Max, panting and weaving through the crowd towards me. He stops at my feet and I kneel so that my face is parallel to his.

'Hi, you gorgeous boy, you,' I whisper to him as I ruffle his fur. 'I miss you. I wish I could have spent more time with you.'

And then for no reason, tears start streaming down my cheeks. I bury my face in his fur and he turns to lick my tears.

And then I suddenly see *him*, off in the distance by the water. Jago Moon, amid his fellow villagers, participating in a community activity. And in a swimsuit, looking like Apollo himself, rubbing his hands together from the cold. Like when he was rubbing my calves to keep my circulation going.

He'd taken care of me. Not taken his eyes off me for a single moment lest I went into hypothermia. But I can't think about that night, the most dangerous and beautiful and exciting of my life. I can't think about it. I will never be as happy as I was then. In the space of two months, I've found – and lost – the love of my life.

As I watch him from a distance, he turns, as if sensing my presence, and in a moment, he's standing before me.

'Emmie…' he croaks, his eyes huge.

I swallow. 'Jago…'

'How have you been?'

I shake my head, unable to answer.

'Can we talk?' he asks.

'Now? What about your plunge?'

'That can wait. I just need to say something. And then, if you never want to see me again, I'll respect that.'

'OK.'

He takes a deep breath and exhales, the cold air forming a cloud around his beautiful head. I can't help looking at him. Or remembering our one night together – the love we could have had.

'You once asked me what I'd do if my girlfriend wanted space. I answered that I'd respect that, but that first I'd make sure she knew how much I loved her.'

'I remember…'

'Well, I *do* love you, Emmie. But there are things that I can't forgive myself for, so I don't expect you to. You need to know, Emmie. I was there when your grandfather had a heart attack. I performed CPR on him and called an ambulance. But it wasn't enough. He was already dead when the ambulance arrived. And when I inherited some of his assets, many doubted my efforts. But we were close friends, like father and son. I loved that old man more than I loved my own dad.'

'I know,' I say softly. 'And Miranda?'

He exhales loudly, as if it hurt.

'Miranda… I should have told you about her. I'm sorry. But I never expected to fall in love with you of all people, Emmie, so *different* from your cousin.'

'You mean not elegant and refined?'

He looks me in the eye. 'No. So warm and loving. Altruistic. You care about everyone. Miranda never cared about anyone but herself. She was impatient. Unreasonable. Jealous of my female classmates in college. I used to be a lawyer. But as it turned out, I hated my job. The dishonesty of it, the bent truth and the mind games. So I decided to quit. Miranda got angry and told me that she didn't want me to be a penniless painter. She wanted me to stay in the firm I worked with in Truro. But I'd already been commissioned for several paintings by the Wickfords – a very rich family who live above St Ives – and I had oodles of requests and orders from their friends.

'Miranda stormed out of the house. I could have followed her, but I was too hurt and angry. She took Nano's river barge out to sea. It sank and she drowned. On Christmas Eve. And still today, whenever I look out to sea, the irrational part of my brain is willing to see them, as they were that day, where I jump in and actually manage to save them.'

I listen to the story I thought I knew and again, my heart aches for him. She had died on Christmas Eve? No wonder he hates Christmas so much. Every year he is reminded of his loss.

He looks up, his eyes rimmed from unshed tears.

'If I'd stayed in that job, she might not have taken the barge out. And she'd still be alive. You can't believe how the guilt weighed on me. For years I battled depression and anxiety, fighting addiction after addiction – alcohol and sex. But both only left me feeling emptier. On the outside it looked like I didn't care. But on the inside I was already dead. She died and it was all my fault.'

'Oh, Jago, don't say that!'

He dashes his knuckles across his eyes and takes my hands in his.

'And then one day, when I was lost in my umpteenth pint of beer, I met you. I fought against my growing feelings for you. God, how I fought! I convinced myself that you should never come near a letch like me. That I could only destroy you. And yet, every time I spent a single moment with you, I went home feeling lighter. For the first time in years, I actually looked forward to something. Even our rows were stimulating. I was alive again, Emmie. Thanks to you.'

He runs a trembling hand through his dark locks.

'But then your grandmother came to see me. She told me to stay away from you. That I ruined everything I touched. And to kill me completely, she told me that when Miranda drowned, she was pregnant. With another man's child.

'I had a chat with Janice, who confirmed the stage of her pregnancy. I couldn't have been the father of that baby. Miranda, of course, kept it from me. And that poor, poor unborn baby went down with her. I couldn't keep either of them safe. It deserved a shot at life, Emmie... But it never got a chance! A *baby*, Emmie! I don't deserve something so precious.'

'Oh, Jago...'

'I was in hospital for months, medicated to the eyeballs for the pain in my lungs. And then from pills I went straight to the drink. Anything that would numb my body and my mind.

'As it turned out, it numbed my soul, too. Because I could never forgive myself for not trying harder. I couldn't save them...' He shakes his head as if to empty it of the memory. 'I just couldn't save them.' He grabs his head, shaking it. 'I just can't get it out of my head. It's a scene that plays itself over and over. *Every* time I go out to sea, I see her, slipping away from me. Just like I couldn't save Nano...'

His head snaps up, his eyes full of a sorrow I thought he was immune to all this time.

'No, Jago,' I whisper. 'You mustn't feel like that. Everyone knows you did all you could. No one blames you.'

He shrugs. 'Tens of therapists have told me the same. I had no role in their deaths, technically. But I can't shake the sense of inadequacy. And you – I know you don't trust me anymore.'

'I don't know that I'm strong enough to start over, to put my heart in your hands,' I whisper as tears sting my eyes once more. 'I'm still hurting.'

'Then let me kiss away your hurts, Emmie,' he murmurs, taking my hands in his.

'Jago,' I whisper, 'my heart aches for everything that you've lost, believe me…'

'Then please give me another chance, Emmie. I love you. And without you, I'll never be happy again. Listen to me – I haven't even felt the *desire* to be happy for years.' He runs a hand through his hair and grins at me through his own tears. 'But if you promise to stick around, I'd like a shot at it, with you.'

He loves me. He wants to be happy with *me*. He wants a second chance. Most people don't deserve one. Like Stephen. And yet, I gave *him* a million chances. Stephen isn't even worthy of licking Jago's boots. Jago loves me. And I love him. Don't we both deserve a second chance?

I wrap my arms around his lean waist and look up into his eyes as his hands circle my hips.

He looks down at me, a tender smile on his face. 'You and me together, a fresh start. How does that sound?'

I grin, laughing and crying at the same time. 'I think, Jago Moon, that that sounds like a plan.'

'You, Emmie Weaver, have made me whole again.'

I hold him close, not caring that we're surrounded by others.

'Oh, I almost forgot,' he says. 'I have something for you.'

And with that, he pulls out a round object wrapped in Christmas paper. I glance at him as I carefully unwrap it.

'I made it myself,' he says. 'Nano taught me.'

'Oh, Jago!' I gasp, for it's a glass snowstorm with a small island and a shack.

Inside the shack, through a window, a fire is visible. And that's all I can see, because now my eyes are drenched in tears.

'I love you, Emmie,' he whispers, taking my face in his hands and kissing my lips. 'Truly I do.'

'And I love you, Jago Moon. It took me a while to understand what my heart had wanted from the start.'

'And now it's you and me, together forever?'

'Oh yes!' I cry, throwing my arms around his neck.

Breathing deeply of the cold morning air, Jago lifts his head and looks around at everyone as if seeing them for the first time. He's like a little boy who's been allowed to run off on his own. A loud, sonorous laugh escapes him as he takes my cold hands in his warm palms. It's such a lovely change to see in a man.

'I feel like I've just escaped a life sentence of misery. And I owe it to you, Emmie.'

In response, Max barks happily, his tail wagging.

'So, shall we jump in?' he says, taking my hand. 'Shall we risk the plunge?'

'Let's,' I agree, closing my eyes, bracing myself.

It's not the first time that Jago and I have faced cold waters together, and we always made it out safe.

Underneath I'm wearing a black pair of knickers and a cotton bra. They're not swimwear, but they'll have to do. Jago's eyes follow my every move as I strip before him and the rest of Cornwall gathered here on the beach. Today is a baptism of sorts. A new start.

'You're the most beautiful woman in the world, Emmie,' he murmurs into my ear as he takes my clothes and holds me close.

'Liar,' I chuckle as I wrap my arms around him.

He lifts me and all around applause explodes like in Hollywood films. He holds me against him, acknowledging the crowd with a big lopsided, shy grin. He's not used to positive attention. Then he looks down at me and kisses me in front of everyone as if his life depends on it. I know mine certainly does. Because if I can't have Jago Moon, I don't want anyone.

'Congratulations, Jago and Emmie! Glad we finally got that sorted!' a voice calls over the megaphone.

It's Dr Janice Miller, standing on a podium, ready for the countdown.

In the crowd, I can see my Coastal Girls with their men and children, and all the other friends I've made here in Starry Cove, from Penny to Laura and Alex to Calvin and Nettie to Martin and the owner of The Rolling Scones, all cheering us on. They're happy for us. Who knew that we could be happy again?

'Is everyone ready now for our annual New Year's Day plunge?' Janice calls.

'Nooo!' everyone calls back.

She laughs. 'Come on, you slackers! And three... two... one!'

And with that, the citizens of Little Kettering, Penworth Ford, Perrancoombe, Wyllow Cove and Starry Cove rush into the waters in one huge wave. Jago does too, pulling me along, and I squeal as our bodies hit the freezing water.

Side by side, we dive in and swim out to the breakwater and back, shouting from the cold and laughing hysterically.

As we climb back to the shore, Jago puts his arms around me.

'You saved me, Emmie, from my own miserable self. But I promise you this. From now on, you're looking at a new and improved man in love with a city slicker.'

'Oh, Jago!' is all I can say as new tears threaten to spill.

But I'm not going to cry. Life is too beautiful to waste any more tears.

'Let's go home and have a nice long, hot bath, sweetheart,' he says.

I wrap my arms around him, rubbing my nose against his. 'Yes. Let's go home.'

And then, like a tiny miracle just for us, a million soft white kisses of snow begin to fall, floating through the universe, over the beach and over Starry Cove.

# Epilogue

*Christmas Day, one year later...*

The village of Starry Cove looks like it's covered in powdered sugar. Even the air smells sweet with baked goods, instead of its usual saltiness that wafts up from the sea. We're at the opening celebration of Emmie's new business, Books on the Barge.

All have come from the surrounding villages to celebrate her efforts. There's food and music and most of all, there's the once contended barge that serves hot and cold drinks while offering books of every kind, from the classics to the newest trends. Emmie loves her books and wants to share them with everyone.

Emmie laughs while I spin her round and round clumsily as our old friends and new look on. They're all here, from her Coastal Girls, as she calls them, to her oldest friend, Maisie, who's now engaged to a nice bloke from Mexico. She calls him Old El Paso. They're getting married in Mexico in the summer.

I've been working in Bend or Bump and painting my portraits and landscapes like mad as I have a long list of commissions. I've also been going to AA meetings ever since and haven't touched a drop for a year now. I don't need to anymore. Because the sense of guilt and loneliness that were slowly killing me are completely gone, replaced only by sheer love. Love for my Emmie – the kindest and sweetest woman I've ever met. And love for our little girl, Felicity. She was conceived exactly a year ago, during that unforgettable night on Tempest Island. The night I knew I could no longer pretend I didn't love Emmie.

I watch, transfixed, as she bends to her grandmother, Mary, holding our baby, and I'm overwhelmed by the beauty of life. We made a life. A human being! And I'm now a father. After losing my first wife and unborn child, I never thought I'd ever accomplish anything so special. I never thought that someone like Emmie could love – and help fix – a broken man like me. But she did. And she does, every single day, with her kindness and her love.

My heart lurches and my throat tightens at the fact that I had almost lost Emmie's love. I will never keep anything from her again. And I'm going to make sure Emmie and Felicity are forever safe and happy and that their lives are always as enchanting and promising as this magical snowy Christmas morning.

# Acknowledgements

Emmie Weaver and Jago Moon would have never seen the light of day had it not been for the hard work of the amazing people at Head of Zeus, and particularly my lovely editor Martina Arzu.

Huge thanks also go to Lorella Belli and LBLA for dealing with all the other stuff that goes way over my head.

Many thanks to my friends Michéle and Eilleen for taking me to Cornwall – and helping me meet Aidan Turner!

Huge thanks also go to my family and friends, particularly my better half Nick, who knows and understands I go AWOL during edits. Thanks for putting up with me!

# About the Author

N<small>ANCY BARONE</small> grew up in Canada, but at the age of twelve her family moved to Italy. Catapulted into a world where her only contact with the English language was her old Judy Blume books, Nancy became an avid reader and a die-hard romantic.

Nancy stayed in Italy and, despite being surrounded by handsome Italian men, she married an even more handsome Brit. They now live in Sicily where she teaches English.

Nancy is a member of the Romantic Novelists' Association and a keen supporter of the Women's Fiction Festival at Matera where she meets up with writing friends from all over the globe.